# THE BOOK *of* CANDY

# THE BOOK *of* CANDY

BY SUSAN DWORKIN

Four Walls Eight Windows
New York/London

Published in the United States by:
Four Walls Eight Windows
39 West 14th Street, room 503
New York, N.Y., 10011

U.K. offices:
Four Walls Eight Windows/Turnaround
27 Horsell Road
London, N51 XL, England

First printing October 1996.



Library of Congress Cataloging-in-Publication Data:

Dworkin, Susan.
The book of candy/by Susan Dworkin
p. cm.
ISBN: 1-56858-078-9
I. Title.
PS3554.W87B66 1996
813'.54—dc20 96-23706
CIP

Text design by Acme Art, Inc.

10 9 8 7 6 5 4 3 2 1

Printed in the United States

*For my mother, May Levine Feinstein*

## ACKNOWLEDGMENTS

I wish to thank Martha Ronk, Suzanne Braun Levine, my husband Moshe Dworkin, and John Oakes for their helpful critical reading of this manuscript. To Rena Lavie of the Hebrew Program at Brandeis University, my thanks for the translation and transliteration of Heimlich's prophecy. Some of the work on this book was done in the beautiful and supportive environments of The Dorset Colony House in Vermont and The Hambidge Center in Georgia.

# PART I

CHAPTER ONE

# THE VOICE OF DELAWARE

IT BEGAN TO RAIN very hard in Atlantic City. The would-be gamblers rushed into the huge hotel, crushed together by their umbrellas. Old ladies descended warily out of buses, clutching each other, watching the cracks between the planks of the Boardwalk with suspicion, asking themselves: will that be the crack that catches my heel, throws me down, breaks my hip, makes me an invalid, finishes me off?

Old men came too, their eyebrows lowered, missing their dead wives, no one to do for them, muttering: never had any luck in my prime; don't imagine I'll have any now; but gambling passes the night and maybe later we'll have a hot meal and a few laughs.

Gambling in Atlantic City does pass the long night.

Lettie and her three best girlfriends had hitched from Paterson with a stern church woman who lectured them the whole way about the dangers of hitching. During the short walk between the car and Orpheo Pastafino's Imperial Hotel and Casino, they tried to save their fabulous hairdos from the rain with newspapers and plastic dry cleaning bags. They were as covered as Shiites in the stormy night. But when they finally made it inside and shimmied their shoulders free of the burden of the weather, you could see they wore pink like bridesmaids and silver like chorus girls, their earrings captured spectrums and reflected rainbows.

They ran immediately for the mirrored walls to check their hair. Okay, they murmured, breathing relief; no sweat; still perfect.

They squeezed each other's hands and headed toward the casino, ready for money and liquor and music and sex. And the old people followed them like docile goslings, assuming that the glamorous girls knew where they were going.

This proletarian melee was what appealed to Heimlich the Comedian about Atlantic City. He distrusted high rollers, having known a few back in California, where he had lived some years before. He liked people who observed precise limits on the amounts they might lose, who played the slots and achieved ecstasy through the appearance of three plums in a row, and whose idea of a madcap spree was buying a glass of Chablis for a stranger. Atlantic City attracted many such folk. And since they could not afford the headliner, they satisfied their entertainment needs with a stopover at the Vancouver Lounge to see the act known as "Heimlich's Schmooze" which occurred at regular intervals, requiring no cover, no minimum.

He told simple jokes which often led to conversations with audience members; ordinary conversations, nothing mean or dirty, nothing Orpheo Pastafino's men would report. . . except that the exchanges triggered by Heimlich's little old jokes often lingered with an individual long after the jingling of the casino coins had ended — sometimes for years, sometimes forever.

Remember that comedian what's his name? people said. That stormy night on the Boardwalk? That was the night I decided to call my ex-girlfriend. . . get revenge on my husband. . . sell out. . . drop out. . . come out. . . what the hell was that comedian's name?

In his act, Heimlich often used a Polish-Yiddish accent, "for old times' sake" he told the crowd. The accent recalled little, gray men in stained fedoras lifting their eyes and palms to Heaven in helpless deference to God's ironies.

Heimlich used the accent for the same reasons that a former head of the Transit Workers had used an Irish brogue and a leader of the black revolution had used an inner city patois — when everyone knew they could both speak English like Walter Cronkite — to stir the blood and trick the pulse of the audience, send them into a time warp so remote from reality that they would hear the message with perfect clarity, no background interference from the complexities of the modern era.

Thus, said Heimlich:

"Yoshke, dat's Jesus to you, folks, Yoshke decided it vass time to make a surprise appearance on de Joisy shore to see if he vass still a popular figure. So, not vanting to test de loyalty of de young — (pause; mean-spirited laughter from the elderly) — he goes to a retirement home and asks one of de ladies: 'Hey lady! Do you know who I am?'— 'No,' she says. 'But if you'll ask at de front desk, dey could tell you.'"

And the workers would strike as though they did not already own blue chip securities and the college students would riot as though they were not already enrolled in law school and the audience would laugh as though the Jews were still harmless antiques without land without hope without hate or guilt or the ever-popular Uzi submachine gun.

* * *

The only person in the Vancouver Lounge to be surprised by Heimlich's joke was Candy Shapiro. "Jerk!" she said to herself. "It was a senility joke! And you thought it was going to be a joke about a face lift!"

Candy was obsessed with her appearance. She was thirty-five years old and five foot two inches tall and she weighed 145 pounds and she thought constantly about losing thirty pounds and having her face lifted. Although her gray eyes already sported genuinely thick dark brown lashes, she added mascara in many separate coats (applied at no less than one minute intervals so that the previous coat should have a chance to dry completely). She used moisturizer, base and then powder to "even out" the color of her skin, which she considered much too sallow. Her round, fleshy cheeks she heightened and shaped with three shades of blush. She had freckles on her nose (if she got sloppy and walked in the sun without a hat and Number 25 sun block, she would have them all over her face). No one could know about these freckles, however, because Candy covered them with a make-up camouflage called "Blanket."

Her least favorite feature was her mouth. There was no indentation in her upper lip. So either she looked like Brigitte Bardot or a lamprey eel, depending on what you thought of her personality. Her gums showed when she laughed. Candy hated that. In some cosmetic millennium, she dreamed of having her lips thinned and sculpted and her teeth removed and replaced with larger ones which would fill up her smile. For the time being, she covered her mouth with her hand whenever she laughed. She never laughed unselfconsciously, Candy Shapiro. Never laughed in peace.

Certain individuals would have been shocked to hear that Candy judged herself so harshly. Her father, long dead, had considered her gorgeous. Orpheo Pastafino had provided the following description to his lawyer, Kevin McCabe, who had been instructed to meet Candy in the Vancouver Lounge.

"She's short and plump by Yuppie standards," Orpheo said. "But she has the face of an angel, sweet gentle eyes, and she wears very stunning clothes and her diamonds are real, you can't miss them. For a white woman, she's got a very complicated hair style. You can't miss her beautiful hair."

Candy's long brown hair alone accounted for about two pounds of the thirty she vowed daily to lose. She contained it in a device known as "A Triple French Braid," by which the hair was woven together not from the usual three but from many tributary sources on each side of her head. For every progression made by the main braid, for every widening and turning, there was a new source to feed it. All the streams of hair wound and intertwined into a mighty mass until right before their end, when they diminished rather suddenly into three small, separate pieces. These were finally wrapped together and united into one lock at the very tippy tip of the braid, which occurred at the blind spot in Candy's back where no amount of twisting would allow her to see herself without a complex assistance of mirrors. This magnificent arrangement was then wound upward and bound by several strong barrettes camouflaged by jewels.

★ ★ ★

When Kevin McCabe approached Candy's table, she panicked. She had lied to her husband, Dr. Martin Shapiro, in order to be in this place tonight by herself. The lie had exhausted her mentally. She had never even thought of what might happen if some man approached her, wanted to sit down drink talk gamble, oh my God! she had never even dreamed of such an eventuality! Candy's legs jumped uncontrollably. A pulse in her neck fluttered.

"I am Kevin McCabe," he said. "Mr. Pastafino's lawyer. Welcome to the Imperial Hotel and Casino."

He sat down.

Candy pressed a long pink fingernail to the runaway pulse. She felt relieved. But she did not smile. Why? Because Kevin wore his Harvard ring on the same finger as his wedding band, and the ring was so much bigger than the thin little wedding band that Candy deduced Kevin must be much more married to his prestigious degree than to his wife.

Kevin might well be a philanderer!

People here might know that about him! Just smiling a polite hello might cause her to be suspected of impropriety, an unthinkable possibility under the circumstances, oh my God!

Candy therefore only nodded formally, as she imagined Margaret Thatcher might have done under similar pressures.

Heimlich the Comedian had long since become aware that he had lost Candy's attention. That nudgied him, like a bunion, like a spider bite. Noting with what coldness she greeted Kevin McCabe, he now saw his chance to re-engage Candy in The Heimlich Schmooze.

"Tell me, pretty lady with the fascinating gray eyes," he said. "Is this man your lawyer?"

Candy turned slowly to look at him.

"How did you know that?" she asked.

"People compare lawyers to rats!" protested Heimlich. "Is this fair?! This is a slander and a calumny! Because there are certain things that rats absolutely positively will not do!"

The room laughed. So did Candy Shapiro, a sudden splitting of the controlled and coated face by tumbling guffaws. She covered her mouth guiltily, darting glances at Kevin McCabe. He was not laughing. At that moment — a beat too late — Heimlich placed him.

"Okay, Mr. McCabe," Heimlich said. "Now take three deep breaths and on the last inhale say to yourself 'I will not demand the execution of this dumb comedian who did not for a minute realize that I was chief counsel to the Pastafino Empire' and then exhale and have another drink. On me. Freddie, bring Mr. McCabe a drink. I got a funny little pain in my eye, ladies and gentlemen, so I'm going to go and give it a bath. Good luck at the casino. See you later."

Heimlich quickly left the Vancouver Lounge. Kevin's irritation followed him; he could feel its sting on the rims of his ears. Also Candy Shapiro's searching look — Who is that comedian? I've met him before. . . — which somehow unsettled Heimlich every bit as much.

★ ★ ★

Orpheo Pastafino's office/apartment above the casino had three walls of blue tinted windows and a vast skylight overhead. If you stood in the center of the office on a clear day, you felt like a drop of water on the inside of a pair of sunglasses. At night, you felt like a star.

The thin strips of steel between the windows were painted the whitest possible blue. Blue cushions padded the traditional English teak lawn furniture. Lavish plantings of gloxinias and ferns softened all the corners. Obviously the decorator had in mind a Victorian conservatory. . . or maybe no room at all but rather a grassy knoll where rich Europeans were about to have a picnic with wine and brie and crusty bread and small pink apples.

On the piano where Orpheo's wife Dorothy had played what were now called "Golden Oldies," the family photographs gathered in a cluster: the dead matriarch, the sons, their children. Orpheo displayed none of the awards, trophies and medals which he must have collected for all his charitable works. No splendid paintings and sculptures showed how rich he was. The only non-utilitarian decoration in the whole office, in fact, was a huge blue glass bowl of fresh cut lilacs. The halogen lights were hidden deep in containers made of white ceramic hands which cupped together as over a well for a cool drink. So brilliantly concealed were these powerful lights that you could have an entire meeting in this place and never realize that the proceedings had been artificially illuminated. The shine on Orpheo's neat desk, on his polished tables and muted blue rugs from China, seemed to emanate from outside in the night over the ocean, maybe from distant galaxies or the slo-mo silent lightning. Every nuance of his environment suggested an outing in good weather regardless of whether the weather was good. And the effect on Candy Shapiro, as she stepped into the room, with the storm swirling harmlessly behind her braid, was that of entering not less than Heaven itself, where storms on earth were seen as movies of storms and no evil spirit could penetrate and nothing could ever hurt her again.

Orpheo gave her a hug.

He was sixty-seven years old, a short square man, not handsome. He had a funny nose, much too small and straight for the rest of his Neapolitan face. He wore a custom-made light gray suit and tremendously thick glasses in heavy eighteen karat gold frames. He had no smell. He rarely smiled, but when he did, he revealed (this was most astonishing in a gambling kingpin) big dimples. This powerful little man seemed so neat, so comfortable in his surroundings that it was easy not to notice that he had lost two fingers on his left hand and the first joints of all his fingers on the right. The fact that he limped suggested a similar deformity of the toes. About half an inch up from the end of his strangely WASPish nose there was a thin scar. You would have had to get very very close to him to see that his ears also were fake and implanted with hearing aids.

Candy Shapiro had known Orpheo all her life and had long ago stopped staring at his injuries. She would never have dreamed of asking for an explanation. Like her mother who came with gigantic hips and her long lost brother Alex who, when they were kids, carried a cross of revolting acne on his back, Uncle Fayo had fake ears. So what? Nobody was perfect.

For his part, Orpheo appreciated that, unlike so many people, she did not recoil at the touch of his amputated fingers. Her father had saved his life. He had known her since she was a baby. He still remembered the evenings when he and Dorothy would visit her parents, and she would come down from her bath smelling like lilacs, dressed in a long warm nightgown, and she would thank him for the doll he had brought her and give him a kiss good night. He could still remember the feel of her little ribs.

The last time he had seen Candy Shapiro was five years earlier, at his wife's funeral. She had come all by herself, with the directions pasted to the dashboard, to the strange church in a strange neighborhood, in a Volvo station wagon with toys in the back. Orpheo guessed correctly that an innocent, protected woman like Candy must have overcome many difficulties to make this sad journey. However, he did not realize that she had come in direct defiance of her husband.

"We have to go to Dorothy Pastafino's funeral!" she pleaded.

"We'll send flowers," Marty answered.

"No no no I have to be there!"

"Don't even think about it, sweetheart."

"Marty! She was part of our family! I called her Aunt Dorothy! I called him Uncle Fayo!"

They were at the breakfast table, on a lovely summer morning at the Shapiro home in Broadbeach on Long Island's North Shore, five years earlier. Candy was wearing an elaborate peignoir, navy with pink flowers, cuffed in lace. She was hoping Marty would notice it, hoping he would say something nice about the fluffy buttermilk rolls she had baked. Also she was waiting for him to be finished with the newspaper so she could read what the reviewer thought of a certain new musical.

"Somebody could start shooting. . . " he said.

"Oh please."

"Criminals get shot."

"Uncle Fayo is not a criminal! Is every rich man automatically a crook?!"

"On some level," Marty answered.

"You're rich," she said.

Marty kept his smile inside his mouth. But she knew it was there.

"If I am so rich," he said, "why does my cute little wife drive carpools and clean silver?"

"Children feel abandoned when their mothers don't drive them to school!" Candy protested dogmatically. "And as for polishing silver, Astrid doesn't do it right! She leaves little gray residues in the crannies!"

The minute Candy said this, she knew how trivial it sounded. Luckily Marty was not paying any attention to her anyway.

"How do you like the rolls?" she begged.

"We have a Porsche, sweetheart," he said.

"Marty!"

He leaned around the corner of his paper, momentarily pricked by her tone. She was nibbling on a roll.

"Why do you nibble with your two front teeth that way?" he asked. "You look like Minnie Mouse."

"I read in a magazine in the beauty parlor that if you eat very slowly, in very little bites, you end up eating less. So there."

He looked at her with a kind of wonder. She tried to drink some coffee. The lace from her peignoir flopped into it. She hoped he wouldn't see that. But he did.

"You only think Uncle Fayo is a crook because he runs a gambling casino!" she cried.

"It's a fair assumption, sweetheart."

"No it isn't! Gambling is legal! Your own mother goes to Vegas with her gin game ladies every couple of months."

"Oh gee," Marty said, frowning. "I forgot to call her for her birthday. . . "

"Not to worry. I called her," Candy said. "I told her you were busy in surgery."

"Did we get her anything?" Marty asked.

"Flowers from us, pictures from the kids, and a new pocketbook from Saks."

He smiled.

"Gee, I wish my secretary had your head for details, Can."

Redeemed by his approval, feeling competent again, Candy poured Marty some more coffee and added warmed skimmed milk.

"I just feel that we should go to the funeral, that's all," she said. "Aunt Dorothy was so nice. She gave us that Lalique crystal vase on our wedding, it's probably one of the single most valuable objects we own. She came to visit Daddy when he was so sick and looked so bad and nobody else wanted to visit, she and Uncle Fayo came and held Mom's hand."

"Sweetheart, listen, please, try to understand," Marty explained patiently. "To the FBI, your Aunt Dorothy was Mrs. Pastafino. Wife of a racketeer and a gambling czar. Who is also thought to be a big dealer in stolen weapons."

"Oh please."

"They will photograph everybody who shows up at her funeral."

"Well, I don't care," said Candy, petulant and final. Her round mouth looked like a petunia when she pouted.

"If you don't care about yourself, at least think about me, my practice, my reputation. Think what the local newspaper will say. 'Wife of Eminent Gynecologist Seen Attending Funeral Of Mobster's Wife!' Gee!"

"I don't see why you feel so righteous and superior," she complained.

"Compared to Orpheo Pastafino, sweetheart, Captain Hook could feel righteous and superior."

Candy threw down her napkin.

"Now you've gone too far," she said. And she stalked away from the table, tripping (but thankfully not falling) over the hem of her voluminous peignoir. Marty burst out laughing. However, his spoiled, zaftig, trivial, clumsy, dogmatic wife had intended no joke.

"She was serious!" he marveled on the following weekend to his girlfriend Pat, an aerobics instructor. "She was seriously concerned that I had besmirched the name of this major mobster by comparing him unfavorably to a musical comedy heavy! She's an idiot! I have allowed myself to breed two children with an idiot!"

Five years later, Orpheo Pastafino — who did not share Marty's low opinion of Candy — poured her a glass of brandy in his crystal office.

"How can I help you, Candice?" he asked "Just tell me."

"My husband cheats on me, Uncle Fayo. Apparently he's been doing that for many years, but I'm such a jerk, I just found out about it. I don't know what to do. Honestly, I don't know whether to do anything. After all, he's such a brilliant guy, a terrific physician, I know I'm probably not interesting enough for him even though I try, you know, I really do. . . I try so hard. . . But on the other hand, I don't want my children to be hurt, you know what I mean? I mean, what if one of these women won't settle for girlfriend status, wants money, has a baby, makes a scandal? I need advice. My father is dead and my mother is old and has to be protected from any more bad news. My wise brother is dead and my other brother is gone. The only accountants and lawyers I know work for my husband. My women friends. . . well, some of them are very smart but they have their own problems and also I would hate to be a topic of conversation at everybody's lunch, you know what I mean? So I came to you."

★ ★ ★

Except for the pain in his eye and the inexplicable Shapiro-fear he had experienced seeing Candy, Heimlich felt very happy. The great singer and current Imperial Hotel headliner Alisette Legrand had paid him a visit earlier this evening and given him cause for hope. She had knocked on his dressing room door while he was having his first eye pain attack. He croaked some awful sound, but anyway she took it as an invitation to enter.

Heimlich sat before his mirror, in his undershirt, his suspenders flopping down around the chair legs, holding a cloth to his right eye and moaning. With his left eye, he took in Alisette as she appeared in the mirror behind him. She wore her low-cut spangled lemon chiffon evening gown and her huge blue-black wig. Although Heimlich thought he had never seen anything as tempting as Alisette's bulging, brown breasts, he was in so much pain that it took all his strength to greet her with suitable enthusiasm.

"Why don't you look as beautiful as this on stage?" he asked gallantly. "You ought to make Fred change your lighting. The lights you got now clearly don't do you justice."

Alisette moved closer, suspicious.

"What have you got in your eye, Abraham?"

"A terrible headache. Like a new kind of headache. When a man forty-eight years old gets a new kind of headache, he worries. What is this, he thinks. A tumor? Shit, he thinks. Maybe there's no time left, maybe soon it'll all be over, this intricate life."

Alisette laughed.

"Answer me this before you die, okay? Would you like to open for me on the main stage? I've got another two weekends here and Pozzo just isn't doing it for me. I'd like to replace him with you. You'd have to tighten up your material, finalize the act more, make some of your conversations with folks less intimate. Don't answer me yet. Think about it. Come see my show. We'll talk later on."

She started to go. He couldn't stand that she was going.

"I thought maybe you came to ask how to discipline your children," he said, "or how to take care of your old grandmother. . . "

"Now why should I want to do that?" she asked.

"Since I used to be a rabbi, women often come to me with questions about personal problems."

She leaned against the door. With one of her coral-lined fingers, she caressed the knob. Right then, in that split second, she decided to stop ignoring her attraction to Heimlich.

"How'd you know I wasn't going to suggest we go up to my room after the show?" she asked.

"I dared to hope. But then I gave myself a slap. . . " Heimlich slugged himself in the face so hard that he fell off his chair and slid under his dressing table. When he came up for air, he was talking with the Polish Yiddish accent. "I said: Heimlich! Heimlich! Vatt are you, crazy?!" He crawled out a little. On the beat. "Did a woman as gorgeous as Alisette Legrand ever proposition you before?!" And a little more, on the beat. "Is something gonna happen to you now that you're an old Jew with a brain tumor that didn't happen to you when you were a young god of thirty who could tolerate caffeine?!"

He had schticked himself out from under the dressing table and now reached for her hand. She pulled him up. She was very strong. Her mouth was inches from his face.

"Give me your answer after my show," she said.

Alisette left his dressing room in a lemon swirl. An hour later, he could still feel the heat of her palm.

★ ★ ★

To reach the nightclub, where Alisette's show would soon begin, Heimlich had to walk across the casino. Drenched as it was in scarlet light, it reminded him of a movie battlefield. The wounded losers lolled around, tossed helter-skelter by this skirmish and that bombshell. The winners hooted and cheered and dragged the losers to safety. And somewhere beyond the ceiling where painted naked goddesses rested on red clouds, fingering their necklaces, patting their hips and grinning slyly,

Orpheo Pastafino the Supreme Commander, builder and owner of all this weaponry and pulchritude, relaxed (perhaps with his favorite lady friend) and ate the freshest possible salad.

The casino folklore about the reputedly lovable "Uncle Fayo" could have filled the notebooks of Lomax.

"They say he has an office above the heavenly orifice of Lady Luck," said Fred the Bartender, pointing to a certain goddess on the ceiling. "Right up there. See the fat broad over the fifth crap table? Now look at her crotch. See those points of light?"

"Those are peep holes," said Fred the Waiter. "They got telescopes in them that transmit everything they see to a television system."

"And Uncle Fayo watches us all on television," said Marge the Blackjack Dealer. "He watches us out of the heels of Sappho, see? Up there, over the roulette. . . "

"He watches us through the nipples of Lilith," said Fred the Sound Man.

"Where where?" asked Heimlich, squinting.

"Look at the snake. Okay?"

"Okay."

"See how the snake slithers between her tits?"

"Yeah. . . "

"Now look at the tips of the nips on the tits."

"Oh yeah! I see! So Orpheo is looking out of those! Who could have imagined such a thing?"

"We are all down here like worms in the dark," said Fred the Light Man, "wriggling around thinking we're independent, when really Uncle Fayo controls everything we do and have, our next meal, our pension funds, the fate of our children. He wants to step on us? We're dead. Just like that. Like nothing. Lucky for us he's a compassionate guy. He takes care of us. It would be good if he'd be President, cause then he'd take care of all the poor people."

"Where do you think he sleeps?" Marge asked wistfully.

"He sleeps where the gorilla sits," said Heimlich.

Like David the King, Heimlich imagined, Orpheo Pastafino could look down on the casino with his thousand television eyes and spot the woman he wanted and have her husband killed and make her the mother of his heirs, just like that, like nothing. Heimlich wondered who she was. What sort of woman becomes the consort of an uncatchable criminal famous for his charitable contributions and his legitimate art purchases? Surely not some floozy. Perhaps a young accountant sizzling with ambition. Or a loyal wife, like Lansky had in the manicurist, someone Orpheo could trust. Perhaps Alisette Legrand is up there now, he thought, perhaps she's rubbing Orpheo's neck and stroking his wavy white hair. Hell, why not? A gifted woman with people to take care of might entertain a tyrant just to win some favors for those she loved. Didn't Tosca do that? Didn't Esther do that? Poor gorgeous Esther.

Like a kid, Heimlich prayed that his cynical vision should not be true.

Please don't let it be that Alisette is really Orpheo's woman and she came to me with his permission, at his bidding, oh please God, if You love me, so all right, leave the pain in my eye, but do not dash the hopes of Your servant!

★ ★ ★

Pozzo, the Wimp of Bensonhurst, opened for Alisette on the main stage. A broken-hearted fat boy, he told Sinatra jokes and Pope jokes, jokes about really stupid body builders and really slutty baby sitters.

Watching from the wings, her arranger and musical director Bo Tye Jamal said to Alisette: "I don't see what you got against this Pozzo guy. He relaxes the Italians, doesn't make too much of an impression, leaves the crowd nice and warm for you."

"But Heimlich would make the audience smart, Bo. Heimlich would leave them alert, ready to remember the lyrics."

"You know what's your problem?" Bo told her. "You did too much gospel as a kid. You got in your mind all your Grandmama's neighbors singing along. Only this is Atlantic fucking City, Al! This crowd don't want to learn no lyrics! Get real. . . "

Alisette did not even hear him. She was thinking about Heimlich's timing, how charmingly he had collapsed his body in the dressing room just to amuse her, and she absently caressed her breasts where they crested the lemon chiffon dress, and smiled. Bo saw that it was no use trying to argue with her now. She had drifted off on one of her dream trips; she always did before a show; most likely dreaming how she was going to sing some damn song, and everybody in the audience was going to know the lyrics, know them cold, just from hearing her sing it just that one damn time.

Power tripping bitch, Bo concluded. What a great fuck she must be.

The audience barely applauded Pozzo and ordered its third round as a voice boomed over the speakers:

"And now ladies and gentlemen, the Imperial Hotel and Casino presents. . . (you expected a drum roll but all you heard was muffled thunder from the increasingly violent storm outside) . . . ALISETTE LEGRAND!"

And there she was in one blue light, wearing what appeared to be a green gown with a floor length shawl. Dustings of sequins from the whorls and swirls of her giant wig sent spikes of light out around her head.

She looked more or less like the Statue of Liberty.

Heimlich was the first person in the club to laugh. Alisette heard his laugh. She knew he was standing at the back of the house in the aura of Fred the Sound Man. She thought of the curly brown hair she had seen in his armpits and his green eyes and his especially sweet, gap-toothed smile.

She sang what appeared to be at first a slow, mournful song about a woman who worked for a rich businessman and served him coffee and balanced his check book and remembered his wife's birthday and only told him she loved him when he was dying in her arms of a heart attack after a savage convocation of stockholders.

Heimlich continued to laugh softly, the only one in the room who understood. . . until Alisette's drummer began to dust the snares, sneakily at first, tipping off the audience to a forthcoming change of pace, and suddenly the boogie woogie beat kicked in and now they all knew it was a joke; Alisette Legrand would never seriously open with a sad song extolling a spineless secretary. And they all began to laugh and clap as the drummer screamed and the lead guitarist jumped and howled and Bo Tye fired the band into high gear and Alisette whipped off her shawl and flicked the first row with its flying fringe and belted out "The Sitcom Blues."

She worked the stage in her four inch heels as though she were Magic in Nikes, holding the microphone so close to her scarlet mouth that businessmen, exhausted businessmen with hostile takeovers and mind-boggling debts, could think of nothing but fellatio.

*I be a fan of the heavies,* she sang,
*A fan of the saints,*
*But for me the show's over*
*When the ingenue faints!*
*Don't you try to cast me in that sitcom, baby. . .*

The lights changed to gold. The dress turned yellow. She simply ignored the resolve and strode right out onto the runway and said "Hello everybody, I am Alisette Legrand. But you can call me. . . Al. . . "

Heimlich wept with desire.

★ ★ ★

Some 50 latecomers were now seated under cover of the applause.

"Guess you folks got caught up in the rain, huh?" Alisette commented.

"It's not just rain any more," said a weary man who had driven in from Philadelphia. "It's a real electrical tempest. The lightning hit the ocean. You could smell the fish frying."

Sang Alisette suddenly in long hawking tones:

*Fried fish.*
*Fry-yigh-yigh-yigh frrrr-eyed fish.*
*Supersonic high electri-fighed fish.*
*Some of us Chrrr-isstians can't abide fish*
(Playfully she depressed the tempo.)
*Cause it remigh-yinds us of Lents gone by.*

The band jammed a reprise; the audience giggled, especially the Italians.

Orpheo Pastafino led Candy Shapiro to the best seat in the house. He held her chair and said: "Order whatever you want, and please, don't ask for a check, okay? I'll come and collect you when the show is over. And don't worry about anything, Candice. Everything will be all right, you'll see."

Candy smiled and thanked him warmly and gave him a kiss on the cheek. All her earlier caution had vanished. She seemed relaxed and comfortable, greeting the other people at her table with the amiability of a family member at home. The maitre d' fawned over her. The waiter hovered.

"Glad you could make it," Alisette said to her, reaching off the stage to shake her hand. "I love your hair."

"And I think you are just the greatest!" answered Candy very seriously. "'The Ultimate Aphrodisiac' changed my life."

Alisette grinned, recognizing a true fan. She concluded, as did many people in the nightclub, that the stylish little stranger with the distinctive mouth and the dumpy figure must be Orpheo Pastafino's new woman.

"What are you so happy about?" Fred the Sound Man asked Heimlich the Comedian.

★ ★ ★

By the time Heimlich went on for his second set, the storm had begun to wash away the shore roads and drown unlucky dogs and cats.

Ignoring the small craft warnings, an independent gunrunner set forth from Delaware for Cape May with a cargo of M16s and Uzis, expecting to drop them where some remote members of the Pastafino distribution system might retrieve them. Far out at sea, he noticed a peculiar calm on the water. The normally choppy waves of a rainy night mutated into gentle swells which grew longer and longer. He rode one for several miles. A single wave shouldn't last for several miles, he thought. And there was another to the starboard and many more behind it. . . strangely slow-moving concentric waves of incredible length. Realizing that he was caught in an anomalous ocean, compelled by underwater signals that spoke to his very bones, the gunrunner dumped his valuable cargo and radioed the Coast Guard.

Watch out, he said. Trouble is on the way. Ordinary everyday tides will suddenly turn dangerous. Watch out.

The local maritime authorities took his message as corroboration of what they could already feel in their own hearts. A tidal wave was coming. Tsunami. Fifty-two hours earlier, a small underwater earthquake had rocked the Aqaba Coast, triggered by a century of relentless drilling for oil in the delicate Bedouin sands thereabout. Of course a distant tidal wave could result, that was a seismic given. But no official warning had been issued as yet. The Jersey shore was still in the dark. The gunrunner, known to the Coast Guard from this moment forth as "The Voice of Delaware," had bought his countrymen four crucial hours with his warning and would soon be a hero, if he lived.

The authorities instantly imposed paramilitary regulations on travel, driving every last soul off the Jersey shore highways with frantic urgency. They evacuated Long Beach Island and Barnegat. They herded all coastal inhabitants safely inland and instructed the people in the casinos to stay put. The old people had expected to catch the 10 o'clock bus home, but the buses had long ago stopped running.

Lettie's three best girlfriends allowed themselves to be seduced by some great looking guys and, leaving Lettie behind, set out for Wildwood in a rented Lincoln Town Car. Like flappers, drinking brandy from flasks and singing, they ignored the police with their Day-Glo slickers and their giant warning lights. After five minutes they were blown off the road and forced to seek shelter in an all-night convenience store where many other terrified travelers already trembled together in the basement among the canned goods and the mice.

With further travel forbidden, the Imperial Hotel and Casino broke out its foldaway beds and announced that it would rent double rooms to parties of four and five. Even so, there wasn't enough space to house all the new-made refugees. Exhausted gamblers nodded off on sofas, snoring and drooling. Dressed up women guarded their money by using their purses as pillows. Orpheo Pastafino's elegant lobby began to look like the Port Authority.

Poor young Lettie, not knowing how unglamorously her friends had ended their evening, sat alone in the Vancouver Lounge, drinking, declaring to any who would listen that her Mama had been right, you could never trust another woman cause your best girlfriend would always dump you for a date with a stranger.

An old man groped her. She belted him.

Heimlich walked out onto the little stage. He had sought help for the pain in his eye from the hotel doctor, Yablonsky of Mount Sinai, and was now operating entirely on the palliative effect of the pills Yablonsky had given him. He didn't like the crowd. Since nobody could drive tonight, everybody was getting drunk, and it was hard to tell jokes to drunks. So he sat down at the piano and sang in the casual patter style of George Burns a semi-dirty ditty called the "The Cross Eyed Pussy Cat."

*She was the cutest little kitten*
*To ever bite the button off a fly.*
*But alas she had a wild and rolling eye.*
*Not roving. . . but rolling. . .*

"I once knew a woman who looked like that," said a furniture mover named Dominick Fabrizi. "Cute and soft and cross-eyed. Ellen Vanczyk."

"Come on," argued Heimlich. "She wasn't really cross-cross-cross-eyed. . . "

"Yeah, well, she was. Really cross-eyed," Dominick continued. "But not all the time, see? Only when she was feeling deeply. She'd call me: Hey Dominick! Yeah you! Because, see, she was the boss's daughter and I was just a piano mover back then — and I'd come running over because I definitely had the hots for her and I'd say: So Ellen, what's on your mind? And she'd look at me with those big baby blues and say: I want you to lift my sofa, hairy fingers. We was both so turned on we coulda made it right there if only her father hadn't been sitting at the desk signing checks. And I guess because of the intensity of the moment, her right eye, the one aimed at my heart, would go rolling out the side of her face like unsecured cargo. . . "

"Maybe you ought to call her," suggested the comedian. "Regret can torment a person."

A platinum blonde from Los Angeles named Spunky Pruitt, who had agreed to spend the night with Dominick, wondered why she didn't feel that Heimlich was out of line. She would remember trying to get a little closer to him, to see into his face, for she was an agent with a nose for talent, and this Heimlich clearly had some special power.

Around midnight, Alisette entered the Vancouver Lounge. She sat down at the bar. Her wigs and spangles were all gone. She wore black and gold, and her real soft African hair. On her naked arm, a gold spiral bracelet snaked round and round, pinching the firm flesh, like the cord of a phylactery. In the darks of her neck, gold earrings gleamed. Heimlich could smell her encores and her ovations, and the shower which had just refreshed her. The smile she cast his way, the glimmer of her teeth and the hot light in her eyes made him shudder. His throat closed. His penis jabbed at his pants pocket like a mugger. He returned to the piano ostensibly to take a slug of his tea, using the moment to lift the piano a little and lose his erection. He felt that he should introduce Alisette — "Look who just came in to have a drink and join The Heimlich Schmooze, folks, our charismatic headliner Mademoiselle Legrand. . . " — but he still could not speak.

Just beyond the entrance to the room, he saw Candy Shapiro surrounded by a crowd of people who were being introduced to her by Orpheo Pastafino. She looked intensely at each new person, clearly trying to memorize the names. Heimlich felt that he had seen her before just this way, as the new girl in the crowd. . . It came to him suddenly. Of course! It was in Patton Pines! She had been introduced to him! Marty Shapiro's girl!

"Mrs. Shapiro!" he wanted to call. "Stop!"

But he could not speak.

The pain moved from his eye through his head.

It seized his arms.

He turned to the people.

The change in Heimlich filled everybody in the room with fear. He looked blind suddenly, and drowned, a man whose head had flooded with sea water. His face lost all color. The green of his irises filled his eyes. His hands floated away from each other, the fingers stretching and jerking spasmodically. From his mouth sprang shipwrecked wisdom from antiquity. It came out in the Hebrew language.

This is a translation of what Heimlich said.

*You have forgotten your mother and sister.*
*You have mocked the work of their hands.*
*Your wife is made sick by betrayal.*
*I am moved by her cries of anguish.*
*Do her justice.*
*Free her from hatred.*
*Call her brother before you call her bride.*
*Or she will be a wasted fortune,*
*Honey melting on the desert sands.*
*And I will harden her heart*
*And she will teach your children*
*To forget your name.*

To the crowd in the Vancouver Lounge, this sounded like gibberish. They thought Heimlich was having some sort of fit. He fell to his knees. His body lunged and jerked, as though tossed from within and without by mighty waves. Then his right eye exploded. Blood poured from the hole in his head. So they thought he had been shot. They plunged under the tables, hugged the walls, dived over the bar and hid.

Alisette raced across their prone bodies toward the stage.

"Help me!" she screamed, pressing a wad of cocktail napkins on Heimlich's eye. "Somebody help me!"

Trying not to be swept away in the flood, Heimlich held on to Alisette with all his strength. He wrapped his legs around her and fastened his mouth to her shoulder. And she did not flinch or cast him off although he drenched her in blood.

Hearing Alisette's cries, Candy Shapiro immediately kicked off her high heeled shoes and ran to help. Orpheo feared for her safety, tried to restrain her. She twisted away from him. So Kevin McCabe tackled her and threw her to the ground with such force that he broke her wrist.

The Atlantic Ocean inhaled and withdrew from the beach, leaving a deep littered canyon, reddish in color. Everyone who glanced seaward at that moment would attest that they wanted desperately to run into the canyon and see what was there. Why? Because to look at the ocean bed is to receive disinterment as a gift, to recognize instantly, even painlessly, dead feelings and buried memories and forgotten wisdom.

The tsunami rose up like a cobra, a tower of water thirty feet high. It paused over the new-made canyon. Then it collapsed slowly, with a deafening blast. The gunrunner who had saved so many pulled in between two helpless Coast Guard boats and watched from far out on a placid sea as the thundering torrent drowned the shore. It made driftwood of the Boardwalk and obliterated the wide beach. For the next several hours, coastal New Jersey languished in darkness. But the Imperial Hotel and Casino was spared, and so was Abraham Heimlich, who lost only his mind for a time, as well as his right eye.

CHAPTER TWO

# THE WITCH'S MIRROR

OF ALL THE GAMBLERS who witnessed Heimlich's prophecy that spring, none was luckier than Candy Shapiro.

The product of a series of historical accidents, she had been born into a blessed time and place, and for thirty-five years, had missed all the catastrophes which might have befallen a woman of her type. Having known no hardship, she expected none. Having met with no evil, she did not recognize its face.

The only daughter of Jack and Maida Deal, sister of Sam and Alex, first wife of Dr. Martin Shapiro, Candy grew up in Gimbel's Inlet, a small town on Long Island which for a time had the highest per capita income in New York State. The town had once flourished as a secluded suburban retreat for the anti-Semitic upper crust. But the highways of Moses probed and opened it, and the inhabitants, stunned by the invasion of their island hideaway, sold fast and escaped to new havens of exclusivity.

"Anyone who thinks they have died out has simply traveled the wrong roads," said Maida Deal to her daughter.

Maida had lost every single member of her parents' French family in the Holocaust. By the time Candy was born in 1952, almost all of Maida's American relatives were dead as well. Her mother died before Candy was born. Her father Reb Ezra Kesselman died in '56, when Candy was just a little girl. And that was it.

Jack Deal's only living relative was Milton, his brother, who had married an Italian girl named Theresa. Aunt Terry spoke fondly of many sisters and cousins, but Candy never saw one of them, for reasons she would only understand when she grew up and bigotry became real for her. Thus Candy Deal lived as a child in a tight family. Small. Defended.

Maida extolled their family's working class past and clucked with pride when it was mentioned at Passover seders that their forefathers had dined upon the bread of poverty. However, the bad old days were more easily invoked than recalled in Gimbel's Inlet. Maida Deal wore her diamond ring to the supermarket. She had housekeepers and seamstresses. She and Jack vacationed in Florida. What poverty?! To Candy's mind, the poverty of her forefathers, in fact, any poverty at all, felt not like a curse but a serious mistake to be swiftly corrected. Bank failure, nuclear meltdown, these things were spoken of by adults (she heard them from her secret places in the shadows on the stairs) but they seemed somehow fictional, like the tornado in "The Wizard of Oz." They tore the world apart, then passed like a dream in a sleep. And when you woke, you were still in Kansas; you were still okay. Hard work fended off trouble, Candy thought. That was the American way. Her Daddy worked nights and weekends, gotta go gotta go, bye bye kiss kiss, and her Mommy smiled the maid out the door, see you Thursday, Lena, then rolled up her sleeves and cleaned the house all over again and cooked the dinner and rewashed the clothes.

"You can eat out of the corners of her bathrooms," said Mrs. Kaplan of Gimbel's Inlet Hadassah, cattily, about Maida Deal.

What she did not know was that Maida also ironed her sons' underpants.

It was the 50s. It was after the war and before the revolutions. Little Candy Deal wore a white organdy pinafore with eyelet ruffles. She had a pink bow in her hair and black patent leather shoes and little white cotton socks with lace on the cuffs. Somebody ran her bath, made her bed, mowed her lawn. She had been named for a famous fashion model to remind fate to endow her with — above all other qualities — beauty. Her father, short, bald, jolly, smelling of cigars and mouthwash, laughed with pleasure every time he saw her and held out his arms so she could run to him. He called her "My knockout! My little movie star!"

She believed that her parents, the children of immigrants, had every right to imprint their culture on the swampy shallows and fields of reeds along the South Shore, and that no one would ever question that right because it belonged to the American promise, the American dream. She pictured her people as in a Chagall mural, lucky Jews with limp limbs, soaring over the Gatsby rooftops and the two hundred year old chestnut trees and embracing diaphanous Liberty. Whoosh! they went. Far they flew.

* * *

Candy grew up in an aristocratic red brick house with white wood columns and a double front door, built originally by Addison Prawn Villiers in the spring and summer of 1833. His descendants had lived in it continuously for one hundred years — but the best of them had died young for the Union, and the remaining members of the family little by little ground their name away to nothing. A creditor took over the house during the Depression and rented it to a series of transitional families, allowing it to deteriorate — the privets untrimmed, the roof leaking, the wide plank floors billowing with mildew and termites.

Jack told his brother Milton that he had bought it for a song. The sly creditor, knowing the history of the house, thought that Deal was paying a fortune. So both men felt happy. And the lucky house, Villiers' pride, fell once again into the hands of a patriotic American woman who respected the significance of its history and relentlessly filled it with pewter from Massachusetts and flowering chintzes of Williamsburg blue.

Perhaps to soften the staunch lines of the facade, Villiers had built circular steps — ten of them leading up to the front door and the pillars — and a circular driveway which curved around a large, kidney-shaped island of grass. This little lawn had come to be dominated entirely by twin chestnut trees. Huge trees, splendid for climbing. Candy's oldest brother, Sam, six years her senior, tied a heavy hammer to a rope one day and threw it over a limb and affixed a board and thus made a swing on which their cute little Candycane flew over the rainbow.

The Villiers family crest was carved above the door. As with the steps and the facade, the strong angles of the "V" were softened with winding ivy, and the space inside was filled by a sleeping lion cuddling up to a smiling lamb.

Jack Deal wanted it off.

Maida said no, it was bad luck to remove symbols of peace from houses.

Jack said: "If we had a mezuzah on the door, wouldn't they remove it if they bought the house from us?"

Maida said a family crest was not a religious icon, and besides the religious source referred to by the lion-lamb combo inside the "V" was The Book of Isaiah, and if Isaiah would approve, who was Jack to say "they" and "we?" Maida further insisted that the house would be worth more if the crest remained. She had this corroborated by her decorator. Feeling confident that her case was now airtight, she smiled with her lips closed and batted her eyelashes. "You'll get used to the 'V'," she said.

"I'll get used to it when my name is Veal," Jack answered.

The crest was removed. It eventually found its way to a famous Connecticut junkyard where nobody bought it.

★ ★ ★

Beyond the patchwork brick back porch, Sarah Villiers' hired men had cut her a star-shaped garden where Candy spent most of her waking hours on sunny summer days and learned tenderness and nurturing and how to take care. A classic Colonial garden, it had four triangular beds, outlined by tiny boxwood hedges, which emanated from a square center bed to form a four-pointed star. The design of annuals and herbs in each triangle reflected Maida's whimsy and her passions of the season. One year she did solid masses of yellow and orange marigolds; one year she did pink begonias. In 1976, the year of the Bicentennial, when Candy was married and Heimlich took up comedy full time, she did blue ageratum, red geraniums and white dusty miller.

Mrs. Horowitz of Gimbel's Inlet Cancer Care commented that Maida Deal had been living among those American antiques for so long that now she had delusions of DARdom and thought her back yard was Bunker Hill.

Candy loved the garden. It reminded her of her own pretty hair, a brilliant embellishment, destined to be done up in a thousand different arrangements, depending on the occasion. She especially loved the garden's square center bed, with its tufts of chives and thyme and oregano shadowed by the statue of The Young Witch.

This statue, about three feet high not counting its pedestal which made it five feet high, represented a shapely woman dressed in mysterious veils of indeterminate origin. Maybe she was Greek or Roman; maybe she was neo-Greco-Roman; maybe she was an Arab or a medieval Catholic saint. Candy's grandfather, Reb Ezra, thought she was Jewish altogether. Maida's efforts to have the statue identified as valuable yielded only this memorable comment from her decorator: "If you like it, keep it. Otherwise, tell your sons to put it out by the curb."

The eyes in the head of the statue were carved of some dark gray stone, not shiny but flat gray like granite, giving The Young Witch a distant look of boredom or possibly regret. She wore no smile, and no frown either. Her hair cascaded in Classical ringlets, like a new perm before combing, and it was wound with ribbons, or maybe snakes, or maybe — as Reb Ezra suggested — seaweed. Her fingernails seemed strangely short to Candy's eyes, for all the women she knew had long nails brilliantly polished. Around her neck she wore a chain of little fishes.

The most interesting thing about The Young Witch was that she was holding a platter. She held it like a waitress, wrist back, with the flat part parallel to the sky. When the Deal kids got tall and curious enough, they climbed up to discover on the face of the platter a weather-worn etching of the head of a bearded man, entirely one-dimensional except for his sharp nose which protruded upward from the platter and served as a sundial.

The man on the platter looked very unhappy.

Candy's brother Sam, lean and Lincolnesque and so much older than Candy that he often seemed more like an uncle than a brother, offered many explanations for this fellow's misery. His head, Sam thought, had just been separated forcefully from his body, and the pain of his loss still colored his expression. Thus, he was really John the Baptist and The Young Witch was really Salome. Or he was really Holofernes and she was really Judith.

Less tall, less brilliant and much more handsome and fashionable than Sam, Candy's brother Alex insisted that The Young Witch's platter was a mirror. The unhappy man whose face appeared on the platter was really a god who had leaned off a cloud to look down and see himself.

"But why is he so sad?" asked Candy.

"Because he hates his new haircut," answered Alex.

As far as Candy was concerned, this explanation blew away Sam's more sober speculations in a twinkling. She entitled the platter "The Witch's Mirror" and so it was called forever more.

The earliest photo of Candy showed her as a delicious baby dressed only in a diaper and a pink bonnet sitting up on The Witch's Mirror and biting her toes.

When she was eight, Candy began the ritual of placing birdseed on The Witch's Mirror on cold winter mornings. Her father soon began to notice an increase in white, runny bird doodoo on his large black car.

"Why is it nobody else in the neighborhood gets bird shit on his car in the winter except me?!" he shouted.

"Because cute little Candycane, your knockout, your movie star, goes out every day and puts birdseed on The Witch's Mirror," said twelve year old Alex, wondering if it were possible that Candy might get yelled at now, the way he got yelled all the time: Put your bike away! Clean up your room! Stop aggravating your mother!

Dashing Alex's hopes, Jack turned to Candy with boundless tenderness.

"Sweetheart, I know you got a soft spot for the birdies, but there's a limit. . . "

"Don't you understand, Daddy?!" Candy protested. "If we feed them in hard times, the birds will come back to our yard in the spring and eat the bugs. So then the bugs won't be around to eat the flowers, and we'll have the prettiest garden!"

Maida arrived. She was rubbing cream on her hands after having washed her everyday wine glasses which had previously been washed in the dishwasher by the maid.

"Candy is absolutely right," she said. "A wise gardener always cultivates a close relationship with the local birds."

Jack Deal and his son Sam laughed, charmed by the eccentric women of their family. Alex wondered why he was the only one who realized that Candy and Maida were lunatics.

So Candy's offering remained on The Witch's Mirror. And cardinals and flocks of hardy little sparrows and mean-spirited blue jays regularly gathered there for the best winter bird dinners in Gimbel's Inlet since the days when Sarah Villiers hung out strips of suet studded with sunflower seeds.

These particular years, when she was literate but not yet menstruating, when her beauty was still unquestioned and her daffiest ideas accepted with love, those years held all the secrets of Candy's strength, and she had long ago forgotten them. So it felt miraculous to her, when, lying sprawled on the marble floor of the Imperial Hotel, her broken wrist engulfing her with pain, she had a memory of being eight years old in Gimbel's Inlet and experienced a thrilling inflow of power.

"I suddenly remembered this moment," she told her daughter Ethel. "It was morning. I sat up in bed. I said: 'My name is Candy Deal. It is November 1960. I am an American which is the very best kind of person to be. John Kennedy, the very best possible President, has just been elected. God will protect Israel and Israel will protect us. When I grow up I'm going to marry a doctor who will take care of me and everything is going to be wonderful. That was exactly what I said to myself, darling. Those exact words.

"Funny, in all the years, I never thought of that moment. But just before the tsunami hit, when I looked out the windows and watched the water pull back from the ocean bed, I was sure I saw it lying there. . . that exact moment, November 1960, and my room, my quilts and pillows, my stuffed animals, the exact words of my thoughts — 'everything is going to be wonderful' — all lying there in the red sand. . . with the litter and the garbage. . . and the poor fried fish. . . "

★ ★ ★

As soon as his revered father-in-law, Reb Ezra, passed from this earth, Jack Deal enrolled his family at the Reform Temple. Maida didn't like the Temple. She said it looked as much like a cathedral as a building could possibly look without actually having a steeple. The organ played. The cantor warbled as though auditioning for the Westbury Music Fair. The rabbi looked like an actor and gave great book reviews on Friday night. Sam the Elder, who had survived bar mitzvah in Reb Ezra's old Orthodox shul, told Alex the Dumber that bar mitzvah would be a breeze in this place. No Hebrew or anything hard like that.

(On the opposite coast, the brilliant social pundit Rabbi Eliezer AvShalom of Patton Pines predicted to his assistant, Rabbi Abraham Heimlich, that such families as the Deals would soon be without form and void, assimilated into non-denominational Never Never Land, that their children would marry equally uncaring Christians, that their grandchildren would be emotionally bereft and that the magnificent struggle of their martyred ancestors to preserve the notion of God's ineffable One-ness would be obliterated in three American generations. What AvShalom and his like never anticipated was that a child like Candy Deal, dressing up as beautiful Queen Esther on Purim, dreaming of herself as the saving grace of her people, would in her way turn out to be just as committed to Jewish continuation as more strictly observant Jews. When he read the figures on the phenomenal growth of luke warm, laid back, half-assed religion in all sects in America in the post-war period, Rabbi

Heimlich laughed and joked to Rabbi AvShalom that there was a time to sow and a time to reap and apparently there was also a time for book reviews. As usual, Rabbi AvShalom did not find Heimlich funny.)

Alex Deal did fine at his bar mitzvah. He certainly looked cute with his dark curls and his red tie, and he sang with a tuneful voice. His big brother Sam read a couple of prayers in Hebrew. His little sister Candy climbed on a box and led the congregation in the singing of the closing hymn.

After the Temple service, the family gathered with no less than 200 of its closest friends in the back yard around The Young Witch and ate large quantities of kosher-style food. This meant that although the meat was kosher in every particular, it was served at the same meal with dairy products, although not on the same table.

The kosher-style caterer, upon hearing that Orpheo and Dorothy Pastafino would be in attendance, came personally to supervise the food service at Alex Deal's bar mitzvah. He watched every morsel that entered Orpheo's mouth, how long it was chewed, whether God forbid it was juiced and spit out discreetly for being too tough. He drove the waiters and waitresses as though they were mules: cut it thicker! serve it faster! make it hotter! replace it sooner! Many bunny rabbits and chipmunks and skunks and squirrels and mammoth black crows waited in the wings behind the azaleas, anticipating glorious nocturnal feasting on the leftovers from this celebration. But the caterer did such a great job that the leftovers were packed into Maida's freezer in a crunchy thicket of aluminum and waxed paper, and the garbage was carried away that very day, leaving the poor beasts and birds without even one upended blini in the trodden grass.

As a bar mitzvah present, Orpheo brought Alex a Bible bound in silver and engraved with raised Hebrew letters that were studded with turquoise. He had been hard pressed to spend his money on what he considered such a meaningless gift. However, Dorothy insisted that traditional gifts took on wonderful significance on these tender family occasions, and if Orpheo wanted to please Jack Deal, he would send his assistant to the Jewish book store to buy this fancy schmancy Bible.

In the shank of the afternoon, Orpheo called Alex aside to speak him a blessing and give him the Bible. Candy watched this ceremony from one of her secret places in the shade of the hydrangeas, assuming — because she was only nine and knew no better — that a similar honor would someday be hers. Orpheo put his arm around the boy's shoulders, said a few kind words about friendship and family values, and presented the Bible.

Alex said: "I cannot accept this holy book from a man like you, sir."

Uncle Fayo's ever-tan face turned pale. His small nose seemed to shrink, that's how enraged he was. Luckily, Jack and Maida Deal did not witness the insult to their friend because they were circulating elsewhere in the large crowd. But Candy felt so overcome by embarrassment that she spilled hot chow mein all down the front of her lacy blue dress.

Orpheo strode over to Dorothy where she was laughing and chatting with a large group of women. One look at his face and she knew they were leaving. Their driver, swapping war stories with the musicians, noticed the Pastafinos heading out. He raced for the big black car and held the door as Orpheo stowed Dorothy in the back seat and started to climb in after her. Candy pulled at the sleeve of his jacket.

"Please don't feel bad, Uncle Fayo, please," she said. "My brother Alex is just a jerk. Don't let him make you feel bad."

And she gave him a hard, squeezy hug around his knees.

Orpheo crouched down and looked into her eyes and stroked her hair.

"You are a good little girl, Candy," he said. "You have a good heart. So you keep this book. It will protect you against evil and so will I."

Candy never really read the silver-covered Bible with the turquoise decorations. She hid things in there, secret messages, mostly about the men in her life. But she never actually sought herself among the ancient braids of history and fiction and narrative and song.

⋆ ⋆ ⋆

When Sam went off for his freshman year at Harvard, Alex began to engage in various experiments of which his older brother would not have approved. One day, he and some other high school juniors got high on pot in the locker room after basketball practice. They sneaked into the biology lab and stole a large frog which had been preserved in chemicals. They laid the frog on The Witch's Mirror. First they watched the crows descend on it. Then they watched the crows die from it.

Alex cried. He roamed the house, sleepless, thinking of the silky black bodies jerking into rigidity, mortal foam bubbling up from their screaming beaks. After that night, he swore never again to take another mind altering drug, or to knowingly poison the earth or its creatures in any way.

He has kept his promise.

A clean man, Alex Deal. A clean and virtuous man.

⋆ ⋆ ⋆

Feeling herself a remnant of the European slaughter, unconnected by blood to any living soul except her own children, Maida made it her life's work to tell every detail that she could recall or infer about her family and her husband's family, so that Sam and Alex and Candy would not be forced to live as orphans in history.

She told Sam her oldest but he was too brilliant to listen to anything twice, and myths are only inculcated by repetition.

She told Alex, her middle child. Somehow he always misunderstood.

"Your grandfather, your father's father, was Pinye Dobkin of Pinsk," Maida told Alex. "He came to New York where he learned to drink like an Irishman, and thus, he died singing under a truck before he was forty."

"Did he sing well?" asked Alex.

"What?"

"Did he have real musical talent?"

"He was a drunk!"

"Well, does anyone remember hearing him sing when he was sober?"

"I don't know, darling!"

"So if you don't know how he sang, how can you possibly know how he drank?"

"You are giving me a headache, Alex!"

"Don't you see, Mom? For the sake of adding color to a story whose veracity you can't even vouch for, you have slandered an entire nation."

"What nation?!"

"The Irish!"

"LUNATIC! GET OUT OF MY KITCHEN!"

Such an adorable child, Alex. So handsome. And talented too. Did she care if he got Cs and Ds? Did she need him to be a genius like his brother? Wouldn't she have done everything to make him happy?

"You're a bigot, Mom," said Alex.

"When you have cleaned up your room, then you can come back and call me names," Maida said.

Candy wasn't so full of herself as Alex. She had humility (a priceless quality in a woman, Maida thought, encouraging it) and that made her the best listener. She wanted to hear Maida's stories again and again.

"Your father's mother, Bertha Dobkin, took in piece work. . ."

"What's that?" asked Candy. She was ten.

"Sewing. She would sew pieces of shirts together at home, them bring them back to the factory next day. She and Pinye lived on the Lower East Side with rats in a four floor walkup. After a while, she became a midwife."

"What's that?"

"Babies. She helped women give birth to their babies."

"Tell how Daddy and Uncle Milton moved her. . ."

"They came home one day, blindfolded their mother and carried her to their car. They didn't let her see where she was going until she was in the new apartment in the Bronx. Then they took off the blindfold and said 'Surprise, Mama!'"

"I bet she was happy."

"She was ecstatic, of course. She became a communist and got a job in a dress store and changed the family name from Dobkin to Deal. She was a hard working woman. Never sat idle for a minute. Even when she was an old lady, snoozing in the sun at the racetrack, she crocheted granny squares." Maida stopped knitting for a moment and spread the back of Sam's new sweater across her knees. "That's how a woman should be," she said. "Always busy. Always producing something."

Candy finished rolling one of her mother's skeins of wool and started rolling another.

"Tell me about Uncle Fayo," she said. "How did he and Daddy become such close buddies?"

Without missing a beat, Maida said: "Daddy knew Uncle Fayo from the war in the Pacific, where they had fought the Japanese together. They saved each other's lives many times. And that is why they are the best of friends to this day."

★ ★ ★

Maida Deal never dressed casually. She never left the house without make-up. She wore high heels and corsets and large dramatic hats. Candy was sure that Maida was beautiful and furthermore that she had inherited those same good looks. She loved her mother's thick chestnut hair and admired the extraordinary care she lavished upon her skin, particularly her hands.

In truth, Maida had few beautiful features. Her forehead was too small for all that hair, and her mouth was too wide for such a narrow little face. Her breasts pointed outward toward her armpits. Her waist and hips were heavy and wide, and she wore her skirts long to conceal thick ankles. Still, for a smart wife, an honorable woman, the daughter of a kosher slaughterer who was commonly called Rabbi, for a productive woman, charitable, above rubies, Jack Deal was ready to settle.

He was in the underwear business. He already knew from beautiful. At the midtown offices where he worked with his brother Milton, the brassiere models would screw you in the toilet in exchange for a nutritious lunch, and they were *all* beautiful. As far as Jack was concerned, beauty could be had for money, like socks and tomatoes. Reb Ezra Kesselman, a tzaddik, a wise and righteous leader, impressed him much more.

Jack made a place in his home for Maida's parents until they died. He gave her the three children: Samuel her prince, Alexander her trial, Candice her comfort. When he died, he left her a lot of money. And although Maida told much of the truth to Candy, she kept certain lies alive, good lies she felt, which would gain breadth and importance as time went on, lies like great rivers that ran through Candy's family, washing and nourishing and drowning.

★ ★ ★

When Candy was thirteen, a high school senior named Jimmy Gottlieb took her to a party. He was forced to do this by his mother, President of the Women's Division of South Shore Hebrew Hospital, who wanted to involve the prosperous Maida Deal in her cause. As Candy's first actual date, Jimmy received more than his fair share of scrutiny from her family.

"He's adorable," said Maida. "He smells like baby powder. He has a nice rosy flush on his cheeks. His hair is not Apache-length like the hair of some 17-year olds I know, Alex darling."

"He's an asshole," said Alex. "He picks his nose. And those rosy cheeks you love so much come from tripping on his mother's diet pills."

For her part, Candy thought Jimmy was as cute as a Beach Boy. She could just die for his blonde hair, his blue eyes, his little nose. ("What is he, adopted?" Jack Deal inquired.)

To Jimmy at the front door, Jack said: "I'm sure you're a nice boy, Gottlieb. But don't test me, okay? Have her back in this house 11:30. Not a half a minute later."

At the party, which was in somebody's furnished basement, Jimmy placed Candy in a beauty contest. He steered her into line with his soft hands and cajoled and convinced her with his soft voice, dusting her neck with little kisses. Afraid to look like a nerd in front of these sophisticated kids, she agreed to strip to her underwear and parade across the shiny linoleum tiles with a lot of other girls while the rest of the crowd sang "A Pretty Girl is Like a Melody." Candy couldn't understand how she could lose this contest because the girl to her right was skinny and pimply and the girl to her left had tiny little eyes and the body of a tree stump and the prettiest girls in the room weren't even in the running. Candy sucked in her stomach, self-conscious that each cup of her bra said "Saturday Night Special" (Daddy's newest novelty item; she had forgotten she was wearing it until too late.) Awarding the prizes was a lovely blonde girl named Ellen. She was laughing so hard she could barely say: "And the winner is. . . "

The winner was the tree stump. Her trophy was a bunch of thorny roses from the garden, with terrified aphids still cowering within. And finally, Candy realized that Jimmy Gottlieb had entered her into an ugly girl contest.

Very quietly, she slipped out of line. She went into the bathroom and looked at herself. She had a large, slightly hooked nose with a smattering of freckles, and gray eyes, a high forehead dotted with small pimples, and a very long luxuriant pony tail. Her lips were thick and round, and she was fat.

She got dressed and called a cab from the kitchen phone and went home. Nobody at the party missed her. Her parents, not expecting her until later, had gone out to the movies. Only Alex heard her come in, and he was holed up in his room at the time, listening to Theo Bikel and practicing on his new guitar. Candy did not cry until she was in her own bed, all alone. Although she had had a few accidents by then — a fall on the tennis court, a finger caught in a car door — she had never experienced any pain more cruel than this humiliation.

Passing her door, hearing her sobs, Alex concluded that Candy's first date had come to a bad end. He knocked on her door, wanting to comfort her, but she wouldn't let him in. Poor kid, to have her heart broken by that shit Gottlieb.

The following Monday, however, at band rehearsal, he heard the whole story of the ugly girl contest from a boy who had heard it from the lovely blonde Ellen, whom Alex sometimes dreamed of fucking. The idea that Ellen had enjoyed a good laugh at his sister's expense made Alex sick with shame. What a stupid cow their cute little Candycane had turned out to be! Stupid cow-slut! If she was going to go out with people who knew him, why the hell couldn't she keep her shirt on?! Seeing Candy as she waddled across the school yard with her girlfriends, hearing her gossip in that irritating nasal whine so typical of Gimbel's Inlet girls, Alex wanted to grab her by the hair and beat the shit out of her. It therefore astonished him that when Sam came home from Harvard for Christmas vacation and heard (from Alex) the story of Candy's first date, he immediately went forth and beat the shit out of Jimmy Gottlieb.

Candy had no inkling of her brothers' differing reactions to her situation. They didn't ask her; she didn't tell them. She never made the mistake of thinking she was beautiful after that night. If her relatives told her she was, she figured they were blinded by love. If some guy told her she was, she figured he was just trying to get her to sleep with him.

She never went out with anyone who looked like Jimmy again. Her dates never smelled like baby powder. They never had rosy cheeks, or soft hands. Once during her college years, she and her friend Roxie Kirsch went down to the University of Virginia Law School for a weekend of parties. In the fastness of a library, a cherubic southern boy forcefully lifted her skirt and plunged his hands into her underpants, kneading her behind and kissing her with soft lips. Candy freed herself by hitting him with law books. Then she ran into the bathroom and threw up — from being drunk, yes, of course, mostly that, but also from physical revulsion. Her husband, Dr. Martin Shapiro, whom she found irresistable, was thin and narrow-shouldered, with the long stringy muscles of a runner. He wore his straight black hair short. He wore dark-rimmed glasses. His hands were so hard, the fingers so phenomenally strong that, if he forgot himself, he could easily leave blue bruises on her body. Candy thought of Marty's hands as mighty little weight lifters. With her make-up, while he was sleeping, she painted faces on them and named them "Lou" and "Rocco."

It took many years for Candy to grow calm enough about her date with Jimmy Gottlieb to be able to look back and understand that she alone among the girls in the contest had divined its true nature. This meant that vanity had not completely blinded her. It meant that she was fairly bright.

The realization that she was smart shocked Candy Deal every bit as much as the realization that she was not pretty.

She kept it a secret for as long as she could.

★ ★ ★

On a typical Saturday during high school, Candy would dress like her mother in a tweed suit and rather high heels and together they would drive to the re-gentrified Long Island Railroad station in Gimbel's Inlet, take the train into Pennsylvania Station and go shopping in the New York department stores.

The distinction between shopping and buying had been made clear to her by the time she was twelve. Shopping was what you did all the time. It was like dusting, a perpetual obligation which women took upon themselves in order to keep their minds occupied and the economy strong. Buying was what you did three or four times a year, at a birthday, or during the Chanukah/ Christmas holiday, or because you had to attend a wedding or go to someone's house in the Hamptons for the weekend and needed a gift. If you had not dutifully done your shopping all year, buying could lead to disasters, impulsive spur-of-the-moment blunders which might well cause deep regret (How could I have paid $280.00 for the blue silk at Bloomie's when Loehmann's had it for $225?!) for years to come.

"Always start with Saks," said Maida. "If you start there, you know how expensive everything is. Then you can look around for a better price. But if you can't find it, you'll know you can go back and get whatever it was at Saks."

After Saks, they would walk uptown to Bendel's, then east to Bloomingdale's. With every step, their toes would plunge deeper and deeper into the pointed fronts of their chic mid-60s pumps, but they strode on despite the pain, accepting it as they accepted sleeping all night in the grip of iron hair curlers, with blithe denial.

And then they would have lunch. Cottage cheese and fresh fruit and melba toast. Watching the hamburgers being served, the milk shakes, the indescribably delicious ketchup, Candy would pick at her curds and curse the very cells of her body. Sixteen years old, and already she had been on a diet for two years. Her mother had been on a diet as long as Candy could remember. Would there never be a meal? she wondered. A real meal eaten out in the open not secretly at night but right out in front of everybody in a restaurant, a real meal with courses and condiments and dessert?!

"The answer is no," said Maida. "I'm sorry to say this, darling, but you might as well accept it now while you're young. We are genetically programmed to be too fat for American fashion. Let down your guard and you can easily look just like Mrs. Khrushchev, who comes from the same basic gene pool. If we lived in Russia, many people would find us cute. But we are Americans, thank God, so we must diet without cease forever."

After lunch, in order to burn calories, Candy and Maida would walk down Fifth Avenue to Bonwit's, Lord and Taylor and B. Altman, and then, with the last of their strength, they would stride back to Penn Station and get the 4:something home before the commuter rush.

Throughout this day, Candy would try on clothes and watch her mother try on clothes. In case she had forgotten that little rolls of fat protruded from under her bra in back, she would now be reminded of them, thanks to the surround-around mirrored walls in all the dressing rooms. Again and again, from every angle, she would come nose-to-nose with her own face, with every pimple and blemish and discoloration; she would be forced to confront the puniness of her eyebrows and the indistinctness of her cheekbones; to inspect the freckles on the backs of her shoulders and then compare them to her mother's, which were much more pronounced, and she would think: "Oh God, it's happening! Soon my freckles are going to spread and grow until I have dotted arms and legs and big brown spots on my back! Just like her!"

Her mother's thighs, puckered and flabby, strained against the tough elastic of her girdle. Her mother's upper arms reminded Candy of the fins on a sea ray she had seen on her class trip to the aquarium.

"Oh God, I'm going to flap!" she thought in horror. "I'm going to ripple! Oh please, let me die before it happens!"

Candy treasured those small details of her physique which she could label as "improvements" over Maida's as though they were lace hankies in a hope chest.

First of all, she had a waistline.

Maida had a rubber tire.

Her forehead was not narrow like her mother's, so her voluminous hair did not drown her face. And she did not have those awful saddlebags of flesh midway between the hips and the knees which made it impossible for her mother ever to wear any skirt that was not dirndl, a style chillingly reminiscent of that preferred by the women's division of Hitler Youth.

Candy would watch the telephone poles of Queens flip by the windows of the 4:something and count and recount these, her bodily advantages, and conclude that she possessed but a pitiful handful, and resolve that as soon as she arrived home in Gimbel's Inlet, she was going to go on that new soybean drink diet, or maybe that new all veggie diet, or the grapefruit diet, or the all-carbohydrate diet or Weight Watchers or whatever and lose twenty pounds and be as beautiful as her father had hoped she would be, at last.

Neither Candy nor Maida could summon the energy to speak the entire way home. They massaged their feet, unhooked their biting garters, laid their heads back and stared out the train window in a waking sleep. Each felt that the other was worn out from shopping. But in truth, they were both exhausted from the orgy of bodily scrutiny which they had just endured, with its lifetime hangover of self-loathing and despair.

★ ★ ★

There was an upside. What was it? It was Maida.

From the first blast of the conductor's "All aboard!" and thence throughout the day, Maida Mao-istically uttered axioms to live by in a complex and dangerous world. Her text was a column in *Vogue Magazine* called "People are Talking About. . . " with additional selected readings from the Arts and Leisure Section of *The New York Times,* which Candy read every Sunday of her life, even when she was on vacation on a tiny Caribbean island and had to pay eight dollars for it. From these sources Candy received her earliest notion of what was important. Television, her constant companion, contributed little to her cultural standards. She felt that television was like the Sunday comics; fun — but you could live without it. The idea of a television elite seemed to Maida, and thus to Candy, oxymoronic. They never considered Lucille Ball an important woman.

Now the theater, Maida said, that was élite. The Broadway musical theater was even more élite. The British theater was most élite.

Fashion was élite. High fashion was more élite. French high fashion was most élite.

Most importantly, people in the theater and in the world of fashion did not seem to be as anti-Semitic as the rest of the gentiles. Why? The homosexuals, of course.

Maida felt that most bigots would never venture into fields where homosexuals abounded as they did in fashion and the theater. Therefore the gay guys served as a kind of first ring deterrent, incidentally protecting all other minorities. A woman would be wise to extend the hospitality of her home to these exceptional young men, who occasionally turned up as the sons of her friends and the friends of her sons, who often possessed an uncanny appreciation for things beautiful ("What fabulous crewel work, Mrs. Deal!") and sat down at the piano after dinner and played and sang their original compositions, soon to be the hit tunes of the Broadway stage.

"Remember," Maida brought down from another context, "to keep the bugs out of your garden, it is wise to cultivate a close relationship with the local birds."

According to Maida, anti-Semites ruled the world. The minute you left New York, she insisted, the spirit of Auschwitz surrounded you. Racial violence roiled dangerously beneath every golden cornfield, every noble river, ready to erupt whenever a big company went broke and laid off lots of workers. You could not breathe free again until you reached Los Angeles, or more correctly, certain neighborhoods in Los Angeles. To make things worse, many good Christians hung onto their anti-Semitic heritage in the name of tradition. When you pointed out to them that the Easter liturgy, the Passion Plays and The Merchant of Venice were Jew-hating, Jew-baiting abominations, they insisted that audiences mentally automatically edited out the bad parts, and besides, wasn't the Easter Bunny cute? Thus did the cancer of racism grab hold of each succeeding generation, disguised as popular culture, sometimes even art.

Wasn't it strange, Maida suggested, that non-Jewish leaders who were not anti-Semitic often died under such mysterious circumstances? For example, had not Pope John the 23rd of blessed memory kicked off with startling swiftness after he cut the deal with Rabbi Heschel, he should rest in peace? "And don't get me started about Emir Abdullah!" Maida said, beating her breast ceremonially with light little punches as she schlepped her packages across Fifth Avenue.

"What a different world we would have inherited if only that courageous man had lived!"

Since most non-Jews, Maida insisted, drank the poison of racism with their mother's milk, the best you could hope for was that, as adults, they would reform their instincts and repress their hatred and behave as though they were not bigots. Mrs. Eleanor Roosevelt of blessed memory was a perfect example. In Maida's estimation, she should have been canonized not so much for what she had accomplished as for all that she had overcome. Less saintly Christians — for example, the British cabinet — repressed their anti-Semitism only if they were kept exceptionally busy with other matters.

"Support the Irish rebellion, darling," Maida said. "It's good for our people."

Candy was told that she could minimize the danger from snobby, upper-crust anti-Semites if she knew how to dress, if she could talk intelligently about the latest play (book, opera, film. . . well. . . maybe not so much film) and if she was married to an absolutely irreplacable doctor, preferably a surgeon, who would one day be needed to save one of *their* lives.

"What about lower-crust anti-Semites?" Candy asked.

"To protect yourself against them, you need a gun," said Maida.

A few years after the tsunami in Atlantic City, when Candy's life had changed beyond her wildest dreams, and she had finally learned some Hebrew, she collected Maida's aphoristic pronouncements, dubbed them *"Pirke Maida"* — "The Sayings of Maida" — and began to pass them on to her own children.

Here is what Maida said.

★ ★ ★

A good son makes a good husband. Your father was very good to his mother. I saw that right away. That's why I married him. Your brother Sam's wife will be the world's luckiest woman. I pity the poor soul who gets stuck with your brother Alex, may he live to be 120.

★ ★ ★

You are well dressed if you have an expensive coat. Wear a shabby coat and no matter what else you put on your back, you look like nothing.

★ ★ ★

Comfortable shoes are always ugly. On the other hand, if your feet hurt, you feel terrible all over. So what's the solution? I don't know. But when you hear of one, tell me, I'll buy the stock. (In fact, the first time Maida saw a young business-woman wearing a gray suit and sneakers on East 53rd Street, she called her broker and bought shares in a large athletic shoe company. Naturally she made money, but only her accountant knew how much. If Candy knew, Candy did not tell, which was another of Maida's sayings:)

★ ★ ★

Don't tell. Nobody needs to know precisely how rich you are except the IRS. Nobody needs to know the contents of your closet or the truth about your sex life or how smart you are either. So just don't tell.

★ ★ ★

Be good to your mother-in-law. Even if she's a bitch on wheels, treat her with kindness and respect, because as men get older, they hold it against a wife if she wasn't nice to the mother.

★ ★ ★

Pick three charities. More spreads a person too thin and helps no one. Pick a disease and something for Israel and something that everyone needs, like the opera or a battered woman's shelter.

★ ★ ★

Leave your husband the first time he hits you. We had a neighbor across the courtyard in the Bronx. Every night she would scream "He's killing me! Oi Oi help he's killing me!"

Nobody took the screaming seriously because this particular woman was sloppy and always muttering.

Then one night she stopped screaming.

He had killed her, you see. When they asked him why he did it, he said because she was sloppy and always muttering.

I think she was sloppy and always muttering because he had been hitting her for so long. I felt that I was to blame for her death. I still do. So don't butt in, but don't ignore a dangerous situation either, because we are all victims of the unacknowledged crime.

★ ★ ★

If you're feeling unhappy, go shopping. Don't go shopping for clothes unless you're feeling very thin that week. But shop for a chair, a table, a carpet, a rare book, something that will bring you comfort and pleasure and boost your self-esteem.

★ ★ ★

Get your hair done every week. Without fail.

★ ★ ★

Get a manicure every week, without fail. Always wear rubber gloves when you're washing dishes. Never even walk into a garden with naked hands, because you will surely see some weeds you will wish to pull. Beautiful hands make you look rich and classy. Beat up hands show the world how hard you work and could embarrass your husband.

★ ★ ★

A person can live very nicely without ever buying anything German. A car can be American, the Swedes make terrific crystal, an opera can be Italian or French. Avoid what is German and you won't miss anything but a horrible pang of conscience which is what the Jews in the BMWs feel every time the motor kicks over.

★ ★ ★

Don't trust other women. Believe me, darling, your best friend will betray you for some man that she will forget in a week. The feminists mean well, I like them, really I do. But sisterhood is wishful thinking.

★ ★ ★

Keep your own bank account. Not that you should steal from him. But say you want to buy him a present, make him a surprise party. . . what are you going to do, take it from your joint account and make him pay for his own happiness?

★ ★ ★

If there had been an Israel, there would have been no Holocaust. If Israel is destroyed, we will all be killed. Not gently assimilated over time, darling. But murdered. Up the chimney. *Tous finis.* So Israel has to live, no matter what. Do you understand me, Candy? No matter what.

★ ★ ★

Expect to make an enemy now and then. We all do. Even if we are very nice, we all end up with one or two serious enemies.

★ ★ ★

Don't envy the beautiful girls who have all the men in the world. All the men in the world never helped anybody. Look at poor Marilyn Monroe, God rest her soul. A decent woman needs only one man, darling. Just one nice man, that's all.

CHAPTER THREE

# WADE IN THE WATER

AS THEY CARRIED HER into the makeshift infirmary near the hotel kitchen, Candy thought "Ow!" about her broken wrist, and simultaneously, she thought: "That wonderful Uncle Fayo! Surrounding me with men who have orders to throw themselves on top of me if there is any shooting! He thinks of everything!"

They laid her out on a long, formica table which had been covered with a sheet. Dr. Yablonsky gave her a shot, and she drifted off into painless twilight while they set her wrist. In her semi-consciousness, she could see the infirmary filling up with people. She had a sense of hysteria, a wild melee being played out all around her — yet masked, depersonalized by the gauzy interference of the damn drugs. She felt that she was falling, but that her heart was pushing upward out of her body, propelled by the same yearning that had made her run towards Alisette's screams for help, the yearning to experience pain and ecstasy, to be adored and avenged, to touch strong feelings and important events.

"Oh let me not be Dorothy in Oz again!" she prayed. "Sleeping through, missing out, dreaming my life, oh please, let me not be Dorothy!" But despite her heart's desires, Candy succumbed to the medication and dozed.

This is what she missed that night in Atlantic City.

Alisette was covered with so much blood that, at first, they thought she had been shot too, just like they thought Heimlich had been shot. So four of them strapped her screaming and flailing onto a stretcher and carried her into the infirmary. Lettie from Paterson, who had banged her head on the edge of a chair and now sported a small bandage, ran after them, protesting: "What are you, crazy?! If a woman's been shot, she don't need four strong men to hold her down!"

They ignored her. They tore off Alisette's clothes, looking for her wounds. "Get your hands off me, you shit brain fools!" Alisette roared. She kicked one in the balls. She punched another in the stomach. She sank her teeth into the arm of a third. The fourth backed off.

Lettie was laughing uncontrollably as she unbuckled Alisette's restraints. Snarling and fuming, Alisette reconnected her underwear. She took the shirt from the attendant who was moaning over his balls and the pants from the attendant who was checking to see if she had broken the skin of his arm. Meanwhile, other attendants brought in other people who had been wounded during the horrible events in the Vancouver Lounge.

Fred the Waiter had been smashed in the face by a falling table. He had a broken nose. Fred the Bartender had been caught and cut in a hale of flying glass as patrons sought safety behind the bar. Dominick Fabrizi, the furniture mover, and his date, the talent agent Spunky Pruitt, had escaped with a few bad cuts. They stared at the pots and the canned olives on the pantry shelves, no longer aware of their stitches, trying to remember what had happened.

Dr. Yablonsky had placed Heimlich on a long butcher block table near the meat cooler. Because so much emergency equipment had been brought in to deal with the ravages of the storm, the doctor had instant access to everything that he could possibly need to treat a bullet wound to the head. Electronic monitoring equipment, clean blood, anesthetics, everything.

Except there was no bullet wound.

Dr. Yablonsky felt himself slipping into a kind of ignorance-panic he had not experienced since his inner city residency, when they would bring in illegal immigrants with rare tropical diseases. His stomach knotted. His hands grew greasy with sweat. Ten years at Mt. Sinai in New York, two years in Vietnam, two at the Hadassah Hospital in Jerusalem. He had seen every wound made by every weapon, and he had never seen anything like this. The erratic heartbeat, the wildly undulating brain waves, the spasmodic jerking of the sedated body, these symptoms suggested a reaction to superhuman physical strain. Had Heimlich run a grueling race? Had he surfaced too quickly after a dive? It made no sense to Yablonsky. He repeatedly checked with the desk in case the hotel was harboring an opthamologist or a neurologist, maybe a sports surgeon, any specialist for a consultation. He went to the freezer where Heimlich's shattered right eye lay in storage, and just stared at it, trying to get an idea.

Alisette took advantage of Yablonsky's reverie to slip past the tubes and wires and get closer to Heimlich. She leaned down over the comedian. He was yelling softly in his sleep, little yells of terror like those you might hear from a man in the distance, down a railroad track maybe or out on the open sea, who was witnessing an accident but could do nothing to prevent it.

On Heimlich's chest, among the nodes and pads that connected him to the machines that recorded his life signs, half hidden by fuzzy hair now matted with blood, was a small, gold medal on a thin, gold chain. Alisette recalled seeing a larger version of this medal on the chest of a Hollywood agent at poolside; also in the ear lobe of a certain saxophone player; she did not know what it was but she decided to place it in Heimlich's hand, as she had seen Catholics do to the dying in films. To her surprise, Heimlich's hand closed over hers, and his grip grew strong. She could not withdraw. So then she had to stay there next to him. One of the attendants brought her a chair.

Orpheo Pastafino walked into the pantry. "Where's Mrs. Shapiro?" he asked.

"She's over there, resting comfortably," said Dr. Yablonsky. "A clean fracture. She'll have a cast to contend with for a while but she'll be fine."

"You're sweating."

"I'm scared I'm going to lose Heimlich."

Orpheo walked over to where Candy lay sleeping, and Kevin stood guard. Kevin hung his head and grinned, embarrassed.

"Don't worry," Orpheo said. "You did the best thing, the right thing. I congratulate you."

Kevin felt as though he had been given a Federal judgeship, which would, in fact, turn out to be the case.

Orpheo gently pushed Candy's thick braid from her arm so that it hung down off the table like the fairy tale rescue rope hair of Rapunzel. He felt her forehead for signs of fever. He untangled her fingers from the sheets.

"Did you hear what Heimlich said?" Orpheo asked.

"No," Kevin answered. "I only heard Alisette screaming."

"Anybody hear what Heimlich said before all the fireworks?" Orpheo asked the assemblage.

"I did," said Fred the Bartender. "I heard every word."

"But I can't remember now," said Lettie.

"Me neither," said Spunky.

Orpheo frowned. "What about you, Alisette?" he asked. "Do you remember?"

"Not right this minute," she answered after thinking for a moment. "But one day it'll come to me."

A pronounced silence gripped the infirmary. Everybody was trying to remember. They all felt that they had understood Heimlich's prophecy quite clearly at the time of utterance. No one realized that it had to have been incomprehensible because no one recalled that it had emerged in Hebrew.

With the expertise of one who had watched a lot of people dying in a lot of hospital rooms, Orpheo surveyed the machines that girded Heimlich. They had begun to record an even heartbeat, a normally functioning brain. "Looks like your patient is getting better," he said to Dr. Yablonsky."

Overcome with relief that Heimlich was not going to die, and strengthened by memories she had recently glimpsed on the ocean floor, Alisette began to sing the first solo she had ever been selected to sing when she was eight years old in Detroit at the church, and the preacher had just recognized her talent.

*Wade in the water* (She sang very slowly, pronouncing the "T"s.)

*Wade in the water, children*
*Wade in the water*
*God's gonna trouble the water.* (Her breath was so deep, all the people could feel it in their lungs.)

*My Lord spoke in a monstrous voice*
*Shook the world to its very joist,*
*Rung through Heaven. rung through Hell*
*My dungeon shook and my chains they fell.* (She closed her eyes. They all closed their eyes. Heimlich opened his eye and heard Alisette singing and felt the gold *chai* in his hand and knew that he had not died. Well, *Baruch ha shem,* he thought. Sanctified be The Name. Then he went back to sleep.)

*Wade in the water*
*Wade in the water, children.*
*Wade in the water*
*God's gonna trouble the water.*

And everybody who heard Alisette sing that night — even Candy in her twilight dozing — remembered the lyrics of that old song forever after.

★ ★ ★

Alisette was due to go west in a few days' time, for a tour that included recording sessions in Los Angeles as well as personal appearances in Carmel, San Francisco and Vancouver. She had long ago arranged for this tour, primarily because her sons Jimbo and Ali wanted it so much.

They attended an exclusive boarding school in western Massachusetts named for W.E.B. Du Bois. Lots of rich black kids went there. For summer vacation, each of the boys had been given his choice: hang out with Dad and his other children or go on tour with Mama. Alisette knew they had chosen her because they wanted to see Hollywood, to meet all the famous people their mother ran with, to see the redwoods, the fog coast, Disneyland, the Universal Studios and the Dodgers from a box with movie stars. She didn't mind that the boys had their reasons. She wanted them with her, especially now, when her soul had been so badly jolted by all the violent upheaval she had seen in Atlantic City, when she had been quite certain for a moment there — hearing Heimlich's voice like thunder, seeing his blood fly — that the end of the world was at hand. She wanted her boys with her because pictures in newspapers fade, and music, even sweet music can be drowned away, but a child is living proof of a woman's power in nature: a child is eternal.

The Western tour had been planned with difficulty and some argument, because of obstacles Alisette herself had raised. First of all, she needed a furnished house with a pool in each town because she would not live at a hotel with those two impossible adolescents. Secondly, she refused to fly. It wasn't just that she had the flusters like Aretha or that she feared to get too close to the judgments of Heaven, as Heimlich had once told her jokingly of I.B. Singer. It was that she remembered still the death of those three boys in the blizzard when she was a little girl.

Her friends in school didn't cry. Her friends in church said Richie who? Buddy what? And meanwhile her cousin, Hank the Trumpet, and her other cousin, Zeke the Sax, were crying as though their hearts had been totally broken.

"There's a third race, Al honey," Grandma Blanche explained. "Not called Black. Not called White. This race is called Entertainer. We in our family is members."

On the several occasions when, from professional necessity, Alisette had dared to consign her soul to the fathomless air, she had looked out the window at the clouds and thought: we are all God's children and He has given us all wings to fly. But what if one day we're up there flying and God suddenly remembers all the shit we have done? The vows we abrogated, the melodies we borrowed, the cards and flowers we did not send to Grandma Blanche when she was ailing, and God gets mad and cracks His thunder and blows away the delicate wings of His angels. . . trillions of feathers fluttering in the wild blue. . .

And with this horrible image in mind, Alisette pulled the little blinds down over the clouds and resolved never to fly again until she felt completely guiltless. That had been — let's see, she thought — a couple maybe three years ago. Since then she had taken mostly trains, toodling on her keyboard while the steel wheels sang in the wide prairie nights between coastlines.

So familiar was Alisette to the people of the railroad that they considered her an advocate and an ally. And when some fool offered up a bill in Congress to cancel the railroad permanently and to condemn all Americans to the road and the sky, she was invited to testify, and her fear struck her elected representatives as so sincere, so deeply *religious,* that they killed the bill in Committee.

"You're keeping a whole antiquated money-losing railroad alive at the taxpayers' expense because of the sensibilities of one rock star!" the sponsoring Congressman shouted to the Committee Chair.

"But 'The Ultimate Aphrodisiac' changed my life," she answered.

In addition to refusing to fly, Alisette further irritated her manager, Megaman Brancusi, and his large staff of accountants by refusing to let herself be booked in coliseums and stadiums.

("Colisea," said Alex Deal, still doing *The New York Times* crossword puzzle after all these years in exile. "Stadia.")

"You must play the big houses," Megaman insisted. "The Meadowlands. The Garden. The Bowl."

"No," she said.

Megaman sat at her dressing room table. Alisette stood in the adjoining bathroom, all dressed for her late night revels, brushing her teeth. With the edge of her eye, she could see Megaman check out his mustache in her table mirror and flick a bit of glitter from one of her costumes off the lapel of his navy suede jacket.

"They want you for the 'Soul in the Bowl' concert," he said, casually reading the letters from her family which she had left among her make-up vials and her earrings. "They want you to jam with Patti and Willy. Quincy's gonna be there, he'll invite you to his house, you will meet Alice there, now I know you admire Alice. She'll come with her 'Al Sings Billie' album and ask you to sign it. You could be on your way, you could rise and converge with the best, rising and converging, rising and converging. Senator O'Banyon's wife could invite you to one of her political soirees. Now just think of it. Andy. Jesse. Connections that could send your sons to the United States Senate, Alisette. But you have got to play the Garden and the Bowl."

"I saw Keith in the Park," Alisette said. "He sounded like he was under water."

"The public didn't think so."

"One speaker goes out and the five hundred people who paid good money for their tickets might as well have been mugged."

"The crew fixes it in a minute, and besides, it doesn't happen any more, they got every wire and circuit computerized."

Alisette strode out of the bathroom. Her mouth was touched with foam.

"I don't want to have to depend on some techie to bring me back to life! I don't want to live in danger like that! I want eye contact! Peace of mind! A small audience!"

"You're scared, that's what you are," stated Megaman.

"Aw, go tell it to my shrink!"

"You are a small-time choir alto at heart, and you are scared of making it big."

Alisette put her arms around him, slipped her hand under his cashmere tie and stroked his heart.

"I *have* made it big," she said softly. "Strangers write me personal letters and tell me their lives."

"You have fifteen minutes, that's what the man said. Just fifteen minutes to become famous in."

"The man who said that is dead, honey. And anyway, he was talking about chic. I am not chic, Megaman. I am going to endure, like Oum Kalthoum. So you book me, two three four weeks at a time, in the good clubs with the great sound, city by city, you book me where my soul tells me to sing, and in the end, you mark me, darling, I shall give you the country."

Megaman grinned. He had always been attracted by Alisette's self-confidence, the grandeur with which she drew herself up and intoned her big plans while fixing him with her dynamite eyes. When he had first realized that she was falling for Abe Heimlich, he had felt downright jealous. He loved her songs and her singing. But there was a limit to how much self-programming he could abide in his clients. He was not going to peddle vibes to a fickle public forever. He wanted to clean up here, get out of the music business and into real estate where the big money was, and if Alisette wouldn't join his agenda, well, so long, sweet thing; Megaman Brancusi had no time for women who wanted to be classics.

For the time being, he kissed her hands and pretended to be her plaything.

"You have convinced me, Al," he said. "I have no more arguments for you. What you want, you get. You'll finish your three weeks here, then we'll send you to San Francisco and Vancouver. In between, we'll maybe take a sound track commission, now how's that sound to you?"

"Wonderful," she said.

"I like to keep my artists very happy."

"Could you ask them to knock out the bad seats here? You know I just hate to have my fans sitting in bad seats."

"Whatever you want, sweet thing."

"Thank you," she said.

She smiled. She had always liked his mustache. He kissed her, looking forward to the moment when her big breasts would tumble onto his face.

★ ★ ★

These were the common fantasies of Alisette Legrand.

1. I am in a red desert, riding a black stallion, leading my troops into battle.

2. I almost strangle myself in the rosy womb, injuring my vocal chords. Therefore I cannot grow up to be a vulnerable artist who cares if the G is true or sour. I must settle for being a mere accountant, with a six figure salary, who routinely tells record producers to stick it.

3. I am in a red room. There is no music. There is love. . . but no music. I am in hell.

"Listen to yourself, my dear!" protested her analyst. "Love without music is hell. Translated that means love not dominated by Alisette's talent is hell. Don't you see? It's your ego that destroys your relationships."

"You are full of shit!" retorted Alisette. "When the men in my band have these fantasies, they are called sexual. When I have them, they are called egotistical. You may send your final bill directly to my manager."

However, in time, Alisette came to believe that the shrink had been right. She had really never loved a man she could not control. She especially loved manipulating talented men who knew exactly what she was doing, could not be fooled by her, and who voluntarily fell under her hand like food in the kitchen just because it was so much fun to be her plaything.

As to race, Alisette did not deliberately seek to mix. Her first husband, an entertainment lawyer, and her second, a famous actor, were both black like most of her lovers. Yet when she had ventured into relationships with white men — (to tell the truth, only twice, and only just for a couple minutes) — they turned out to be surprisingly similar to black men. They peed the same, snored the same. Their greed had the same damp heat.

Alisette would never admit she had stopped believing that white men were different from black men. In these separatist times, it would not do for an established African American singer to appear to have adopted some sort of grand sexual philosophy that overrode distinctions of color, oh no, it would not do at all. But because of a telltale softening of the heart that persisted, she went to see Heimlich the Comedian one last time.

He had been moved to a small, modern hospital far enough inland to have been untouched by the tsunami. He was out cold. The battlefield surgery which had been performed on him by Yablonsky of Mt. Sinai in the pantry of the Imperial

Hotel had been subjected to some revisions and refinements, so he now had a new incision and new painkillers.

Limited to no more than a five minute visit by the physicians, Alisette viewed him through a thicket of equipment. What could she say? He snored in her face, sputtering spit. A snotlike tube snaked out of his nose. The purple veins on his one exposed eyelid repelled her, as did the chalky pallor of his toes. Nauseated from smelling medicines, she could not for her life recall what she had found so attractive about Abraham Heimlich only two days earlier, and she left the hospital without even sitting down.

Soon she was splashing in the Pacific with her children.

Jimbo was chunky and thirteen. Ali was lanky and fifteen. They wore funky sunglasses with rubberized frames of iridescent green and orange. They both had big strong teeth and flat top haircuts. In another couple minutes, they would be taller than Alisette. As it was, their needs — for things, for clothes, for long mornings of sleep and long nights of inquiry and unmitigated selfless mothering — simply overwhelmed her.

She had all she could do to remember herself that summer, much less Heimlich the Comedian. So when exactly he left the hospital, she did not know. That his daughter Rivka came from Yale Law School in the middle of exams and took him out in a wheelchair and flew him to California where his daughter Rachel met them, this Alisette did not know.

She did not even know he had daughters.

Potential lovers and partners, Alisette and Heimlich now lost each other, bound up as they were in their private lives and unique ethnicities and the destinies of children so different from each other that they would have been astonished to discover that their parents had ever even met.

# PART II

CHAPTER FOUR

# ALMOST TOUCHING

MARTY SHAPIRO WENT TO LOS ANGELES for a conference on breast cancer. Although he never brought Candy to these things, he would have liked to this time because L.A. was his home town and his mother lived there and Candy had wonderful ways to occupy and entertain his mother. However, Candy had broken her wrist at a Hadassah meeting in Atlantic City, falling when she caught her heel between planks of the Boardwalk, and could not travel with the cast. Too bad, he thought. He would have to deal with his mother one on one.

The elder Mrs. Shapiro had moved from Patton Pines in the Valley after Marty's father died and now, at seventy-seven, lived alone in a splendid high rise cooperative on the beach. There she waited for her beloved son, the healer, savior of women and babies, she waited for him to call or visit. His wife called twice a week and often put nine-year old Ethel and six-year old Sam on the phone. However, Martin, her Martin, had given up his whole personal life to tend to his fabulous practice, and he rarely had time to say more than "Hiya Mom, how are you?"

Mrs. Shapiro told all her friends about Marty's forthcoming arrival. She told strange joggers who happened to plop down next to her on the Palisade path where she sat reading *The Los Angeles Times* with her new 20-20 lenses recently implanted during cataract surgery. "My son is coming to see me," she said. "He's a brilliant diagnostician, an overbooked surgeon. Women force their tumors to wait for him. My son."

⋆ ⋆ ⋆

Martin's courtship of Candice Deal had always struck Mrs. Shapiro as much more pragmatic than romantic. She was sorry about that, for she had wanted her only child to find true love.

Then just finishing his residency in New York, Marty had reported no social life to his family back in Patton Pines. He seemed to work all the time and wouldn't discuss the details. Thus when he merely mentioned that he had met a nice girl at a party, Mrs. Shapiro got all excited. Her husband — already sick with cancer and completely humorless — called her an idiot and told her to calm down and bring him a Hershey Bar. Happily, when Marty came home to visit, Mr. Shapiro was hospitalized and heavily sedated and could not interdict her eager questions.

"So do you have interesting cases?"

"No. Well, yes. Mostly trauma."

"What do you mean?"

"Let's not talk about it. I really don't want to talk about it, Mom, okay?"

"But what does that mean: trauma?"

"Emergencies."

"Oh, you mean like miscarriages. Last minute Caesareans."

"Like rape, Mom. And battery. And kitchen table abortions."

"Oh darling. . . "

They went to see his father. Identical faces. One almost dead. Mrs. Shapiro often wondered — in fact she had asked Rabbi Heimlich point blank — if a son's anger and hatred could tip the scales of luck and push a father into the grave. In typical fashion, Rabbi Heimlich had answered: "You will never know the answer to that, Mrs. Shapiro. Other people are always mysteries, even your own children. All you can hope to know is whether *a wife's* anger and hatred can push a husband into the grave."

Mr. Shapiro woke up. He stared at them as though they were strangers. (Well, they *were* strangers.) He asked them for some Non Pareils, crumbled into a spoon, the tiny white pellets mashed together with the chocolate, sweetness being the only taste he could tolerate at this point. In a funny way, the same seemed to be true of her son.

"Candy is a nice girl," he said that night, at dinner. "She smells good. She's warm and cute. Not complicated. An ordinary everyday New York JAP."

"I wish you wouldn't use that term, Martin."

"She has some gopher kind of job in the Broadway theater. Her father is in the underwear business. Her brother was killed in Vietnam when she was in college. . . "

"A military man?!"

"A surgeon. Orthopedics. There's another brother. Ran away from the war. Far away. Apparently beyond reunion."

Mrs. Shapiro smiled. The picture had now become quite clear to her. This Candy was the last hope of her parents. Probably she felt pressured to make up for the fate of her brothers. Probably she wanted to get married and have babies. She wouldn't say "Let's wait until I get my doctorate," or "Let's wait until I make partner," or "Let's just live together and see," like those other girls Martin had known, those other mean, dreadful girls who had broken his heart.

"To tell you the truth, the most interesting thing about Candy is her hair," he joked. "She's got this hairdo which is as complex as the DNA molecule, and I'm really only taking her out because of scientific curiosity, to see if maybe someday I can break it apart and analyze its structure."

Mrs. Shapiro hugged him. He was all her joy in life. She was thrilled when it turned out that Candice Deal, this so-called ordinary everyday JAP, had an infallible memory for birthdays and other minor occasions, an extraordinary ability to give great dinner parties, wonderful taste in furniture, and endless patience with the kids who drove Martin quite crazy. The house which she had bought in Broadbeach, on Long Island's North Shore, had a capacious deck facing the Sound where Martin could read his Sunday paper, a pristine lawn where he could putt in peace and a specially equipped music room where he could enjoy the best possible audio reproduction of the sonatas he loved so much. In Mrs. Shapiro's estimation, Candy had turned out to be the most suitable wife a successful gynecologist could possibly have. And if she had pretended to be maybe a little dumber and more helpless than she actually was in order to break down Martin's fear so that he would marry her, well, what could you do? A smart girl dissembled. It had always been thus.

Candy had warned Marty that his mother would cook. He said "Oh come on! She can barely stand!" and made a reservation at a chic restaurant. But as always in matters domestic, Candy was right. The minute Marty walked into the apartment in Santa Monica, he smelled the brisket. His mother wept with joy when she saw him. He thought she looked like a sparrow, balancing on twig limbs. She made him wash his hands before dinner.

He ducked into the bedroom, called and broke the dinner reservation, called his girlfriend Cecily and told her he'd get there late. She sounded annoyed. She had this party she wanted to go to. Marty said he wouldn't be long, that his mother could not possibly require more than an hour. Then he glanced around at the dressers, the night tables, and noticed the pictures, dozens of pictures in dozens of variegated frames, a menagerie of moments from his life and the lives of his children.

"I take it back," he said to Cecily. "I will be more than an hour. Go to the party without me. I'll catch up with you there later."

The brisket had been bought from a butcher with connections to the best cuts on the West Coast. It had been roasted and basted with whole Vidalia onions and baby carrots and the heart of the celery. Mrs. Shapiro cut the meat into broad slices dripping with warm, salty juice and served it with brown potatoes and apple sauce tinged with cloves, and when Marty bit into it, he felt like he was on vacation from his adult life.

The lovely dinner eradicated the years. Mrs. Shapiro once again looked into his heart as through an open window, as in the days when he was still her soft-skinned boy.

"So tell me what the problem is, Martin," she said. "Tell me what is troubling you."

He dropped his glasses into his hands and rubbed his eyes.

"My patients don't like me, Mom," he said. "They only come to me because they're so sick, they don't care if they like their doctor. They have heard in the supermarket, on the job, that I saved somebody's ovaries, or I removed somebody's fibroids and she conceived, I mean, my achievements as a surgeon are really . . . well, they're real, Mom. But I don't know how to tell bad news. I tell it wrong somehow. My nurse quit because she said she was sick and tired of comforting hysterical women whose hearts I had broken. And last month, one of my patients hit me."

"Oh darling. . . "

"I told her she had a tumor in her right breast that would probably replicate itself in her left breast inside a year, so even though the left was still clean, she ought to have them both off at once because one general anesthetic was a lot less dangerous than two, not to speak of the enormous savings in money."

"And you don't know why she hit you?"

"To tell you the truth, she beat me up, Mom. I had a shiner and I lost a back tooth."

"A big woman."

"Thirty maybe forty pounds overweight."

"This blindness is a gift you inherited from your father, darling. You should seek help."

"I called my lawyer, Phil Brinks."

"Not that kind of help!"

"We were going to sue her for assault."

"Oh Martin! No!"

"That's what Candy said. Imagine the headline, she said. 'Eminent Gynecologist Sues Desperately Ill Patient.'"

"She was always a sensitive girl, Candy."

"She went to see the woman. They straightened it out between them. The woman took my advice. She went to a friend of mine for her surgery, and he showed me the reports, looks pretty good, I think she's got an excellent chance of becoming a very old lady now." He dug into his apple cake. Scrumptious it was. As far as Marty was concerned, at Spago, at Lutèce and La Chine, they had nothing to equal it. "But I tell you, Mom, I went out of my way to attend this conference on breast cancer because I was hoping I would meet someone here who really understands how to tell bad news, who has made that his sub-specialty as it were and who can give me some advice."

Mrs. Shapiro served his coffee and poured just the right amount of heated skimmed milk into it.

"Why don't you go see Rabbi Heimlich?" she suggested. "He was always good at that sort of thing. He got me through your father's illness. He got your father through your father's illness. I haven't seen him since that awful trouble with Rabbi AvShalom about the funeral, but I'm sure he will remember our family, and he will certainly remember you."

Marty suddenly grasped his mother's twig hands and kissed them.

"What a wonderful idea, Mom! Gee! Rabbi Heimlich! Of course!" He beamed at his mother. "A great idea! And a great meal!"

Mrs. Shapiro lived on that kiss, that beam, that compliment, for the rest of her life.

★ ★ ★

Candy's decision to go see the woman who had assaulted her husband was based on no hunch, no suspicion, no fear, just a general desire to be an honest broker between two obviously innocent parties.

The woman's name was Maureen Holiday. She lived on the Queens border and had traveled some distance to see Marty at the medical office building he and his partner Harry Wang now owned on the Suffolk border. According to eye-witness reports, Maureen had listened to his diagnosis, nodded meekly, started to leave his office, then turned with a horrible scream which endured like a siren, a pulsing scream nobody would ever forget, and leaped at Marty, plunged over his desk, straddled him as he sat in his chair and punched him repeatedly. As four (it might have been six or eight) people tried to pull her off him, she screamed "You miserable shit! I'm going to kill you!" and other words to that effect.

They called Maureen Holiday's husband at his place of employment, a truck rental agency, and asked him to come and take her home. He said he was too busy and suggested that they call her a cab.

Phil Brinks, Marty's lawyer, would have been perfectly happy to help Marty sue this crazy woman. However, Candy came out of the kitchen with coffee and those little rolled up Jewish cakes with honey and nuts and raisins which Phil loved so much, wearing her apron and her diamond locket, smelling like nutmeg, and she defended Maureen Holiday until Phil and the bruised and aching Marty too could see how a punitive action might make them look like hard-hearted cyborgs in court. Therefore, they decided not to sue.

"There's only one thing still," said Marty. "She ought to do what I told her. I mean she's sick. If she doesn't do what I told her, she's going to give the cancer a chance to recur."

"Send her a letter," Phil suggested.

"Um. . . um. . . a letter is a little on the cold side, fellas, you know what I mean?" Candy said gently. "Why don't I go and talk to her?"

So Candy went to see Maureen Holiday on the Queens border. A hefty woman with reddish hair, wearing dirty jeans and a bleach-blotched red shirt, she initially closed the door in Candy's face. Candy waited patiently on the stoop of the small house, staring out at the neat yard, clearly determined not to budge. Finally Maureen came out and sat down beside her. And this is what she said.

"You want a cigarette?"

"I stopped," Candy answered.

"Why? You think that's going to keep you from dying?"

"Please. Don't be bitter with me. I am not your enemy."

Maureen sighed. She exhaled smoke like a rocket.

"A few years ago," she said, "I went to your husband on the advice of a friend."

"I thought you were a new patient!"

"Shut up and listen or I won't tell you," Maureen said. "I had had a tubal ligation and somehow it didn't work and I was pregnant again. But my own doctor said that he could not have screwed up the sterilization, that I was just overcome with guilt at having tied my tubes and that I was not really pregnant again but hysterically pregnant.

"My husband believed this doctor. I tried to believe him too. When the doctor prescribed strong sedatives, I took them. But still, I was sure I was pregnant. I needed to see a doctor outside of my community, far away, away from my husband, which was why I went to Marty.

"He told me sure, I was right, I was pregnant. He thought that with all the drugs I had been taking, my baby would probably stand a good chance of not being normal. He recommended that I go back to my incompetent son-of-a-bitch doctor and demand a free abortion and another tubal ligation because, see, the tube had not been cut through all the way and had re-canalized, that was the term he used, re-canalized; the tube had regenerated from that little microscopic spot where my incompetent son-of-a-bitch doctor had not cut it all the way and the sperm had just sailed through.

"I went back to my doctor. He got really mad. He called up Marty and accused him of being disloyal to a fellow practitioner.

"Marty called him an asshole and threatened him with exposure if he didn't do the abortion and the new surgery. So he did. See, the son-of-a-bitch had no choice. He was nailed.

"When it was all over and I was healed and I finally couldn't get pregnant any more, I stopped by at your husband's office to say thank you.

"It was a really great thank you, Mrs. Shapiro. We had an affair that lasted a week. He was a very considerate lover, I am sure you know that. Not like my Vincent who can barely find a breast in the dark much less anything smaller and who was mad anyway that I would only have five children and not eight like his poor mother.

"I wanted to celebrate my sterilization, and my husband wanted to mope about it. That's why I took up with Marty. To celebrate my sterilization.

"And then, when I got sick, I went back to him. Five years had passed. I went back to him with my mammogram results and he examined me and he did a biopsy and the tests came back positive for cancer and he told me what I ought to do, and all that time, he had no idea who I was! He had sex with me! A whole week of sex! And he had completely forgotten that he had ever known me!"

Maureen Holiday had begun to cry.

"It wasn't him I wanted to kill, even though I was hitting him," she wept. "It was me! And my life, my stupid wasted life! The unimportance of my most important decisions, to be sterilized, to betray my husband! The unimportance of my breasts!"

Candy put her arm around Maureen. This was hard because Maureen's back was so much wider than the length of Candy's arm. She sat that way for many minutes until Maureen stopped crying.

"Well, but you must think about survival now," Candy said. "I mean the idea of importance doesn't mean much without survival, am I right? Martin is a very good surgeon, really the best. If you want him to, he will still do the mastectomies you need. You ought to have them, to save your life. Because you have children. They're more important than anything. Your life is vital to them. And if you don't want Martin to operate, which I can certainly understand, than I could give you the name of another man, a colleague, he's very good too. . . "

Maureen wiped her eyes and peered at Candy.

"You are some cool customer."

Candy did not smile.

"Do I have choice?" she asked.

She drove around for a while after leaving Maureen's house. She picked up Ethel from ballet school and dropped off Little Sam at baseball. Then she went to see the nurse who had, during the previous month, walked out on Marty Shapiro. The nurse was watering her marigolds. She and Candy had a long talk.

* * *

On the evening of the day that Candy discovered her husband had been constantly unfaithful, virtually from the inception of their marriage, she sat down in the living room with the lights off and ate a box of Oreo cookies. Her children were sleeping. Marty had said he would be working late at the hospital, although she would never again be able to believe that. All she could think of was violence. Profanities that lurked in her subconscious, that had never seen the light of mind, surfaced suddenly like horrible sea monsters. She imagined Marty's hands on dinner plates, and Sam and Ethel devouring them, finger by finger. She saw his severed penis lying on the baby blue carpet like a piece of dog shit. She thought of flying to Florida and surprising her mother, strangling her old mother with nylon knitting yarn and feeding her into the garbage disposal, then flying to Los Angeles and becoming the Pacific and dashing her mother-in-law against the rocks. The treacherous old hags! They knew! They were as guilty as Cordell Hull and Roosevelt! They knew! And they had not told!

Candy's tears fell like poison on her lips. She spat them out in a fury; she tore them off her face. Screw crying! she thought. Never again! Over and over she played "The Ultimate Aphrodisiac," a pissed off, stomping number in which Alisette scraped her tambourine with her fingernails and grunted in counterpoint with the bass guitar as though she were in the act of fornicating.

*If you're gonna shoot for the top of the tower, girl,*
*Make sure it's built of stone.*
*If you're gonna get high on power,*
*Make damn sure it's your own.*
*Oooh. Oooh. Gimme-it. Gimme-it. Oooh. Oooh.*

Candy's housekeeper, the stately Marie de Grenouille de Port-au-Prince, who usually retired in dignified silence after the dinner dishes were done and had never been seen when not perfectly dressed and coiffed, appeared in a battered green chenille bathrobe. She wore pink flip-flops. She had grease on her face and droopy rag curlers in her hair.

"Is there anything that I can bring you, Madam?" she asked.

Candy took her hands and danced with her a little.

"Wisdom," she whispered. "Bring me wisdom!"

"Will you settle for a glass of brandy, Madam?"

Candy polished off the bottle.

As she was losing consciousness that night, she guzzled mouth wash and slathered her whole upper body with mineral ice to mask the brandy smell and fell into bed reeking of spearmint and eucalyptus. Marty — who usually slept with her breasts in his hands and her hair in his eyes — was so thoroughly repelled by the stench that he spent the night in the guest room. When he left for work the next morning, Candy managed to be in the shower behind a wall of spray and steam. "No one needs to know. . . " her mother had said, and so Candy hid her misery through every means at her disposal, hoping to get through the hours one by one, hoping that time would clear her mind so that she would be able to decide upon a course of action.

She took aspirin and vitamins for her hangover and drove the carpool in total silence. Then she went to New York.

Her appointment that morning was with two young men, Jock Silver and Slim Price, who had produced a small Broadway comedy, soon to be in previews, and would cut her a good deal on a theater party for Broadbeach Hadassah. Candy wore her purple silk suit and matching amethyst barrettes. Not one centimeter of her real face showed through her make-up. And over her eyes, she wore lavender lens sunglasses.

Candy explained to Jock and Slim that in Broadbeach Hadassah, there were eighty-seven women who felt personally responsible for rescuing the Ethiopian Jews. They needed to raise money to bribe the greedy colonels and ransom these benighted descendants of Sheba and Solomon so that they could emigrate to Israel. A Broadway theater party was clearly the best way.

Slim offered her the balcony at a Wednesday matinee.

Candy tried to explain that the women of Broadbeach Hadassah would not sit in the balcony, that they needed excellent orchestra seats. "Otherwise they won't like the play," she said.

Jock said that excellent orchestra seats would cost her $30 each.

"Look," she said. "You know you will probably get a bad review. *The Times* hates your star. When she did 'Twelfth Night' in the Park, he called her 'a prancing monkey,' am I right? The only way you are going to be able to pull the show past the reviews is if you have great word of mouth from the previews to sustain you while you advertise. Besides, you've got another show running downtown and you're trying out another one in Connecticut this summer, and I do four theater parties a year. Give me a break and I'll send you my business ad infinitum."

"She's adorable," Jock said.

"Let's take her to lunch," Slim said.

"Give me 150 good orchestra tickets at $15.00 and I'll take *you* to lunch," Candy said.

They settled on $18.00 and took her to Joe Allen's. They introduced her to an actor who was currently performing as a supporting player in a British musical. Candy told him she had loved his performance as The Gentleman Caller in Stratford, especially since she had schlepped out there to see a certain actress who played The Sister whose performance had turned out to be terribly disappointing, making her appreciate this fine actor's work all the more.

"She's fabulous," the actor said to Jock and Slim. And he sent over a couple of other show business people to meet her.

The meeting with Slim and Jock made Candy feel stylish and *au courant.* So she regained her strength a little. While driving home, she made a mental list of all the possible advisers she could consult to help her deal with her new knowledge of Marty's infidelities. First eliminated were her best friend Roxie Kirsch, who would surely fly into a vengeful, feminist rage, and her mother. Candy could just imagine the conversation with Maida.

"Did Daddy ever cheat on you?" Candy would ask.

"Never," Maida would answer. "His friends, his brother, they all cheated plenty. But not my Jack. He adored me. Once he married me, he never looked at another woman."

Candy could not bear the thought of this exchange. No, she needed a less romantic adviser, someone who would be cold, who would think primarily of her children and advise her over time, for the long run, like a banker. The answer came to her on the Triboro Bridge. That evening Candy told Marty that she had decided to attend an Hadassah Regional Board meeting in Atlantic City.

He believed her because she had never lied to him before.

★ ★ ★

Marty listened to an excellent paper on fibrocystic disease of the breast. During a lunch with his learned colleagues, he instigated a potentially lucrative relationship with a French plastic surgeon named Danton Moore. Finally he headed out over Beverly Glen to the old neighborhood, to the synagogue where as a boy he had attended Hebrew school and studied for his bar mitzvah.

Nothing had changed. Everyone remembered him. The synagogue secretary, Cassie, now grown old, had the same pictures on her desk, the same cascades of bougainvillea in the same insipid vase that he remembered from two decades before. The caretaker, Boris (a.k.a. "Crocodile") Badchan, a burly Russian immigrant, still trundled through the halls spreading the stench of ammonia, with the enormous, jingling ring of keys that signaled his coming long before he could be seen, as in Captain Hook's crocodile.

"Still married to that beautiful New Yorker, Marty?" he asked. "Lucky son of a bitch. When I saw you walk in here with her, you miserable little bastard. . . what was it?. . . ten years ago?"

"Eleven years," Marty answered.

"Eleven years ago when you brought her to your father's funeral and we all got to meet her for the first time. 'Shapiro's son is engaged to a girl from Gimbel's Inlet, no less,' that's what they said and I nearly peed in my pants laughing. I said to them, that nasty little prick gets himself an MD and lookit, the treasures of the Jewish nation fall into his arms!" The powerful Badchan belted Marty heartily between the shoulder blades. "God sure has strange tastes, don't He? Did she give you children?"

"Two."

"Healthy?"

"Smart and cute and healthy, a boy and a girl."

"You lucky son of a bitch!"

Rabbi AvShalom, whom Marty had always disliked, greeted him with a careful formality. They had not seen each other since Marty's father's funeral, in the spring before Marty and Candy were married. At that time, AvShalom was hostile and angry because Marty's dying father, a former president of the synagogue and one of its most cantankerous and disrespectful members, had asked the junior Rabbi Heimlich to officiate. By the time Marty's father finally died, Rabbi Heimlich had been fired and had moved to another city. He called Marty's mother, saying that he could not officiate because of the conflict and discord it would create in the congregation, and he pleaded with Mrs. Shapiro to apologize for the insult to Rabbi AvShalom so that he would willingly preside at the funeral and the Jews of Patton Pines would be able to live in peace once more.

Mrs. Shapiro had apologized — but really only because Rabbi Heimlich had asked her to. And Rabbi AvShalom had agreed to pontificate over her husband's remains — but really only because the board had begged him to. Since then the old lady had paid her dues, supported all expansions, behaved with nothing if not respect for Rabbi AvShalom. However, all her efforts were obliterated when, after 120 seconds of niceties, her son Marty the Direct said to Rabbi AvShalom: "Actually, I'm looking for Rabbi Heimlich."

AvShalom lifted his palms to Heaven.

"Why?" he asked (God, not Marty). "Why?"

"Uh. . . .to talk to him. . . "

"Once a month some ex-congregant comes around asking for him," said AvShalom. "What did he do to you kids? Give you drugs? Set you up with starlets?"

"Oh please. . . "

"He became a slightly successful comedian."

"No kidding!"

"That's why we fired him, because he was always such a big comedian!"

Marty Shapiro laughed and shook his head.

"Oh please, AvShalom," he said. "We're both adults. We both understand. You fired Rabbi Heimlich because he was popular and charming and everybody loved him and he had no respect for you."

Rabbi AvShalom stood up. A short man with a fat face and thick gray beard and a kind, rather vacant smile, he was often selected to mediate disputes within the Jewish community, for he was famous for his judicial brilliance and his ability to remain calm despite the most outrageous provocations. At this moment, however, he looked so much like Maureen Holiday raging that Marty raised his arms to defend himself against a physical attack.

"He told your father a couple of jokes during his terrible illness!" Avshalom roared. "He sat with your mother in the hospital and explained that if your father would make some large bequests to charity in his final hours, he might expect to spend eternity at the right hand of God! Which was bullshit! Because everybody knew, your father was a dominating, self-centered bastard who treated the people around him like dirt!"

"I don't have to listen to this. . . "

"I can recall one or two occasions when you yourself had to be coaxed and cajoled and even bribed to go back to living under your father's roof! "

"I was twelve years old, for God's sakes!"

"Heimlich got your father when he was dying! Believe me, it was his best time! When he was in good health, nobody could stand him!"

Marty straightened his tie. He smoothed his smooth black hair. He put on his glasses, something he always did when needing to reduce the size and strength of a difficult patient.

"I am going to leave here now," he said.

"You think you can say the unspeakable to people and they will have nothing to say to you in return?! Are you such a fool, Shapiro?! I gave my life to this congregation! Carrying the day to day, building the library, the Hebrew School, putting up with the Sisterhood, the Young Couples' Club and then the Israeli immigration and then God help me the Russian immigration and now the Persian immigration, this onslaught of Persians who chase each other around the seder table with scallions! And after all my work, my devoted work, your mother, whose lousy cooking I endured at countless potluck dinners, walks in here and right to my face tells me that your father wants Heimlich to officiate at the funeral!"

Marty had finally summoned enough will to reach the door of the Rabbi's office. AvShalom was still screaming.

"With his dying breath he manages to dishonor me in front of the whole community! I could have killed him! Don't you realize that the Second Temple was destroyed and our people dispersed because of just such an outrage as this?! You ignorant putz, how dare you come in here and open an old wound so casually?! Oh, you are too cruel, you Shapiros! You were always vicious bastards who felt it was your right to humiliate the people around you! No wonder it's so easy for you to spend your life lopping off the breasts of women!"

★ ★ ★

Marty drove his rented Saab convertible directly to his girlfriend Cecily's office in a small seagreen glass building on Ventura Boulevard. She was busy on the phone arguing with some agent. When she saw his face, she got off the phone and told her secretary to hold all further calls. She locked the door. She fell on her knees before him. He couldn't get hard. Really all he wanted was for her to hold him, just hold him, but it was in the middle of a business day and much easier for a record company executive to give you a blow job than to give you comfort and sympathy when she had so many phone calls to answer and tapes to hear and meetings to take.

Anyway, Marty realized that he didn't want to have sex, he actually wanted to cry. More precisely he wanted to pray for his despised father and cry.

Cecily was at a loss. She straightened her hair and her tiny little skirt. She was crazy about Marty Shapiro. She loved his old fashioned paisley ties, the powerful cars he always rented when he came to see her, the way his narrow body fit precisely into her narrow body like the precision crafted clasp on the 18 karat gold bracelet (with lapis) he had bought for her birthday. She would do anything for him! Absolutely anything!

Marty strode directly into the office of Cecily's boss, a dapper fellow with suspenders. Ordinarily this important man's secretary would have prevented such an intrusion. But since she happened to be in the ladies' room, commiserating with Cecily just then — *What do these men want?! What the fuck do they fucking want?!* — Cecily's boss's door was left unprotected.

The boss was sitting at his gigantic desk. He had swung his chair around so that he faced his window and could enjoy a panoramic view of the San Fernando Valley in smog. He was talking on the phone. He did not see Marty enter.

Marty closed the door. He faced the wall. He said kaddish for his father and drenched his custom-made shirt in tears. Then he left. Cecily's boss never got off the phone.

★ ★ ★

Eliezer AvShalom stayed in his office all that night, rummaging in his bookcases among texts of distress and rapture, seeking comfort if not guidance. Marty's visit had left him breathless with anger. He felt that it had given him cancer. The lumpish swelling in his throat was surely a symptom. He felt that it had thickened his blood, would clog his arteries, send him a stroke, a heart attack.

Even after this panic abated, reality remained. People were still looking for Abraham Heimlich. More than a decade had passed since he had fired that impertinent yutz, and still, people showed up to seek his counsel.

Heimlich had come to the congregation in Patton Pines after a brief emigration to Israel which had turned out tragically. Although he had never held a pulpit in Israel — non-Orthodox rabbis rarely did — he had done a lot of social work there. And Rabbi AvShalom needed an assistant who would specialize in pastoral counseling, leaving AvShalom free to write and lecture on issues demographic and moral. He had expected Heimlich to cope with illness, divorce, unwanted pregnancies, homosexuality, academic failure, adoption, senility, inter-marriage. But he had not expected the junior rabbi to enter the hot scarlet dreams of the congregation.

Battlefields aflame with sunset; wombscapes decorated in rich blood-red; the russet canyons of hell itself; these were the dream locations Heimlich harvested from the collective subconscious of AvShalom's flock.

AvShalom didn't want to hear about it.

"Please Abraham, enough with these fantasies!" he protested. "Battlefield, womb, hell. What's the difference?"

Heimlich pointed out that a battlefield dream was good because, to even have it, you had to survive the battle. And a womb dream in scarlet, signal color of appetites, was yet better since everyone knows you'll never be that rich again. But explicit dreams of hell were bona fide nightmares, he explained, legitimatized by Christian artisans and made real for non-believers by the friends of Hitler. Here the screams of the damned muted the screams of the other damned. So the only screams you could hear were your own.

"These are the nightmares of our people!" Heimlich persisted. "Nightmares about the loss of community. The failure of congregation. For God's sake, Eliezer, listen to what they hear! All they hear is their own screaming. They have ceased to believe that they are lucky compared to their ancestors so they are leading a comfortless existence. They are in hell!"

AvShalom chuckled at what he considered Heimlich's highly over-dramatic presentation.

"People who laugh at the pain of others ought to be forced to visit them in their nightmares," Heimlich continued mercilessly.

Rabbi AvShalom quite rightly took this as an insulting personal reference to himself. He told the board that Heimlich was an impertinent yutz and demanded that he be cast out. Seeing as Heimlich had humiliated the senior rabbi in other ways as well, especially as concerned the imminent death of

Old Shapiro the Stinker, the board felt it had no choice but to fire Heimlich.

They pleaded for his sympathy. Couldn't he see what an awful bind they were in?

"Yeah yeah sure, I see," Heimlich said. "This is the kind of trouble you get when you hire a rabbi who thinks he's a Highland Chief and Av is Mac."

Reporting this further insult to AvShalom, the board now agreed that Heimlich was an insufferable putz, as well as an impertinent yutz, and voted (twelve to nine, but that's another joke) to launch his comedy career.

Heimlich had been gone for more than ten years. And still the comfortless were looking for him, not just old students like Marty Shapiro, but strangers more recently affected.

A woman named Spunky Pruitt had stopped by unannounced. She scared Cassie for she was clearly a lesbian, with her platinum blonde butch haircut and her oversized bow tie and trousers and oxford shirt. Ms. Pruitt said that Heimlich's manager had given her AvShalom's name. The manager did not know where Heimlich's daughters had taken him, didn't actually want to know after all the mess, the canceled dates, the deposits which had to be returned. The manager was sorry for Heimlich but he wasn't sending him flowers. It took time to build a career, and Heimlich's career was clearly over. All that time had been wasted. What a pity. Poor guy. Now onward.

This Spunky Pruitt, apparently an agent of some repute in Los Angeles, sat with her hands on her knees. She smoked thin brown cigars. "He was in the middle of his act," she told Eliezer AvShalom. "And then suddenly his voice changed and he spoke like they say in tongues. Or maybe it was in a real language that none of us there that night happened to understand. I am a godless woman, Rabbi, but I swear to you, it was as though he had been seized by a spirit. His brain seemed to explode. I wish I could remember what he said but

I was blinded by his voice. It would mean a lot to me to know that he's not dead, maybe to talk with him. . . His manager thought you might know where his family had taken him."

The sincerity of her quest, the apparent unforgettability of her experience, touched AvShalom, but he put his feelings of sympathy aside. "Heimlich and I were not friends," he said. "So his daughters have not kept me informed."

Spunky Pruitt's visit was followed in short order by that of a thin man named Fred. He wore a plaid shirt and weathered jeans and said he was working on a television show in the area. Having received this address from Heimlich's manager, he had just stopped by because everybody in the gang back East at the casino had asked him to. "We all liked Heimlich," Fred said. "He was better educated than most of us, a kind of house philosopher, you know." He placed an envelope on Eliezer's desk. "This is a get-well card signed by all of us. If you'd pass it on to Heimlich, we'd be grateful."

"But I never see him; I don't know where he is."

"Well, you've sure got a better chance of finding him than me," Fred said, smiling.

And then in walked a famous black blues singer, dropped off by a silver limousine, on her way to a recording studio, asking if this was the place that Abe Heimlich had once worked and did the rabbi happen to know whether he had recovered? Unlike the previous visitors, this woman seemed not awed or obligated by her experience with Heimlich, but rather heartbroken because of it.

"We were going to work together. . . " she said, shaking her head. "Truth to tell, Rabbi, we were going to mean a lot to each other. I feel so sad about it. . . to almost touch someone and then to be lost from them. . . "

A wash of tears made Alisette's eyes shine. The gold of her earrings shimmered in Eliezer's serious brown leather office long after she had left.

And now Marty Shapiro of all people. Rabbi AvShalom had raged at Shapiro as he had never done before at anyone, and he knew, because he was a brilliant and self-examined man, that his rage was not so much against Marty as against his wasted life in the rabbinate, his blasted dreams of greatness. He knew that if he heard only his own cries of anguish and did not heed the cries of these others like Spunky Pruitt and Fred the Sound Man and Alisette Legrand, he would be all alone forever, and he knew that because Abraham Heimlich had told him so. So in the clarity of early morning, he took up the one fact that he possessed about Heimlich's family, which was that Rivka attended Yale Law School, and he started calling. Although she was not in, a man named Chuck told him the name of the place where she and her sister had taken Heimlich. It was called Playa del Ruach. AvShalom phoned old Mrs. Shapiro and told her this.

★ ★ ★

Armed with the new information his mother had received, Marty decided to spend an extra day in California and give the hunt for Rabbi Heimlich a try. He had already lengthened his stay by two days because of Cecily's passion for him, her desire to take him out and introduce him to her friends so that they should all see she did not have just a phantom lover whom she had invented as did so many professional women but a real consort, a flesh-and-blood physician with a big practice and children and a wife and the wherewithal to pick up a sizable tab.

Marty decided to blanket his two Cecily days under the cover of his Heimlich day, since the truth was always best.

"I've been trying to find the assistant rabbi, this guy Heimlich," he said to Candy on the phone. "Mom thought he might be able to help me with my communication problem, and I agreed with her, so I've been trying to find him, but it isn't easy, he left the synagogue when Dad died and apparently became a comedian."

"Of course!" Candy exclaimed on Long Island. "It was the same m. . . "

"You were introduced to him at the funeral, when we were engaged and I brought you out here."

"That's why he looked so f. . . "

"Anyway I think I have located him. He's up north. It means I'd have to stay an extra day. But I don't have any surgery scheduled. So unless you and the kids need me."

"We don't n. . . "

"The kids okay?"

"Wonderful. Sam got a trophy for boating at camp. And Ethel can now sing the entire score to 'Gypsy.' Last night at dinner, she put on Mom's underwear and did 'You Gotta Have a G. . . '"

"Great great okay give them all a kiss for me. Oh yeah, how's your wrist?"

"Dr. Wickes says the c. . . "

"The janitor at the synagogue remembers you fondly. He thinks you're beautiful."

Candy laughed.

"That's because he's a R. . . "

"So take care, I'll be home in a day or so."

"Send my love to your m. . . "

That night, at one of those important parties-by-pools Cecily loved to take him to, Marty found himself wondering, for the first time in their marriage actually, what Candy had been about to say all those times he had interrupted her. A wave of joy swept over him as he realized that for the first time, he had actually heard himself being callow and thoughtless, that somehow during the course of this strange day, he had become sensitized, he had grown as a man! He was very pleased and proud. He felt that one day he would conquer his problem in communication with his patients. He felt that people would one day really like him, that he would have friends for friends instead of work for friends. Interesting how a hate-filled outburst like AvShalom's could trigger such positive results.

He poured Cecily a drink and made her a little blini with caviar and eggs and sour cream and served it to her and kissed her on the cheek affectionately. Other women in the entertainment industry, just as beautiful and successful, observed how tenderly Cecily's lover treated her, and they felt so lonely and so jealous and so desperate for love at the important party that they ducked into the bedrooms and bathrooms of the luxurious house and wept.

★ ★ ★

On the Pacific Coast Highway heading toward Ventura, Marty stopped and called Ojai information to find a number for the private hospital run by Dr. I.R. Dellarue, the name he had been given by his mother. He figured the hospital itself would provide him with more exact directions. But Ojai listed no such person as Dr. Dellarue. Since the weather was so good and the view of the Pacific so splendid, Marty pressed on. He reached Ojai at eleven. He had lunch in a little coffee shop which also sold horoscopes and outrageously expensive teas in hand-painted brown paper bags that were themselves advertised as incidental works of art. Across the room he noticed a beautiful girl who sat alone at a table, reading the Calendar section of *The Los Angeles Times.* She had black hair and gigantic eyes and really astonishing skin.

In an effort to get a little closer, Marty took his lunch check and moseyed over to the counter to buy some fancy herbal tea for Candy and a couple of horoscopes for his kids. To his disappointment, an older man now sat down at the same table with the beautiful, black-haired girl.

He sure was a handsome old guy.

His perfect white hair had been recently fluffed, his red golf shirt clung to a well-muscled chest, his legs and arms were bronze. When she saw him, the beautiful girl folded up her newspaper and smiled ecstatically. She had teeth like chiclets. She must be an actress. Had to be. And the old guy with the biceps was a movie mogul who could probably have any woman he wanted, any time, for any purpose, no strings (Marty's undying adolescent dream).

Because of his new proximity to the beautiful girl's table, and the changed configuration of her newspaper, Marty now got a good look at her hands. They were his mother-in-law's hands. Wrinkled, spotted, clawlike, the red nails like the talons of vultures.

He laughed out loud. The saleslady, who had just read him the outrageous price of his lunch plus the tea and the horoscopes, thought Marty was laughing about that. She had the good taste to be embarrassed.

Marty turned to the mogul and the beautiful girl who was really a 62-year old woman with four grandchildren.

"Excuse me," he said, "I hope you won't think I'm too bold. My name is Martin Shapiro, I am a gynecologist and a surgeon." He handed the man his business card. "At the recent conference on breast cancer in Los Angeles, I met a cosmetic surgeon named Danton Moore, whom I am considering recommending to my patients. I wondered if you had heard anything about him."

The woman's incredibly large, nearly lidless eyes grew yet wider with shock. A complete stranger had accosted her in a public restaurant and asked her to discuss her plastic surgeon! Her unlined lips quivered a little.

"Moore is the best, the absolute best we've got," said the handsome, white-haired man quite amiably. "Not only did he do my wife's face, he also did her ass and her thighs. Stand up, honey, show Dr. Shapiro your beautiful new butt."

The woman did not move.

"If you really want to be impressed, get a load of this!" continued the enthusiastic man. And he pulled up his trousers and stretched out his legs so Marty could view them from every angle. "All my life, I looked like a wimp playing tennis because I had skinny legs. I worked out, I did weights, I got shoulders, arms, a great back, but legs? Total shit. Now look at those calf muscles. Would you have any idea they were implants?" He smiled, creating a dental glare. "Danton Moore's work," he said. "You can't go wrong recommending Moore, isn't that right, honey?"

His wife's eyes brimmed with tears. Otherwise her expression did not change. She walked quickly out of the store.

"I upset your wife," Marty said. "I'm so sorry."

"Don't worry about it," the man said, brushing away the bad moment with a wave of his hand. "She never likes me to talk about her surgery. Why is it she's so embarrassed about it and I'm not? You're a gynecologist, Shapiro, you deal with women all the time, can you explain that to me?"

"No," said Marty. "In fact, that seems to be my problem, that I don't know any more about women than other men and everybody expects me to. Have you ever heard of a Dr. I.A. Dellarue? He has a mental hospital near by."

"Only mental hospital around here is the Playa del Ruach."

Silently, Marty castigated himself for having risked one of his immensely valuable days on a phone message taken by an old lady.

"Some Israeli told me it means Windy Beach," the mogul said.

"*Ruach* isn't quite windy. . . it's more spiritual than that. . . " Marty explained. "If you have a lot of *ruach,* you have verve and enthusiasm. . . or an evil feeling, bad vibes, that can be called *ruach* too. . . it's the feeling, the emanation, the breeze that stirs the soul. . . "

"Are you Israeli?"

"No."

"You know Hebrew. . . "

"No, I only know *ruach.*"

The man smiled. He really liked this Shapiro. There was something tremendously appealing about a doctor with humility.

"Take the fork after the light," the man said. "Double back down the dirt lane to the left go over the bridge under a long stretch of Douglas pines, maybe three miles, you'll see a little red barn on the right, don't turn there, turn at the next right and stay right down the hill. At the bottom of the hill — not the very bottom — but almost to the bottom you'll see a pebble road on the left that seems to go nowhere. Take it. Trust me."

"Thank you," Marty said.

They shook hands.

The man went after his wife, to comfort her.

Not for many years had Marty felt such comradely warmth from a total stranger. He was sorry he had neglected to ask the man's name. He was sorrier yet, an hour and a half later, when he had become hopelessly lost in the mountains (because he should have made the second right after the little red barn not the first right, said the snotty receptionist at the Playa del Ruach when she finally picked up the phone) and he would have liked to call the asshole with his artificial calf muscles and tell him what a prick he was for giving out with such serene confidence the wrong goddamn directions!

By the time Marty worked his way back into the vicinity of Ojai, with his new directions in hand, it was two o'clock and he had a five o'clock plane to catch and a car to drop off and the last thing he wanted to do was sit at the feet of Abe Heimlich and castigate himself for insensitivity. So he abandoned the whole project. He sped out onto the Freeway. Unfortunately, the traffic was backed up for miles. Some woman had opened the car door and entered the fast lane while her husband was driving. The removal of her body and the other car wrecks which her decision to self-destruct had caused had virtually closed down the highway.

Marty didn't arrive at LAX until 7:30. But he didn't miss his plane because it had not yet come in from Chicago because of unseasonable electrical storms in the upper midwest. There would be a two hour delay at least.

He called Cecily, to ask her to come have dinner with him at the airport. She wasn't home. He called Candy to say he would be very late. Marie said she was out with those sweet young men Monsieur Jock and Monsieur Slim from the theater and wouldn't be home until very late.

Pissed at both Cecily and Candy for not curtailing their evening's activities on his account, he called his girlfriend Lisa the art dealer in Manhattan.

"Oh Marty!" she cried. "I'm so scared! Somebody broke into my house and opened all my drawers and went through all my photo albums and letters and didn't take anything!"

★ ★ ★

It was morning when Candy came home. Jock Silver and Slim Price had taken her out for the evening, prelude to their offer to make her a partner in their newest venture. They had driven her all the way up to Connecticut to have dinner and see the show which they were thinking of moving off-Broadway. Then they took her to a party where the cast and its agents and managers romanced them all shamelessly. Stupefied with wine and weariness, Candy snoozed as their driver cruised them back to Manhattan where Jock and Slim shared an East 60s brownstone.

"Silver, Price and Deal Productions," she thought. "Sounds solvent."

Revived by a second wind at six in the morning, she pulled her car out of their garage and drove the empty highways home.

She found Marty returned from Los Angeles, asleep in his clothes. Little Sam remained in his bed, but Ethel had curled up perpendicular to Marty's feet, almost touching, almost.

Ethel loved her father.

How could a decent woman leave a man whose children loved him so much?

Burning with weeks of neglect, hating that the only male company she had was that of two men who loved each other, Candy locked herself in the bathroom. She took off all her clothes and looked at her body. And the most hideous monster of all lunged to the surface of her mind and attacked.

"It's because I'm ugly," she said to herself. "My husband philanders because I am ugly. My nose is freckled, my cheekbones don't show, my mouth is too wide and there is no indentation in my upper lip, my breasts are too small, my stomach protrudes. Notwithstanding a hundred million situps after childbirth, my stomach still sticks out. My behind is flabby and shapeless, I have stretch marks on my hips, my calves are thin, my upper arms are fat, my neck is short, I have dry skin. Tons of cream and I still have dry, rough skin on my elbows and my ankles. The hell with my hair. What's a nice head of hair on a dog? I have failed at the only thing I was ever given to do, which was to look good enough to keep one man interested. My life is worthless because I am ugly."

On the phone next to the toilet, she began dialing information exchanges in various Canadian cities, to see if there was any Alexander Deal listed anywhere. But he wasn't in Montreal, or in Toronto, or in Ottawa, or in Halifax or in Calgary or in Stratford. Devastated by failure, she scavenged in the medicine cabinet for a clipper and savagely snapped off her fingernails. Then she stroked her own body until she achieved a small orgasm that provided no relief at all.

At nine-o'clock she put on a robe and went down to the kitchen and ate a bagel and read the newspaper and said

"Have a good weekend" to Marie who was just leaving. Marie looked gorgeous. She was wearing white linen. She pressed Candy's hand warmly and said she would return late Sunday night.

When the kids and Marty came down, she made them pancakes with real maple syrup and fresh-squeezed orange juice. Marty gave her the canister of tea he had bought in Ojai. She seemed to like it. He did not notice that her fingernails were gone.

CHAPTER FIVE

# PLAYA DEL RUACH

ITS FOUNDER, Dr. Manuel Herskovits of Mexico City, had named Playa del Ruach for the state of mind created by an afternoon on the west terrace, where patients sat comfortably beached in the mountain mist, enjoying a delicate breeze.

From the outside, Playa del Ruach looked like one of the local houses — a sprawling *ranchero* with russet tiles for roofing and an old, carved wooden door and an interior patio hiding verdantly behind the dun-colored adobe walls. Dr. Herskovits kept the place small — no more than 15 patients at a time — and very badly marked so that only those who were desperate to find it could find it, and people like Marty Shapiro with planes to catch and other priorities would eventually give up and go away.

Here in this place, the wounded Heimlich bedded down, consigned to wheelchair walks, routines of medications, changes of dressing. He sought Alisette in his dreams. Too bad that every time he glimpsed her, she was galloping away on a black stallion and could not hear his shouts of greeting. But he could not avoid Candy Shapiro. She slashed at his peace of mind with her diamond locket. He obsessed about her calm gray eyes. "Empty vessels!" he cried. "Waiting to be filled! Time is wasting! Waste is catastrophe!" He ranted on and on in this manner until one of the attendants finally got an order for a needle and put the crazy comic back into his customary stupor. The shiningly bald Dr. Herskovits tried to talk with Heimlich, but without success. After these few early mutterings indicating a paranoid fear of rich housewives, the comedian lapsed into silence.

It was Heimlich's daughter Rachel, at twenty-six pregnant with her fourth child, who had discovered the Playa del Ruach. While her younger sister Rivka was making arrangements for Heimlich's transport from the East, Rachel journeyed down from Mendocino where she lived, did the deal with Dr. Herskovits and rented a small apartment nearby for herself and her sister. It was over the garage of a psychic named Harold Bettancourt. Because Harold was homosexual, Rachel suspected that someone might have recently died in the apartment. So she re-cleaned it even though Harold always kept it immaculate, *kashered* the kitchen and put very sweet-smelling soap in the bathroom.

"Please don't be shocked when you meet my younger sister Rivka," she said to Harold as they sat watching the summer evening from the front steps of his house. "She goes to Yale Law School. Her every thought and deed is an abomination in the eyes of the Almighty. And just watch! She will come after I have filled the refrigerator with all the things she likes to eat, after I have stocked the bathroom with all her favorite toiletries, and then, having paid for nothing, she will complain about my housekeeping. She is brilliant and stingy and personally very dirty, I warn you."

Shortly thereafter, Rivka arrived, with her mammoth masses of dark and unkempt curls, her hiking boots, knapsack and laptop. She and Rachel embraced. But that night, Rivka mixed up the *milchick* spoons and the *fleischick* knives. A terrible fight ensued which shook the little house and disturbed the entire block. Besieged with phone calls of protest from his neighbors, Harold started up the stairs, intending to evict the Heimlich sisters at once. In the dark, he bumped into Rivka the lawyer who was clumping down the stairs carrying a swishing parachute silk sleeping bag and wearing what looked to Harold exactly like men's underwear.

"Sorry we woke you up," Rivka said. "As you have undoubtedly noticed, my sister Rachel has returned to 13th century Polish religion. She will not brush her teeth unless she prays first. Even her spoons are fucking sanctified. I cannot stand the stench of the soap she uses. Tonight I shall sleep in your back yard in my sleeping bag, if that's all right, and tomorrow I shall go visit my poor demented father one last time and then I shall return to New Haven where the people are better adjusted. Good night."

Rivka did not keep her promise to leave. She and Rachel stayed on together that whole summer at Harold's house. Every night, Rachel telephoned her husband Bernie the Furniture Maker and her children, Max, May and Leah. She made frequent journeys north to see them. Rivka kept calling Yale to say she'd be back in a week or so but that did not happen. Her patient boyfriend Chuck sent cheese and crackers and fruit in a basket covered with crinkly transparent gold paper which Harold kept to wrap his crystals.

For Harold Bettancourt, the fighting Heimlich sisters provided a welcome diversion from the misery of his friends, whose lives had become case studies in the management of catastrophic illness. His customers, the purchasers of his psychic expertise who kept him in rent and groceries, had proven to be no diversion at all. They were mostly Hollywood women who came on the weekends to seek crystals and curses and charms and other assistance with problems so insignificant by comparison to death by AIDS that it was all Harold could do to keep from throttling them.

This bizarre clientele had come to Harold by a series of mysterious flukes befitting his lifestyle. Once he had decided to acknowledge his clairvoyance by giving up accounting and living the life of the spirit, he had naturally assumed that his customers would be mostly gay men trying to settle their estates sensibly by knowing a little more about the events to come. But one day, Spunky Pruitt got lost looking for a certain spa at Ojai. Seeing the words "Psychic" on Harold's elephant-shaped mailbox, she decided that it was fated for her to have lost her way. So she dropped in on Harold just at the moment when he had had a cancellation due to death, not an uncommon occurrence in these grim days of plague.

On this occasion, Spunky was wearing a tight red dress and cowboy boots. She lugged her 60-pound briefcase into Harold's house because she was afraid to leave it in her car, because somebody might swipe it and read the top secret contracts inside.

"Relax, Spunky," Harold said. "You're an agent. That doesn't require a security clearance."

"How did you know my name?!"

"It's written on your boots."

Harold looked at her for a full five minutes. He saw immediately that she was working herself to death as a punishment for having perverse sexual inclinations which she had not yet accepted. But what else was there about this garish woman? He could feel something else. . .

Finally he spoke. He told Spunky that her father would soon have a massive heart attack. That she would soon find a fabulous condo at a sensational price in just the right neighborhood. That she would meet a magical prophet — this was what Harold had felt so sharply — and that the sound of his voice would melt her frozen soul, and she would learn to love herself at last.

Harold gave Spunky a crystal because she was terribly afraid that she would accede to evil impulses and become a liar like other people whom she knew in her business. The crystal, he said, would remind her of how much positive energy abounded in the world. She must wear it on a chain around her neck, to hang like a light before her heart and guide her in the paths of righteousness.

Spunky began to cry. She cried for several minutes. Then she and her briefcase ran out of Harold's parlor before he even had a chance to tell her how much she should pay him. He felt foolish and ripped-off. But he soon forgot his pique. There were surely worse things in this life than being stiffed by a sad woman.

Almost a year later, in the summer after that awful storm in Atlantic City that killed so many poor little dogs and cats, a courier delivered Harold an envelope with $1000 in it and a note from Spunky Pruitt.

"My stepfather always hated me," she wrote. "He called me a dyke whore and threw me out of my own mother's house. I have not thought of him for twenty-six years. Had no idea he was even alive. He just had a massive coronary and died and left me a building in Toluca Lake with four fabulous apartments. I am in the process of moving into the most fabulous. The rent on the other three guarantees that I will live essentially for free.

"On the night that I heard the voice of the prophet, I slept with a piano mover from Queens. In the morning, I knew I would never sleep with a man again. What a relief to accept the truth at last! I never take off my crystal. Thank you, Harold. Guard your health. I shall send you customers."

And so she did.

A steady procession of women from the television and film industries soon began coming to see him. They ranged in age from thirty to sixty. They were as lovely as the entertainers they tended to and lived among, but strangely, they were never entertainers themselves. Harold admired the beauty of their clothing, the smoothness of their skin, the androgynous ripple of the cultivated muscles in their hips and thighs and buttocks as they walked ahead of him into the parlor. They were the most contemporary women in America, and yet, as they drove north from Los Angeles, up into the hills that leaped away from the Ventura coast, something happened to them, some millennial makeover, and by the time they arrived at Harold's house, they had become as superstitious as sixteenth century Spanish gypsy girls, ready to slather their money on amulets and aphrodisiacs to make themselves financially successful and to win the hearts of men.

At least Rachel and Rivka loved each other, he thought. At least they had people where they lived who missed them. Rachel waddled up and down the wooden stairs to the apartment with Rivka supporting her from behind, and all the time they bitched and argued, but they did not leave. They neglected their personal lives and their other obligations to see their old man through his nightmare.

Good girls, Harold thought. If I had been a father, I would have wanted good, strong, loyal girls like that.

★ ★ ★

Leah Heimlich, mother of Rachel and Rivka and Little Yehudit who was called *Motek* or Sweetness by everybody who knew her, lived in Venice Beach as a young girl. She sold T-shirts painted by her Aunt Bea and rollerskated through the sand-drenched streets, licking pink yogurt in a cone. Like Aunt Bea, she had enormous hair. She fastened it with a plastic bike lock. She spiked the volley ball toward Malibu, her brown legs with their gold down gleaming. With a playful grin (and an unmitigated overbite, for Bea thought braces were like corsets, relics of the old slavery), she snubbed the brazen skate boarders who called to her: "Hey Lay-ah Bay-beeeee. . . ."

Heimlich caught her when she was young and he was a surfer. He noticed her while upside down in the blithering spray, noticed the undersides of her thighs as she bent over one of her skates to scrape gum off a wheel. Schlepping his board onto the beach, he wriggled out of his wet suit and collapsed at her feet. She smiled at him. He told her he was the son of an important Hollywood lawyer. She believed him. He told her he was going to New York to aggravate his father by studying for the rabbinate. She followed him.

They were very poor in New York. Leah worked in a hardware store. Heimlich did social work in Bedford Stuyvesant and disc jockey comedy part time on the Jewish station. Sometimes Aunt Bea sent cash in a manila envelope to help them out. Sometimes Heimlich received a check from his stepmother, a former starlet.

He squeezed Leah from behind as she stood in the tiny kitchen on the Upper West Side baking chale for shabbat and called her "Lay-ah Bay-bee" to remind her of her old life.

One day, Leah asked Heimlich her husband to go to the kosher butcher and buy a brisket. Loving these errands — for they sprang him from his eternal books — he whistled himself through the West 90s to Bradley's Kosher Meats. There he found many customers waiting.

"Where's Bradley?" he asked.

"He must have stepped out," they said.

"How long has it been?" Heimlich asked.

"Half an hour," they said.

"That's too long for Bradley to step out," Heimlich commented.

He led a search party into the back of the store, to see if maybe Bradley had banged his head against a side of beef and knocked himself out or something. There he was in the freezer. He had been shot through the heart. A pious Jew. A man with children.

Heimlich's teacher at the Rabbinical Seminary gave a sermon. He said the Jews of New York should not eat meat again until the kosher meat business was no longer used as a front for organized crime and men like Bradley the Butcher could no longer be slaughtered for refusing to act as intermediaries in the activities of gangsters. Few people listened to this wise man. However, Leah Heimlich, new at kashrut and still open-minded about it, accepted his instruction and decided that she and her husband would eat fish and veggies from that moment on. (Aunt Bea wrote from Venice that it was the best idea in any case.)

During her third pregnancy, when Leah craved steak so that she cried for it, Heimlich went out and bought a USDA prime London broil at Shoprite.

"It may be traife, but at least it's not Mafia," he said.

Leah would not touch the protein-heavy scarlet slab. So Heimlich took her to Jerusalem and found them a little apartment in Rahavia where they settled with their first two daughters, Rachel and Rivka, and Leah could eat kosher steaks imported without moral taint from Argentina.

How the Heimlichs loved Jerusalem! They had no trouble adjusting except for a few minor items. Specifically, it took them two full weeks to realize that the large rattan fan hanging from the balcony was not merely a decorative object but in fact an essential rug beater. Also they missed lettuce terribly. And it surprised them that most of the people they befriended were North Americans, for they had no idea until they lived abroad the range of specific characteristics which set Americans and Canadians apart from other ethnic groups.

For example, on the occasion of an election, their newly-arrived Russian-born neighbor had a minor nervous collapse. She could not comprehend why so much political literature suddenly stuffed her mail box. She didn't know what to make of the truck-mounted loud speakers blaring the appearance of this or that candidate. The party lists with their staggering array of choices gave her a migraine. One day Leah came home from shopping and found the poor woman huddled on her doorstep, clutching her children and her jewelry, crying: "I can't stand it! I don't know who to vote for! You're an American! You're used to this chaos! Tell me what to do!"

"Wow," Leah murmured. "This is a very heavy trip for me, I mean like voting is complicated, you know. Maybe you should talk to my husband the rabbi. Why don't you come on in and have a root beer and chill out until he gets home and then he'll explain everything, okay?"

Initially, the neighborhood women found Leah just too loony. It was the early 70s, and they had not progressed enough to readily accept a grown woman rollerskating around Jerusalem as though she were one of her own little girls. However, she made lollipops from scratch in her own kitchen and gave them out with an open hand. She barbecued zucchini on her terrace and freely lent her adobo seasoning. She kept photographs of David Ben Gurion and Aleph Daled Gordon in her front hall, along with baby pictures, as though they were uncles. Eventually — in a matter of weeks actually — all the neighbors had grown very fond of her.

Leah's favorite Jerusalem place was the Kennedy Memorial. She took the girls and their friends there for picnics. The Memorial itself was constructed as a large tree, cut off in its prime. The emblems of each of the American states decorated it like a necklace all around.

"That's us," Leah would say, pointing to California. (She also resolutely spoke English at home, so that Rachel and Rivka would not forget the Old Country. Even so they pronounced the sound of "r", represented in Israel by the letter *resh,* as an "l." They said *"Ima v'Abba m'Califorllnia."* Long after they were back in California, they said it that way.)

As sunset approached, the city below Leah and her daughters took on its world-famous glow. Maybe it was because of the way the cool mountain air combined with the rays of that particular desert sun, maybe it was because the Mayor and the Council of Jerusalem had mandated that every single structure must be built of a pinkish-gold local stone whose molecules reflected the sun's rays with an extra special compatibility. But undeniably ("No shit, Aunt Bea,"

Leah wrote. "Like really. . . ") the city of Jerusalem glowed. Generations before her had seen this glow; she was not crazy.

"The glow has its disadvantages," Heimlich explained to Aunt Bea who had come to visit. "Because you see, the loony tune Jews look at it and they say to themselves: *We have seen the glow and it is us.* And so, as a race, we have this ridiculous need to shine, sometimes like a star, sometimes like a searchlight, to show things up, illuminate the way. Whether our stuff is good or evil, it is exemplary. We cannot hide ourselves. If we make a mistake, the whole world learns from it."

Leah's Aunt, who had raised her according to the will of her dead mother, inculcating liberal philosophies, rejected Heimlich's idea. She said the Jews were not a race at all, but a nationality past its prime whose major task now was to disappear and thus improve the world's chances for peace.

Leah, however, believed her husband. She believed she was a crystal in the dark world and that her decisions were crucial to the world's future. If she ever missed her carefree life on the Venice streets, no one who loved her saw it. The tears that stained her face as she stood overlooking the glowing city were, her daughters knew, tears of joy.

"Thank God I am here," she would say in her heart. "Thank God I have a cool husband with a sense of humor, and I am an American who knows how to pursue happiness. Thank God most of all that I live in Jerusalem where the light begins."

★ ★ ★

Heimlich continued his studies in Jerusalem. However, he never worked as a rabbi there. Most mornings, he sifted dust at an archaeological dig near the site of Solomon's Temple, where an ecumenical babble of divinity students and history buffs was excavating an ancient library.

Here he found fragments of a letter that told of a ship sinking off the coast of Aqaba, near the port of Eilath. The ship carried dyes and wool and green glass goblets and slaves, among them a woman who had been sold by her family for being too troublesome. She shouted and cried and threatened so incessantly that the ocean was driven to turbulence and the ship went down. But who was she? the workers at the dig wondered. And what could she have said that would create such a mighty storm?

Some afternoons, Heimlich did time as a social worker to counsel deprived and dangerous young people at a drop-in center. The Israelis at the archaeological dig couldn't believe that Heimlich went every day into neighborhoods where they would hardly ever venture. Whispered Heimlich to a professor from CCNY: "What do these people know about mean streets? Have they ever been to Mednorth in Queens?"

On Saturday night, he did stand-up at a comedy club, specializing in re-enacting great scenes from Jewish history to which he gave stentorian titles, such as "In the Wine Cellars of Rothschild, Pinchas Sapir Invents the Spritzer" and "Golda Meir Tells Meyer Lansky To Fuck Off."

Even with these three jobs — sifter, social worker and comic — Heimlich couldn't make ends meet in Jerusalem.

Leah tried to get a job as a saleslady in a boutique, citing her many years of experience in T-shirts in Venice and hardware in New York. The proprietor responded that he never hired Americans because they reported all their income, thus confounding his (in fact, the nation's) tax accounting system. So Leah became a waitress and worked for cash.

Every morning, she dropped her big girls (Rachel four, Rivka two) at the pre-school and Little Yehudit, who had just passed her first birthday, at the *Gan* or Day Care Center. Then she took the bus to the central station, whence she walked to Leviathan, an important place to have lunch.

Leviathan was a large, noisy cavern with thick walls. It offered the cool of centuries and the most eclectic menu in the Middle East. Its owner, BenZion Shachar, an ill-tempered gourmet, loved to taste the rare and perfect the ordinary. The scion of a family which had lived in Israel continuously since the days of Solomon, BenZion had joined his nation's foreign service as befits the well-born and had spent the 50s in Africa. In one particular West African country, he had personally trained the entire upper middle management of the national bureaucracy, in anticipation of Independence. But when Independence came, these fine young men who could have been rivers to their people were all murdered by an evil dictator. Grief-stricken, BenZion gave up the foreign service and went into the restaurant business. He decked Leviathan with the artifacts his students had given him, masks and spears, feathered talismans and symbolic carvings to ensure fertility in peace and victory in war.

BenZion's wife, Astarte, was a Durrellish Egyptian Jewess who knew twelve languages. She naturally became his business advisor. "Hire Anglos," she said. "They know how to wait on people because they have all been waited on at some time, but because of their political background, they don't feel it demeans them the way we do. They know how to count. And they know how to hurry. Hire observant married women, with covered heads and naked faces, who look men in the eye and mean nothing by it. These will be the best waitresses in Jerusalem."

With his wife watching over the kitchen and the help, BenZion went forth to entice the customers, a unique, macho mob from the bureaucracy, the military, the business community.

Astarte made a great fuss over the occasional visiting movie actress, or high fashion model, or female professor. An autographed photo of Barbara Tuchman hung over her desk in the kitchen. But on the whole, the only women in the place were, like Leah Heimlich, waiting on the tables.

The men who ate at Leviathan spent their lunchtime gossiping about politics, glad-handing, catching up, dropping hints and putting out feelers. Will this contract be signed? Will that manager be dropped? Will Kissinger go for it? Will the French screw it up yet again?

As their guests, they invited wary Europeans, factory managers, owners of groves, who could not, even now, after all these years, eat comfortably with Jews, and toasted the deal just made with tea and tangy cider which Astarte imported from upstate New York. They brought Americans from the Pentagon and the aircraft factories who relaxed and drank buckets of beer and wondered aloud, back in Memphis and St. Louis, why the sun-wrinkled Israelis were so much easier to take than the better-educated Jews who abounded in the scientific establishment and the universities at home.

("There is another race," Astarte told Heimlich and Leah one autumn evening before the Yom Kippur War. "It is not called Jew. It is not called Arab. It is called Soldier. The members of the Soldier Race communicate in ways the rest of us will never comprehend, even when they are bitter enemies.")

In the custom of the region, Leviathan's customers ate substantially at their midday meal. They ate humus and tehina with little green olives and fresh pita bread. They ate vermilion Rumanian soup containing seven discernibly different vegetables, tender flanken streaming with noodles, mixed grill so expertly blackened and seasoned that it was hard to believe it was kosher, California pasta salads and Vietnamese turkey burgers invented by BenZion's head chef Huang Binh.

A wizened man of fifty, Huang Binh took complete credit for introducing lemon grass to Israel. He swore that he had immigrated in the regular manner, through the airport.

However, everyone knew that he had been happened upon at sea, one of forty starving refugees in a small boat. The specially equipped Israeli military vessel which rescued him and his friends could never admit to having been in those waters at that time. So like many important historical incidents, the saving of Huang Binh had really never happened. Now his three daughters were married to Israelis. Among them, they had twelve Jewish children.

The maitre d', Yitzak, had grown up near Arad in what Heimlich referred to as "The Middle South" of Israel. He had injured his back in a tractor accident and had moved to Jerusalem to be near his physical therapist. He said that the best thing about his back injury was that it got him out of Army service.

Nissim and Shaul, and the Arab twins, Hamid and Yaza, had dropped out of school to work as busboys and dishwashers and help support their many brothers and sisters. Shaul was the smartest one. Heimlich had found him at the drop-in center. Someone had robbed his father's fish stand and Shaul had chased the man, caught up with him, and hit him with the fish, breaking his nose. Now the man's sons were after him, and Shaul had no place to hide. So he was hiding in the drop-in center. He was fifteen.

Heimlich immediately got him a job at the restaurant.

"Do you ever wonder," mused Leah, "why we Americans are like the only people in this country who think getting a job is like a solution to anything?"

Shaul learned self-discipline under BenZion's iron hand and self-restraint from Heimlich. Leah was fond of him. On the weekends when she baked, she always saved him some peanut butter cookies, and, after Heimlich got through reading them, she brought him the *Sports Illustrateds* and *Rolling Stones* which Heimlich's stepmother, the former starlet, regularly sent.

One day in the men's room, Shaul caught a member of the international press corps hiding in a stall, attempting to secretly record a conversation between two diplomats who were standing at the sink.

"Hey. . . " said Shaul.

"It's not a bomb! It's a tape! I swear!" screamed the journalist. He pressed the tape into Shaul's hands. "Look! See?! See for yourself!"

Quick to realize how he could take advantage of this fool's terror, Shaul narrowed his eyes and "confiscated" the state-of-the-art tape recorder as though he were an agent of the Mossad. To Heimlich at the drop-in center, Shaul bragged about how much the fancy little machine would bring on the black market. The American rabbi clucked like a mother, simultaneously tender and stern. Shaul sighed. "Okay, okay. . . " he complained. The next day, he returned the tape recorder to its mortified owner.

Leah had a friendly relationship with the other waitresses, Jenny from Glasgow, and Doris from Capetown. It amused her to be lumped together ethnically with women so completely different in background. Jenny's father and mother had been industrial wage slaves of the Marxist variety. So Jenny and her brothers studied agriculture and settled in Galilee, putting the grim, gray world of Glasgow behind them forever more. As soon as her kibbutznik husband finished his degree at the Hebrew University, Jenny intended to take her children back to their alfalfa fields in the north and spend her evenings knitting and enjoying the stars. Doris had been raised in Capetown in medieval luxury. She and her husband left South Africa one step ahead of the police. He now worked in the accounting department of the Hadassah Hospital. Their oldest daughter had just gone to the Army. It was not likely that Doris would ever live in luxury again.

Shaul the busboy marveled that a lucky woman like Doris could leave a life so pleasant and comfortable for this rathole of a country with its perpetual poverty and eternal war.

"These Anglos are all crazy," he commented to the Arab brothers.

★ ★ ★

One day, because the day care center was closed, Leah brought Little Yehudit, called Motek, to Leviathan and parked her in the kitchen in her crib near the canisters of sugar and the bags of rice. She arranged for Heimlich to come over from the dig on his break and pick up the baby so that she would not disturb the restaurant during its tumultuous midday rush.

However, even a pre-lunch visit from Motek was too much for BenZion. How could Leah have dared to bring this adorable little girl in her diapers cooing and gurgling like a siren, tempting all the help to play with her, just exactly at the busiest time of the morning, when everybody should be giving their undivided attention to the job of setting up?!

"Stop tickling that baby, Shaul, and go outside and bring in those boxes of tomatoes!" BenZion commanded.

"Give the boss a kiss, Motek!" Shaul whispered to the giggling baby as he played the local version of Inky Dinky Spider on her little belly. And then he held her up for BenZion to smooch.

"Enough!" BenZion commanded, averting his face from the tantalizing flesh. "Put her back in the pen! We have forty minutes to our first sitting! Go outside, unload the tomatoes!"

Shaul ran outside, laughing. Seeing him depart, Yehudit stretched out her hands to have him back and began to cry.

"Oh, she's crying!" exclaimed Doris.

"Poor lambie!" exclaimed Jenny.

Yitz the maitre d' reached for the baby.

"Motek Motek, do not cry," he crooned. "Forget Shaul, he is young, he will break your heart. What you need is your old Uncle Yitz to take care of you and give you kisses and squeezes. . . " and he kissed her and squeezed her and made a great show of chewing on her knees until the baby was choking with laughter and BenZion was in a full throttle rage. And a small bomb, which had been placed in a canister of sugar, went off.

The explosion occurred too early to hurt any of the men who were expecting to lunch at Leviathan that day. Instead it tore off the head of Yehudit Heimlich and eviscerated her mother and killed and maimed her admirers.

At this time, Heimlich was only a few hundred feet away, on his way from the dig to pick up his little girl.

He heard the roar. He saw the flames.

He sees them still.

Washed up on the Playa del Ruach, too far away for his cries to be heard, he sees his people's last surviving repositories of hope and good nature exploded into the streets of Jerusalem, their children bereaved and hardened, and he calls to his adored wife, his golden girl on roller skates, his brilliant crystal lighting the dark world: "Lay-ahh. . . bay-bee. . . "

⋆ ⋆ ⋆

Rachel and Rivka went to the Playa del Ruach every day and waited for Heimlich to be wheeled out of his room into the patio. He smiled and kissed them and patted Rachel's belly but he would not really converse. All day, the three Heimlichs sat there in the shade of the avocado tree. Rivka would pace the grass, hitching her jeans and scowling. Rachel would remain calm until after lunch, when the silence finally got to her and she would often shout "For God's sake, Daddy! Say something!" and tear the bandanna off her cropped brown hair and send messages of *agitta* to her baby, waking him and making him squirm. The consequent heaving of her stomach really pissed off Rivka, who accused Rachel of being inconsiderate of the poor little doodle and who threatened to smoke(!) if Rachel did not calm down.

Heimlich would snooze, or listen to music on a headset. The dressing on his eye finally came off, and Dr. Herskovits presented him with a Dayan-type patch, hoping this would amuse the comic. Heimlich remained silent.

Then one day in the early fall, right before the Jewish New Year, he said "*Shemesh.*" Overjoyed, Rivka raced his wheelchair into the bright September sunlight. Heimlich lifted his face to the sky and took a tan.

All through that year, Rachel and Rivka journeyed back and forth between their lives and their father. The baby was born, a big healthy boy named Rashi, and Rachel set him on Heimlich's lap. Heimlich smiled at his grandson but could not speak to him. When the sisters came in January right after the American New Year, they found that Heimlich had reached the magazine stage. He was reading everything from *The Atlantic* to *Good Housekeeping* to *Vanity Fair* to *Essence* as well as *Variety* and *Ha'aretz.* He read them one after another, as though he had been away forever, a hostage suddenly freed, and needed to regain his country, to catch up with every single type and style of person in the land.

Sometimes Heimlich got tired from recovering, and dozed off like an old man. Sometimes he laughed — usually at a cartoon or a hairstyle. His face was pale where the bandage had been, brown where it had not been, a bi-color effect which made him look half-disappeared. The right side of his hair, from the sideburn past the ear, had not only turned bright white but had lost its curl.

Rivka put sun block on his nose. Rachel showed him pictures of her kids and her husband's hand-hewn chairs. At six o'clock, the two sisters would be sent home by Dr. Herskovits. And the song of their argument would begin again and continue into the night.

"If you wouldn't hock him with those pictures. . . "

"If you wouldn't smear him with guck. . . "

"If only Mom hadn't died, he wouldn't be crazy."

"She wouldn't have died if Daddy hadn't taken us to Israel."

"He wouldn't have taken us to Israel if Mom hadn't become convinced that much of the kosher meat in the United States was controlled by the Mafia!"

"Well, it is!"

"Oh please!"

"That's what I heard."

"All you hear is the neo-conservative Orthodox claptrap that filters up to your spot in the balcony!"

"What is wrong with the balcony?!"

"Women should not be exiled from the service!"

"Oh, and I suppose you get closer to the Almighty at that Marxist terrorist feminist minyan in New Haven!"

"At least I'm counted as a member of the congregation!"

"At least I know who I am, Rivka!"

"Do me a favor, Rachel, go fuck yourself!"

Harold would beat on the ceiling with his antique walking cane and call softly: "Girls. . . oh girls. . . how about a cup of chamomille before retiring?"

And they would descend the rickety wooden stairs, Rivka bounding, Rachel schlepping the new baby, and drink tea with their landlord and pray for their father that he might return to them a well man.

CHAPTER SIX

# THE JAPRAP

ON HIS DOCTOR'S ORDERS, Rabbi Eliezer AvShalom took a vacation from his troublesome congregation and went north into the mountains to consult with King Solomon as in the days of his youth.

"Why is my life so unhappy?" he asked. "Why has all my wisdom brought me so little joy? Why is it that all the questions are known, and all the answers, and still the mystery of self persists?"

*Envy destroys the world,* the great king answered. *Jealousy is cruel as the grave. The coals thereof are coals of fire.*

Staring inward at his conscience with renewed interest, revitalized by guilt, grateful to God for his guilt, AvShalom now decided that what he had to do was pay a visit on Abraham Heimlich. At least he had a pretext. After all, weren't there messages to deliver? He passed the coffee house where Marty Shapiro had met the mogul and his wife. He turned right where the mogul had told Marty to go straight. At the entrance to Playa del Ruach, he suddenly experienced stomach flutters. What if Heimlich had died? What if he was insane? Even just unforgiving?

He found Heimlich sitting under an avocado tree, looking about seventy years old. Not expecting visitors — for his daughters had now returned to their lives — he had flipped his patch up on his head to let the mountain breeze refresh the empty socket. It was a horrible sight.

"I have a get-well card here," said his old enemy. "Delivered by Fred. Signed by Fred, Fred, Fred, Marge and Dr. Yablonsky. Also you were asked after by the following women: Spunky Pruitt and Alisette Legrand."

Heimlich just stared at him.

"It's me. Eliezer AvShalom. Do you remember me?"

Heimlich nodded.

"Please tell me what happened to you," Eliezer pleaded. "Tell me everything."

Heimlich sighed.

"A voice came out of my mouth which was not my voice," he answered. "I don't remember what it said. However, its passage through my brain blew out my eye and bleached my hair and gave me a nervous collapse."

"Jeez Louise," said Rabbi AvShalom.

"So sit down and I'll tell you the details," said Heimlich.

They embraced. They shed tears. For the whole day, they sat and communed in the mottled leaf-shade, laughing at their own foolishness without overt laughter, rather with wryness and irony like the old Jews, and Heimlich told the following story.

"When I came back to California, after my wife Leah and my little Motek were killed, it was very hard for me. I was used to having a wife to hold me and take care of me, and now I was back in my loneliness with no property, no prospects and two small daughters. In short, I was the average woman's idea of the catch from hell.

"Leah's Aunt Beatrice came to my aid. She couldn't manage both girls at once, but sometimes she would keep Rivka at her T-shirt emporium in Venice. My stepmother would take Rachel. The Chassidim were very powerful among some Jews she knew in show business so she sent Rachel to a

Chabad nursery. How could I explain to my well-meaning shiksa stepmother that I wanted a day-school for Rachel but not a Chassidishe day-school? Poor soul, she thinks we're one people! I was so busy making a living, trying to date women who might mother my children and distract me from my loss, that I was uncritically grateful for any help I could get. Did I say to myself: Heimlich, watch it. Rivka is going to turn out a secular humanist with unshaven legs and Rachel is going to turn out an orthodox housewife with a wig?"

AvShalom heaved a sigh and raised his palms to Heaven.

"And if Leah had lived, can you be sure your children would have turned out the way you wanted anyway?" he asked rhetorically.

"Can one ever be sure of anything?" responded Heimlich in kind.

"So did you find a woman?"

"No," Heimlich answered. "And I was very angry about that. The women all disliked me. They wouldn't go out to dinner with me twice. They wouldn't sleep with me."

"Not even the Hollywood executives?"

"Not even them. They would date actors! Sometimes even agents! But me they shunned."

"Perhaps you were too pitiful," AvShalom philosophized. "Did you whine?"

"Oi, did I whine! Sometimes I moaned. I wheezed and moaned. The only thing that comforted me was to hear other people's problems. My major emotion was sympathy. It was at this time that you fired me."

"It was for this reason that I fired you," amended AvShalom. "Also because my major emotion was jealousy."

"You were jealous of me?!" exclaimed Heimlich.

"Am I a saint, Heimlich? I repent my jealousy."

"And don't I repent my sympathy?" concluded the mad comedian, and finally they both cracked a little smile.

Heimlich reached into his *GQ* and pulled out a small flat bottle of vodka which he had hidden there. "Will you join me, Eliezer?"

"Is it all right? I mean, will it conflict with your medication?"

"We won't ask and we won't know and it won't be a problem."

The rabbis threw back a couple of shots from little paper pill cups. Then they thoughtfully walked together around the avocado tree, their hands clasped behind their backs.

"So," said Heimlich, "My heart filled up with hate against the Jewish women who were rejecting me, women who had grown up with my advantages but who had not walked out on them as I had done, and who were therefore much richer than I was. In my heart, I said to them: I gave my wife and my daughter, my priceless treasure for the preservation of your national home and still you over-privileged JAP bitches spit in my face. Well, fuck you, I said in my heart. I'm gonna getcha.

"And since I had now decided to become a comedian full-time and I needed AN ACT, I took my energized hatred on stage and made all the women who had rejected me ridiculous in the eyes of the audience. My act was called THE JAPRAP. I did it in university towns. I did imitations of the JAPS. I made fun of how they examined their fingernails and shopped for stringbeans and pulled the bottoms of their brassieres loose from under the weight of their breasts. I made fun of how they ate cottage cheese and melba toast nibble nibble like Minnie Mouse."

"But everyone makes fun of how they eat," said AvShalom.

"In the previous generation, everyone made fun of how they fed," Heimlich said. "I never did that because I had never been fed by a Jewish woman. Because my mother ran away. She told me that she ran away because she didn't want to become a

Jewish mother going 'eat eat' and making her husband constipated and her son a misogynistic monster. So she ran away from who she was. From the ridicule. . . Because so many comedians in her generation made fun of who she was."

Eliezer cleared his throat. "Precisely the path which the anti-Semite lays down for us so we may easily abandon our heritage and embrace our own destruction," he elucidated.

"You got it, Eliezer. But did I get it in the 70s? I needed AN ACT. Did I think of my mother?"

They had arrived in the vine-covered patio of Playa del Ruach where personnel and patients and their guests habitually sat to drink cappuccino and eat cold pasta on small paper plates. The assemblage looked up at them — two rabbis after all — and immediately paid attention.

"Be the MC," said Heimlich. "Introduce me near Brandeis on Homecoming Weekend."

"And now ladies and gentlemen, for your giggling pleasure," said AvShalom, not missing a beat, "the Waltham Laugh Riot presents Homecoming Weekend's leading comic figure, the recently sacked Assistant Rabbi from Patton Pines, Abraham Heimlich and his JAPRAP!"

The crowd at Playa del Ruach applauded.

"And I would come out in a business suit with a white shirt," said Heimlich, "no tie, with a black kipah on my head, looking very modern Orthodox, and I would say to the assembled college students, almost all of them Jewish, I would say:

"Good evening, boys and girls. Wonderful to be on the East Coast. I am here to tell you about my sister Stacey the JAP. Who may be among you, give a look to the right and the left, you never know, Stacey is everywhere! You may even be God forbid poo poo poo dating Stacey!

"Stacey could always tell you how to solve life's little problems. You wanna control your weight? Eat 16 quarts of fruit and cottage cheese but in very little bites. You wanna change a light bulb? Order a Tab and call Daddy.

"Stacey was the apple of Daddy's eye. She had the ideal JAP body. Big round cantaloupe shaped tits that only Thomas Wolfe could love. My father thought she was gonna be a movie star.

"I said 'Dad! What're you, crazy?! With that nose?!'

"'So we'll fix her nose,' he says.

"'With that ass?!'

"'We'll fix her ass,' he says.

"'With that pussy?!'

"'What pussy?!' he says. 'No daughter of mine has a pussy!'"

The crowd at Playa del Ruach laughed and groaned simultaneously.

"Stacey was a tireless worker," Heimlich continued. "She could do Saks Bloomies Bonwits and Loehmann's all in one day. Her husband Norman was lucky if she did him once a month.

("Did we used to laugh at these jokes?" asked a guest of a patient.)

"Her husband Norman married her in a moment of passion. For my father's money.

"I said to him: 'Norman Norman, what do you think you're gonna get from a woman who won't lend her brother an Art Garfunkel record?' But did he listen? Not Norman. He never listens. That's why he could stay married to Stacey for three years."

Heimlich paused so that an orderly could check his pulse. As soon as Dr. Herskovits gave him the go-ahead, he continued.

"Stacey had a fabulous relationship with our mother," he continued. "JAPS always do. They call their mothers every day, import their mothers for holidays and keep them for weeks afterward. They go on marches with their mothers to liberate women from the burdens of being a mother when you have full-time live-in help and a laundress who comes in once a week to iron the underwear.

"One morning Stacey called up our mother. She said 'MA-AA-AAA!!'"

Despite themselves, a few of the people, even AvShalom, began to laugh, so perfectly had Heimlich captured the sound of his mythical sister's voice. So Heimlich did it again.

"'MA-AA-AAA!!'

"'What's the matter, darling?' says our mother when she hears Stacey's agonized yowl. 'Tell Mama. Mama will make everything better.'

"'Oh Ma!' says Stacey. 'How shall I begin?! Bertha overcooked the creme caramel so that it stuck to the bottom of the pan so I had to fire her! Now I will have to go out and buy a dessert for the Hadassah girls who are coming here to lunch to discuss a theater party to raise money to save the six Jews who remain in downtown Detroit!'

"'Not to worry your lovely head another minute, Stacey darling,' says Ma. 'I'm coming right away. I'll bring my very own apple crumb cake for dessert and my very own Lena to clean up afterwards. I'll even bring a couple of your father's ties for Richard.'

"'Richard?' says Stacey. 'Who's Richard?'

"'Richard is your husband.'

"'But my husband's name is Norman!' cries my sister. 'Oh my God. Is this 362-7858?!'

"'This is 362-7859,' answers Ma.

"'Oh my God!' screams Stacey. 'Does this mean you're not coming?!'"

Nobody laughed now, even with nostalgia. Heimlich was sweating and his hands had begun to shake.

"The crowd at the Laugh Riot was really rolling by this time," Heimlich said. "With my peripheral vision, I detected that one melon-breasted girl was slipping away, perhaps just to pee but perhaps in anger. Have I gone too far? I asked myself. Hurt some feelings?

"Hey honey, I call. Where're you going? Don't tell me I insulted you! This is all in fun! I love Jewish women. My accountant is a Jewish woman. So was my high school history teacher. So was my first wife.

"I met her the other day; she looked great. I said: 'How's about a night of passion for old time's sake?' She said: 'Over my dead body.' I said: 'Why should anything be different now than it was before?'

"The audience roars. The girl stumbles out of the night club. Guilt gives me a zetz in the colon but I cannot stop, I must continue with MY ACT. I must make a living to feed my children by concentrating on the majority of the audience which remains helpless in my hands, like clay, Eliezer. Like clay in the hands of the potter. Mindless, lumpish clay."

Heimlich suddenly leaped to his feet and roamed among the people, scaring them.

"A few years back, my sister Stacey decided to find me a Jewish wife," he announced. "And she fixed me up with her friend Barbara.

"Now to understand Barbara you've got to understand that appearances mean everything to JAPs. 'Am I right sweetheart?' I say to the girl beside me. She blushes and smiles. 'What's your name, honey?' I ask. She says her name is Cheryl. 'Isn't it true, Cheryl,' I persist, 'wouldn't a JAP rather die than go shopping in comfortable shoes?' She giggles and blushes.

"This Barbara had sex once a month, I say. So she went to her shrink to curb her nymphomaniacal tendencies.

"Luckily for me it was that time of the month.

"I get Barbara into bed.

"She says more to the right now up now a little to the left not inside, outside, you fool, didn't you read *Our Bodies Ourselves?!* My shiksa girlfriend would have been screaming in ecstasy by now but not Barbara. From her I get a syllabus!"

Heimlich gripped Rabbi AvShalom's shoulder, seeking support.

"And then this voice comes out of the dark," he continued. "'The syllabus came from Hadassah,' says the voice. 'A national directive on how to get through a night with the average narcissistic schmuck like you. The alternative is faking orgasm which was the directive sent out by the National Council of Churches. Obviously the bedtime reading of your shiksa girlfriend.'

"Well, of course this woman was getting laughs. Making a fool out of me. Ruining my ACT.

"I said: 'What're you, running for office, lady?'

"And she said: 'No, but my husband is. My name is Carol O'Banyon, and I hope you will all vote for Senator Frank O'Banyon next November.'

"So feeling that I had no real choice, I started applauding. 'Let's hear it for Carol O'Banyon!' I hollered. 'In the age of Pat Nixon, it's good to know there are still some politicians' wives who won't shut up!' And that got me into my political stuff, my Golda Meir - Meyer Lansky scene, and I survived the night.

"I never performed THE JAPRAP again, but I didn't need too," Heimlich continued. "The damage was done. I had made my contribution. In the ensuing years, I saw joke books about JAPS that had variations on all my jokes in them. I saw JAP cocktail napkins.

"My youngest daughter went off to college. One weekend, she attended a football game. Big stadium. Ten, fifteen thousand people. And near the section where Rivka was sitting, a girl — one of those girls with Stacey's body and Stacey's voice — called up to her friend: 'DI-YANNE! DI-YANNE! DO YOU WANT A DIET PEPSI OR A TAB WITH LEMON?' And somebody in Rivka's section started laughing and yelling 'JAP JAP' and the thing spread around until the whole section of the stadium was yelling 'JAP JAP' like a like a like a ch..ch..chant or a ch.. ch. . . cheer like 'GO GO WIN WIN' there must have been thousands of people chanting this thing and at first the girl didn't get it; Rivka said she looked around sort of puzzled; and then her friends who were laughing said 'It's you, Judy, it's you.' They didn't think anything bad was happening, but poor Judy was unsure, not sure, not sure at all whether she was supposed to smile and take a bow for all the people yelling 'JAP JAP' or run for her life because maybe the next thing they were gonna do was lock the door and throw in the gas and pull the switch."

"Shhhh, Abraham. . . that's enough now," Eliezer said.

"In the inner cities, in the fascist outbacks of the mountains, even in the universities, our people are maligned again as they were in the days of our childhood!"

"It was always that way, when was it not?"

"And I myself have added to this mortal danger! Painted my own stripe on the nightmare! Somehow I think that what happened to me in Atlantic City was punishment for that, I don't know how quite but I feel it. . . I feel it. . . "

The patients and their guests and the orderlies now drifted away from Heimlich as from old material, not wanting to be responsible.

"The thing is, Eliezer," he said, "I made up Stacey. I didn't have a sister. But somebody does. Somebody out there has a sister. She's a housewife now, with children, and she is no longer confused like the girl at the football game. She knows they are making fun of her. She knows that they want her to take the path laid down by ridicule and stop being who she is.

"If we keep making fun of them, they won't want to be who they are, and they will run away from being themselves, like my mother ran away from being Mrs. Portnoy, and when they run away, who will take care of us? Answer me that, Eliezer! Who will take care of us then?!"

CHAPTER SEVEN

# WARS

THE JEWISH NEW YEAR brought both grandmothers to the Shapiro home in Broadbeach. As the honey flowed, as Ethel entertained them all with her latest number, Maida Deal could not help remembering the sweet singing voice of her Alex, and she excused herself to dry her tears and repair her make-up. Old Mrs. Shapiro, faded beyond recognition, incapable of staying attuned to this world for more than an hour at a time, dozed off on the deck, among the embankments of mums, her face to the sea.

Candy pleaded with Marty not to allow his mother to go west again. But the old lady insisted, she was fine, nothing wrong, fit as ever, and Marty the Stern turned into a little boy before the eyes of his children and could not cross her. So Candy called the most prestigious agency in Los Angeles and hired a full-time housekeeper to live in the luxurious Santa Monica apartment and shop and clean (what was there to clean?) and see to it that Mrs. Shapiro took her medication on time.

It was convenient for Marty to fly back with his mother and acquaint her with her new keeper because he had to deliver three lectures on endometriosis at the UCLA Medical School.

Candy knew exactly how much time he would spend lecturing. Orpheo's staff, under the direction of Kevin McCabe, had sent her pictures of Cecily's apartment. She had seen Cecily's jewelry box. Somehow she had never dreamed that Marty would be so generous with his mistresses, that they would have from him framed paintings, designer bathrobes, authentic jewels. She continued to swallow her anger and say nothing, hoping that the affair with Cecily would end as the affair with Lisa the art dealer had apparently ended, with anger and recrimination, in the fullness of time. However, to her fantasies of mutilation she now added an obsession with accounting, with defining what exactly she owned in her marriage, since it was clear that those outside it owned so much.

Her wrist had healed. The new Broadway season was beginning. Her mother, staying on for a few weeks, required cheering up after the low of the holidays. Candy told Marie de Grenouille that a night at the theater would be the ideal way to entertain Maida. A major shopping trip might further divert her. (Marie — herself an inveterate browser in the world's stores of comfort — understood that it was not Maida who needed to go shopping.)

Candy drove into New York in her new Volvo with Maida and Ethel, now a wiry, near-sighted ten year old with a big smile. Ethel possessed her father's thick, straight black hair as well as his slender build. Despite old Mrs. Shapiro's objections, she had been named for Ethel Merman, to tempt fate to bless her with a unique singing voice and perfect pitch, and the charm seemed to be working.

Having instructed her decorator to call ahead and make appointments, Candy now surged through the most exclusive furniture emporia on the East Side of Manhattan. The acute young Ethel observed, and unconsciously memorized, how her mother was transformed while shopping. Candy adopted an air of haughty imperialism toward the sales help. They seemed to adore her for it. Her voice sharpened. Her soft mouth flattened over her teeth. She did not remove her sunglasses. She examined the undersides of brocades and velvets, picking at the weave. She looked at every hutch and sideboard, sat in a hundred dining room chairs, consulted Maida without words, with looks that said "Too heavy?" and "Yes, but it will wear well." And she bought nothing.

On their lunch break, Candy said: "I think I'm going to go back to work."

"But the children are still little. . . " Maida protested.

"They're both in school whole days. The garden is established. I can change my volunteer hours at the Homeless Shelter for weekends and drive the evening shift of meals-on-wheels."

"Marty. . ."

"Might have more respect for me if I earned some money."

Maida nodded, not surprised to hear this said of her son-in-law whom she had always feared more than liked.

"Where would you work?"

"In the musical theater where I used to work."

"I didn't know you stayed in touch with those people."

"I didn't. These are new people."

"Are they honest?"

"I think so. Jock Silver and Slim Price. Nice guys."

"Gay?"

"Of course, gay."

"Will you be their secretary?"

"No, Mom. I will be their partner."

Ethel had remained silent all this time, her mouth — filled with semi-chewed hamburger — hanging open in rapt attention. Now she swallowed at last and screamed for joy. "Yayyyy!" she hollered. "Yayyyy! Mommy's gonna be a Broadway producer!" She climbed into Candy's lap and hugged her enthusiastically.

Maida was much less delighted.

"What did you do?!" she cried. "Did you sell the bonds?! My God, Candice, those bonds were supposed to be for a rainy day!"

Candy reached around Ethel and gave her mother's hand a little squeeze which said "That day has come." Maida's eyes filled with tears which she — tough old lady — immediately wiped away.

"This is gonna be terrific!" Ethel rambled on excitedly. "Wait'll I tell the kids at school! Can I come with you to your office?! Can I come to rehearsals?! Oooh please lemme come to rehearsals!"

Before dinner, Candy cruised the West 40s, sending Ethel into theater after theater until they found three tickets to a show they might like. Actually only Ethel liked it. Maida thought it wasn't as good as "Oklahoma" (by which she had measured every show since. Why not? A standard is a standard.).

Candy used the dark to rest and collect her many thoughts. She found herself imagining Alisette Legrand in the role of the eccentric American chess champion, wondered if Alisette had ever considered Broadway — and that reminded her of some lyrics she had heard in a dream in a sleep:

*Rung through heaven rung through hell*
*My dungeon shook and my chains they fell. . .*

"Mom. . . " Ethel whispered.

"Candy darling. . . " Maida whispered.

"Would you please stop singing?!" hissed the woman behind her.

★ ★ ★

By that magical subconscious process so familiar to brilliant shoppers, Candy Shapiro finally decided what she wanted to buy. One morning, without Maida or Ethel, she went back to a certain furniture store in New York and acquired a wall of mirrored cabinets for her living room. It measured ten feet high and eighteen feet long and twenty-two inches deep, and was divided into six units, each three feet wide, four doors per unit. The latches to these cabinets were hidden so well that when they were all closed, you could not detect any but the slightest distinction between the doors.

The cabinets were completely mirrored. The interior back wall of each cabinet was mirrored and so were some of the shelves. Other shelves were made of clear glass, so you could see the surrounding mirrors *through* them. Candy figured this would be a perfect hiding place. Every time you walked into the house, you would see yourself in the cabinets. Therefore you would see nothing else. Into this fortress of reflections, she intended to secretly stash all her personal precious objects and household goods. "I will build myself a high tower," she said to herself. "If it comes to all-out war, I will be ready. Not one teacup or silver spoon that rightly belongs to Sam or Ethel will fall into the hands of the next Mrs. Shapiro."

Like a lunatic ordnance officer, Candy tallied the stuff to be secreted in the mirrored cabinets: the crystal and china, the tableware and photo albums, candlesticks, coffee pots, carafes and decanters and hand-hewn pots and serving platters, linens she and her mother had embroidered, damasks and brocades and all the appurtenances of Passover, *haggadot* that had belonged to her French grandmother and still smelled of cinnamon and wine, Reb Ezra's battered prayer books and the silver Bible Uncle Fayo had given her with the promise of protection.

Her diploma from Boston University.

The original medical diary which had become her brother Sam's posthumous book "The Bones of Parris Island."

The priceless (to Candy) documents declaring her grandparents to be citizens of the United States.

Love letters from men whose very existence she had forgotten in her passion for Martin Shapiro.

"I will build myself a high tower," Candy thought. "And even if I die under this torture, my children will have remnants of me to point to with pride: that was Mom's, they will say; those were her gifts; that belonged to my mother."

In preparation for the arrival of the mirrored cabinets, Candy surreptitiously retrieved all her music from the music room. Soon the soundtrack of her life had disappeared from places were it had lived for eleven years. The Peggy Lee the Alisette LeGrand the James Taylor and Carly Simon the musicals from Porter to Sondheim, the Aretha, the Barbra, the Paul, the Paul and Art, the Sweet Honey in the Rock, the Abba, the Ofra Haza and Yoram Gaon, the Phoebe Snow, the Meatloaf and Bessie Smith and collections of arias by Sutherland and Domingo and Willie Nelson. All this and pounds more just sort of evaporated, like the Jewish people from a Polish town.

Look! I have nothing of yours, she would be able to say in case it came to that. Not one of your precious Horowitz CDs. Not one.

* * *

Candy returned from buying her cabinets early in the afternoon. She felt strong. She was looking forward to spending a couple of hours in the garden. Instead of entering her home through the garage as she usually did, she parked in the driveway and walked around to the back, holding her shoes so that the heels would not dig into the grass and become discolored.

Thus by chance that day, Candy made no sound coming home.The brightly colored leaves of autumn were reflected in the pool and scattered across the lawn, flying from the banks of Broadbeach into the Sound and swiftly sailing out to sea. The garden had turned out beautifully. The ice blue asters matched the sky. Candy was content. She felt that she was suffering less today, that she had learned to manage her husband's disloyalty the way the people at the Homeless

Shelter managed their humiliation, like glaucoma, arthritis, a chronic illness. Okay. So it hurt like hell. But it was not going to kill her.

Noticing that the sprawling hedge roses needed pruning, she set down her pocketbook, slipped on the gardening moccasins which she kept stored on the deck, donned her canvas gardening gloves and apron and took up the heavy limb lopper. The glass doors that led from her deck to her dining room were open to their screens, for Marie had been washing the small rugs and had hung them over the deck rails to dry. Candy pressed her nose to the screens, to see if Marie was there, thinking to call "Hello! I'm home! Wait'll I tell you what I bought!"

She saw a man. His back was to her. His arm was raised. He was holding a knife. His other hand encircled Marie's neck. A hideous wheezing emanated from her compressed throat. Candy slid open the screen door and hit the man as hard as she could with the limb lopper. The man screamed, clutching the side of his head. He dropped his knife. Pushing the blood back from his face, he turned and jumped at Candy. She swung the lopper at him with both hands, horizontally, as though it were a baseball bat, and caught him in the ribs. He said "*Merde!*" and kept coming.

Marie had retrieved the knife. Before he could seize Candy, she attacked the man from behind and stabbed him in the shoulder. He staggered past Candy onto the deck. So much blood from the first blow of the limb lopper was pouring into his eyes that he could not see. The wound in his shoulder gushed.

Candy raced into the kitchen and called the police.

The man was heading toward the lawn. Screeching like a crow, Marie ran after him with the knife.

"No no no!" Candy shouted.

Marie stopped. Candy held her, to calm her trembling. They stood together at the door and watched the man trying to escape. He stumbled over the chair that held Candy's pocketbook. Maybe he couldn't see which way to go; maybe he was too badly wounded to be quite conscious, for he was trying to escape by the wrong route. He lurched past the pool, down to the water, and stood on the shore, looking for the street, for the car he had parked under the neighbor's weeping willows, sure that he had parked a car around here somewhere, and then he collapsed. And then the police came.

★ ★ ★

Marty did not understand the violence that surrounded him. He squinted, unbelieving, at rapists and batterers who were brought to the hospital in chains to be identified by their victims. How can they do it? he asked the cops. To hit a woman, Detective, a soft woman. God. . .

The cops patiently explained about rage pent up, pressurized, then bursting forth like Yellowstone. But why? Marty asked. Up to his armpits in gore, he marveled that anyone could maliciously shed blood. His own rage had burst forth in explosions of straight As, perfect med board scores. Having done it himself, he could not understand why other men were unable to twist and plait their anger into something more useful to the world than a show of force.

For this reason, he had very little sympathy with Candy when he came home from Los Angeles and found that she and her Haitian housekeeper had almost killed an intruder.

It seemed that this man had a political vendetta against Marie's husband back in Haiti. He had meant to assassinate only Marie, and had carefully waited until she was alone in the house so that no innocent American bystander would be hurt. Rug-washing day with its open deck door had provided him the opportunity to attack. He had a small camera in his pocket for he had intended to take pictures of Marie's body and drop them in her husband's mailbox. The man, an illegal immigrant, was quickly imprisoned, patched up and deported. He would spend the remainder of his life a semi-invalid, partly because of his serious wounds, partly because of the terrible psychological trauma he suffered as a result of having been overcome by a couple of women.

"The minute you realized he was in the house, you should have run next door and called the police!" Marty insisted to his wife.

"There was no time!"

"But to attack him physically, an armed man twice your size! How could you be so stupid?!"

"Did I have a choice?" Candy answered.

★ ★ ★

In fact Candy, who had only fantasized violence, had resorted to it instantaneously, without a second thought. Why? Because she had been trained in violence by the movies, and the news, the blood-drenched news.

She had never met the people who were blown away in the bombing at Leviathan, but she felt that she knew them personally. Hearing of the incident at Boston, on an icy path near her college dorm, from another Jew who had never even spoken to her before, she began to weep. The tears froze on her lips. Such bombings had occurred with regularity from the time Candy was a little girl. They punctuated her calm, luxurious life every six months or so, like distant thunder. Her father would bring down horrible curses on the heads of the murderers, disregarding Alex's reminders that they were also somebody's national heroes. Her mother would weep and keen as though her own relatives had been killed. So that was how Candy felt about the Israeli dead — that these school kids on buses, workers in orchards, passengers in airplanes, waitresses in restaurants, were her own relatives.

From their fate, she unconsciously developed an acceptance of the perpetual need for standing armies. Even in the serene security of Gimbel's Inlet, she believed that no Jew remained alive in this world who had not been somehow defended by physical force, and when her house was attacked, she was ready.

Candy was a Zionist.

She thought of Israel as another American state in which a branch of her family lived. She did not believe in God but she was sure that He watched over the Israel Defense Forces.

When she was sixteen years old, she stood on the dining room table, having the hem adjusted on her pink lace sweet sixteen dress, and it was announced on the radio that the Syrians had bombed Haifa; refineries in flames; tens of thousands killed. Her efficient, pontificating mother, who had just arrived from the beauty parlor with perfect hair, fell apart. She screamed. She ran around the dining room, literally beating her breast and crying: "Oh where shall we go?! What shall we do?! God my God who will take care of us now?!"

Thinking Mrs. Deal had gone mad, the seamstress dropped her pins and began to pray. The maid ran in from the kitchen and stood in the doorway, massaging her apron, at a loss, shifting from foot to foot like a kid with a need to pee. Candy leaped down off the dining room table, grabbed Maida and slapped her three times in the face.

"It's a lie," she said, her eyes like winter's ice. And of course, it was.

Given her modest religious background, Candy's deep feelings for her fellow Jews were nothing short of miraculous. Uneducated in those observances by which Leah Heimlich had brought form and order to a bohemian existence, she still felt powerfully the bonds of nationhood, the ancient tribal bonds. *Kaddish* was one of the few prayers she knew in Hebrew, and she prayed for the victims of the Leviathan bombing and all the other bombings with familial intensity. With each segment of television news recording dust-covered

Israeli soldiers prying bodies out of the rubble, she grew more resolved in her loyalty to the Jewish state and more absolutely convinced that its enemies would one day be vanquished and the peace of Jerusalem guaranteed forever more.

★ ★ ★

Candy visited Israel for the first time during the summer after her graduation from high school, on a tour with a group of equally wealthy Jewish girls from towns like Gimbel's Inlet. They had a wonderful time. They took pictures of themselves between the sky and the desert. They thought the boys were cute and couldn't get over how sort of loose and slutty the Israeli girls looked, with hairy legs and Cleopatra make-up on their eyes and tight skirts, no stockings. Compared to these uncorseted Levantines, Candy and her pals felt like goyim from Minnesota.

On a bus to S'dom, she fell to schmoozing with a nice Israeli girl. Her name was Dalia. She was on her way home for Shabbat, a weekly ritual of reunion in her family. Dalia felt dumb and provincial when she heard that Candy would imminently begin attending university. Candy felt weak and silly when she heard that Dalia would soon be serving in the Army. Dalia taught Candy to recognize the word *motek* and the word *cusamok* which was so dirty Dalia almost didn't know enough English to explain what it meant. With these two words, she said, Candy could know whether she was being courted or cursed by the Israelis who spoke to her.

At the Dead Sea, where a million pillars of salt all claiming to be Lot's wife rose up to greet them, the American group got off the bus. Candy inhaled the mineral air, the spiced past that she and Dalia shared, and with a sudden rush of sisterly sentiment, ran back onto the bus and gave the Israeli girl all her make-up. By local standards, this was a year's supply of eye shadows and liners, lipstick and mascara and blush (unfortunately for Dalia, in colors suitable only for the sallow skinned and pale-eyed). The girls exchanged addresses and vowed not to forget each other. And even though they did not meet again, the memory of their happy journey endured, a slender thread but strong.

The Israeli boys prowled after the American girls, who thought it was great fun to lead them on ("I love you! I want your baby!") and confound their ambitions ("My Daddy owns the Chase Manhattan Bank. Sure, he could give you a job.") and leave them gasping with frustration ("I'm not really Barbra Streisand's favorite niece. So long, schmuck."). It was fun because it was a taste of power over men, something the spoiled, untrained girls could never expect to have at home. From the moment of sexual maturity, they had been chased for their money. They could recognize greed when it was still on the phone asking for a date. And when they wiped the floor with the naive boys whose families had come from Iraq and Morocco, they were really scoring a couple of points against the med students and law clerks and brokers from Scarsdale and Shaker Heights who less clumsily but no less single-mindedly dug for Daddy's gold.

It never dawned on Candy that to marry one of these Israelis might be to rescue him from death by war.

Far from making her a less intense American, as some traditional anti-Semites suggested would happen, Candy's Zionist fervor only intensified her commitment to American "patriotic" causes. This horrified her brother Alex, whose country was Peace. He could not believe that a sister of his might doubt the wrongness of the Vietnam War and would actually vote, in her very first election, for Richard M. Nixon!

During the week of intensive buying which followed weeks of intensive shopping and preceded her departure for college, Alex interrupted Candy's labors to ask her to sign a petition calling for more effective control of handguns. Candy refused, saying that it was an American right to bear arms.

Furthermore, she announced, gun control was bad for the Jews.

"How do you figure that, little Candycane?" Alex asked, laughing.

"The cops keep their guns. The crooks keep their guns. The anti-Semites never give up their guns," she answered. "So comes the Day of Judgment, we're the only gunless group because our knee-jerk liberal brothers told us that gun control was wonderful, and va-voom! it's the Warsaw Ghetto all over again."

"Ah CandyCandyCandy!" cried Alex, doing Cary Grant. "What has happened to Daddy's pretty little movie star, our angel, our gentle dove?!" He pulled on Candy's braid as he had done since he was nine. "One summer in the Holy Land and va-voom! a lifetime of JAP values goes out the window!"

"Sammmm! Tell him not to call me that!" Candy yelled, hitting Alex playfully in the arm as she had done since she was six.

"I don't know why I'm suddenly worried about Candy's ideological life," Alex said to his girlfriend that evening. "The whole idea is oxymoronic to begin with."

"It's a phase," said the girlfriend. "She'll get over it."

But Candy did not get over it. She had watched her mother raise the colors of the flag out of the earth on the Fourth of July. She had grown up surrounded by the possessions of women who had nursed the rebels in Massachusetts. Their furniture, their bric-a-brac and counted-thread cross-stitch had decorated the safe interiors of her childhood. She believed that this Republic of Washington and Jefferson was the greatest country in the history of the world, and could not do wrong, impossible, unthinkable, and with uncomplicated logic, she bought the whole package: freedom of speech and the right to bear arms and the pursuit of happiness, all of it. When she visited Masada during that pre-college summer in Israel, and then the Revolutionary battlegrounds near Boston, she said to herself of herself and her brothers: "Here, our forefathers fought most bravely to defend our way of life. Our nationality is American. Our race is Jewish."

Candy's patriotic amalgam included a different definition of "race" than that commonly held by the rest of her countrymen.

What others called race, Candy called merely color.

She thought of The Blacks as a different race, but she did not include among them the Jews of Ethiopia who she felt were part of her race. It was her Zionism, her belief in a multi-colored Jewish race, which, in a racial war, would make Candy — for all her political conservatism — a less than trustworthy ally on the white side. Most Americans, black and white, did not realize this. Unlike Alisette's Grandma Blanche, who knew there was a special race called Entertainer, and Astarte Shachar who knew there was another called Soldier, they did not realize that one might come upon many multi-colored races during the course of this intricate life.

★ ★ ★

Alex Deal once quipped to a fellow Peace Marcher that Boston was "an easy JAP school for easy JAPS" which was why such fools as Candy went there. True, Candy and her friend Roxie Kirsch were not serious students. At least they didn't think they were when they arrived on Bay State Road with dozens of sweaters.

Roxie studied English. Candy studied American History. Roxie's favorite thing was Graham Greene. Candy's favorite thing was Gettysburg. Neither of their mothers knew they had already had sex quite deliberately, with boys they had quickly forgotten, and that they shared a common incredulity at what all the excitement was about. They were both short. They were both chubby. But Roxie gave up trying to girdle and slim herself when she was twenty, and Candy was still at it on the day she died.

Maida and Jack Deal liked Roxie. She came from a well-to-do family in Brookline. Jack felt that she had somewhat more Jewish education than he preferred to see in a girl. However, Maida liked that Roxie was less beautiful than Candy and would probably never take a man away from her. And Roxie always did the right thing. She brought candy and wine and flowers and, on one occasion, marvelously scented soap in a reusable jug. If Alex had been home, they would have urged her upon him. But Alex was in Canada, escaping the war, while Sam was in Asia, attending to its casualties.

The pitched battles that occurred in the big house in Gimbel's Inlet during the Vietnam Conflict woke the dead, releasing the political furies of the Villiers clan, so that the walls shook with ghosts of old fights and unquenchable betrayals. The gold standard fight, the trade union fight. Mexico. Slavery.

The house was a mess after Alex and Jack stopped fighting, after Maida stopped screaming that they should stop fighting. Pillows were strewn, sofas tumbled, papers flown everywhere. All the drawers and doors seemed to fly open as generations of Villiers sided with one or another of the Deals. But as usual, Candy saw and heard none of this because, as usual, she was out of town, in this instance away at school.

She did not see her little father standing at the top of the staircase while Alex stood below him, a foot taller than he was, looking him right in the eye.

"It's a shitty war," Alex yelled. "A stupid war. I am not going to give up my life so that the United States can massacre innocent people and be dishonored for all time."

"Bullshit! You're a coward!"

"Don't you dare to judge me!"

"Your brother went to serve his country!"

"My brother is an orthopedist! He sits in a hospital, and they bring him the wounded to repair! He's safe, Dad! I'm going be a foot soldier if I go! I'm going to die!"

"I was ready to die for my country!"

"It was a different war."

"They came at me with bayonets, the crazy, screaming Japs! *They* were ready to die for their country!"

"So long, Dad."

"Coward!" Jack screamed.

Alex turned to descend the stairs. Jack grabbed his pony tail and twisted him around and nailed him with a mighty right cross, sending him tumbling down the steep staircase, with flying legs. Maida screamed at the bottom. She tried to gather Alex in her arms. But he would not be gathered.

Candy called home the next day and was told by Maida that Alex had run north and that he had said to say goodbye. Maida was crying. Jack had gone off with Milton and Orpheo, to drink and otherwise console himself. So Candy consoled Maida. She said all the right things. She said: "Don't worry, Mom. Alex loves you, he'll stay in touch, he'll find work in Canada, he's not lazy, he'll write."

When Candy hung up the phone from consoling her mother, she asked her friend Roxie: "Why didn't he call me?"

"Because he was running away. You don't stop to call when you're running away."

"But I'm his sister. He should have called me."

"Maybe he'll write to you."

And he did. A letter soon came from Canada.

"In case of emergency," it said, giving a secret "416" number.

Much relieved to have not been forgotten, Candy also felt deeply honored that Alex had entrusted her with the key to his whereabouts. She wrote the telephone number in the silver-coated Bible, in the margin next to the Battle of Ramoth-gilead when Ahab was killed, next to his grave site in Samaria. A random choice of pages.

★ ★ ★

Later on, during the winter of her sophomore year, when news of Sam's death arrived in Gimbel's Inlet, no one immediately thought to call Candy. In the grief and sedation, she was completely forgotten.

Other women who saw the military vehicle in the circular driveway and heard the first cry of anguish ran through the open front door and collapsed on the floor with Maida, rags of mothers moaning together. One of them called Jack's brother Milton who went to find Jack in the showroom. Milton's wife, Theresa, reached Sam's fiancee, Miriam. And all of Gimbel's Inlet had gathered under the chestnut streets before anyone dared to say:

"What about Alex?"

"Shhh, he's in Canada, a draft dodger, don't mention his name."

"But what about Candy?"

"Oh my God! Candy!"

She was in class with Roxie, hearing a lecture about the Civil War. She was imagining the pride of the Villiers clan, dying in a heap in Pennsylvania. The children they had not raised as a result of that terrible battle were the children who could have saved a fine Long Island family. At that moment, the Assistant Dean of the School of Liberal Arts entered the classroom. Snow glittered on her green tweed coat. She took Candy by the hand and led her outside into the hall. She said: "I am so sorry to have to tell you this, my dear. Your brother Sam has been killed."

The Assistant Dean was a harpist by profession. She looked somewhat like Ethel Kennedy, with those large teeth. And she spoke with the same regional accent as William F. Buckley. When Candy's knees gave way, she prevented her from falling.

"I am sure you must try to be strong now," she said, "to comfort your poor mother and father."

Roxie packed some clothes. The Assistant Dean drove them both to the Back Bay station and put them on the train to New York. Roxie hailed them a cab at 34th Street and paid for the expensive ride out to Gimbel's Inlet. By the time they walked into the Deal house, the family had been sitting *shiva* for a full day.

But why didn't you tell me? Candy asked her Aunt Theresa, her Uncle Milton. Why didn't you tell me the minute you heard? she asked her neighbors who had known her since babyhood. Why didn't you tell me? she asked her poor mother and father.

They stared at her with blank faces. They didn't know what she was talking about. They barely knew who she was.

She and Roxie drove to a pay phone near the supermarket and called the number Alex had sent. A girl took the message. Alex soon called back.

"Please come home," Candy said.

"How did it happen?"

"The hospital was hit. . . "

"Did he suffer?"

"I don't know! How could I know that?!"

"They say that people who are hit by bombs die instantaneously."

"Mom is hysterical. She's been drugged. Dad is in a stupor!"

"Where are you going to bury him?"

"We haven't even got him to bury yet! We're sitting *shiva* but it'll take weeks before we get his body. Tell me, Alex, what should I do?"

"Do what you want, Candycane."

"But how could I know what I want?!" she cried.

"My uh my brother Sam is gone. . . " he said to someone in Toronto.

"Talk to me!" cried Candy.

"They killed my brother Sam. . . "

"Talk to me!" She heard murmurs of friends comforting him. "Alex! Please! I can't bury Sam all by myself! Help me!"

He hung up. She called back but the number was busy and remained so. Candy went home. She leaned on the solid, angry Roxie. All around her, people came and went on tides of food, babbling. For the first time in her life, she saw how stupid women look, potchkying with coffee cups, slicing rafts of bagels, transported by their trays, saying "Eat something, darling. You have to keep up your strength."

Her Aunt Theresa, still extremely beautiful, sat down beside her and pressed into her hand a copy of the words from John about the Resurrection and the Life, and suggested that they read it together. Candy refused. "Just because we've had a tragedy doesn't mean we're going to give up and become Christians, Aunt Terry," she snapped, wounding the well-meaning woman, making Theresa feel keenly the pain of a lifetime spent among strangers. Immediately, Candy apologized, hugging her. But what was said was said.

As evening fell, the handsome young rabbi tried to gather ten men to say *kaddish* in Sam's memory. There were only eight in the packed house. Roxie and Candy offered to stand in. The rabbi politely declined, completing the necessary quorum with two boys who had just arrived with a delivery of yet more food from the local delicatessen.

Her mother sat on a box. For days. The ugliest woman in the world on a box in a room without mirrors.

"Talk to me, Mom," Candy said.

"What?"

"It's me, Candy, tell me what I can do for you."

"Bring me back my prince, " Maida said. "My darling my first-born, bring him back to me."

Candy went to see her father. He lay on Sam's bed in Sam's old room. She sat at Sam's desk.

"Don't sit there," her father said.

She stood.

"Talk to me, Daddy," she said. "Tell me what I can do for you?"

"What?"

"It's me. Candy."

"Oh yeah."

Jack took a deep breath.

"You just be your own sweet adorable self, baby," he said. "Get yourself a nice husband, bring me some nice cute grandchildren." He smiled absently and patted her hand. "My beauty. My little movie star. Look how grown up you got."

She and Roxie went to see Sam's fiancee, Miriam, a thin young woman who worked in a laboratory. Miriam thanked them for coming. She poured them all a glass of scotch, like they were men. She gave Candy a "secret" telephone number which Alex had sent to her, where he could be reached in Toronto.

On the platform of the train which she was about to take back to Boston, Candy's good friend Roxie said to her:

"Look, there's a couple of wonderful things about not being taken seriously. First, you're never held responsible. And second, when you finally make your move, you can count on the element of surprise."

⋆ ⋆ ⋆

In Gimbel's Inlet, the young rabbi rang the doorbell. It was almost three weeks since news of Sam's death had reached the Deal family. He was a benevolent, well-intentioned guy, this rabbi, really he was, although his name would be hard to remember in years to come. When Candy saw him at the door, she did not invite him in.

"Uh. . . your parents. . . "

"What do you want?"

"I'd like to speak to your parents."

"They're sleeping. Tell me what it is."

"Well, Sam's remains have arrived," the rabbi said. "And so we have to arrange for burial. Your family has space at Beth Chayim."

"My brother is being buried at Arlington National Cemetery."

He could not prevent a breath of shock.

"Did your parents want that?"

"My parents are non-functional. They will do what they are told to do. They are patriots. They agree that this is best."

"Shall I call Alex?" asked the rabbi. "I have a number. . . "

"Apparently everybody does."

"He sent it to me in case of an emergency. If you would like, I'll get in touch with him."

"Why didn't you get in touch with me?"

"What?"

"Nobody called me. For a whole day, nobody called me."

"Listen, Candy, in a time of trial. . . "

"It really doesn't mean anything to be a sister, does it Rabbi?"

"I see how hurt you are. I'm sorry. . . "

"You run your temple like a Unitarian church and still you wouldn't let me and my friend Roxie make a *minyan* for *kaddish*."

"It's a tradition, Candy, please. . . "

"Eat shit, you wimp," she said and closed the big front door solidly in his face. Even now he feels the cold wind of that closing. It frosted up his glasses and almost knocked him off his feet.

So Candy and Sam's girl Miriam buried what remained of Sam's tall strong body in Virginia with a Hebrew prayer from a chaplain in uniform and a bugler playing taps. The army gave Jack and Maida the flag that draped his coffin and his personal effects. Miriam kept the letters she had written him and the half finished love letter with snapshots which he would soon have sent to her had he not been bombed to death in the afternoon.

Candy held on to the medical diary which Sam had kept. She entitled it "The Bones of Parris Island." She showed it to Roxie. When in years to come, Roxie was running her own little publishing company, she published it as a kind of ancillary text for surgery students. It sold rather well, so acute were the observations of the young orthopedist, so vast the variety of fractures incurred in war.

It sold very well in Israel.

★ ★ ★

The second time Candy saw Jerusalem was when she and Marty went on a Young Leadership Mission. They had been married eight years at the time. The trip was Candy's idea. She told Marty it was long overdue. Of course the Mission would cost them; they would be expected to pledge many thousands to the UJA-Federation campaign. But why not? Candy said. They had prospered and should now "pull their weight" in the community.

Marty's father had been much less charitable than Jack Deal. In fact, he had not given away very much of his money at all until his final hours, with Heimlich goosing his conscience. Marty might have allowed his own affairs to work out this way as well, except that Candy insisted that people as wealthy as they were simply had to give away at least twenty per cent of their income. Not to do so was a scandal! She wouldn't be able to bear it! She would be ashamed to show her face in the supermarket!

He knew that she was active in Hadassah, that she organized the theater parties for their kids' school and their growing Conservative synagogue, that she was on the board of the Homeless Shelter and the Cancer Society, that charity was how she got her kicks. So finally, to shut her up, and because he kind of liked the idea of being “A Young Leader,” Marty agreed to the Mission. He and Candy went to Israel.

The Mission turned out to be made up mostly of other physicians and their wives.

“I guess it’s hard to find businessmen under 45 who can give away a lot of money without asking Daddy for permission,” said one particularly smug dermatologist. “We, the professionals, are the only self-made men around.”

Marty preferred the company of a cardiologist from Boston and an endodontist from Florida and the odd man out of the Mission, a genius named Dick Glick who had revolutionized retailing by concocting an inventory control clamp which could only be released by passage across a precoded magnetic field; no more cumbersome unlocking machines; no more damaged goods. Dick’s wife, Charlotte, was six inches taller than he was. She was a nice nerd, just like Dick. And an accountant. What this accomplished woman saw in Candy, Marty would never understand, but they soon became close friends, clambering over the windswept battlefields of the Golan with binoculars, Charlotte in her safari jacket and weathered jeans, Candy in her ironed Calvins, her high-heeled boots and her angora sweater with the beaded embroidery.

Led by a savvy guide, the rich, young Americans rode up the trails of blood, imagining that they felt the bones of fallen warriors grinding beneath their wheels. They chatted with officers, contemplated Syria and experienced the horrid thud of military aircraft passing overhead. They climbed into a tank and then quickly climbed out.

All except Candy. She closed the hatch and locked herself in. The guide beat on the gun turret. He could not rouse her.

Marty was embarrassed."Okay. Enough, sweetheart. Out you go!" he called.

No answer.

"She must need to be in there," said Charlotte Glick sensibly. "Let her stay a while."

They took an hour's walking tour, and when they returned, Candy was sitting cross-legged on the sand-colored war machine, her eyes distant. The freckles which appeared when she neglected to protect herself against sunshine were beginning to speckle her nose and cheeks.

"We thought we lost you for a minute there," Marty said in a jocular way, more disturbed by her distress and dishevelment than he wanted to let on.

"I'm sorry," she said. He hated that. He hated when she needed him, and he didn't know how to help her, and she apologized.

The Young Leaders headed south to the luxurious hotels of Eilath to wash away the dust of the battlefields. But Candy would not idle with the group. Somehow she found a gang of chipper British military history buffs who had taken a sentimental journey from Tobruk to El Alamein to Port Said and were now trundling through Sinai to examine the battlefields of 1967. Since there was plenty of room on their bus, Candy bought a ticket and went along. She made no effort to disguise her origins to better fit in with the frumpy crowd. She wore gray green mock alligator hiking shoes with immaculate yellow socks, yellow mesh sweats, large silver earrings inset with green stones, and a floppy golf hat that sported a protruding green plastic shade.

For the first time in his married life, Marty Shapiro began to think of Candy as an eccentric. Dick Glick, who fell asleep in the middle of conversations and awoke ten minutes later refreshed and never ate anything but brown rice and raw vegetables, could be forgiven his eccentricities because he was so incredibly successful. But Candy was a nice Jewish woman! A suburban housewife! The mother of his children! And to see her being handed up onto a bus at the Egyptian border by a pudgy Arab who bowed and leered at the same time, to see her surrounded by crusty old imperialists in walking shorts, this gave Marty's heart a terrible turn. What if she fell into a political discussion with one of them?! She was such a jerk, she might just blurt out her sympathy for the Irish rebels! He disliked the bizarre melancholia which pulled her to the sites of so much death and suffering and caused her to neglect her appearance. Why couldn't she just be calm and safe and contented in Israel the way she was at home? With all his heart, Marty Shapiro wanted to drag Candy off the damn Brit bus!

He distracted himself by snorkeling with the cardiologist from Boston and the endodontist from Florida. He tried to be fascinated by the spectacular colorations of the fish. Under the water, in the coral caverns among the sunbeams, they bumped into a Senator's wife. She had come to Israel on a political junket. In the manner of politicians, she quickly made friends with the three physicians. Her name was Carol O'Banyon.

Carol showed up again that night while the Young Leaders were having dinner on a terrace. She tugged by the hand her handsome husband, the Senator. Marty and his co-snorkelers introduced the couple all around the Mission. Although the Senator had few constituents in the group, he was clearly interested in making friends with people who were rich and generous and likely to be impressed with his stalwartly pro-Israel voting record when he announced (as he planned to do in the fall) his candidacy for the Presidency of the United States.

Carol O'Banyon sat down between Marty Shapiro and Dick Glick, and had a glass of wine. A tall, limber-legged woman in her late 40s; she had once almost been a movie star, one of the several statuesque blondes chosen for fame by Alfred Hitchcock. She had given up a potentially phenomenal career to become the Senator's second wife. Actually, however, her retirement to marriage had made Carol even more of a celebrity than she might have been had she stayed on Hollywood's short leash, for now she was the most successful hostess in Washington, and the most brilliant *saloniste* since Mabel Dodge Luhan. If you were rising and converging, as Megaman Brancusi had instructed Alisette, you eventually ended up at Carol O'Banyon's house. She was witty and literate, and never invited a writer to her home without first reading his books. She served scrumptious buffets. The layout of her living room invited jam sessions. When her husband started to look a little bit too old for this high life, Carol sent him to her surgeon, Dr. Danton Moore, and got him a subtle, Parisian face lift.

She had a way of introducing people to their causes — a certain rock singer to the rain forest; a certain chicken heiress to the non-proliferation of nuclear power plants. And she had not the least hesitation to call up the most remote academics in the world, astronomers down from the night skies, behaviorists in from the jungles, and set them lecturing about their research to boggled Congressmen in her living room.

"Many people get real high on power in Washington," she said in her charming Charlottesville drawl. "So I feel it is my patriotic duty to remind my guests that they do not by any means know everything there is to know."

Marty Shapiro and Dick Glick were amazed that a woman who was so much older than either of their wives could look so much better. Carol kept her long body uncorseted, her clothes simple, her lightly curled blonde hair clean and free, her fingernails short and invisibly polished. Not one serious word passed her thin lips. When she laughed, it was low in the throat, and her teeth barely showed. She reminded Marty of Grace Kelly and Kim Novak, heroines of his earliest childhood fantasies, and so he felt young again in her presence.

It was hard to believe she had once been Jewish.

"Please," she drawled, "I'm in agony in this country. Ever since I got off the plane, I've been on a guilt trip. The women here all remind me of my aunts in Virginia saying,

'Carol honey, how can you give your life to that Irishman? You'll have to sit in a closet and confess your sins! You'll have to eat scones!'" Everybody laughed. "My husband of course has turned out to be the greatest friend the Jews ever had. So the next time Israel gets a hundred million in military assistance, I ask you all to observe a moment of silence for those of us who have been sleeping with goyim lo these many years to make it all happen."

The whole group now fell into the rhythm of Carol O'Banyon's sophisticated patter and everybody was telling funny stories and drinking wine when Candy returned from Sinai. She was a mess. Dusty. Sweaty. Her elegant outfit had been stained with rust from moldering armored vehicles. Still, Marty had no choice but to introduce her.

"Let me get this straight," said Carol. "You came to Israel on a Young Leadership Mission and then when they finally let you out of the tanks and off the trails and gave you a day to luxuriate in the Gulf of Eilath, you left your gorgeous brilliant husband here and took off for Egypt to look at more battlefields!"

"You got it," Candy said, smiling.

"But what about your hair, my dear?! Why it got all messed up! What about your beautiful shoes?! Look how dusty and dirty they are!" Carol laughed. "You are my heroine, Mrs. Shapiro! Sit down here next to me. Somebody bring this terrific woman a glass of wine."

In her entire life up to that moment Candy Shapiro had never been so deeply flattered. She blushed beneath her freckles.

At one point, when they were freshening their drinks at the bar, Senator Frank O'Banyon asked Candy what she had seen in Sinai.

"I saw dust," she said. "I thought it was pathetic, the way those Englishman dragged around the desert, looking for their wars."

"But what were you looking for?" he persisted.

"Me?"

"You too were dragging around the desert."

"Oh, I was looking for my brothers," Candy said. "But I think it must have been too complicated, too personal, you know, like taste in music. I'm never going to find them. All I saw was dust."

In this manner, Senator Frank O'Banyon became the only man in the world to ever hear the truth of Candy's heart on the matter of Vietnam, the conflict which had destroyed her family. He died of a massive stroke six weeks later, in the cold stone corridors of the Capitol, immediately before announcing his candidacy for the Presidency, with Candy's knowledge of futility still trapped in his body.

CHAPTER EIGHT

# A WOMAN OF VALOR

A YEAR OR SO AFTER HER HUSBAND'S DEATH, Carol O'Banyon moved to New York. She bought an apartment in Manhattan's glitziest high rise, and took a fund-raising job with Safe Earth, the most stylish environmental protection group in the metropolitan area.

Candy promptly sent her a huge basket of fruit and jam and candy and nuts. "Welcome to your new home!" the card said. "We'd love to have you to dinner. Give us a call when you're settled. Your old friends from Israel, Candy and Marty Shapiro."

Many weeks later, Candy was thrilled to receive a handwritten card: "Thanks for the fabulous goodies!" it said. "It was wonderful meeting you in Israel. Much love, Carol."

"She remembered us!" Candy beamed at her husband.

"Now which one was she?" he asked.

To augment her income, and possibly launch her own political career, Carol hired writers and added to their skills an unfailing ear for exhortatory rhetoric and made herself one of the most attractive public speakers on the circuit. If you could get her to speak at your function, you were sure to raise money.

She won the respect of many women by personifying fashion independence. No designer could call Carol his own. Eschewing the tailored look then so popular, she opted for clothing which flowed in classic, pre-Raphaelite folds. (Reading *Women's Wear Daily* in Tampa by the sea, Maida Deal noted that it was her daughter's good friend Carol O'Banyon who pioneered the ringless finger, the short fingernail, the small earring.)

Carol went to Lincoln Center to see the opening of a new American work. A newswoman asked her to comment about the gala crowd that swirled around her.

"This night will go down in history, mark my words," Carol purred. "'A fabulous affair!' scholars will record. 'A triumph for the renaissance of American music! And in keeping with the style of the season, virtually every woman there was dressed as a whore.'"

This witticism caused much hilarity among the members of Broadbeach Hadassah, for Lee Kreinick, Marsha Chomsky and Candy Shapiro too had noticed the whore trend. What else could you say about a fashion in which the skirts were short and tight and black, the tops were low and tight and black, the stockings black lace, the heels high, the hair and earrings gigantic? Decent women who valued good taste had found their new champion in Carol O'Banyon. And she was Jewish! And she was Candy's friend! Maybe Candy could get her to be the keynote speaker at the New Year's lunch to raise money for the Soviet Jews!

"Don't do it," said Roxie.

"Why not?"

"Because I hate her."

"She's adorable!"

"She's an aging queen bee who doesn't take anything seriously unless it has balls."

"Oh come on. . . "

"First, she almost became a movie star. Then she really did a bang-up job as a hostess. Now she became a rich widow with great clothes and a sinecure at a not-for-profit. B-i-i-g fucking deal! My mother had the same life and she died in despair because she knew she had accomplished exactly nothing."

"Oh Roxie, you're so mean!" Candy laughed.

"I hate Carol O'Banyon," said Roxie. "She never marched with us when we marched on Washington."

"Well, she was the wife of a Catholic Senator! He had Presidential ambitions. How can you blame her?"

"Come on, Candy, you gotta stand up and be counted when it counts. This woman is just not a sister."

Candy closed her eyes and smiled in that self-satisfied way her mother had perfected to annoy her father.

"It's hard to be a 'sister' when you're a Zionist."

"Now don't start. . . "

"I know you'd prefer not to hear this, Roxanne, but unfortunately, the feminists are anti-Israel. There. I said it. The truth is the truth. First they attack us for being volunteers. . . "

"Who's *us* ?!"

"Then they denigrate us for being housewives. And then they say Zionism is racism."

"Who's *they* !? That was an international conference!"

"Don't take this personally, you know I love you, but the Jews in the feminist movement are a bunch of knee-jerk liberal self-haters who don't know what's good for them, just like my brother Alex." (Candy waved her fingers toward the north.) "Wherever he may be."

"Since when is Carol O'Banyon a Jewish communal leader?!" Roxie protested. "She married an Irishman! She went to Mass!"

"Only for the sake of appearances. You would have done the same thing."

"I would not!"

"What I'm really worried about," Candy continued, "is that the environmental movement is going to turn out to be another left-wing front where they want every species to survive except the Jewish people. What will we do then, Roxie? I mean the environmental movement is much too important not to join. It has to be made Jew-friendly. I think Safe Earth needs a good relationship with Hadassah. So I'm inviting Carol O'Banyon to be our keynote speaker."

Roxie groaned.

"She won't be interested. You're not chic enough. She doesn't even know who you are."

"We spent a whole evening together in Eilath."

"B-i-i-g fucking deal!"

"She'll remember the basket of fruit I sent her. It was fantastic. You should have seen those dates! Those pears! The size of those pecans!"

Candy called Carol's office every day for two weeks. Carol's secretary dutifully took the message — "She knows me; we met in Israel" — but no answer came. Suspecting that Roxie may have been right about the "balls" part, she asked Marty to call.

"How can she remember me when I don't remember her?" he asked.

"Oh stop. As soon as she hears 'Doctor', she'll think you're calling to warn her about the viral history of one of her ex-lovers and she'll take the call."

Marty laughed. Candy could certainly strike him funny sometimes. He wondered what had happened in recent days to make her so much more acerbic than she had ever been before. He asked his secretary to call Carol and, if she wasn't in, to leave a message.

Carol didn't think Marty was a doctor calling to report on one of her ex-lovers. She thought he *was* one of her ex-lovers. So she called back, leaving her phone number at home. Which was where Candy reached her and asked her to address Broadbeach Hadassah. It was not until this moment that Carol O'Banyon recalled Candy Shapiro and identified her as the source of those extraordinarily large pecans.

Carol named a very high fee. Candy met her price without flinching and ordered the invitations. When Carol canceled (so that she could spend the weekend with a man who would soon be the Chief of Detectives), she offered Candy a substitute speaker and figured that would be the end of that. But Candy would not take a substitute. She insisted on an alternative date. Carol said that one would not really be available until next year. Candy said she would wait. Unable to blow off this tenacious Hadassah lady, Carol agreed to the speaking engagement.

"They're wonderful women," Carol O'Banyon said to her speech writer. "But since they give away so much of their money to worthy causes, everybody knows how rich they are. So they are magnets for jealousy, derision, even hatred. Even their fellow Jews call them JAPS and belittle them for their special blessings. So they feel insignificant. So they try to make up for that by becoming 'Women of Valor,' you know, the one in the Bible whose price is above rubies. She goes to business, sews coverlets, never idle, covers her husband's name with honor while he sits in the gates and become famous for his wisdom. So now, after thousands of years, these wonderful women are incredibly productive — and completely powerless." (She smiled.) "Why don't we try to make them feel good about themselves for once?"

★ ★ ★

Broadbeach Hadassah ate the loss for printing on the old invitations and the deposit on the hall for the old date. Candy had new invitations printed. She hired a new hall that seemed to be much too big at first (but turned out to be almost too small), ordered the food, decided on the flowers, inveigled fabulous doorprizes out of local merchants, spent six weeks juggling the seating arrangements so that only a few women were really angry, told all the other speakers what they had to say and how long they had to say it in and rehearsed them in her kitchen to make sure they sounded smart. She sent out press releases and personally enlisted the cooperation of half a dozen environmental groups on Long Island, so that they too sent out press releases.

When Carol arrived at the luncheon site, she found that Candy had arranged photo opportunities with every meaningful political figure on Long Island. Then Candy ushered her into a room where 1800 women — including two hundred who had never attended an Hadassah function before, and would become members before the day was through — sat chatting at their tables. Many of them had announced large pledges in addition to the considerable fee for the luncheon itself. Their food was fancy salad. Clearly these women were much more interested in the charity they had come to support and the speaker they were about to hear than in the food they were about to eat.

They were really something, Carol thought. Out of sheer respect, she gave it everything she had, and the luncheon netted many thousands of dollars to help resettle the Soviet Jews.

At the end of the day, Candy invited the luncheon committee and Carol back to her house where Marie and two new Russian immigrants who were trying to start a catering business stood guard over a sumptuous smorgasbord, a great idea since everyone was starving from having eaten such a teeny lunch. Carol asked the Russians for their business card. They had not thought to print one. However, Candy had.

"Tell me, Candy," Carol asked, "what do you do when you're not saving the remnants of our people?"

Candy answered seriously: "Well, before I was married, I worked as a gopher in the theater, and I recently became a financial partner in an off-Broadway producing organization. But basically, I don't do anything. I'm just a housewife."

Carol seized Candy's hand and called out loudly to everyone in the house: "How often have I heard this bullshit?! Our Candy exhibited skills today in public relations, banqueteering, financial planning, personnel management and theatrical producing that can bring a person a six figure salary! And can you believe this?! She says she doesn't do anything! She says she's just a housewife!"

Candy blushed. It was the second time her existence had been validated by a woman she considered semi-great. Strength and self-confidence set a fire in her blood.

★ ★ ★

One day, old Mrs. Shapiro called her son at the office to ask him if he would arrange to have flowers sent from her for Candy on the occasion of her being elected Woman of the Year by Broadbeach Hadassah. It was lucky she called, because Marty had completely forgotten the occasion. His mother — who was the one who was supposed to have reached the age of forgetfulness — expressed shock. "A woman brings honor to your name, and you forget the honor?! Gee, Martin darling, you really are turning into your father."

As guilt trips go, it was a solid ten. Marty raced from his office in the middle of the day to make an appearance at the Hadassah luncheon where Candy was being honored, and ended up arriving late, standing in the back with Roxie Kirsch. He was surprised to see her. She must have come out from Manhattan, a major schlep. It flashed briefly in his mind that there might have been other occasions in Candy's life which he had missed and Roxie had schlepped for.

He had never particularly liked Roxie. Short, dumpy, with electric frizzy hair and gray clothing, she reminded him of Communists in the 30s. She couldn't seem to stay married.

She had her own publishing company and did quite nicely (he had the feeling that Candy had invested.) For Candy's sake, he tried to be friendly to her. But Roxie was not friendly back.

A woman stood up to read Candy's award.

"For dedicated service to the community," it said, "for giving herself wholeheartedly to the task of resettling the Soviet Jews who have come to us virtually destitute, for running our theater parties and benefits for years without once booking a show we didn't like, for driving kosher meals on wheels every single weekend to the elderly and homebound, for linking us into wonderful alliances with the environmental coalition as well as the Broadbeach family shelter program. . . "

Naturally, Marty knew about all these activities in Candy's life, but he had never imagined that a room full of similar women would give her a standing ovation for them. He began to feel kind of proud.

She got up to thank them. She had a speech prepared and appeared confident. However, to Marty's eye, she looked garish and over-garlanded as a hula girl because she was wearing *both* the corsage which her mother had sent from Florida and the corsage his mother had sent from California. He wondered how he would be able to get her a present so she wouldn't know he hadn't gotten her a present.

"You are all wonderful people and I am really grateful to know you and to have you for my friends," Candy began. Marty grinned and waved to her to catch her attention and show her he was there. The speech fluttered in her hand. "Oh. . . there's my husband. It never occurred to me that he would be able to make it. Um. . . well, I'd like to introduce my husband, Dr. Martin Shapiro, who makes it possible for me to give so much time and money to this great organization. . . "

They all turned to Marty. He smiled. They applauded. Roxie closed her eyes and sagged against the wall.

"I had a speech," Candy continued, "Um. . . but I am. . . I think it would be best if I just said that I love you all and I thank you from the bottom of my heart."

She kissed Lee Kreinick and Marsha Chomsky and they all applauded again and she sat down.

That afternoon, Marty sent out his receptionist to buy Candy a pair of earrings. She came up with pearl clusters on gold leaves. Little Sam examined the earrings very closely, wondering how you learned to pick out these kinds of things for girls. Ethel carried on over the earrings and made Candy try them on immediately and then tried them on herself just for fun, and Candy thanked Marty and kissed him. But she seemed sad about something.

"What's the matter?" he asked.

"Lee Kreinick called me really pissed off. She said I should have made a nice encouraging speech and instead I made everybody at the luncheon feel like shit. Like there would be no Hadassah except for the sufferance of rich men. And if my work meant so little to me, then all their hard work must be for nothing too."

Her eyes filled with tears. Ethel's eyes filled with tears.

"Aw baby. . . " Marty said, stroking Candy's hair, holding her tenderly. "That's ridiculous come on shhhh she's just jealous come on don't let some nasty JAP make you feel bad."

* * *

She hated him. She just hated him. Every time he did something nice to show that he loved her, he filled her plate with fresh heapings of humiliation to show that he despised her, and every time she thought she had made peace with her own loathsomeness and knew why he despised her, he did something nice to show that he loved her.

She knew exactly how his affair with the record company executive had ended. During the UCLA lecture series. At a cocktail party in Venice. Cecily went home crying, alone; Marty went out with Danton Moore and a couple of fashion models. Marty's model was wearing white leather pants. This report did little to raise Candy's hopes, because Marty was being such a shit these days that even if he had been faithful, she would have hated him.

He did surgery every other day, sometimes every day, five days a week for weeks on end. His feet hurt him. He needed orthotic inserts in all his shoes. He suffered from eye strain and shooting pains in his neck. If the kids interrupted him while he was reading, he gave them that look of condescension and disgust which could whither the soul and which had repeatedly caused nurses to quit his employ despite the good pay. So now the kids were afraid of him. Ethel never practiced the piano when Marty was home without first asking his permission. Little Sam never asked for help with his homework unless Marty was out of the house, because if Marty volunteered to help him, Sam would inevitably end up in tears, and like his mother, he hated to cry.

Fascistically clean, Marty would run his index finger along the upper rims of the picture frames to check for dust. Candy had already fired two housekeepers whose dusting had failed this test. Unable to bear the thought of being parted from Marie, Candy now took to re-dusting the picture frames right before Marty came home. (It dawned on her that her mother's much-parodied tendency to redo housework already completed by her maids might have originated in exactly the same way.)

Unemotional by day, Marty often seemed to experience horrible pain in his sleep and soaked the sheets with sweat. Marie and Candy changed them every morning. Once when he was whimpering in the night, Candy woke him. He grabbed her by the arms and shook her and yelled "Get away from me! Don't touch me! I hate you! You disgust me!" When she told him what he had said, and showed him the bruises on her arms, he showered her with remorseful kisses, begged her to forgive him.

How could she not, when his work demanded such heroism and he was under such terrible pressure and she loved him so much?

One of his patients, six months pregnant, was killed by a drunk driver, leaving behind two other little kids. Marty saved the unborn baby.

Over the past few years, he had performed three operations on a woman who was desperate to have a child. Finally she became pregnant. So she loved Marty. In her fifth month, she discovered by amniocentesis that the baby would be retarded. So she hated Marty.

The women in the free clinic, where he donated two afternoons a week, labored to give birth, screaming for strength, and no one would come to help them because no one wanted to touch their blood. The AIDS babies, born astride the grave, lay suffering in their incubators.

A fourteen-year-old girl was brought in with a raging fever. Marty found a baby rat in her vagina. He performed an emergency hysterectomy on a woman who had been knifed in the stomach. Then he went back to his private practice, where the women were rich and presumably safer from abuse, and he found that the daughter of one of his patients had been gang-raped at a fraternity party and so severely kicked and beaten that Marty had to remove her ovaries.

If someone had asked him what he wanted in life, he would have said he wanted Dick Glick to invent a surgical glove which could not be pierced by a needle before all the doctors and nurses in America were infected by the AIDS virus.

Candy begged him to take a vacation. He said he had no time. She tried to rub his neck. He said he'd really rather have a professional masseur. She hired one, a Russian who had worked on the stars of the Kirov. After ten minutes, Marty declared the man incompetent and ordered him to get out.

Candy made potato pancakes the way his mother made them. She bought a CD player for their bedroom and inlaid it with the Chopin he loved. She came to bed wearing an ice blue teddy with no crotch. Marty laughed and melted and began to kiss her. But the phone rang. Somebody was bleeding.

He asked Candy to drive him to the hospital so that he could sit in the passenger seat and concentrate on talking to the emergency room staff on the car phone. Candy wasn't used to the new BMW. Repeatedly, she stripped the gears. Marty became so furious with her that, as soon as they arrived at the hospital, with the whole night staff watching, he asked an orderly who happened to be leaving then to drive his incompetent wife home.

Candy cowered in the car. She clutched her bathrobe around her, terrified that this stranger would glimpse the stupid blue lace thing in which she had started out this horrible evening. Of course he repeatedly stripped the gears because he couldn't drive the BMW any better than she could. He was sweating with embarrassment. A brown-skinned guy. From the Dominican Republic. Handsome, sort of, and young. As he pulled up at the bus stop near her house to drop himself off, Candy thought — for the very first time actually — that it might really be fun to make love to Dr. Shapiro's orderlies or his ambulance drivers or, better yet, one of his caddies at the golf course, and finally at long last bring some serious dishonor to his fucking name.

★ ★ ★

Marty left for Paris on a January morning. His new friend Danton Moore had invited him for a week, to attend a conference on drugs which might prevent AIDS from crossing the placenta. Candy remembered that when her brother Sam had gone to war, he had kissed her goodbye in the same vacant way, his mind already soaring forth ahead of the plane that would take him to his life's heart, to his work, his awful, thrilling work.

Candy clung to her husband for an extra breath of a second.

He pulled away, almost annoyed.

"Sorry," she said. "I didn't mean to irritate you with my minor needs."

"What could you possibly need that I don't give you?" he snapped.

"A better kiss."

Indulgently, he kissed her again, and the cab took him away. Candy remained standing on the front steps for a long time.

CHAPTER NINE

# A BETTER KISS

IT WAS A LOUSY DAY IN BROADBEACH when Marty Shapiro took off for Paris for the first time. Dark, dirty clouds hung low over the houses. Bitter cold withered the rhododendron leaves. The grass had the look of lead shavings. Down at the end of Candy's back yard, the black water smacked the pilings. The relief of snow did not come.

Candy could have gone to work. However, Jock and Slim were vacationing in Key West. The office would be dull and deal-less until their return. She thought of taking Roxie to lunch, for it often helped, when you were feeling blue, to comfort somebody who was even bluer. However, just at that moment, Lazard Goldberg of the Lazard Cares Moving Company called and said that he would soon be bringing over the cabinets she had ordered so long ago.

The mirrored cabinets! The beautiful cabinets she had bought to be her fortress last October were finally arriving, and just in time to save her from a fresh depression! She and Marie immediately began lugging the living room furniture out of the way so that the workmen could beat a path from the front door to the wall where the cabinets were to reside, without breaking any wonderful nut dish or antique vase. To avoid impatience while waiting, they baked six dozen rugulach. And since they had extra dough, Marie defrosted some apples they had harvested from their own trees and baked a couple of pies.

When the truck bearing the cabinets pulled up into their driveway, on schedule, just as planned, Candy could barely contain her excitement. A strong, grizzled man came to the door.

"Lazard Cares Moving Company," he said. "I'm Lazard. We got your cabinets."

Candy immediately assumed her forbidding shopper's demeanor.

"Please put something down on the floor to protect the carpet," she commanded.

"Shaul!" he called. "Bring the plastic!"

A younger man soon appeared at the door carrying a pile of folded plastic drop cloths. He had dark olive skin and tightly curled hair of shiny black, and although he wore two heavy sweat shirts, gloves and a muffler, he still looked cold. At his first whiff of the pungent house, this young man warmed like a candle. His nose grew moist; his heavy-lidded eyes closed automatically. He stood in the foyer, just smelling for a few seconds, before getting down to work.

Candy and Marie hung back in the kitchen doorway, watching. When he was finished rolling out the plastic, Shaul looked up at them.

"Where do you want the cabinets? On this wall?"

Candy nodded. He walked out the front again, hitching back the screen door so that it would not impede the entry of the furniture, and leaving black fingerprints on the woodwork. Marie went to get a cloth to wipe them away.

"Not yet," Candy said. "There will be more fingerprints before these men are finished. Let's wait to clean them up all together."

In a few minutes, the young man called Shaul and his boss returned with the first cabinet, just the shell, no shelves, no doors. They placed it against the wall and brought in the other five. Each cabinet was wrapped in protective plastic, a lucky thing because, at one point, Shaul scraped the end he was carrying against the door frame.

"Hey, watch it," Candy said.

He rolled his eyes with an elaborate display of disgust.

"You want to do this?" he asked.

"No, I don't. But I want you to do it correctly."

"I do it the way I do it."

"Just do it correctly."

"I wasn't always a moving man, you know," Shaul said. "My brothers and me, we had a restaurant in Afula."

"Don't try to impress me," Candy answered. "I've seen Afula. Just install the cabinets and be very careful."

Shaul and his boss Lazard Goldberg exchanged a look of resignation. They began to expertly attach the cabinets to each other and then to the wall. When they were finished and heading back outside for the shelves, Candy tried to shake the cabinets. Then Marie tried to shake the cabinets.

"Maybe you want to bring Arnold Schwarzenegger in here to see if he can move it. . . " Shaul snapped.

Candy and Marie laughed — "Macho jerk!" they were thinking — and took the rugulach out of the oven.

Shaul and Lazard came back with the shelves. Installation took some time. Candy paced back and forth as they worked, watching every move. They could see her in the mirrors on the back walls of the cabinets. She wore spotless white sneakers and spotless white socks with the cuffs turned down and cozy sweats of heather blue. Her bouncy gait reminded Shaul of big black Americans leaving the basketball court at half time. Her braid bobbed in the center of her back. Her chubby buttocks quivered with every step.

"Is she checking my work or my ass?" Shaul asked his boss in Hebrew.

Lazard answered in Hebrew. "Don't flatter yourself. Her husband is a doctor. She's beautiful. She's a rich American. To her, you are a piece of shit. Let's just get the job done."

Candy drifted into the kitchen.

"What do they say?" asked Marie.

"All I understood was American and shit."

"Nobody likes to take shit from Americans," Marie interpreted. She gave Candy a taste of the new made apple pie. Candy lifted her eyes to Heaven.

Shaul and Lazard brought in the mirrored doors. They had begun to sweat because of the heaviness of the work. Without asking, Candy set down a tray of ice water and some rugulach. The older man took a drink and said thank you. Shaul drank a whole glass and ate three rugulach and drank another whole glass and said good. Then the two men began to affix tiny hinges of miraculous strength and install twenty-four doors on the front of the cabinets. Candy hovered at their backs, ready to protest the slightest nick or scratch.

"Stop!" Shaul protested. "You make us crazy looking like that!"

"Tough nuggies," she said.

"What?"

"I paid. I watch. You'll live."

Lazard now laughed, thinking that this was some cool customer, this Shapiro woman.

Scowling, feeling outnumbered by the Americans and betrayed by his boss, who was still one of *them,* even if he did speak Hebrew, Shaul turned back into the cabinet. He could see her in the mirror, conferring with her maid. Their laughter tickled the small of his back. It occurred to him suddenly that Mrs. Shapiro and her maid might be lovers. He dropped a hinge.

Candy had a well-trained suspicion of guys who looked like Shaul. She recognized the seasoned arms, the eyes still so young, innocent by contrast with the battered hands. This was the kind of guy who had followed her through the streets of Yaffo, offering to buy her a coffee, when she was a young girl. When she was young. Before everything. Before Sam and Alex and Daddy and Marty. Before everything. Before Sam.

"Too bad," she murmured.

"What did you say, lady?" asked the boss.

Candy blinked a spurt of tears from off her eyelashes and said "Nothing. Just a memory. Sad memory. Nothing."

Lazard shrugged and turned back to his work. Shaul stared after her as she walked into the kitchen, watched as she placed the remaining rugulach on a silver tray which she covered with an embroidered linen cloth. Her split second of weeping had made him tremble, a hot breath of feeling on a cold day.

When the cabinets were done, Marie called to her: "Madam Shapiro, *tout est fini!*"

Candy rushed back from the kitchen, her forearms now dusted with powdered sugar. Her face was flushed. A lock of hair had fallen out of her braid and dangled before Shaul, tantalizing. Where did it fit? She looked over the cabinets and smiled and said "Great! You did great, fellas."

Lazard gave Shaul the delivery receipt for Candy to sign. Somehow, Shaul forgot to do this. The next day, he called in sick and returned to the fancy house in Broadbeach. It was a Thursday. Marie's day off.

"My name is Shaul," he said. And seeing Candy's concern that she might mispronounce the strange name, he said it more clearly. "Sha-ool." She waited. "I. . . um. I forgot to get you to sign this ah. . . paper. . . " She worried her bottom lip with her teeth. "What does it mean, 'tough nuggies'?" She smiled but she did not answer. "I make a study of American slang. I want to become an expert." Still she said nothing. Still she made him stand there like a beggar. "I was really in bad shape yesterday," he continued. "Homesick. Cold. I never was cold like this in my life. But then I came in your house. And it smelled like Heaven. And I couldn't stop thinking about you."

So she let him in.

★ ★ ★

Shaul Beit-Halachmi and Candy Shapiro began their love affair with a minimum of talking, mostly because they had so little time. He came to her house only once a week, between 12:30 and 2:00, his lunch hour, usually on a Wednesday, which was the day Lazard took off. Like the previous foreign intruder into the Shapiro home, he parked his vehicle down the street in a glade of willows. His approach to the house was hidden from the prying eyes of neighbors by acres of landscaped grounds to the right and left. Marie let him in, grinning at him furtively like a witch. She made him remove his large, dirty shoes and his socks (to her mind, the stinkiest parts of a working man) and leave them in the front hall. He took the stairs two at a time.

At first, Candy dressed for Shaul as for a lunch date. Her hair was done, her silk blouse was pressed, she even wore stockings. He never undressed her. He kissed her and pulled down her pants and entered her and then he undressed her, a feat of self-containment in which he took great pride.

Soon enough, Shaul realized that Candy wasn't coming. So the following week, he loosely tied her hands to the headboard with a couple of Marty's neckties, thus preventing her from being able to touch him, and then he spent his entire lunch hour kissing and fondling her body, whispering in a hoarse voice the words of love songs that had awakened the desires of women for millennia. And the next week he did it again. And the next week on the brink of April (when Marty returned to Paris for an ovarian cancer detection conference), Candy greeted Shaul in her little blue lace, and rode him like a kid on a bicycle, her breasts flying, her eyes tearing, and he put his finger into her behind and experienced for himself the uncontrolled pulsing of her heart.

He was the very first man she had ever met who openly cared about her feelings. Was it good? he asked. Are you all right? Are you content?

No, she laughed. More. Again. More. *"Tikaness,"* she said in Hebrew. "Come inside. *Achshav.* Now oh now now. . . "

As spring bloomed, he began bringing her presents. He brought her perky potted plants with large flowers whose juice he squeezed into her belly button. Candy called this the "Naval Nectar Caper." He brought her small cakes topped with whipped cream that he smeared on her vagina and then sucked off with a mind-blowing lack of haste. He looked at her face as she moaned toward climax. *"Motek,"* he whispered. He had whipped cream on his nose. He was absolutely the cutest guy she had ever known in her entire life, and Candy gladly went down on him with a laugh and a tickle, something of which her husband would never have dreamed her capable.

Soon, the lunch hour wasn't enough. Candy gave Marie the afternoon off and the keys to the car and money for a movie and told her to be back at three in time for the kids' arrival home from school. Shaul put off the mid-day deliveries for early evening. They made love on the living room floor in front of the mirrored cabinets. She turned on the stereo and lip-synched the entire score of "Pajama Game" — apparently some sort of American classic light opera, Shaul told his brother Shimshon. When they got to "Hernando's Hideaway," even though she was naked except for the new high heels she had purchased on sale at Geller's, even though he was naked except for the gold *chai* hanging around his neck and the apron he had put on while making brownies, she taught him the tango. Why not? Maida had sent her for lessons. She knew the cha cha cha and the mambo and the meringue as well. Since no one ever danced these dances any more in her crowd, she was teaching them to Sergeant Beit-Halachmi, the terror of Lebanon: it shouldn't be a total loss.

Through bad planning one day in April, Candy's children found Shaul in the kitchen chatting with Marie and drinking Gatorade. Because of the truck down the block, they assumed he had delivered the new lamp which had actually been delivered by somebody else. Sam sat down with Shaul and drank a glass of Gatorade too. They spoke of baseball. Candy came in from the garden with daffodils. Marie served warm cookies. Shaul pulled a series of three nickels out of Sam's ear. Candy entitled this stunt "The Nicklear Proliferation Trick." Sam pleaded that Shaul should show him how to do it. The directions for doing that trick, said Shaul, are in Ethel's lunchbox. So they looked there and found three more nickels.

The kids called him "The Funny Israeli Moving Man." They told their father about him that night at dinner. They said he yelled *Yoffee Yoffee* which was sort of the Hebrew equivalent for *Bravo Bravo!* when Ethel did the soft shoe she had just learned in musical comedy class. They repeatedly asked their mother when he would deliver something else.

By the end of June, Shaul had begun to need Candy.

On the anniversary of the Leviathan bombing, he asked her to meet him at a bar in a Bronx neighborhood where women of her class were never seen. She drove there in her Volvo. She parked on the streets, walked alone in the dark, ignored the vile gestures of hoods who tried to frighten her, sat with Shaul while he sobbed: "I was saved by being sent outside to unload tomatoes! What does this mean?! Why me and not the Rabbi's little baby?! Does this have any meaning at all?!" She stroked his hair and kissed his face, thinking all the while: "Oh God, I am such a foolish woman! Who am I to rage against my husband for his peccadilloes when there are so many unfortunate, impoverished, drunk, addicted people in this neighborhood and my lover is haunted by such terrible memories?!"

* * *

When Shaul went to work as a schlepper for Lazard Goldberg, founder and president of The Lazard Cares Moving Company, he had no legal right to work in America. Dominick Fabrizi, Goldberg's chief competition, would have paid Shaul half the minimum wage like he paid the equally illegal Hondurans. But Goldberg could not shortchange a fellow Jew, a brave boy, he thought, veteran of the Lebanese War and the soul-destroying Intifada, who had taken the sins of battle on his own head so the rest of us could live on with a clear conscience, giving charity, feeling good about ourselves. Thus Goldberg — expecting not gratitude but. . . well. . . a little recognition — paid somewhat more than the minimum wage to Shaul.

"So I live like a poor American instead of like a poor Israeli," Shaul joked to his brother Shimshon on Candy's phone.

"Don't call on her phone," Shimshon cautioned. *"He'll* find out."

"He won't even notice," Shaul laughed. "He works like an ox, he's never home, and he shits money. If he notices a phone call to Israel, she can say it was Hadassah business."

"Who's Hadassah?" asked Shimshon.

The two brothers had owned a restaurant once, in Afula where they lived, with their third brother, Yosef. They called their place "The Bread House," after the family name. They wrote it in English because that was so chic, but they didn't know how to write English so they wrote "The Bredd Howse," attracting much more attention to themselves than they would have if they had spelled it correctly.

Centrally located and very cheap, "The Bredd Howse" catered to farmers from the kibbutzim and moshavim that greened the fields of Galilee as well as Army kids hitching their way through the large station town. Nothing fancy. Mixed grill and chips and salad and felafel. Fifteen little tables that seated four-to-six people each. But it took all the money which the three brothers had saved from working, and all the money Shimshon's wife Yaffa and Yosef's wife Zahava had brought in marriage, plus the hands-on labor of every single one of them to own and operate this little place.

As the oldest brother, Shaul insisted that his years of experience under the tutelage of BenZion Shachar had qualified him to be the boss of the enterprise. His brothers and their wives agreed. He promised to make such a fortune for the family that they would be able to build separate houses and own yachts.

Trying to remember how BenZion had done it, he appointed Yosef the cook and Shimshon the bus boy, and made waitresses of Yaffa and Zahava. Himself, he handled the money and controlled all managerial decisions. Somehow, things did not go smoothly. Yosef was a wasteful cook. Yaffa and Zahava hated waiting on tables. If a customer ordered without proper deference and respect, the lovely Zahava would ignore him and the feisty Yaffa would tell him to go drown. When the blonde Scandinavians and blonder Dutch girls stopped by on their travels, Shaul generally tried to charm them and take them home, ignoring the cash register, creating economic chaos.

They worked haphazardly and fought constantly. Shaul fired at least one of them at least once a week. Customers seeking a laugh were known to come in just to hear the Beit-Halachmi clan brawling in the kitchen.

In the sixth month of its existence, the well-situated little restaurant began to show a profit. With a great flourish, Shaul divided this small sum equally between the three brothers. Yosef and Shimshon demanded a larger share on the grounds that their wives were also working in the restaurant. Shaul declared that he was acting in a prince-like manner for not himself demanding the largest share since he was the founder and boss.

The dispute soon grew so bitter that it had to be adjudicated by a rabbi. He demanded a large fee which he then split with a fundamentalist political party. This made Shaul furious. He might defer to the *rabonim* on matters of ethics. But he firmly believed that if you let them into the government, they would outlaw war on Shabbat and depend on God to defend Israel, and the Syrians would soon be pissing on the Temple Mount. So he got his family's money back by storming into the rabbi's study and threatening to break his neck.

Hearing of this incident in the bus station, the progressive kibbutzniks said to themselves: "Good for Beit-Halachmi." And they began patronizing "The Bredd Howse" with greater fervor, making the cash register sing. Shaul and his brothers went back to work, their differences forgotten.

And then Yosef was killed during a routine patrol near Jenin, and it made no difference that his unit chased the killers into their own graves within minutes, because he was gone. Beautiful Zahava was a widow, sitting in the darkened apartment, spitting on patriotic consolations. "The Bredd Howse" declined into bankruptcy, the savings of the brothers, the dowries of the wives all lost to an existential paralysis. For what was the point of going on now? What was the point of breaking your back, planning for tomorrow, imagining houses and yachts?

Shaul sold all his possessions and gave the money to his mother and Zahava and went to America to work to repay the members of his family for their fruitless investment. He had hoped to find Abe Heimlich, his old counselor, who had once written him a postcard giving a California address and offering a welcome. However, the people at that address said Heimlich was sick, like Menachem Begin, sick with a death-rattle melancholia brought on by the collapse of dreams. And since Shaul had no green card, minimal education and very little English, the only one who would hire him at something more than the minimum wage was big, strong, sloppy Lazard Goldberg of The Lazard Cares Moving Company.

★ ★ ★

Initially, Shaul had expected to live with his friend Udi in the Bronx. Udi worked as a cab driver and itinerant clarinetist while studying music in Manhattan. It turned out that his life was not worth sharing. The Bronx apartment was tiny. The food was tuna. You couldn't go anyplace without taking the subway. And Shaul, who had chased shadows through hate-filled towns with mines beneath his feet and the sons of Ishmael shooting at his head, Shaul was terrified of the subway.

Udi laughed at him. He pointed to schoolchildren and old ladies and young women unescorted, all blithely entering the black pit full of sparks and roaring. Shaul thought they were crazy. He sweated and hyperventilated in the subway, hugging his brawny arms to hide their trembling.

One night Udi succeeded in bringing one of his fares home with him. She seemed like a nice Jewish girl actually. She had that smart, secure American air, those pretty shoes and immaculate hands which Lazard Goldberg called JAP-PY and which Shaul and Udi found irresistible. What was so terrible about a woman who knew where her next meal was coming from, who read the newspaper, dressed well and never did her own hair?

"They break your balls," explained Lazard, who had already been divorced by one. "They want everything. Then they want more of everything. More car more house more university. Nothing you do is ever good enough for them. That's why so many of them are frigid! They can never be satisfied not at the bank not in the bed no way no how. Do yourself a favor, boychik. Take a poor girl from a religious family or an academic with no religion at all, but don't take a JAP!"

The young woman whom Udi had brought home smiled nervously. In her slightly whiny voice, she said she was from Woodmere and lived in Manhattan and worked for a fashion magazine. When they offered her a drink, she asked for Tab with rum but gladly accepted Chianti. She glanced repeatedly in their small mirror, concerned that she might not look all right, and when she sat down, she crossed her legs tightly. Shaul and Udi could tell that she was an innocent girl, not accustomed to going home with cab drivers, even Israeli cab drivers who said they were musicians, and that she was scared that she had been lured to the Bronx with a line of bullshit: she was scared to death.

Wisely, Udi broke out his clarinet and played. The jolly klezmer beat relaxed her. She laughed. So he *was* a musician! Then Udi played her a J.S. Bach number, to show her that he was a serious musician. By the time Shaul left them, the delightful girl from Woodmere was sipping her second glass of wine, and she had uncrossed her legs.

Shaul went to sleep in the bus station. A man tried to slip his wallet out of his pocket. Shaul woke up and broke his nose. He told this story at work the next day, convinced that he had to find another place to live. But where could he afford to live in this hellish city?

"I got it!" Lazard yelled, slamming down his fist on his incredibly sloppy desk. "I got the greatest idea! Boychik, I am saving your ass right this minute! Wait'll you see where I'm gonna get for you to live!"

Lazard called a woman he was dating. Her name was Barbara. She taught English in the public schools. She owned a home in a Queens suburb which had been so completely taken over by drug dealers that it had lost its original name and was now called Mednorth. Short for Medallin, North America. Barbara could no longer live in her spacious, pleasant house for it had been robbed twice. Twice more, she herself had been mugged while walking home from work. During the last mugging, the assailants had thrown her down on the pavement and kicked her in the face.

"Fucking kike bitch," they had said.

Now at the age of 43, Barbara was back living with her old parents in Brooklyn. She was seeking a buyer for her house. Until one could be found, she would settle for a tenant.

And wouldn't she rent cheap to a tough kid? Lazard smarmed on the telephone as Shaul watched. A brave boy. Two wars. Left hook like a sledgehammer. "Do yourself a favor, Bubbeleh," said Lazard Goldberg. "Take Beit-Halachmi as a tenant and the crackheads won't dare come near your beautiful house."

Barbara said yes yes yes.

Shaul spat on Lazard's dirty office floor.

"I can die in Israel!" he yelled. "I came here to get a rest from dying. Take your lousy crack house and shove it up your ass."

"Hey hey don't get so excited," Goldberg laughed. "Am I insisting? I was trying to help."

"Bastard."

"I'm sorry."

"Scumbag."

"Okay okay, lighten up, Shaul, come on, come on, you don't want to go live in Mednorth, fine, we'll find you a room by me in Bensonhurst. You don't like Italians, fine, we'll find you a room with a family in Ocean Parkway. You don't like black hats, fine, we'll. . . "

"Shit neighborhoods," Shaul said.

"Where do you think the Jews live, my boy? We can't all be doctor's wives with two wooded acres on the Sound in Broadbeach."

That was a shock. Shaul had not realized that Lazard knew about his visits to Candy.

"What do you think is the reason for a man to leave his country and his people and live in America?" Shaul asked."So he can ride in the subway and get a preview of hell? The whole purpose of America is to make money. You ask the Haitians and the Koreans and the little Hondurans who are breaking their backs for Dominick Fabrizi. They all think the only reason to be in America is to make money."

"It takes time to do that, Shaul," Lazard said patiently.

"I have no time. My brother was dead at 30, I have no time. You sell me fifty-one per cent of your business. I'll bring my other brother over here. We'll double the numbers of your clientele in six months."

Lazard nodded with mock respect.

"I see you got big plans," he said.

"Don't laugh at me, *mamzer.* I'm taking over your company."

Lazard slapped his desk and roared.

"Oi, please please, cut me a little slack here! What ever happened to 'Clal Yisrael?' 'Never again?' 'I gave at the office!' 'We are One?'"

Lazard was making himself giggle uncontrollably with these obscure American references.

"I'll give you $5,000 down and you can take the rest out of my salary and my brother's salary," Shaul said. "In two years we'll pay you off, and you'll still own 49% of the business and you'll be a much richer man because your 49% will be worth five times as much as your 100% is worth today."

Lazard raised a callused hand. "Okay okay, don't get a hard-on, Trumpface, I'm not selling you nothing. Stop with the schvitzing and the crap. You want a raise? Fine. You want me to give your brother a job? Fine. Bring him over. If he works out, I'll give him a raise too."

"I want to earn $60,000 a year base pay and ten per cent commission on any new account I take from Dominick Fabrizi," said Shaul.

"What are you talking about?! Please please. I built this business from nothing. I make a payroll here. Five families depend on me to keep them in their jobs. I worked in this business every day for twenty years and I don't make 60 grand." Lazard leaned forward. No anger. No recrimination. Honest advice. "And do yourself a favor, boychik, don't ever forget what I am saying to you right this minute. Nobody takes an account from Dominick Fabrizi. Nobody."

Shaul whistled with condescension.

"You're such a schmuck, Goldberg," he said. "You're scared of the Italians. You're scared of the blacks. That's why you're not rich. You could be rich in this business, but you're a schmuck and you're stupid."

Lazard finally stopped suspending his disbelief.

"Go down to the bookkeeper's office and pick up your check," he said.

"It'll cost you to fire me, Lazard. I'll sue you for severance."

"How much do you think you're entitled to?"

"I'll sue you for six months' pay, watch me. Even if I lose, it'll cost you plenty to defend yourself against me, it'll take time and time is money. Anybody'll tell you, you're better off settling out of court."

"Oi vay! He's been watching 'L.A. Law!' I am trembling with fear!!"

"Don't laugh at me, Goldberg."

"Then don't say funny things."

Shaul said: "Okay. So I'll move into the Mednorth house. But she'll have to pay me as the caretaker."

Lazard shook Shaul's hand.

"So long, my boy. Good luck to you."

"Okay, so I'll pay her a hundred a month including utilities," said Shaul.

"She wants eight hundred a month, plus utilities."

"You fucking son-of-a-bitch capitalist exploiter," Shaul said, because he had been told long ago by Abe Heimlich that American Jewish liberals hated to be called those things.

Lazard Goldberg, however, was not a liberal.

"Okay," Shaul agreed. "Three hundred a month including utilities."

"Who taught you how to make a deal, boychik?" Lazard asked as he dialed Barbara's number. "Abu Nidal?"

* * *

In Barbara's house in Mednorth, Shaul found four bedrooms, two full bathrooms, a living room with a fireplace, an eat-in kitchen, a finished basement with laundry machines and a back yard big enough to play a small soccer game in. All within walking distance of the subway. He immediately rented the three smaller bedrooms to Gad, Reuven and Efi who were all working their way through college. Udi gladly gave up the Bronx to sleep on a fold-out sofa in the living room. It helped the lonely young men to live together in a house where Hebrew could be spoken and friends were always present.

No one had a car so no one used the garage, a large, disattached structure covered with ivy and filled with gardening tools and summer furniture that was so old, it wasn't even plastic.

Since the Israelis said hello pleasantly on their way to work and school and were never seen staggering or glassy-eyed, the children were permitted to ride their tricycles past Barbara's house. Udi would play his clarinet for them. Gad showed them his artificial leg. Reuven, who had a way with machines, got the ancient air conditioners to work, so the house was now cool in the summertime, tempting people to visit. Soon the neighborhood girls began to take that route to the subway and smile and talk and maybe stop by for a coke and a kicking lesson in the back yard. Efi gave a party. Some white girls came. Some black girls came. There was no trouble.

Their across-the-street neighbor, a voluptuous lady named Rita, asked Shaul and his housemates to help her move an old refrigerator into her basement. She had been wanting to accomplish this for five years. It took the Israelis maybe five minutes. It broke the ice. From then on, Rita always made extra soup for them. She told her friends at church they were nice boys. The neighborhood grew friendlier.

One morning in the summertime, Shaul invited Candy to see his new house and to give him some advice about starting a garden. Rita was watching from her window, absorbing every detail of Candy's appearance, impressed with her nice car.

In order to access the gardening tools, Shaul attempted to open the garage door — but it wouldn't move. Candy laid down her pretty purse and tried to help him. *Achat, shtayim, shalosh!* they counted, putting their shoulders to the task. The old rickety door had the dead weight of solid steel.

Shaul pushed Candy behind him and backed away. He stared at the garage with awakening fear, as though it were an old enemy recognized in a new setting. Something about the reinforced quality of that door. . . some steel feeling behind the moist boards. . . He called for help. Rather, he barked an order. Gad and Reuven, who happened to be home at that time, recognized his tone and came running.

Candy was sent across the street to sit on the curb near Rita's front door, like a little girl. She pouted. She was just about up to here with sitting on the sidelines — but how could Shaul have known that?

While he picked the lock, Gad and Reuven guarded his back, facing not the garage but the street. It took a few minutes. The lock finally gave. Shaul opened the door slowly, releasing a dry wind from the interior, a dry, hot wind and a billow of oily dust.

The gardening gear and the lawn furniture had disappeared. The garage was packed floor to ceiling with crates. Several of them had been opened, and in them lay weapons, gleaming. M-16s. Remington 780s and 870s, 44 Magnums, like little brothers in their plastic diapers. Electronic sighting devices, launchers, projectiles. Shaul squeezed down the narrow aisles between the crates, and for a moment, he forgot who he was now and remembered who he would always be and re-experienced an old moment of elation. We found them! We found the fucking guns! Enough for twenty wars! Let's load them up and take them home and march them through the streets for all the people to see! He remembered the cheering crowds in the streets of the northern towns, the feel of an old man's hug. These are the guns that would have killed us, the old man said. These are the rocket launchers that kept us pinned in our shelters, caused us to abandon our homes. And you, our hero sons, you have found them and brought them back to us as prisoners. *Yoffee. Yoffee.*

It was the only glorious moment he had ever enjoyed as a soldier, and he had been soldier half his life. And now, it was ruined forever, because the guns had come back. They were in Barbara's garage. Like metal straps around a wine barrel, they girded the world, and though the world disintegrated in their embrace, they lasted.

He closed the garage door, and refitted the lock.

Within an hour, all the inhabitants of Barbara's house had been informed that they were back in a war zone and must evacuate. Within three hours, they and all their possessions were gone.

* * *

Candy gave him the money he needed to move into a new place in Brooklyn. Just gave it, knowing how much he would need, sparing him the embarrassment of asking. A real mensch, his Candy, he told his brother Shimshon, who was preparing to come to America.

"Now what?" she asked.

"What now what?"

"The guns."

"What about the guns?"

"What are you going to do about the guns?"

"What can I do?"

"You have to do something!" she insisted.

"Ah forget it," he said, pulling her back down into the bathtub where they were both soaking. "They don't bother us, we don't bother them."

"When it was your country, they bothered you!" she yelled, twisting away from him. "That was an arsenal in that garage! That was to kill people! What if the weapons are sold to gangs and the gangs have a war in the streets and the children in the streets are killed in the crossfire?! Think of the little kids on their bikes riding by! Think of your neighbor the soup lady!"

"Candy. . . *motek*. . . please. A treasure of weapons. A dangerous business."

"A crime! An unacknowledged crime!"

Shaul squinted at her. In the six months they had known each other, he had never seen her angry.

"Come on, take it easy, chill out, it's not your neighborhood."

"It's my country, you unfeeling creep!" Candy surged from the tub and wriggled into her clothes. They stuck to her wet body. "It's my city! My people! My city! And this is my house, and you are going to leave it right this minute!"

She raced out of the bathroom as he roared with laughter. *Her* people! Those *mamzerim* who had attacked Barbara and used her garage for an ammunitions dump! Candy stormed back into the bathroom and threw his clothes at him. Because he could not see an alternative, Shaul got dressed and went downstairs. She was on the phone.

"It's a garage. At the corner of Vine and Mercer in Mednorth," she was saying to someone. "Packed to the ceiling with military hardware. I know because I know. I heard however I heard; what do you care how I heard?!"

Shaul grabbed at the phone.

"Hey! Stop it!" he yelled. "You want to get us all killed?!"

Candy hit him in the face with the receiver. He backed off, surprised.

"Do it now, Carol. Bring the whole press corps with you. Just make sure you take all the credit. Don't forget yourself and say on television that it was me who tipped you off." She laughed. "Oh, I would so love to win for a change," she whispered. "I am so dying to beat the bad guys just once, just once!"

She hung up.

"Candy. You don't understand. These are serious businessmen, these gun runners. They will not forget such an attack. They will take vengeance. Candy. . . "

He reached for her. When he touched her, he found that her anger was gone, replaced by a vacant coldness.

* * *

At first Carol O'Banyon couldn't quite believe that Candy Shapiro the Suburban Superwoman was giving her a tip on a gun stash in Mednorth.

*But how do you know?*

*I know because I know.*

*But how did you hear?*

*I heard however I heard; what do you care how I heard?!*

Carol's heart pounded. This could be exactly what she had been waiting for, all her life on the sidelines in politics. A major event. A launching pad. What the murder of Kennedy had been to Dan Rather. What the assassination of Harvey

Milk had been to Diane Feinstein. A way to become the center of attention in an hour of need.

The first thing she did was to call a certain public relations man with whom she had once been intimate. Then she paid a sudden visit on the new Chief of Detectives with whom she had more recently become intimate. He authorized surveillance on Barbara's house. Immediately, the cops took up their positions in the nooks and alleys of Mednorth, waiting. With a few calls from public phones, Shaul warned his neighbors that there might be trouble. The streets emptied. The young girls kept down and inside. Rita camped out in her basement. No tricycle toodled past Vine and Mercer. Amazingly, not one person in the neighborhood seemed to be in cahoots with the gun-runners. No one told the gang. When the guys showed up for their stash, they were arrested and three million dollars' worth of weapons was confiscated by the grinning Queens police.

The public relations man went into action. Carol O'Banyon became a heroine. She posed for the cameras in front of cases of weapons and explosives. The Chief of Police shook her hand repeatedly. The frazzled people of New York, who had come to believe they were living at the sufferance of brigand kings, celebrated her like a birthday and embraced her in the streets.

She went to the opera with a charming broker. (It was reported they might marry.) In a moment of unprecedented public gratitude, the audience gave her a standing ovation, and so did the orchestra!

Everybody thought that Carol's hair looked great. Nobody could believe she was 55 years old. Everybody said she was now a shoo-in for the Congressional nomination.

"I know you can't name names, Mrs. O'Banyon," said the news anchor. "But tell us, what sort of person calls a political figure like yourself and gives out this sort of information?"

"A patriot," Carol answered.

CHAPTER TEN

# FRENCH MEDICINE

SINCE THEIR FIRST MEETING IN LOS ANGELES, the debonair cosmetic surgeon Danton Moore had managed to inject a certain amount of fun into Marty's life, and nobody had ever been able to do that before.

You are a big doctor, my friend, Danton would say. With an excellent reputation. Perhaps you do not yourself understand what obligations that places upon you. You must invest in real estate. Refuse even to consider the less interesting cases. Say goodbye to the 14-hour work day. Spend some time with a woman who is at least half as challenging as your practice. Come with me to dinner in Provence. We shall go there by barge. *Allons!*

A man so personally handsome that many people took him for an actor, Danton Moore was tall but rumpled and rather round shouldered. He smelled of limes. His thick hair (which he unabashedly highlighted with ash and gold) flopped over one eye, raising the possibility that he might be kidding. His lower lip drooped sensuously. His upper lip sported a mole (or was it herpes?) He had the smile of a Caravaggio. Sleepy. Wicked. Delicious. His worst enemies were gay men who had been misled.

Danton had been raised in England and France with more style than money. He lived with his wife Adrine in a floor-through apartment in the 18th *arrondissement.* Luckily for Danton, Adrine had inherited her Armenian family's real estate fortune. She managed the Paris branch. She loved beautiful things. So Danton bought them all the time. He bought rugs from the Orient, piling them on his floors and tables like a desert sheikh. "Not to go shoeless in my home is to miss out on *pied paradis!"* he announced to Marty at the front door. He bought one-of-a-kind goblets from glass blowers and instead of placing them in a sunny window where the light could play, he filled them with wine and drank.

After the conference on fertility in Nice, Danton took Marty and two other big doctors from America out to dinner with four of the best looking swimsuit models on the Riviera. They told jokes, drank beer, tossed their beepers against the stone hearth R.A.F.-ishly. At Danton's insistence, they flew off to Dublin where they bought yards and yards of a certain special snow white linen. Then they flew off to Como to a certain special super terrific tailor who made them suits which were ready by the time the Gynecological Institute convened its annual conference in Boston. At the penultimate session, where they were all featured speakers, they appeared in their white linen suits to lecture on breakthroughs in dealing with ectopic pregnancy, looking, noted the HERS column in *The New York Times,* like a quartet of Latin American dictators.

Danton always did exactly what he wanted. Adrine certainly didn't try to stop him. His work was no impediment either, as it often was to Marty. Since Danton's patients were all *electing* surgery, they never beset him with emergencies. His patients were never sick. They made their surgical schedule at Danton's and their own convenience. He charged them a fortune. And they paid in full — no third party reimbursements for a nose job or a tummy tuck. Most wonderful of all, they loved Danton forever because he had made them pretty, which was a lot more thoroughly appreciated (Marty observed this ruefully) than making them well.

When Danton introduced Marty to Odile Ste. Jacques, he put his arm lightly around her shoulders and told Marty she was a brilliant scholar but *helas!* the mistress of a powerful German industrialist who, *heureusement!* came to Paris not so very often now because he had been shot in the knee by a vengeful stepson masquerading as a political assassin.

"Everybody loves Dr. Moore," Odile told Marty. "At Scaasi and Patrick Kelly, the beautiful young models call him 'Monsieur Printemps' for he brings only joy."

To the interested onlooker (there were many in the small world of world-class medicine), Moore and Shapiro seemed to be ideal partners. The dazzling Frenchman and the workaholic American, they were a great combination, *helas!* separated by an ocean but, *heureusement!* less frequently these days since Mademoiselle Ste. Jacques had entered the picture.

However, the exchange between Danton and Marty was much more technical and complex than that. They needed each other. They saved each other.

As a consultant on a breast augmentation, Marty had prevented Danton from blithely inserting an implant into tissue that would soon be invaded by malignancy. It was one of those mistakes which — if Danton had made it — could have cost him his practice. On another occasion, Marty had insisted that a woman who wanted the excess flesh of her stomach removed first be checked for the liver disease he suspected. As usual, he suspected right. In eighteen months, the poor woman was so thin from being sick that she couldn't even recall what excess flesh was like.

Danton's great gift was that he could talk to people. He had a way of explaining things which made patients calm, even forgiving. For this reason, Marty asked his help in explaining to a very distraught husband what Candy would entitle "The Infamous Midwinter Semen Screw-up at Blessed Mother."

Not glibly, yet not completely overlooking the intrinsic humor of the situation, Danton explained that the brilliant Dr. Shapiro had succeeded in implanting a fertilized egg in Madame's womb. Congratulations, Monsieur! You are going to be father at last! However, there is one thing you ought to know. Because of a mix-up in the lab at Blessed Mother, your child will be half-Chinese.

Of course, this was not anything that Dr. Shapiro could have known or prevented. It was a laboratory malfunction, pure and simple. The imbeciles at Blessed Mother were now hiding from Dr. Shapiro, who has been so incapacitated with rage that he could not even be here with us today, Danton explained, to make this explanation. If the (speechless) husband wished, Dr. Shapiro would be happy to abort the pregnancy at no cost and attempt another insemination as soon as the womb was receptive once again. On the other hand, after ten tries, maybe it would be better to keep the kid. Especially since the real father was rumored to be (but of course one could not prove this, it was just a rumor) a real rocket scientist.

The husband talked to his minister and his shrink and his wife and decided to accept the child, allowing the terrified administrators at Blessed Mother to continue as they were, without lawsuits or adverse publicity.

Marty was grateful to Danton and enormously impressed with his communication skills. "I just couldn't have done that," he said humbly.

"And I could not have produced life in that womb with anybody's semen," remarked Danton to Odile Ste. Jacques. "What a cruel joke, that God has blessed these damn Hebrews with such extraordinary healing powers, so that nobody ever really dares to wipe them out completely."

★ ★ ★

There was this one problem. Danton hated Jews. Every time he allowed Marty to cross his threshold, two thousand years of Church dogma told him that he had just unleashed a plague of rats upon France. He had to summon every ounce of strength to repress these feelings. Sometimes he broke into a sweat from the effort. Even on the coldest days, he could be seen mopping his face at the moment Marty Shapiro walked through the door in Paris and said "Hiya!"

Marty was not fooled for a minute. "Danton's a high class bigot from the Old Order," he told his lawyer Phil Brinks. "And the rest of them are no better — a despicable lot of cowardly fops who gave up their country in a few weeks to the Nazis in order to save their museums. Which are filled mostly with decorative art, let us not forget that. Their whole over-praised culture is about grammar and manners and fashion and the fancification of surfaces, just like Danton Moore's practice. And let us not forget that when it suited the Frogs, they turned in their Jews like empty soda cans."

Phil was overwhelmed. "So why are you dealing with them?" he asked.

"Because I have enormous respect for French medicine," Marty answered.

When he returned to France to attend the hysterectomy conference (it was his third trip in one year), he was feeling pretty good. His wife Candy, for all her fatuous dingbattedness and vulgar materialism, was doing a nice job with the kids. And he finally had a brilliant mistress who waited for him like Larissa for Zhivago at her calm, ivory-colored apartment.

Odile looked great. A slender blonde, she wore only pastels. With her Ph.D. in Epidemiology, she had become one of the leading French medical statisticians, quantifier of death certificates, spotter of exceptions to the prevailing trend, tracking the AIDS virus with her fine, thin nose and her sharp eyes behind wire-rimmed glasses.

The sheer simplicity of Odile's flat calmed Marty's spirit. The walls were bare except for one astounding red-on-red graphic and a large picture window facing the pigeon-crowded roof across the street. The kitchen never seemed overrun with dishes and mixing bowls and half-chopped onions and apple peelings in baskets and lunches in plastic like Candy's kitchen. Odile's white dishes were always neatly tucked away. Her copper pots gleamed. No mess of magazines cluttered her bed. No mint-filled chatchkies from Mafia wives distracted the eye in her living room. How much easier it was to cope with the addling complexities of a medical career when you could return at the end of a day to this spotless haven with blonde furniture and one scarlet tulip in an unfaceted vase!

Marty really liked Odile Ste. Jacques. Just as Danton had predicted, he enjoyed being with a smart woman. But he never quite spent the entire night in her embrace. Though he felt drunk with weariness, some still living fear of closing his eyes among these people always compelled him to drag himself back to his hotel to sleep alone.

★ ★ ★

At the hysterectomy conference, Danton suggested that cosmetic removal of the scar should be performed immediately after the surgery, actually as *part* of the surgery. He even suggested a way to make this cost-effective.

"Why should a woman who has to lose her womb also have to endure the disfigurement of her belly?" he asked with touching concern. "It's not fair, don't you see, my friends? Women value their beauty. So must we who dare to cut into their flesh."

Marty met Danton later at his office. What an office! It faced a park that flowered with lovers and painters. And it was *pink,* with pink marble floors and baroque side chairs and continuously playing New Age music. Fashion magazines and flowers decorated the end tables. Rose-tinted mirrors decorated the walls. Danton came out to greet him wearing his white coat and his wonderful smile. With a navy linen handkerchief, he mopped his wet forehead.

"*Ah bon,* it is my dear friend Dr. Shapiro from New York! How honored I am to have you once again here in my city!"

"Hiya."

"Where do you get your ties, my friend? They are. . . *comment devrais-je dire. . . ?*"

"Where do you get your ideas? If I worried about the ugliness of scars while I was operating, gee Danton, half of my patients would bleed to death."

"You see, ladies," Danton said to the two lovely young patients in his waiting room, "Dr. Shapiro here has no time for delicate questions of aesthetics. His patients are suffering! They develop complications! He snatches them daily from the jaws of death itself!"

One of the women crossed herself. The other smiled seductively.

"May I use the phone?" Marty asked. "I've got a woman on the guarded list back in New York."

They met Adrine for lunch. Taller than Danton, she had a big nose and strong, thick, black eyebrows. She wore designer suits, and important jewelry. By comparison, Marty thought to himself, Candy would look like a Cabbage Patch doll with mascara. You had to hand it to these people. They had style.

It seemed to him that everyone in Paris stopped at their table. At each visit, Danton introduced Marty like he was the risen Dr. Schweitzer. When the coffee came, Danton pulled his chair very close to Marty's and got serious.

"I have a proposal to make to you," he said. "I am building a clinic on the beautiful Caribbean island of St.

Maarten. I want you to invest a million dollars and serve as chief medical consultant to the staff."

"But what about Paris? You have one of the largest practices in the city!"

"I do not enjoy operating here," Danton explained. "I find myself frightened when I operate — not of the surgery; that I do better and better all the time — but of the recovery. As I grow older, I feel the pain of recovery much more keenly, I dislike the bleeding and the tears. In beautiful surroundings, by the immaculate sea, it will be easier, for my patients and for me."

"This project is already begun," Adrine interjected. "We own the land; we have the plans. The tax incentives for investment in St. Maarten are excellent. . . "

"And I shall have no trouble raising the rest of the money if you are my partner," Danton said. "Not only do I want your financial participation, I also want to be able to say that all incoming patients will be examined by you, so that we may have the benefit of your notoriously conservative views on whether or not they are good candidates for the surgery they desire. Thus, our investors and clientele will be satisfied that they are in the very best hands. And we shall flourish. So. What do you say?"

Marty cracked his knuckles. He ate ten or twelve consecutive mouthfuls of his excellent lunch.

"I say: if you want a triple bypass, go into the clinic business. You will spend your life collecting bills and chasing down addicted nurses. The insurance liability alone is out of sight. And if God forbid something goes wrong, no amount of damages paid will save your reputation."

Danton laughed. "You are my insurance policy, Martin."

"That's very flattering. But it's bullshit, if I may be so bold."

Danton would not be deterred.

*"Écoute, mon cher ami,"* he said. "You and I cannot possibly go on working as hard as we do. We have to be able to charge

much more for the operations we perform. . . so that we can afford to perform them less often. This clinic is a way to achieve that goal. We charge for the scenery. The mimosa, the ocean, the birds of paradise, the luxury service. We charge for the recovery, my friend, and that makes the surgery worthwhile."

Marty imagined six or eight weeks in the Caribbean every winter, not cutting, just consulting. Just consulting! He imagined a small, luxurious house with a deep pool and a hot tub in the corner of the pool and Odile Ste. Jacques in the hot tub and time to read thoughtful prose and listen to Mahler, and Candy back in Broadbeach, growing into a charitable and gracious middle aged woman, going to the theater with her witty partners, attending to her garden and his terrific kids.

"Before I make any decisions, I guess I'd better take a look at the place. . . " he said, making Danton smile.

* * *

Kevin McCabe sent a note to Candy at her office.

"Odile Ste. Jacques," it said. "Epidemiologist. Thirty-three. Never married. Never pregnant. Supports her old mother."

Really, she should have expected nothing different. She should not have been surprised, and really she wasn't surprised. Except that she couldn't get out of bed.

* * *

Shaul called. I miss you, he said. I'm sorry we fought. I want you so much. Forget my fears and my caution. You and I are not about caution.

*Not now, not now, I have to think, I can't think when you're in my life. Go away.*

Concentrate on frivolities, Roxie said. Shaul wants you. He says you're beautiful. Does he have to say it? Maybe he says it because he means it. Think of that. You don't like him any more? No sweat. There's more where he came from. You're a desirable woman. Now get out of bed.

*I hate that I still want Marty. Is it possible to want a man just because he's a terrific surgeon and your mother told you to want one of those? I never judged him as a lover. He was my husband, that was enough. But now that I've been with Shaul, now I think he's cold and white and unpleasant to smell. And I still want him! How is that possible?! What am I, some kind of pervert? Do I really just get off on power like in the Alisette Legrand song? Oh my God. I have to think. I can't think.*

Ethel has the lead in the seventh grade show, Roxie said. She's playing Joseph, no less. She needs a costume, a many-colored coat. Concentrate on Ethel's costume.

*I'd better get a divorce.*

Stop stop! You're not thinking clearly! I got divorced and all it did was make him rich and me poor. Besides, now I'm lonely. Don't get divorced. Get revenge. Call Shaul. Take him up to the Concord. Suck his tongue on the dance floor. If somebody tells Marty, you've scored. If nobody tells Marty, you've scored.

*Shaul only wants me to help him be successful here so he can go back to Israel like a sheikh and raise his family out of poverty.*

So what?! You've got money; why not help a poor immigrant boy? He's a great fuck, right? Therapy. Laughs. Little Sam adores him. What was it? Nicklear Proliferation. . . .

*My back hurts. I can't get out of bed.*

Candy. . .

*Leave me alone.*

No, said her very good friend Roxie.

⋆ ⋆ ⋆

Mommy's sick this morning, said Marie, sending the children into Candy's bedroom to kiss her goodbye before they went off to school. Sam felt her head and took her pulse and recommended a diet of ice cream and cake. Ethel got right into bed next to her, holding her tight with strong, thin arms until the honking of the carpool wrenched her away.

★ ★ ★

Where is she? Jock Silver asked Marie.

We need her here! Slim Price insisted. How can we make a decision about the show in New Haven without her? What do you mean, she's sick? Sick with a fever? What hurts her? What do you mean, her back? Where in her back? In her shoulders? In her lungs?

Please God, Jock whispered.

What do you mean she's weak? Slim asked. How weak? How long has her back been hurting? Is she coughing? What else hurts her?

She has a pain in her heart, Marie answered.

Candy's partners breathed relief. For a moment, they had shared a terrifying thought. After all, she was sleeping with some guy nobody really knew anything about. And she was married to a surgeon.

They hired an actor who showed up at Candy's door in a Jackie Mason mask and sat on her bed and told Jewish jokes.

★ ★ ★

People need you! Roxie hollered. Think about the Russian immigrants, how much they have left behind, how much they endured: poverty, silence, midnight visits from the KGB! Shit, Candy, get real! Compare your problems to somebody else's! Hear somebody else's screams, for God's sake! The Russians have nothing zippo nada nada nada! They need dishes glasses mops pots chairs jobs Shabbat dinners! Invite them to dinner on Friday night! You have children! Partners! Friends! People who depend on you! Get your ass out of the fucking bed!

★ ★ ★

Marie brought her a cup of tea. It tasted bitter but she drank it down.

"Roxie called and yelled at me and we have to make a decision about the New Haven show. So I'm going to work," Candy said. "We'll have company for dinner Friday night. Russians Jews. They speak no English. The wife is a physicist. The husband is a physicist. She's babysitting. He's working in a warehouse. Let's make them some good chicken soup, from a chicken."

"*Bien.* No problem."

"What's in this tea?!"

"Slivovitz."

Candy laughed and kissed her.

"This is what I worry about," she said. "This newest woman in Paris, what if she gets pregnant? I mean, thirty-three years old; a trained professional; successful. Maybe she's feeling desperate, thinking she'll never marry, never have a family of her own. Maybe her old mother is putting pressure on her. Imagine. *'Odile, ma cherie, je te supplie, donne-moi un petit avant que je meurs. . .'* Odile may become pregnant, just to be a good daughter, just to be a mother. And then the kids will eventually have to contend with another little Shapiro."

Marie considered the situation for a moment. She knew that Candy had good reason to be afraid, that some evils were unstoppable by ordinary means.

"Can you get me a photograph of the Frenchwoman?" she asked.

★ ★ ★

Odile wanted to come along to St. Maarten, feeling that she would have something to contribute about the set-up of the clinic laboratories. Marty said no. He had the feeling that Adrine Moore might be more comfortable with Candy, with The Wife, and immediately Odile realized that he was right. He loved that about her, that she didn't argue.

Excitedly, he called home to ask Candy to pack her bags and join him for a few days, thinking how happy that would make her, confident that Adrine would love her just as Charlotte Glick and the increasingly famous Carol O'Banyon had loved her.

She reacted ecstatically. "Oh thank you for inviting me, honey!" she cried. "It's just what we need! A vacation together!"

Marty felt very satisfied.

Then she astounded him by calling back and saying she couldn't make it, that her long lost brother Alex had suddenly re-established contact, out of the blue, and that she had decided to go to Portland to see him.

Marty felt kind of sad. Once he might have asked Candy to put off the reunion with Alex. . . but he had grown as a person in the last couple of years, he felt sensitized to her needs, more understanding, more generous. "I understand," he said. "You have to go. So what shall I bring you?"

"Nothing."

"Nothing?"

(Nothing?! said the voice of Roxie Kirsch in the inner ear of Candy's mind. Are you wacko?! You may not be divorcing this man, but please remember that if and when you do, you can be sure of keeping only that which he gave you before you divorced him. So while you're still married to him and putting up with his grubby little affairs, get everything you can get!)

"Okay," Candy said. "I'd like a briefcase. Brown or gray, not black. And not so thin that it can't hold a contract. Ask Danton's wife or some other stylish woman you may know there to pick it out. And when you're in St. Maarten, get sweatshirts for Sam and Ethel that say 'Marigot University' so they can wear them the first week at school and say 'This is what my father brought for me.' Sam takes a child's large and Ethel takes an adult's small. And bring perfume for my mother and your mother and a very fancy lace handkerchief for Marie. Don't forget Marie, please."

Marty laughed and rolled over against Odile's long white back.

"The trouble with asking a JAP what she wants for a present is that she always knows, exactly."

"What does that mean, JAP?" she asked.

"It means Jewish American Princess."

"Ah, so it is an anti-Semitic remark, an ethnic slur."

"No. It's a joke," he said, pulling her close.

"Will I always be your mistress, Martin?"

"Always, sweetheart," he answered, kissing her throat. "Have you got time to pick out a briefcase at Gucci?"

★ ★ ★

The St. Maarten clinic site, a hillside overlooking an empty bay on one side and a patchwork of hanging gardens on the other, took Marty's breath away. Who would not recover more quickly in this pungent air, above these fragrant forests of mango and palm? The steel outlines of the buildings suggested spacious state-of-the-art facilities with so much privacy for the guests that no patient's pain would ever impinge upon her neighbor's recuperation.

Having negotiated for the real estate, arranged the bank loans, the tax abatements, and probably all the necessary bribes as well, Adrine now climbed forcefully across the rutted clay roadbeds, wearing sensible shoes and beige linen. Clearly the mother and spine of this entire project, she bantered with the Caribbean workmen and their French overseers as they slowly crawled their tractors over the earth. At midday, when everyone else was frolicking in the ocean, she could be found in a puddle of shade inside the hotel, talking on the phone in her husky voice and pecking at her calculator.

Danton led Marty and his other potential investors across the site, through the potential rooms, down the potential halls. They stood on the potential terrace, where patients could get better while enjoying the view of the green sea. In a thatch-roofed restaurant by the petite harbor of Marigot, the handsome Danton drank cognac and promised that the operating theaters would be tailored to Marty's specifications, a thrilling notion.

Marty found it unsettling that so many of the other investors seemed to be waiting on his decision, for although he knew he was good, he didn't know yet how good other people thought he was. It hit him suddenly that Danton's flattering introductions were not just mere Franco-banter but real p.r. — and that they had worked. Many people now believed that Dr. Martin Shapiro's participation was key to the profitability of the Moore Clinic.

He did not doubt that he could raise a million dollars. However, he had never invested in anything that was not held firmly in his own strong hands, and he did not trust Danton. He trusted Adrine much more, but then again, he didn't trust his trust because he knew it was based on an ethnic affinity for Armenians. Even though Adrine was just about the Frenchest woman anyone would ever want to meet, Marty did not think of her as French. He did not blame her even subconsciously for the murder of his mother-in-law's family.

On the beach, surrounded by women with small bare brown breasts, and little children with platinum hair cut long, Marty began to feel the tightness in his chest undoing itself, like laces loosening. For the first time in a dozen years, he had been on vacation from his work for fifteen days. Fifteen days without the stench of blood, the blipblipblip of failing hearts, without the screams, the groans of women suffering from huge incisions, without the infections, the oozing, the darkening before flesh dies. Fifteen nights of uninterrupted slumber, without the terror of the corridors, where the survivors lurked curse-like, waiting for his footfall, ready to pounce, begging for an answer: tell me, doctor, be a god be a titan be the Baal Shem Tov and tell me true: is there anything that you can do? For fifteen days, no son's mother had breathed her last on his watch. And so for the first time since he could remember, Marty Shapiro began to feel okay. Tension burned off his body like a fog finally lifting. He slept unprotected in the sun for hours.

The spectacle of the sharp surgeon from New York snoring on the sand prompted Danton Moore to comment that to know that these damn Hebrews were really devils, all you had do was take one with you to a tropical island and watch him roast in the sun without noticeable discomfort or ill effect.

Adrine Moore glanced up from her calculator, a gleam of disgust in her black eyes.

★ ★ ★

When Marty awoke, it was near sunset. The beach was empty. A stillness pressed the water absolutely flat. Not a wave, not a ripple, nothing. Green glass the ocean seemed, lit from within by the translucent bodies of billions of protozoa. Large-billed birds swooped without sound onto the water and flew away with their dinner.

From behind the line of palm trees that separated the beach from the pink hotel, island music and happy hour laughter could be heard.

Marty waded into the sea. He floated on his back. He lightly sang an old Broadway song he had learned from hearing his wife Candy sing it in the kitchen.

Suddenly, as though summoned, a fat man rose up beside Marty, not scaring him. He spat out water, like leviathan spouting, and smiled. This man was dark brown. He had the face of an antiquity: carved lips, oval eyes. His ear lobes were long and studded with many tiny earrings. Around his neck hung a necklace of fish.

"Ah, this is a good sea," the fat man said. "Still clean."

"Do you come here often?" Marty asked.

"Whenever I can take a rest from my business."

"What business are you in?"

"Shipping."

"So you know this place well."

"Very well."

"Should I invest? An associate of mine is building a clinic. . . "

"Are the roads in?"

"Not yet."

"Don't invest until the roads are in."

With these words the fat shipper smiled farewell and once again disappeared beneath the surface of the sea.

Danton Moore came down to the beach to look for Marty. He carried dry towels and two daiquiris. Marty took the towels and turned down the drink.

"I slept on it," he said with his usual delicacy. "And the answer is no."

"Ah but Martin. . . "

"Don't argue with me. My wife does that."

⋆ ⋆ ⋆

Candy was setting the Shabbat table when Marty called and asked her to join him in the islands. His offer filled her with joy. She danced around the table, tickling the crystal with the silver to make it sing. The option of going to see her brother Alex, who had phoned suddenly, also lay before her now, like an extra plate. She might eat from it or not, as she wished, but what was important was that she had the option of a brother again. Of course, she would put off Alex. If Marty was coming back to her, then Alex could wait another fifteen years for all she cared. Throwing open the doors of the mirrored cabinets with a renewed sense of security, she plucked out her grandfather's prayer book and the brass candlesticks that Sam's girl Miriam had given her for a wedding gift, determined to make this the most beautiful table ever.

And then Kevin McCabe called. He told her that during his last trip to New York, Marty had enjoyed a brief fling with a woman named Angie Lichtman, the wife of his accountant, who had a huge apartment on the Upper West Side filled with priceless antiques and a couple of major paintings. "I tell you this to comfort you, so you don't think your husband is more loyal to his French mistress than he is to you," Kevin said in a jocular way. He figured she was about at the end of her rope.

In a twinkling, all that Marty had begun to hope for — stability, security, the reflected glory of successful children, an interesting middle age with an exciting girlfriend and a well-connected and productive wife — all of it fell to pieces. Nothing Roxie Kirsch could say would help him now.

Candy had her hair done and her nails done and called Mrs. Lichtman.

"Hiya," she said. "I am Candice Shapiro. My husband and your husband do quite a lot of business together. I understand that you have a very large and beautiful home and that your husband is a supporter of liberal causes and candidates. I am calling to ask you to give your home for a cocktail party to support Carol O'Banyon's campaign for Congress. I was thinking of perhaps $1000 per couple."

"I. . . I. . . I. . . I will have to ask my hu. . . huh. . . ." Angie croaked. Sweat exploded at the back of her knees.

"If you like I could call your husband and ask him directly," Candy said.

Recovering her wits, comprehending the threat in Candy's voice and the enormous risks involved in not accepting her suggestion, Angie said: "It won't be necessary for you to call my husband, Mrs. Shapiro. I am sure he would be agreeable. When would you like to do this?"

"After the end of the summer," Candy said. "When I return from visiting my brother in the West."

CHAPTER ELEVEN

# FAMILY BLOCKING

ALEXANDER DEAL INVITED HIS SISTER TO VISIT HIM because of a new song that Alisette Legrand sang during her August gig at the renowned Oregon mountain nightclub, Aunt Dorothy's. Personally, he preferred folk music. Baez, Bikel, Dylan, Seeger, these were his minstrels. He would not have chosen to drag down from the little town of Briarbush to see Alisette except that his wife, Belle, was a big fan, and she prodded and insisted without cease.

Once famous for the flamboyance of her wigs and outfits, Alisette had now changed her style. No more lemon yellow dresses with yards of lace; no more spangled shawls. This year, she dressed in white like an angel of the Lord, but sequinned. Belle gasped when she appeared in her dazzling gown with her diamonds flashing and her skin darkened to Masai-color by the Pacific sun. She sang them "Stardust" and "Deep River", and "Many a New Day" real slow, mostly *a cappella,* and then, when they were toasted by her warmth, she sang "Fried Fish" which had become a hit single, and "The Ultimate Aphrodisiac", now called by the disc jockies a bona fide classic.

Belle sang along with that one. She and many other women just all of a sudden started dancing, singing "Gimme-it Gimme-it" and wagging their hips and clapping, delighting the men they were with. Maybe because they knew the words, or because they danced, and she saw that they were such loyal fans of hers and loved her so much, Alisette gave them her new song. Bo Tye drove up the tempo; the back-up singers flew out from Alisette's body like wings. She looked like a cosmic angel, enveloping them all. Alex thought she actually looked like Amnesty.

> *Who is we?* she sang.
> *Who is we?*
> *We is our families whose blood we share but where do we go from there?*
> *Oooh baby oooh baby*
> *Wanna be part of your scene*
> *Oooh baby oooh*
> *Wanna be part of you.*
> *I thought we was my honey and me,*
> *But he stole my VCR.*
> *I thought we was the economy*
> *But it repossessed my car.*
> *So I said we is the city*
> *And the city said that's fine*
> *But not where the bankers have brunch, girl,*
> *And not on the streets after nine.*
> *We're a team til we lose the game.*
> *We're of one mind til we don't think the same.*
> *If we is a color, the future is bleak.*
> *If we're a religion, it's up shit creek.*
> *Oooh baby oooh baby*
> *Wanna be part of your scene. . .*

The people had caught the refrain and sang along "Oooh baby oooh Wanna be part of you. . . ". Even Alex stood up and clapped his hands as in the old days. Then the rock beat stopped. Only the keyboard man played. Alisette sang out in her Mahalia voice:

*I spent my whole lifetime*
*Learning who I am,*
*And what is expected of me.*
*And now that I know it*
*How do I bestow it?*
*Where do I take all my loving and caring?*
*Who are my people? What says my nation?*
*Who do I get to call we?*

Belle touched Alex's shoulder. He was crying. "Call them," she said. She had said it many times before but now Alisette had finished the job for her absolutely. "Call your mother and your sister."

★ ★ ★

Alex Deal had become a tall, hunched man with long gray hair that he tied back with lengths of rawhide. He wore faded mountain plaid flannel shirts and jeans and old boots stained with blackberry juice. Belle liked how clean he kept himself. She loved what she called his "deep-feeling Jewish eyes." Ten years earlier, his tenderness to her little daughter had won her heart.

The big problem was that Alex's brother, Sam, came to him at night, dressed in American military fatigues. He sat down on their bed and squeezed his nose twice, then sniffed, then breathed a little steam on his glasses and cleaned them with a tissue.

"If you look at the matter logically," Sam said, "no matter what decision you make, you are causing someone's death. If you go and you fight, you will inevitably kill some mother's son. Even if you are assigned to ordnance, you will do that. Even if you become a nurse. Because to work in the apparatus of war is to contribute to its purpose, which is the slaughter of the enemy."

"Shut up, Sam," Belle said.

"If you don't go," Sam continued, "then someone goes in your place."

"Shut up."

"Another American. Someone too poor or uneducated to resist the draft. Precisely the same people you say you want to help, Alex. They will die in your boots."

"Get out of my bed!" Belle said.

"I am a doctor now, it's my life, it's all I think about," Sam continued. "I'm not the master of my soul any more. I'm just a set of life-saving skills. So I'm in a different spot than you, I understand that, I really do. The rest of the guys at the hospital refuse to go to the war. But if I look at the matter logically, I see that the war will go on without me, and perhaps if I serve, some of the people who would otherwise die or be crippled forever will have lives and jobs and families."

"Shut up!" Belle raged. "Let us go to sleep."

"Each of us is all alone in this thing," Sam said. "I can't advise you. You have to do what you want."

"How should I know what I want?!" Alex cried.

In a fury, Belle finally slammed on the light. The sight of her large white body scared Sam's ghost from the room.

Naturally, he returned. The morning after Alex and Belle heard Alisette sing at Aunt Dorothy's, Sam materialized in their restaurant, on the counter next to the yogurt machine. Alex was wiping off the tables, preparing for the lunch of the regulars. Sam wanted to talk about their mother. At first, Alex refused to be drawn into the conversation. He insisted that he didn't miss Maida, that he hardly ever thought of her, that she was not his main parent any more than Candy was his main sibling. If, to borrow Alisette's lyric, "we" was "they", if "they" were all he had to call family — those lesser lights, supporting characters, two silly JAP shoppers in the east — then he might as well not even call.

"You are lying to yourself," Sam said.

"Shit, you sound like Belle."

"Belle is right. You have to go back to them."

"Why why why?!" Alex asked. "They were both on Dad's side."

"That wasn't such a bad side to be on."

"It was the side of evil and stupidity and slaughter."

"Okay okay fine. But you can't blame Dad for that. He was an old-style patriot."

"He was a pimp!" Alex yelled. "He took the girls out of the showroom and introduced them to Pastafino's boys, he appeased the mob with them. And this pimp, this low-life, this slime bucket dared to stand in judgment on me!"

Belle called from the kitchen: "You're yelling at yourself again, honey."

"Don't you miss Mom? Come on. . . "

"I don't miss her. Shit."

"You have to go back to Candy," Sam said.

"I don't even remember what Candy looks like. I don't even know her married name."

"Shapiro," Belle called.

* * *

With the indomitable Belle standing over him like another snow-capped mountain, Alex called Maida. It was after midnight. Listening to the phone ring, he tried to figure how old Maida was; she had to be pretty old by now. Early on in his exile, Aunt Theresa had often been in touch to plead for a visit on some special occasion — the unveiling of Jack's headstone, Maida's birthday, Maida's minor heart attack. Somehow, Alex had always managed not to go. And now he bore so much guilt at having ignored his mother these many years that he felt dizzy with fear that she might soon answer the phone. Oh my God! She'll be asleep! I will have awakened her! She'll sound old! She'll be frail! Oh my God!

A sleepy voice said that someone else lived there now; Maida had long ago moved away. The receiver crashed angrily back into its nest. "I can't find her," he said to Belle.

"Try your sister."

He called information for Shapiro. There were 104 of them in Candy's area code.

"Martin," said Alex.

"We have seven of them," said the operator.

"He's a doctor."

"Well, several of them are doctors. What kind of doctor is he?"

"Um. . . um. . . .I'm afraid I don't know what kind. Thanks for trying, Operator. Bye."

Alex hung up.

"He's a gynecologist," Belle said.

So then he had to call information again and this time he got Marty's office number.

"Dr. Shapiro is out of the country," answered the all-night answering service. "Dr. Wang is covering for him in case of emergency. Is this an emergency, sir?"

"I'm his brother-in-law," Alex explained.

"Dr. Wang's?"

"No, Dr. Shapiro's. I need to reach my sister."

"Is it an emergency?"

"Well. . . almost. . . "

"I suggest you call her at home, sir."

"I've uh misplaced their home number."

"We do not give out Dr. Shapiro's home number."

"Please. . . it's important."

"What is important is for me to keep this line accessible to patients who are in need of emergency care, sir!"

The answering service hung up.

Alex told Belle it was impossible. He couldn't find them, they were just lost, it was a bad idea anyway and they should forget the whole thing and go to bed.

"Call your Uncle Milton."

"No."

"He lives in a town with a grotesque name." She succeeded in recalling it. "Great Neck. There will only be one Milton Deal in Great Neck. He'll give you Candy's number, and he will know where your mother has moved."

"It's two in the morning there."

Belle sat on the desk, glowering at him. She was seven years older than Alex. She had lived with him for a decade and borne him two children and taught her first child to call him Daddy and now that they had built a successful business together, she wanted him to introduce her to his first family. Like Maida in years gone by, Belle longed for relatives. She had no one on her side any more. Alex's family was all she could hope for, connective tissue for the kids. And anyway, she could not bear to see him tortured by guilt this way. A man who had risked everything to do the right thing should be able to go home and enjoy his victory, Belle felt. Hadn't everyone else?

"Call your Uncle Milton and ask him for Candy's number," Belle said.

"You don't understand. He's a semi-hood. He'll break my balls and make me feel terrible."

"You already feel terrible."

"Get off my case, Belle."

"Coward," she said.

The magic word.

★ ★ ★

To his relief, it was Aunt Theresa who answered the phone. Having no children of her own (a punishment for the sins of her youth, she said forthrightly,) cut off from the children of her own sisters who had never forgiven her for marrying "that sheeny underwear salesman", she had always doted on Maida's kids. Alex remembered her kissing his forehead like a blessing and slipping candy into his pockets.

"How're you doing, Aunt Terry?" he began enthusiastically.

"Oh Alex," she said. "Hold on."

"Wait Aunt Ter. . . "

Milton came on the phone.

"What do you want?" he asked.

It had been fourteen years since Jack died. Thirteen years since Candy had married.

"How are you, Uncle Milt?"

"What do you want?"

"I want to reach Mom and Candy."

Milton immediately provided Maida's new number in Tampa and Candy's on Long Island as well as at work in Manhattan.

"She works? Candy? What does she do?"

The click of the phone informed Alex that even Milton and Theresa hated him now. He decided that it was going to be much too hard to ever see his family again. Big scenes. Recriminations. His mother would scream. And if there was anything in this world he thought he could not bear to hear, it was Maida screaming.

"A rebel yell," he told Belle while they were baking bread the next day. "Blood curdling, with a vibrato, high-pitched. . . "

"Like this?" she asked, and she began to scream like his mother.

So at four o'clock in the afternoon, even though he had her work number, he called Candy at home in order to avoid having to speak with her. Ethel answered.

"Are you the Uncle Alex who ran away to Canada and never came back not even after Amnesty?"

"The very same," he said. "Although I live in Oregon now. . . in the mountains. . . "

"So why are you calling?"

"I got a directive from a singer."

"Which one?"

"Alisette Legrand."

"Oh! She's my favorite!" cried Ethel. "I just love her! Don't you just love her?! I know all her songs." And she began to sing. *Fried fish! Fri-eye-eyed fish! Supersonic high electri-fied fish. . .*

"Ethel. Please. Is your mother home?"

"Certainly not. She's at work. Do you have children?"

"I have two little boys six and eight and a girl who is my wife's daughter by her first uh. . . uh. . . husband who is fifteen now."

"Well, to tell the truth, Uncle Alex," Ethel said, "Mom never speaks of you except with revulsion. But she's basically a mushy person. And if you tell her about your children, she might soften up. I'll ask her to call you back when she comes home."

Candy refused categorically to call him back. However, like her Aunt Belle, Ethel had a certain way of insisting.

* * *

Alex drove down to the coast in his Isuzu pick-up on an afternoon of fog and rain. Belle told him to get the truck washed. For some reason, he wanted to leave it dirty. She told him to bring Candy home for dinner, and began to bake a blackberry pie.

"Candy is going to hate you," Sam said.

"Why?"

"Because you treated her like shit when she was thirteen."

"Oh come on. She should have known better than to undress in a strange basement."

"She was a kid."

"What happened that was so terrible? Nobody raped her. They put her in an ugly girl contest. So what? She was an ugly girl, a big fat blob. What can you do? She came by it naturally. Our mother is no beauty either."

"If you hadn't stopped me, I would have killed that son-of-a-bitch," Sam said, sniffing and growling like Sonny Liston.

"Didn't you ever do anything mean to a girl?" Alex asked. (He had always wanted to ask Sam that question.)

"Yes," Sam said. "Yes, I did. But luckily for me, she wasn't somebody's sister."

Sweet-faced Jimmy Gottlieb walked across the mountain road, carrying his clarinet, heading for the athletic field adjacent to the high school. The band had been practicing and now sat around on the bleachers, taking a break, watching the majorettes swirl their flags. It was a beautiful day.

"Gottlieb?"

"Yeah?"

"My name is Sam Deal. I am Candy's brother."

The band went on the march again, tubas and trombones bleating, while Sam beat Jimmy bloody with the clarinet.

"Enough Sam. You'll hurt him too much. Enough."

Twenty-three years later in Oregon, Sam said "You should have let me at least break his nose."

"For what?" Alex asked. "For the family honor? Shit, the only person in the family who ever behaved honorably was me when I came to Canada and sold candles on the streets of Toronto and ate the bread of poverty for convictions I still hold, to this day, Sam, I still believe that I was right and you were wrong."

"You can say it forever, Alex, but you'll never make me agree with you," his brother told him for the millionth time, before disappearing into the dust blue skies.

★ ★ ★

When Candy told Maida that she was going to visit Alex, Maida acted unconcerned. She had invested several years in the hard work of forgetting her son; an exorcism of sorts, quite deliberate, very difficult; she was determined to make it stick. She did not ask to come on the trip. She sent no presents along for the ride. However, she did immediately loot her carefully organized photo albums for just the right selection of pictures to trigger fond memories of sibling bliss, and then sent them to Candy by courier.

During her poor Jack's protracted death, Maida would have been grateful to have Alex around. She had thought he would come then, his love for her re-ignited by the imminent loss of the parent who had rejected him, if only to drive her to the hospital and sit with her there and give her advice about what to do with her future and her possessions as sons are supposed to do. Since he didn't come, Candy filled all those needs of Maida's, helped by Theresa and Milton and Dorothy Pastafino (a devoted friend, poor woman, what a horrible life she must have had, she should only rest in peace.)

When Candy married, Maida still would have been delighted to welcome Alex into the festivities. She had heard from friends in Los Angeles that Marty's father was disliked in the community. What if Marty turned out to be a chip off the old glacier? A husband with a genetic predilection to meanness might forget himself and behave less than lovingly toward a wife who had no brothers around to protect her.

"Even if you no longer care about your sister," Aunt Theresa had pleaded on the phone, "come to the wedding for the sake of appearances. So that Candy won't seem quite so vulnerable, you know. . . alone. . . on her wedding day."

But Alex did not come.

Maida remembered him as her pitiful son. He seemed to have a knack for ignoring the people who adored him, and adoring the people who despised him. He was forever standing in front of the open refrigerator, staring at two hundred dollars worth of food and complaining that there was nothing to eat. She remembered screaming at him that he had to clean his disgusting room, and he promised he would, but he never did.

Maida had a scenario in her mind of how dinner ended in the days when they were all together. Jack and Sam would be arguing about ethics and public policy. They would get up from the table, yelling and laughing. Little father. Tall son. Alex would follow them, trying to say what he thought.

"Let the boy speak, Jack. Give the boy a chance to be heard," Maida would call, as her father Reb Ezra had always done when he was alive. But Sam and Jack didn't hear her, and most important, Alex didn't hear her either. It made absolutely no difference to him that his mother was on his side.

When Maida described this memory to her daughter, Candy entitled it "Family Blocking," a phrase which Maida did not quite understand.

"Where was I?" asked Candy. "In the family blocking at the end of dinner, where was I?"

"I suppose you went off in a different direction," Maida said, "I don't remember because I was watching Alex."

"The Heartbreak Yid," Candy mused.

Maida gave Candy's hand a couple of smooches.

"Anyway, you are my daughter, you are competent and stable, just like me," she said. "You never needed watching."

In her most haunting memory, Maida saw Alex tumbling down the stairs, his pony tail flying, a trace of blood on his face where Jack had hit him so very hard. How disdainfully he shook off her comforting arms and sneered at her tears! He left his telephone number with Candy with the rabbi even with Sam's girl Miriam but not with her, his mother. And even after Amnesty, when other women's sons were rushing back to them, desperate for their cooking, the smell of their laundry soap, the sound of their slippers on the stairs, presenting them with adorable little Canadian babies, Alex never came.

So enough, Maida thought. She had two children who loved her. One had lived to give her two grandchildren who loved her. Enough mourning over the other one in Toronto or wherever he was now. Enough.

★ ★ ★

When she suddenly took his arm, as he waited in the airport, he honestly had no idea who she was. Who could have imagined that dumpy little Candycane would grow up into this bejeweled broad with scarlet-framed sunglasses and tons of make-up and a fucking humongous fox coat?! Who did she think she was, Imelda Marcos? Their mother may have been a pain, but at least she affected the Eleanor Roosevelt look. At least she had taste!

Gulping his disapproval, Alex felt he should probably kiss Candy warmly. However, she did not permit him to, holding herself back from him and limiting herself to pursing her bright red lips at the air beneath his ears. He really hated that. He could not prevent himself from saying: "You should be ashamed to wear that coat," for he was the vice president of the Briarbush Animal Shelter and had often led demonstrations against trapping.

"I like my coat," Candy said.

"Ask the little foxes if they do."

Candy laughed. "Not to worry, darling. It's a fake."

"That's a fake?!"

"Isn't it great?!" She swirled around in the airport, catching eyes, inviting disapproval. Nobody else in Portland believed it was a fake either. "I paid a fortune for it at Saks."

"Come on, Candy, are you going start telling me right away how rich you are?"

"It was worth every penny," she continued, "because besides looking real and keeping me very warm, it has the added advantage of provoking hostilities with knee-jerk fox-lovers like you."

In this manner, the surviving Deal siblings kicked off their first meeting in fifteen years. They disliked each other so thoroughly that within minutes, they both needed a drink, which was why they ended up in the Wild West Saloon and Steak House, a neo-Victorian emporium, with burnished wood and brass fittings and scarlet velvet upholstery. The bartenders wore arm garters and large mustaches.

"Travelers come here to feel nostalgic about 'Gunsmoke' and the good old days," Alex said, rubbing his faded flannel elbow on the table as though to shine it like a part owner.

"It's true, the place does actually remind me of Amanda Blake," said Candy.

"Excuse me?"

"Did you hear she died?"

"Uhh. . . wait. . . who are we talking about here?"

" 'Gunsmoke.' She played Miss Kitty the saloon keeper. Red hair. Died of AIDS."

Candy leaned forward, her face suddenly charged with grief. Her words, so carefully chosen heretofore, now rummaged forth in a blather of fear and confusion.

"We have this plague going on at home, Alex. Do you have it here too? It's so. . . so targeted. . . like on the junkies and their children and on the gay guys. It's carrying away our most gifted people. Every time one of my partners stays home with the flu, I get crazy. The whole reason my husband even started with the French is because he was called in on so many cases where the. . . the. . . thing had crossed the placenta and the poor babies were born dying."

Candy's voice had grown shrill; tears glazed her eyes; she had that look leading to hysteria which Alex remembered so well in their mother. He got scared.

"So how's the rabbi?" he asked.

Candy stared, her outpouring stopped.

"What? Uh. . . what? Which rabbi?"

"The one I gave my number to, what was his name?"

"Oh him." It was all coming back to her now. Brother Alex. Changing the subject. Dodging the painful. "He made *aliyah.*"

"What?"

"He went to Israel to live." Alex's unfamiliarity with what Candy considered an everyday Hebrew term suddenly gave her a shocking thought. "Oh my God, Alex. Are you still Jewish?! Did you convert?!"

He sighed. Sam had warned him that he would have to endure a certain amount of hostility. "Waiter!" he yelled. "Better bring us another round."

Candy also ordered a plate of buffalo wings. Her heart was pounding. She hoped that if she occupied her face with eating, she would be able to conceal her disgust at his gray pony tail and his string tie. Who the hell did he think he was?! Willy Nelson?!

Alex drained his glass and ordered another. He knew he had to win her sympathy somehow. He could not bear the thought of going back to Belle and saying: "Candy hated me. She hated me so much that I lost her again, and we have no sister, we will have no mother no wider home no family."

"Do you remember Reb Ezra?" he asked.

"How should I remember him?"

"Right of course you were what. . . six. . . seven when he died. . . " Alex grinned. "A little cutie with bunches and bows and fat legs."

"You had to say that."

"We called you 'Thunder Thighs.'"

"I still have them."

"Come on, Candy, where's your sense of humor?"

"My husband's many mistresses got together for lunch and ate it. G'head g'head, so tell me about Grandpa. . . "

Warmed by the liquor, and greatly gladdened to hear that her life was not absolutely perfect, Alex relaxed and began to tell Candy a story which she had never heard.

"Everybody liked the old man, Reb Ezra Kesselman our grandfather," Alex said. "He looked like Abe Lincoln. Tall with jutting brows, and an abnormally large jaw. Sam used to say that he had the basic distended bone structure of a giant, but something had gone wrong, bad nutrition, crowded beds, low ceilings, sick chickens, the usual shortcomings of the Pale. A failed giant, that was Reb Ezra. Saintly and wise in a butcher shop on 47th street west of Ninth, quoting Torah and Talmud to stagehands.

"I was his favorite. 'Let the boy speak, Jack,' he used to say. 'Give the boy a chance. This boy has understanding. What good is wisdom without understanding? Let him speak!' he used to say. My defender. If only he had lived. He used to take me to the shop, when I was like eight years old, on Sundays. I'd sit by the counter watching him cut cutlets.

"One Sunday, a local hood comes in. He wants Reb Ezra to pay him to have his store protected. So naturally Reb Ezra asks why? Was somebody threatening the store that he should need protection? If the man wanted money to feed his wife and children, he should just come right out and ask and not make up these phony protection business excuses. And with that, Reb Ezra takes a five dollar bill from the cash register and gives it to the hood and says: 'Go with God, young man. Don't be discouraged. You'll find work soon.' "

Candy laughed, charmed.

"So that night, we tell the story of the hood to Dad. Mom becomes hysterical. She's screaming to wake the dead. . . you know that piercing but grating prolonged but staccato scream. . . "

"If you don't like the way our mother screams, you should not have broken her heart," his sister interjected.

"Hard to imagine breaking the heart of a woman who stood by while her one surviving son was cut off like a gangrenous toe!"

The buffalo wings came. Candy began to suck the sauce off them, then she stripped off the skin, then she ate the thin little strips of wing meat. A disgusting sight, Alex thought, those manicured fingers in all that spicy gunk. Candy noticed him staring.

"What are you, a vegetarian?"

"Yes," he said.

"I should have guessed. So g'head with your story."

"Well, of course, Dad and Milton run out immediately and hire their hood buddy, Fayo Pastafino, to protect the store. Which was precisely what Reb Ezra didn't want to do in the first place. Reb Ezra says no. They tell him to shut up and be quiet, he's a *tzaddik,* a holy man, a learned man, what does he know?

"And then one Sunday, we go into the store as usual. But Pastafino the Great Protector has screwed up."

Alex took a breath.

"What?" Candy said.

"In the window. . . "

"What. . . ?"

"Under the kosher sign. . . "

"What?!"

"In the window under the kosher sign, crabs are crawling." Candy cried out in horror. "Inside there are pigs little pigs running around squealing and defecating." She shoved a napkin into her mouth, pressed her chest to keep the gorge down. "Reb Ezra grabs me, drags me away from there. We run and run down the street. Then suddenly he sits down on the curb and begins to throw up. I didn't know what to do. I mean, I'm a little kid. I've never seen a grown man throw up on his shoes."

Candy clasped her hands together over her heart, then intermittently clapped them together, without making any sound. She rocked back and forth.

"Somebody in the neighborhood must have called Dad, because he and Milton came and got us and put us in the car. Reb Ezra kept yelling that the pigs were innocent creatures and shouldn't be left to die, so they put the pigs in a bag in the trunk. God, what a racket they made. I looked out the back window as we left and I saw smoke coming out of the butcher shop. Dad and Milton had set it on fire.

"We stopped near a church. Dad dropped off the pigs and then we went home. The cops came and arrested Uncle Milton and Dad for arson. Did you know they did time? Or was that something else our mother managed to spare herself from telling you? I understand they got a very light sentence; couple months. Pastafino may not have been able to prevent the desecration of our grandfather's shop, but at least he had some pull with the judges.

"Grandpa got sick after that. He never got well. He died from a broken heart, because your Daddy had given his nice clean kosher shop over to the protection of criminals."

Candy exploded.

"You're such a wimp, Alex! Don't you see? Grandpa was just plain naive! Daddy and Milton and Fayo were trying to help him!"

"Bullshit! Fayo was getting Dad to make the payoffs Grandpa wouldn't make!"

"That's impossible! Daddy and Fayo fought together in the Pacific War! Fayo has feelings for our family! He brought you a Bible on your bar mitzvah and you wouldn't even take it!"

"Because he was a crook! A goon! A two-bit hood who caused the death of our grandfather the *tzaddik* the one who used to say 'Let the boy speak, Jack! Give the boy a chance to be heard!'"

"All you care about is your own wounded ego! For God's sake, grow up. See things clearly for once!"

"I see that you're making excuses for a man whose association with our family is a disgrace!"

"You're the man who disgraced the family, you putz! Uncle Fayo and Aunt Dorothy held Mom's hand when Daddy died, and you didn't even show up! She cried for you! Where is my baby? she cried. How can I bury Jack without my son to help me?! And you didn't even call!"

Alex snarled at this vision of his suffering mother, to scare it away. "Oh, give it a rest! All you JAPS talk about is how helpless you are. (He imitated Candy's whine; Heimlich himself could not have done better.) 'I'm all alone, help me, oh help me, I can't bury Sam alone, how am I supposed to bury my Daddy all by myself?' Shit. I'm lucky I didn't go home. I would have been buried too by now and you and Mom would still be groaning and moaning about how hard it was to dance on my grave!"

Candy put on her coat.

"Why take it out on me just because you were the unexceptional son?" she asked.

"Christ, you're a bitch, Candy. No wonder your husband cheats on you. Anything to get away from the jingle of your bracelets and the sound of your voice!"

"Oh fuck you, you prick! You cowardly selfish prick, fuck you fuck you!!"

Candy leaped at Alex as brawlers did in the days of the wild west, shattering glasses and plates. He fell over backwards, surprised, and she clambered onto his legs, beating at him with arms like wiper blades. She took off her spike heeled shoe and hit him and hit him and hit him until her braid came loose and her make-up ran like lava and her coat was matted with buffalo wing sauce and vodka and snot from her running nose. It took both bartenders to rescue her brother.

* * *

Candy sat in her hotel room, in the middle of the bed. She watched a television show. It featured a beautiful older woman who, like Carol O'Banyon, had kept her body slender and fixed her face and now looked at least twenty years younger than her actual age. From room service, she had ordered a steak and a banana split, and she had eaten it down to the last smear in five minutes, and she was still starving. Because she was afraid that her brother Alex might try to say he was sorry, she had given the desk instructions to let no calls through. She couldn't talk to him now. She had to think.

Candy ordered a bottle of vodka and a tin of caviar and drank and ate. Soon she was so sick that she had to crawl to the toilet on her knees and vomit. There, facing the hopeless stink of her own gut, she said to herself quite simply: "I am all alone."

She who had so recently been raised from the bed of depression by the interventions of her friends now felt that she had none, not one, who was not primarily interested in her money. Look at them. Marie got a great salary for almost no work, why shouldn't she be nice? Jock and Slim would have been broke except for her bail-out investment, why shouldn't they hire itinerant comedians to cheer her up? Shaul thought of her as a free loan society; why shouldn't he tell her she was beautiful and make love to her on the stairs? All he really wanted was to call Afula on her phone. Roxie wouldn't have a publishing business if Candy hadn't invested again and again. Lee Kreinick and Marsha Chomsky appreciated her mainly for the amount of money she could raise. So did the Russian Jews. So did Carol O'Banyon. Candy figured if she showed up at the soup kitchen and said *please, I have helped you, now help me,* the hungry, the homeless and the working poor would laugh in her face.

"I am all alone," she thought.

For the first time, she got so depressed that she began to seriously consider whether hers was a life worth continuing. She sealed herself into the silence of her own bones, the sarcophagal silence which she had developed especially for these occasions when wakefulness became unbearable, and she slept without dreaming on the bathroom floor. When she woke, it was early morning and the call button on her phone was flashing.The desk operator told her that her husband Dr. Shapiro had called from St. Maarten, leaving the date and time of his return as a message, and that her mother had called from Florida and that her sister-in-law Belle had called three times.

She knew she had to call back her mother and that she could not accomplish that without first somehow pulling away from this latest, most terrible seizure of darkness. So with great effort, moving arthritically like an old lady, Candy washed and dressed and braided her hair and went shopping.

For a whole day, she roamed Portland. She looked and looked for something to buy to lift her spirits. The stores of the city rejected her completely. We cater aggressively to tasteful, plain women, they said. We have not even a handbag or a string of beads that would remotely suit your gaudy persona.

In the window of a store that sold local arts and crafts, Candy saw pretty quilted vests with designs embroidered on them. Candy bought the vests for her children, assuming this would be a help to some poor person. Even though she did not particularly like these layered totem patterns of the northwestern tribes, she respected them for they represented a culture, a whole way of looking at the world. The way was round and padded. Circular ice houses, blubber laden sea lions, curving tusks and heavy haired dogs. Moon faces framed by soft halos of fur. This art represented the truth of a certain way of life. It validated the people who lived that way; it made them feel real. Wasn't that what culture was supposed to do?

What was her culture? Candy wondered. What were her local arts and crafts? Hadn't somebody once made necklaces out of miniature hardened bagels? Maybe that was her culture. Maybe she should buy a heather gray sweat shirt at Saks and then embroider the word "SCHMUCK" all over it, maybe that would express her way of life.

Rejected by Portland, wishing she were an Eskimo, despairing of ever being comfortable in her own flesh, Candy walked on a stone path alongside a small park. Her feet hurt unbearably from all the years of shopping, so she took off her shoes. She snagged her stockings on the stone and ripped them. Since a well dressed woman cannot wear ripped stockings, she peeled them off in tatters, inviting the stares of passers by, and walked on with naked legs. Sam fell into step beside her and told her not to walk that way on the pavement, that she would get a serious cold.

"Get away from me, you stiff," she hissed.

A man walking a dog took offense at that. The dog pulled him onward before he could fashion a retort for Candy.

She sat down in a small, outdoor coffee house adjacent to a park. She ordered a hamburger, french fries and a chocolate milk shake and a piece of apple pie. While she was eating, she noticed that her nails needed doing. So out of her large pocketbook, she dumped nail polish, nail polish remover, clippers, emery boards, hand cream, and began to give herself a manicure. She nipped her fingers with the clippers, making herself bleed. She ordered a glass of water. She squeezed some blood into it until the color changed and then took a little drink. No taste. Not even salty. She ordered more water, dipped her napkin into it and began wiping the make-up off her face. For twenty minutes she did this, long after all the make-up was off. Candy soon realized that two women at a nearby table were staring at her, obviously concerned. Had she been talking to herself? Did she appear insane? She instantly became defensive.

"What?!" she asked. "What what what?!"

The women were embarrassed.

Candy put a $50.00 bill on the table and, leaving her manicuring paraphenalia, stalked away on bare feet. A boy rode by on a bicycle. Something about the thin black tires made Candy imagine an endlessly elongating dick coursing through cities like a snake, poking its one-eyed head into offices, saying "Hiya." She laughed and laughed.

"What's so goddamned funny?!" somebody yelled.

Candy looked down at a fenced-in bed of roses, trying to find which rose had yelled at her. These were larger and brighter than the roses she grew at home. With their glorious color, and large thorns, they pricked many tiny holes in the madness defense. Reality began to leak in. She saw that she needed her shoes. Where had she left them? Back down the path, perhaps. She turned to find them. . . and the boy on the bicycle rode by in a different direction and handed them off to her without a word.

Well, that was thoughtful, she thought.

On a stone at a corner of the rose bed, there was a little plaque. The roses, it said, had been donated by a large company, famous with gardeners like Candy, whose breeding fields were only half a day's drive down the highway.

She raced there like a dying woman after a miracle cure.

★ ★ ★

The sky over Oregon was so gray and dense with rain that she had to keep her lights on most of the way. The mountain miles took forever to traverse. She almost despaired. She almost forgot what she had set out to see. And then she floated over a small hill and saw acres and acres of roses.

The grandiflora fields went from white to ivory to gold to sudden bursts of scarlet, fifteen different shades of scarlet. The climbers supported trellises and arches with sagging wands of pink, thirty different shades of pink. Candy strolled among the the experimentals; the purple hybrid teas, the orange floribundas. And finally in a field of medieval Belgian hedge roses, peach tinted pink with ivory hearts, and giving off a perfume that would make the angels in Heaven drunk with joy, she sat herself down and took a little rest.

She stayed there until nightfall, baffling the watchmen, imagining that she was a child again in Sarah Villiers' garden without a care, loved by all, safe in her Daddy's arms. She remembered The Witch's Mirror and the picture in some album of herself, all pink and bows, placed there by loving brothers as an offering to the sky. It had taken her a lifetime — almost forty years — to understand that all the conjectures of Sam and Alex had been simply wrong. The lady of stone was not some cruel classic from the annals of ancient folklore. She was rather just a married woman, maybe even Jewish as the wise Reb Ezra had discerned, with children and a home and an old mother and responsibilities, whose task it was to hold up a mirror to the men who controlled her life from their godlike heights and say look, look, how you have fucked up, mister, look how you have taxed my reason and wasted my love.

★ ★ ★

"Where are you?!" Maida screamed on the phone. "I have been calling your hotel all night! I have been so worried! I called Marie, Marie was cagey. Your husband came home, nobody picked him up at the plane, he wanted to know if I had heard from you, what was I supposed to say?! Belle called again and again, she expected you for dinner, she was so upset, she was crying! And I didn't know where you were! How could you not call me?! How could you not go to meet Belle? How could you not tell me about my Alex?!"

"Shh Mom, stop yelling, it's okay," Candy said. "Alex is fine. He and Belle have three beautiful children and a very successful restaurant. He has a nice truck. He's charitable. Vice president of a respected environmental protection organization. If Sam hadn't been killed, he would have come home long ago, anyone can see that. He loves you. Please stop crying. He wants to see you. He's just embarrassed to call you because he didn't call you before. But he loves you, Mom. He misses you and loves you. And I'm sure that if you ask them, and maybe help them out a little with the fare, he and Belle will come to see you very soon with the children, because it's clear that she really wants to be part of our family."

CHAPTER TWELVE

# THE DEAL

SHAUL GOT HIS GREEN CARD because he had once worked on a *moshav,* a semi-collectivized agricultural settlement. His job there was to wrestle sheep to the ground and paint their behinds red, so, when they wandered away, they would be easy to find. During one particular period in the history of American immigration, such experience was enough to legalize its owner — especially if you had a good lawyer, which Shaul did, thanks to Candy.

From the moment he became legal, Shaul did not cease the pressure on Lazard Goldberg. He demanded a raise. When he got the raise, he demanded fringe benefits. When he didn't get those, he threatened to quit. When Lazard accepted his resignation, Shaul changed his mind and said he wasn't quitting. So Lazard fired him. Then Shaul sued him in small claims court, because he said Lazard had fired him without cause. And he won. Five hundred dollars. Lazard cheerfully handed over the money in a greasy wad that stained Shaul's pants from within his pocket. "It's worth every nickel, boychik," he concluded. "Just to have you out of my life."

Shaul sent the money home — and he was broke again. Two years working like an ox in this cold country and still he had not found the soft spot in the capitalist monolith where a poor boy might slip in. He held down two jobs — one as a waiter, one as a bouncer — and he went to school too. Soon he would have his high school equivalency. Then, he thought, he might take a business course, so he wouldn't have to be a waiter and a bouncer all his life, so he could be a boss, like Lazard, like BenZion. Baffled and frustrated, he tried to study the system. He faithfully followed the lives of the rich by reading the gossip columns on page six of *The New York Post.* They said that Carol O'Banyon, Candy's friend, had spent more than $100,000 on clothing every year for the past ten years, a fact which placed her in the same league with movie stars. How was it possible for one woman to wear so much?! Shaul wanted to know. He saw that Charlotte Glick, Candy's other friend, wife of the inventor of the inventory clip, had outbid major museums for six medieval Hebrew manuscripts and then had donated them to the library of the Jewish Theological Seminary. How could one little gadget make somebody's wife so rich?! He read that the new album from Megaman Brancusi's new record company was soaring off the pop charts, making millionaires of the six brown teen-agers pictured on the cover. Why them? he thought. Why not the group that BenZion used to contract with to entertain at private parties at Leviathan? They were teen-agers. They were brown.

He told his brother that the American system was based on a kind of perpetual greed riot. You could never allow yourself to achieve a sense of sufficiency here. You had to *want* constantly. If you didn't want the whole pie, you couldn't even get a slice. If you didn't hustle every minute, it was as though you were standing still, and if you stood still, some other hustler ran past you. It was exhausting — but what was the alternative? He rented films like "Wall Street" and "Working Girl" just to feed his dreams about what the offices and the meals and the women were going to look like when he finally made it big.

"He will never get what he wants," Shimshon wrote to his wife Yaffa in Afula. "He will sit here dreaming and earning a little more than the minimum wage and spending it all on videotapes until he is an old man, past his strength. And then he will finally give up and come home and sit in the sun again and spend the rest of his life telling our children how much better it really is in Israel than in America."

Every day Shaul got a new idea by discovering a new mistake he had been making and would now, he vowed, never make again.

For example, he had made a terrible mistake with Candy. He had thought she was most concerned about her sex life. In fact, he now realized, she was most concerned about the children. She was a mother first. That was why she had taken such an incredibly foolhardy risk in setting up the Mednorth bust, to clean up the community, so that the streets would be safe for the children. She stayed with her awful husband because she didn't want to hurt her children, who loved him. Obviously, what he should do was to send presents to Ethel and Sam on their birthdays. He should waylay them on their way home from school, invite them for hamburgers at the restaurant where he now worked, regain the mother by seducing the children.

On a certain summer day, drawn by the sound of their merry voices in the pool, he slipped along the fence on the neighbor's side, completely undetected in the vastness of the Broadbeach grounds, thinking he might call to them, that the Shapiro kids might recognize him, that he might be able to say that he had been delivering a bed next door and had come to see how they were doing. They were such adorable kids, he thought. He dared to imagine that they might be happy to see him, that his favorite, Little Sam, would give him a hug.

Shaul parted the branches of the short scarlet maples, seeking just one more taste of family, good times, the only good times he had ever had in America, their giggles, her smell, her wonderful smell. . . and he came face to face with Marty Shapiro.

Marty had entered the border bushes to look for a golf ball which he had putted off course. He was wearing a yellow knit shirt. His thick glasses gave him enlarged eyes. His watch alone could have paid for the year's study that was needed to help an impoverished foreigner acquire the skills necessary to get a good job and make a real living like a mensch at last.

Shaul looked right into his face.

*He looked right into my face, Rabbi, and I sensed nothing, not even his envy, that's how oblivious I had become to human emotions and the appeal of pain.*

Marty assumed that Shaul was the neighbor's gardener and asked if he had seen a yellow golf ball.

* * *

Having rented all three parts of "The Godfather," Shaul concluded that all the Italians in New York were Mafia, and that was why Lazard had been so afraid of Dominick Fabrizi. However, the Italians were honorable people — this could be clearly seen from Pacino's relationship with Brando's old retainers. You could make a deal with them, and if you kept your part of the bargain, they would be fair with you.

"This was my mistake!" Shaul announced. "I always thought of Fabrizi as the competition. When of course he is the natural ally of anyone who wants to take over the business of Lazard Goldberg."

Without telling Dominick, Shaul and Shimshon systematically called all of Lazard's customers and offered them drop-dead prices if they would switch to Fabrizi.

"What if Dominick can't make these prices?" Shimshon asked.

"Then we take the customers ourselves."

"But we haven't got a truck. . . ."

"If we get ten jobs, it'll be worth it to rent a truck."

Of course, Lazard immediately found out that Shaul and Shimshon were calling on his customers because his customers told him so. Trying to remain calm, he went to the beach, to shul, to the *schvitz* and then to a singles' dance where he picked up a nice woman. Only then did he take himself to the brothers' apartment.

Shaul seated him ceremoniously at a table, offered him beer and cookies. He fully expected that Lazard had come to make a deal.

"I gave you a job," Lazard said. "I gave your brother a job. You do nothing but make trouble for me, and when finally I am forced to break with you, you make more trouble. Why? Are you so top heavy with good buddies? You wanna be out there alone in the world without a friend? Please stop pushing me."

"Sure, okay, I'll back off," said Shaul. "But you've got to sell me 51% of your company."

Seeing that it was no use, Lazard drank down his beer.

"I was good to you," he said sadly. "You spit in my face."

"Don't take it personal," Shaul said. "Business is business." (He had heard it said in some movie.)

* * *

One morning Shaul and Shimshon showed up at Dominick's office, bearing half of Lazard's customers like a great gift and expecting to be rewarded.

"There's only one trouble, fellas," said Dominick. "I can't service these accounts for the prices you offered."

"You do it once, once is all, then you got the account forever," Shaul said.

"It doesn't really work that way," Dominick said. "Besides, I don't like people going out and speaking in my name without my knowledge and making me appear as a dishonorable man before my old competitor."

"You're making a mistake, Fabrizi," Shaul said.

"Oh yeah?"

"Because these customers have been taken away from Lazard now, and if you won't pick them up, I will."

"Oh yeah?"

"Come on, Fabrizi, work with me. . . "

Dominick's wife, a cute little woman who had not spoken previously, looked up from her desk. She was obviously upset. Her right eye slid slowly off to the outer edge of her face.

"Take yourself and your turd brother out of here before we have you flushed away," said Ellen Vanczek, the cross-eyed sex kitten of furniture moving.

And then Candy called from Oregon. She sounded drunk.

"Can you loan me and Shimshon some money?" Shaul asked her. "We want to go into business."

"I don't want to make a loan," she answered. "I want to make an investment."

Shaul covered the phone with his hand.

"What should I do?" he asked his brother.

"Give her what she wants," said Shimshon. "She's a housewife. How much trouble can she make?"

Shaul uncovered the phone.

"Candy? We're prepared to sell you 49% of our business."

Candy laughed raucously in Portland.

"Please, darling, try and shake off the grip of your ridiculous Levantine machismo and see things clearly for once. I know what I am doing, and you do not. I had a father who hired and fired drivers and schleppers every day and you did not. I know every woman on Long Island who is redecorating her house and you do not. I have money, and you do not, so I will own 100% of the business. In a couple of years, when we're in the black and I'm tired, you and Shimshon can think about buying me out. Meanwhile I run the company."

Shaul covered the phone with his hand.

"My mistake was that I always underestimated American women," he said. "Look at that Mrs. Fabrizi with her crossed eye rolling. I bet you anything, she's the one who's going to give the order to have us killed." (Israeli humor is like that, Heimlich told Eliezer AvShalom. Dark and grim and ghoulish.) "Okay, Candy," he said into the phone. "You've got a deal. But you have to promise to sleep with me."

★ ★ ★

Since his break with Danton, Marty no longer received so many invitations to French medical conferences. However, he had grown addicted to the calming effect of Odile's love, and he missed her terribly, and couldn't imagine continuing his life without her. So he invited her to New York.

She came in October, Manhattan's best month. He set her up in a small, luxurious hotel, gave her money to buy whatever she wanted, took her to dinner and the symphony. She fit in perfectly at those places he never went with Candy. At intermission in Carnegie Hall, she fell into a spirited argument with a perfect stranger about the relative merits of Yo Yo Ma and Jacqueline DuPre, and the man invited them to join him and his wife for a drink after the concert, and they had a wonderful time. Because of a connection through one of his patients, Marty brought her backstage at the ballet, and a great Danish dancer kissed her hand.

She knew just how to have her hand kissed, Odile. She was a cultured woman, a real lady, elegant, soft-spoken, wise.

She locked her long legs around him, warming his lungs. *"Reste avec moi,"* she said. *"Reste ici."* Misunderstanding as always, Marty stayed inside her as long as he could. But still he would not stay the night.

Even in his own city, among his own people, she sobbed to Danton, he would not stay the night.

*I lived in their guts, Rabbi, and I never understood them, not one of them, not even her, and I loved her so. . .*

★ ★ ★

Candy told him at breakfast that her theater business had been placed on hold, that she and Jock and Slim had passed on the New Haven show and were now looking for a new property. She was bored, she said. Needed something to do. So she had taken a part-time job in a moving company, called Achim Movers. Really it was just to put her back in a business situation so she could keep up with her secretarial skills.

Marty said fine, it was okay with him — even though she had not asked for his permission.

Suddenly, Candy was busier than ever before in her life. Busy busy rush rush gotta go gotta go notes on the refrigerator — "The BMW man called and said the tires have to be rotated and the oil changed. I'll be home by eleven. Don't wait up." — notes on the bedroom mirror — "I'm catching up on billing. Lots of other people with me in the office. Don't worry."

Had he ever waited up? Had he ever worried? For the first time, he thought maybe he should — but then he didn't.

Marty generally figured Candy for a secret eater, because she stayed *zaftig* despite the fact that she never ate in front of the family. Lately, however, even the pretense of dieting went out the window. She sat down at the table with the children and ate whole meals, with courses, and condiments, and dessert. He figured it was in the genetic cards. The wives of many men he knew were getting fat at forty.

At least twice a week, Candy would come home from work and pick up the kids and sometimes Marie as well and go shopping. She spent thousands and thousands of dollars that fall, on things like a canoe for the house she was planning to rent next summer by a lake in Vermont, and a grand piano for

Ethel who had seemed perfectly content with the spinet up to now, and the best stove in the world, fit for a great restaurant. (Its installation necessitated the reconstruction of the entire kitchen.) She bought "The Encyclopedia Britannica" and skis and cashmere sweaters and CD players for each of the kids. Marty told Odile that Candy had turned into some kind of materialist machine. When she finished with the newspaper, he noticed, it was inevitably folded to the financial section. Reminded him of the wife in a Saul Bellow novel he had once read long ago, when he still had time to read fiction.

As if her new business didn't keep her sufficiently occupied, Candy now plunged into Carol O'Banyon's campaign for Congress with an energy that Marty thought bordered on the pathological. As a kick-off, she threw a fund-raiser at Nat and Angie Lichtman's house. The normally cool Angie seemed nervous, and constantly beckoned him to join her for a secret talk in the pantry. Naturally he didn't go. Nothing was better forgotten than their moment of passion in the Pierre (or was it the Park Lane?)

To make matters worse, Carol fawned on Candy, draping her long, graceful arms around Candy's shoulders and introducing her as "The Suburban Superwoman" to gallery owners and retauranteurs and fashion critics.

"Come on, Carol," Marty whispered. "Give it a rest."

"What's the matter, Herr Doktor? Afraid that your wife might learn to enjoy not being treated like a helpless JAP?"

"Don't insult me, Carol. I'm the one who wrote the check."

"I'll be sure to tell Candy you said that."

She laughed and kissed him to show that she was not serious.

One morning at the beginning of December, he backed out of the garage, past the basket of clothes Candy always collected to bring to the homeless shelter, where she was now a member of the board. In the basket was the briefcase from

Paris. It still had the tags on it. Marty had never really noticed that Candy had not used the briefcase. . . but now that he saw it ignominiously piled on top of Ethel's old sweaters, he became irritated. Just because Candy didn't share Odile's excellent taste didn't mean that the pretty leather thing should go directly to the destitute! Marty grabbed it and took it to the hospital.

It just so happened that the hospital administrator was having a birthday that week. So Marty had his receptionist wrap the suitcase lavishly and present it to the administrator as a gift. She was thrilled, and shocked. The staff cafeteria buzzed. Something wonderful was happening to Dr. Shapiro!

★ ★ ★

Why did Candy turn into a materialist machine that autumn? Why did she immerse herself in a (now clearly losing) political campaign and eat like six horses and throw away her husband's gifts? Because with his persistent blindness, his need to distract himself, to be a pasha like his father and parade his women openly, to feel *free,* Marty had made Candy precisely what she had so desperately desired not to be: a topic of conversation at everybody's lunch.

"It was the husband I met first," said Carol O'Banyon while eating a four lettuce salad at Crunchies on the Upper East Side. "He was swimming around the reef in the Gulf of Aqaba and so was I, and the sight of his wrist with one those sort of electric green underwater watches on it really turned me on. But of course, my husband Frank was alive then so the only place I could even entertain a lascivious thought was underwater."

Her friends giggled. They had just come from a low impact aerobics class. They were a television executive who knew Spunky Pruitt; a celebrity journalist who knew Roxie Kirsch; an interior decorator who often employed the Lazard Cares Moving Company.

These accomplished women had seen Candy at fundraisers for Carol's campaign. But she didn't live in Manhattan or summer in the Hamptons or Westport or go to their gym, so they didn't really know anything about her except that she was one of those JAP suburbanites with lots of money and awful taste. The only reason they remembered her name was that nobody else they had ever known personally was called Candy.

They were in their 50s, healthy, slender, attractive and, each in her way, an important person, well-known among people who mattered. The younger women who worked for them admired them and wanted to become them. But just at that time of life when they felt most needful of it and most entitled to it, these women were not having a whole hell of a lot of good sex. And so they looked forward to a salacious story, which they could tell was coming because of the leer on Carol O'Banyon's thin lips and the wicked tapping of her nails on her glass of papaya juice.

"Well," Carol continued in her titillating drawl. "So it's evening in Eilath. We are all gathered on one of those incredible terraces overlooking the sea which make you think you're in Cannes with the transvestites instead of in hell with the Israelis. . . "

"Oh Carol. . . " they laughed.

"And Dr. Shapiro turned out to be a completely humorless gynecologist whose charms stopped at his great wristbones. — Could I have a plain seltzer with lemon, Lulu? Don't give me some fancy water. Just plain seltzer. — And suddenly out of the desert comes the wife. Candice Shapiro The Suburban Superwoman. With the earrings and the boots and the matching this and that, but covered with dust and sweat, she actually stank! She had gone off to Sinai on a bus with no air conditioning and no shocks to look at battlefields. You should have seen the husband! He was so embarrassed."

Carol squeezed her lemon into her seltzer and drank.

"Mmm," she said, enjoying the little bubbles. "Cuts the grease."

"So what happened?" asked the interior decorator who sometimes used Lazard Cares.

"So then Frank died and I could finally escape from Washington and move to New York. And from the moment I arrive here, some strange woman from Long Island is plying me with gifts and invitations, driving me absolutely crazy with her attentions, because for some reason she thinks I am her friend. And it turns out to be Candy Shapiro.

"She gets me to address her Hadassah group in Broadbeach. Of course I resist, but she is incredibly persistent. And in the end, I'm glad I did it because I have helped Candy raise an unprecedented amount of money for the Russian Jews. I mean, this is a good woman. Concerned with the environment, the destitute, the peace of neighborhoods, a woman with political convictions. So despite the beads on her sweaters, I make her co-chair of my finance committee."

The television producer who knew Spunky Pruitt was getting nervous.

"Shit, something's gonna happen with the husband. . . I can feel it. . . don't tell me I don't want to hear. . . "

"I go to the BAM opening of the Osaka Company's 'Trojan Women' in October," Carol continued. "And who do I see there but Dr. Shapiro? He's with a charming Frenchwoman. She's hanging on his arm, nibbling at his silver temples. . . "

"Oh Carol. . . " they laughed.

"Of course I hide, I duck, I hug the shadows and thank God, he's so engrossed in his girlfriend that he doesn't see me."

"I really don't want to hear any more," said the interior decorator, and she started to go.

"Wait. It gets worse," Carol laughed.

So how could the decorator resist? She sat back down.

"The next month I go to Paris to buy some clothes," Carol continued, "and who do I see at Scaasi but my old friend, the most charming fabulous man, I adore him, Dr. Danton Moore. I swear there wasn't a pair of tits in the place that Danton hadn't personally sculpted. And who was he with? The very same Frogette who had appeared so mad for Dr. Shapiro at BAM. And what was she wearing? A loose fitting cotton frock that barely concealed the pronounced swelling in the front of her body."

The celebrity journalist who knew Roxie Kirsch winced and said: "This is not a funny story."

"My reaction exactly," Carol continued. "Whose baby is this? I ask myself. Is the co-chair of my finance committee being outbred by a combination of sawbones? Suddenly I am filled with sisterly solidarity for the Queen of Russian Jewish Resettlement. And so when I get back to New York, I call Candy Shapiro."

"You didn't tell her!" cried the interior decorator. "You didn't tell the poor woman!"

"Of course, I didn't tell her, what do you take me for? I'm telling *you* but I wouldn't tell *her!*"

"Oh Carol. . . " they laughed.

"And we have lunch," Carol said. "Candy eats steak for lunch! Can you imagine?! No wonder she's built like a panda.

"But never mind. She wants to talk. She needs to unburden her heart. She tells me that her husband is an inveterate philanderer and she's heard from people she knows that he has now brought his current mistress to New York and she's feeling extremely pissed.

"Leave him! I cry. Take him for everything! Make him suffer for his sins!

"Well, she looks this way and that way, and when she's satisfied we aren't being overheard, she leans forward and says: [Carol tried to imitate Candy's brittle whine but somehow it didn't come out so funny this time.] 'It's cheaper to get revenge than to get divorced, and a lot easier on the children. So I have invested in a moving company. It's a young moving company. It's strong and lively and hungry. It's very moving.'"

*I keep wondering Rabbi, if I had known about him, if I had known that she was bragging about him to her friends, screwing him in my bed, would I have cared? I guess she was trying to get my attention. . . but nobody carried the message to me. . . nobody said 'Hey Shapiro! Look!' I guess because nobody blamed her.*

"So you see, girls," concluded Carol O'Banyon, "in case you are ever overwhelmed with pity for these poor women from the suburbs with their charities and car-pools and cheating spouses, think upon Candice Shapiro and save your pity for the poor."

★ ★ ★

On Hannukah, Candy and Marie made a feast that went down in the history of the Broadbeach Jews as the most splendid and celebratory of its kind ever.

They made gefilte fish from scratch, its jellied sauce floating with red onions and tinged with curry. They found fresh ducks and stuffed them with wild rice and glazed them with mandarin oranges. Their potato latkes ought really to have been called potato souffles because of their incomparable lightness (Maida confided to Belle that the secret ingredient was seltzer water. "Don't tell!" she whispered.) Golden wax beans and sugar snaps frozen fresh from last summer's garden were mingled with sun-dried tomatoes and capers and arranged on wreaths of curly endive. The guests refreshed their palates with a little brandy and coffee. An hour or so after the main courses had been finished, Candy served long coffee breads braided with apples and honey and a chocolate cake which was so high and light and fancifully decorated with burnt sugar snowflakes that Little Sam took a picture of it with the new camera Jock and Slim had bought for him and sent the picture in to a "Beautiful Food" contest and won his first award for anything.

The guest list included Marty's lawyer, Phil Brinks, and his wife Virginia and their two children, Dick and Charlotte Glick and their four children, four Soviet immigrants with five more children, a couple of homesick Israeli brothers named Shaul and Shimshon who ran the moving company where Candy now worked.

The kids were happy to see Shaul. They called him The Funny Israeli Moving Man. They asked him to do tricks. He demurred, for he was apparently a shy fellow embarrassed by his lack of facility in English. He and his brother left early.

For the first time Marty could recall, Roxie Kirsch did not show. She and Candy had fought about something. The absence of the familiar aunt-like figure might have upset the children except that, miraculously, in keeping with the spirit of the holiday, Roxie had been replaced by Alex's wife, Belle.

The return of Alex Deal to Long Island involved maybe twenty minutes of nervous anxiety before becoming a forgive-and-forget festival. Alex lost his fear. He kissed Candy and hugged her and didn't tell anybody that she had attacked him. Candy went along with that. In the days preceeding Hannukah, she had gotten to know her sister-in-law Belle, a woman so kind and good natured that it would have been unthinkable to make her suffer any more by catching her in the sibling crossfire. Therefore, throughout the evening, Candy repeatedly checked her reflection in the mirrored cabinets, fixing her make-up, composing her face, and packed away her anger with all the rest of her stuff.

Everybody loved Belle, and she loved Broadbeach. She toured the town with her three freckled kids, stretched out on the leather sofas listening to Candy's Broadway show CDs. Maida took her shopping in stores for over-sized women, wanting to buy her things. However, Belle would accept no money, only advice. She showered Maida with daughterly attention, which included enrolling herself and her boys (the girl wouldn't go; everybody understood) in a class for converts to Judaism. She won over Ethel when she displayed her autographed collection of every single song Alisette Legrand had ever recorded. She seemed to be leading Alex back into the family, covering his reluctance and his embarrassment with her enthusiasm. Everybody welcomed her except Aunt Terry who said she was just a shiksa gold digger trying to get her brats into Maida's will before it was too late.

Maida didn't think so, and even if it were true, she wouldn't have cared. She had her boy back, her Alex, the sensitive sweet sad funny one. All through the great Hannukah dinner, she did not let go of his hand.

★ ★ ★

Roxie Kirsch refused to attend the dinner, because she said it was "an obscene charade." Candy defended herself with righteous ferocity.

"He brought her here! To my city!" Candy raged. "Slim and Jock saw them on 56th Street! Your friend the journalist told you that Carol O'Banyon saw them at BAM! So when I was pouring out my heart to her, she was keeping her mouth shut to spare my feelings, but she already knew. . . *she already knew!*"

"Aha!" said Roxie. "That's why you're so upset! The Great O'Banyon knows! Well, big fucking deal."

"I don't understand you," Candy protested. "You're the mega-feminist. You say: be strong, Candy; people need you; don't get divorced, get revenge. And when I really get it, in Marty's house, according to Marty's rules, you say, oh well, I didn't mean for you to go that far, Candy, gee whiz golly, buying enough cashmere sweaters for the next forty years is okay but inviting Shaul to dinner, now that's really dishonorable."

Roxie winced. "But it is," she said wanly. "It is dishonorable to parade your lover in front of your husband in front of your children and so I am boycotting your dinner!"

"You'd rather be alone on Hannukah?" Candy asked her old friend. "You'd rather stand at your kitchen counter and eat tuna fish out of a can? You don't want to meet this terrific Russian chemist I thought you might like? So all right. Stay home and object to the way I parade my lover. At least I've got a lover."

Roxie staggered from that blow. "Bought and paid for!" she yelled.

"Yeah yeah," said Candy, "So what else is new?" She heaved herself into her new ankle-length shearling coat. "The trouble with you liberals is that you can't handle victory. That's why you never really put up a good fight to the death. Because you're afraid you'll win."

★ ★ ★

The Hannukah feast was one of those occasions when Marty Shapiro knew he had done the right thing by marrying Candy. He loved the way the board groaned and the feastless came to feast at his table. He loved the honor.

Candy looked especially beautiful. She wore a low-cut black dress. Her cheeks glowed from the heat of the cooking. After dinner, she presented each of the children with a small embroidered sack containing hundreds of pennies, including some Israeli ones and incidentally some French change she had gathered from Marty's pockets over the past year. With these "chips", the kids played a spirited game of *dreidle* on the living room coffee table. One of the Russians who was now making his living as a garage mechanic sat down at the new piano and played Rachmaninoff's greatest hits. Then Ethel sang Richard Rogers.

"Marty!" exclaimed Dick Glick. "Get this kid a vocal coach! You've really got something here!"

That night, as Candy stood in the bathroom, braiding her hair, Marty approached her from behind and kissed her.

"I am so proud of you," he said, expecting her to smile and bask and warm and rise like bread as she usually did when he made the first move. Instead, she turned to face him and kissed him hard with her teeth bared. He backed away, startled. She pulled down her bra so that her breasts lunged out at him. He turned his back.

She laughed. "No foreplay?" she said derisively. "You just want to fuck, hanh? Well okay. . . "

She reached into a drawer in the bathroom commode and pulled out a package of Trojans.

"Don't be ridiculous," he said.

"Why not? You're a surgeon. You travel a great deal and you operate on a lot of women and they have complex lives and you wallow in their blood. It seems only sensible for you to wear a condom. I'm afraid I must insist."

He became very angry. It was her tone.

"What is this 'I'm afraid I must insist' crap?! Who do you think you are, Margaret Thatcher?!"

"Oh please, don't get all self-righteous and superior. All I asked you to do was wear a condom."

"You're such an idiot, Candy. Gee! Do you really believe I am like other men? I know everything that is going on in my body. My blood is so pure, you could bathe a baby in there and he'd come out smelling like Ivory."

She wouldn't budge.

"I don't want to have sex with you unless you wear a condom."

"Bullshit! You just don't want to have sex! You're like an old JAP joke from Sigma Alpha Mu! 'Gee, that whore was dead, Mister.' — 'No kidding! I thought she was Candy Shapiro!'"

And so it ended.

*Before my eyes, Rabbi, I swear, she turned to stone.*

The old joke finished it for her. It was being the star of the joke that she just couldn't bear any longer.

She wiped off her make-up. She washed her face. Her skin looked sallow and blotchy at the same time. The tight underwear had left red creases on her flesh. Her heavy thighs were puckered. She had stretch marks on her hips. She was about to be forty years old.

"I'm really tired, Marty. Why don't we just call it a day?"

"What?"

"Let's get a divorce."

"Candy?"

"I figured I could take it as long as it was just women and they kept changing, I figured you were under a lot of pressure and I'd be sophisticated and hang in and sort of inherit in the end what was supposed to have been mine all along. But then you brought her to New York and people who know me saw you with her. I mean I'm not such an important woman that I can withstand public humiliation. And now you're raising another family. So I can't manage it any more. I don't want to feel bad any more. I want a divorce."

Marty steadied himself against the bathroom door.

"What are you talking about?"

Just from observing his expression, Candy suddenly realized that, thanks to the watchdogs of Orpheo, she had found out about Odile's pregnancy before Marty, and this caused her to laugh loudly and openly, without covering her mouth.

★ ★ ★

In the tiny chapel in Brooklyn where she went on her day off, Marie de Grenouille de Port-au-Prince kept a picture of Odile Ste. Jacques which was now electric with prayers of ill favor.

Marie had nothing against Odile. She cursed her as a matter of loyalty to Candy. Before Candy had taken her in, she had lived in America illegally for three years, hiding like a ferret, never signing her name. Back home, there was nothing but terror. Her father had been killed; her husband was a hunted man. Candy made her legal and safe and paid her well enough so that she could bring over her children, and when one of her husband's enemies tried to kill her, Candy had saved her life.

Had Candy realized that the assassin would gladly have killed her in his next breath after killing Marie? Did she have any idea how dangerous it was to attack him? Marie thought not. Candy seemed never to have had any experience with bad people; she had no knowledge of evil. She did what was necessary with a kind of clear-cut courage, as though she expected God or something to protect her.

She was not stupid, Marie explained to her children in Brooklyn. She was just ignorant.

Marie felt that she owed her life to Candy Shapiro, it was that simple. So she welcomed the young Israeli workman who brought Candy so much happiness unlike the cold, exhausted husband. And when Candy wept about the Frenchwoman, it touched Marie's heart, and for Candy's sake, she summoned all her powers to confound Odile's hopes and destroy her future.

★ ★ ★

Far away in Ojai, Marty's old girlfriend Cecily, now Vice President of a different record company, sat weeping in Harold's beaded parlor. She laid the lapis bracelet on his little table. She spoke of how Marty had used her and then left her, without even an explanation, for his wife, no less, his wife whom he had ridiculed and called idiot, he went back to his wife and his children, leaving her alone in Hollywood with only this damned bracelet to remember him by. And every time she went to sell it, she couldn't. Because it was the only thing she had to remind her that she had ever had any long relationship with any man at all. If only Harold would give her access to an evil wish, she pleaded, then perhaps something terrible would happen to Marty Shapiro, something really terrible to pay him back for the heartbreak he had caused.

Well, of course Harold threw her out.

"I am a psychic, not a witch!" he yelled.

However, Marie was a witch.

And there was a witch up in the hills named Evelyn who gladly sold curses to these poor souls from the entertainment industry. "What the hell," she explained to Harold. "How can it hurt? The accursed is safe because the curses don't work. The cursee gets some comfort from having vented all that hatred; and I make a living."

Thus when Marty Shapiro went to Paris in the late winter after the great Hannukah feast, the spirit of falsehood which Evelyn had conjured and the spirit of loyalty which Marie represented flew alongside him in the sky.

He went to break off the affair. He wanted out, he said. He was really sorry that Odile had decided to become pregnant, he said, without asking first, without discussing, then without telling, so that his wife should be able to find out even before he knew. He was so mad, his jaw was so tight, that he could barely speak.

"All that it means is that you underestimated Candice," Odile said gently. "You spoke of her as though she had no importance and presented no danger, and look, she is like the Central Intelligence Agency, the Brigatta Rossi, the wrath of God."

Odile, who was now five months pregnant, confessed that she had not told him earlier because she did want to hear him ask her to have an abortion. She wanted the baby regardless of his role in her life. More than anything she wanted to have a child to make her imprint on the world. Although she herself had tested HIV positive, Odile knew there was some chance that the child would be born healthy, and that she would be able to spend perhaps a few years with the child before she died, and she could not think of anything more important than that.

"Forget it," she said. "It is not your problem. Very likely, it is not your child. What is important is that you are not sick, and your wife and your patients are not in danger. I have friends to keep me, and a mother who will always love me, and I shall be able to manage everything."

★ ★ ★

Marty called Danton repeatedly. The maid kept saying he was busy, he would call back, but he never did. Was he still angry that Marty had refused to join him in the St. Maarten project? Was Adrine angry that Odile was pregnant? Did it present some embarrassment to her in some remote Parisian social way? Finally Marty just went to the office. The beautiful flower-filled pink waiting room was not only empty but dusty. The nurse said Danton was at home.

Marty went there. The maid said Danton was out. Marty pushed her out of the way and strode into the living room, calling Danton's name.

The apartment was dark. Where were the one-of-a-kind goblets? What had happened to the rugs, the heaps of Oriental rugs — *pied paradis?* The place seemed so empty; had everything been sent out for cleaning? And it smelled not like Paris but like some pungent Eastern city; the sour bite of cumin hung heavy in the air.

Adrine was in the kitchen with her aunts. Like them, she wore a big wraparound apron and a scarf to cover her hair. They were making *sarma* for a large family gathering. Hundreds of grape leaves. Pounds of rice. Danton sat at the kitchen table, a napkin tucked into his shirt at the neck. He was thin. And his skin had a grayish coloration. And he coughed. He was reading the newspapers, and he wore half glasses which made him look old. It was as though Paris had disappeared around him, and he was now living in exile, his life controlled by women jabbering in an exotic language.

He did not rise to greet Marty. After all, when you have given a terrible disease to a man's mistress, it would be insensitive to maintain an automatic cordiality.

Adrine explained that Marty had been quite right to eschew investment of money or time in the St. Maarten clinic for it was now doomed, clearly didn't have a prayer of completion, already the tendrils of the jungle reached for it to squeeze out the last drop of life.

"It was the roads," she said. "Some instability in the ground made the road beds impossible to finalize. Springs bubbled up everywhere; there was no controlling the water table. Sudden torrential downpours would eradicate a week's work on the mountainsides."

"And what about the thievery?! And the incompetence!" Danton interjected. *"Ah Dieu,* these blacks are ineducable! They have no concept of private property or the obligations of a salaried job, even after centuries of tutorial French rule!"

Adrine sent him to his room.

"My husband should never have spoken ill of the blacks," she wept. "They must have heard him. They must have made a doll, and on the face, in red letters, they must have painted his name, and then they must have stuck the doll with needles already infected with plague. Otherwise, how could he have caught it? How could he have caught it, Martin? Such a healthy man, so strong and smart?

"Perhaps the Jews took a vote in their synagogue and decided by a majority to pray for his death. After all, he is a terrible anti-Semite, everybody knows that, a racist and an anti-Semite. Perhaps this plague was wished on him. How else could he have caught it? Such a strong, smart man. . . a physician. . . Monsieur Printemps. . . *ammann. . .*

"Perhaps it was the homosexuals. So many of them were angry at him. They said he led them on with his style and his looks, his flirtatious looks. Perhaps they put something in his tea."

Marty held her tight. Dark rings engraved her eyes. She was shaking. Her aunts muttered and fluttered their hands.

"How could he have endangered his patients and his colleagues this way? How could he have endangered me this way?!" Adrine cried.

She had herself tested. She was fine. Lucky that she always insisted that Danton use a condom. One could not be too careful after all, when one was the wife of a surgeon and a notorious philanderer.

★ ★ ★

There is a point when no more blame can be laid on any head. And the sharp rap of tragedy on the door seems to come finally from nowhere, from out of the blue, arbitrary and random. Maybe somebody forgot to mark the door with the blood of the lamb and the Angel of Death did not know, therefore, to pass over. Maybe the twin spirits of loyalty and falsehood really can be conjured by mere women, and they met over the rooftops of Paris and collided, and smashing each other's atoms, created catastrophe.

Marty did not return from Paris. He attended lectures, haunted the obstetrical labs, imaging the virus and cursing it as Marie and Cecily had cursed Odile, same technique, same old religion.

Women in America, told that Dr. Shapiro would be honing his skills abroad for some months, put off their surgeries if they dared and otherwise assigned themselves to the capable hands of Harry Wang.

"You are much missed," he wrote to Marty.

"We're doing fine without you, Dad, don't worry about a thing," wrote Little Sam. Shaul had taught him how to build a wooden box. They were going to a soccer game together. He was learning Hebrew.

"Too bad you couldn't come to my concert," Ethel wrote with a poisoned pen. "But Uncle Jock and Uncle Slim came, and they wore tuxedos, and they sent me roses like I was a star. And Shaul sat with Mom so everybody thought he was my new father."

And all the while, he attended on this woman who didn't need him or want him, in this hospital where he was not authorized to practice, in this country he despised, waiting for the birth of a child who might not have been his anyway.

Odile did not let Marty see the little boy. The minute she knew, she rose from her bed and went into the nursery and killed the child and killed herself. She never even said goodbye to her mother.

# PART III

CHAPTER THIRTEEN

# ENTERTAINER

SEVENTEEN PEOPLE DEPENDED FOR THEIR LIVELIHOOD on the talent of Alisette Legrand. And that did not include Jimbo and Ali, Grandma Blanche (now hospitalized, sometimes senile), the Detroit Free People's Emergency Loan Fund, the All Saints Liberation Baptist Church of Southfield Building Fund and Megaman Brancusi himself, he did real well off Alisette's singing for a while there.

The accountants and the public relations people, the happy-go-lucky major domo at her home in Detroit, the dedicated housekeeper at her home in Malibu, her personal assistant Kisha who helped her dress and answer the mail and keep her appointments, the lawyers, the producers, the musicians and the back-up singers, all of these people supported Alisette's career, seeking to fulfill her vision of how her act should play and what mood and message her records should convey. They called themselves her friends. Close as kin, they said. But she knew they listened to the vibrations in the stage to detect any weakening of the applause, and that if she should begin to fail, the swiftness of their departure would probably stop up her ears. She took pride in her reality fix. . . and loved them all anyway.

Meanwhile she guaranteed her security with wise investments in stocks and tax-free municipals and real estate. She owned a couple of other condos down the beach on the Pacific which she rented out with ease. She had an interest in a great steak house for vacationers on Michigan's Upper Peninsula. Any other singer who wanted to perform one of her songs paid plenty for the privilege. That was Megaman Brancusi's doing. Alisette herself would gladly have given away her creations free of charge, a small enough contribution, she figured, for the satisfaction of having them interpreted.

Megaman lectured her incessantly about the necessity for artistic distance. He supported the moat of blindness between audience and performer that was created by lights and microphones and make-up and public relations.

Alisette knew he was probably right.

Still, whenever she could be sure Megaman wasn't looking, she walked out among the people and encouraged them to sing along, and in her dreams, she sang naked, with her heart on the outside of her body.

⋆ ⋆ ⋆

A girl named Lettie who had seen Alisette on the night of the tsunami in Atlantic City applied for a job as Megaman's personal secretary. The events of that night had changed her life. She had blown off her high-flying, man-crazy friends, finished a business course at the top of her class, quit her hospital job in Paterson and migrated to California. For almost 18 months now, she had bided her time in two different entertainment industry organizations, all the while pressing her application at Brancusi Management, in case something should come up, and it finally had. She had finally achieved her goal, which was to meet up with Alisette, her idol, once again.

Like Alisette, Lettie could not remember one word of what Heimlich had said that night.

"Some sort of mumbo jumbo," she reported to Megaman at her interview. "But I tell you, Mr. Brancusi, that comic would be dead today if it was not for Miss Legrand, and that's the truth. I saw it with my own eyes. He was attacked by the devil. Hell was coming out of his head. And she stood at the river of fire with her arms outstretched so that poor man's soul could not be carried over, and that was how she saved his life."

Megaman rocked back in his maroon leather executive swing chair and ho-ho'ed like Santa Claus. Here was this spiffy little girl from Jersey, had a body like Shari and 200 words a minute on the machine, talking devil and rivers of fire, just like his Aunt Delia doing her religion in the chicken coop. Incredible! Instead of passing away like other antiquated foolishness, the old religion had hung on, propagated by these crazy damn women. It looked like the old ones had taught the young ones, and now the black ones were teaching the white ones. Megaman knew an otherwise tough-minded agent named Spunky Pruitt who wore a crystal on a chain around her neck, like the Barbadian women from the projects used to wear herbs and stones, to ward off evil, and she sent other intelligent females like Maxine the drummer and Kisha, Alisette's assistant, up to Ojai to buy curses and blessings from some faggot swami they all thought could tell them the future!

Megaman hated superstition. He hated the old world, the chicken coop, the projects. He would never have hired this Lettie except that she sounded like a New Yorker on the phone, which lent class to an L.A. office, and she never forgot anything, even Megaman's dentist appointments and the safe places he put things so they would never be lost. Besides, Alisette interceded for her with tender pleadings, like the Virgin Mary. How could he resist?

Just about the time that Lettie came to work for Brancusi Management, Alisette once again mounted her campaign to spend the whole summer up in the mountains of the north, singing at Aunt Dorothy's. She had first heard about this place years before, from Joan at a charity luncheon. Joan said that she had loved playing Aunt Dorothy's, that she would gladly give up Vegas to go back. She described a capacious shed among the redwoods, with the best sight lines and acoustics of any comparable club in the west. The performance space, she said, was set in the middle of the floor. Its multilevel design allowed for unlimited varieties of stagings. The audience gathered around in a horseshoe-shaped embankment of semi-circular tables. There was room to dance in the aisles.

Paul had played Aunt Dorothy's before "Graceland;" Billy Joel before "Allentown." Eric told Alisette at a party at Quincy's one night that once when he was playing Aunt Dorothy's, he had noticed Bjorn and Benny in the audience and had asked them to come up and sing some of the songs from their forthcoming Broadway musical. You could do that kind of thing there, he said. The management didn't freak if you blew your regular program. Maybe it was the mind-expanding freshness of the air, Eric conjectured, and the towering trees.

Most importantly, a very attractive drummer named Nacoochee told Alisette after a concert in Atlanta, Orpheo Pastafino's people ran the place with the same efficiency you could count on at the Imperial Hotel in Atlantic City. There were never any bothersome drunks, never any waiters who didn't get their tables cleared before the opening chords. The mob at the dressing room door had always been picked over by Orpheo's men, only the very best apples in the barrel had been selected, Nacoochee said, so you didn't have to worry that your ex-wife was gonna come and shoot you after the show 'cause of you not paying child support for sixteen years.

A gaffer on a movie for which Alisette had recorded the soundtrack told her that because of a brilliantly planned intersection of angles above the stage at Aunt Dorothy's, the lights did not blind the performer! If ever she sang there, he assured her, she would be able to look into the eyes of the smallest person in the last row.

For Alisette, this was the ultimate temptation. She believed the stories about the lighting at Aunt Dorothy's because she had seen Orpheo Pastafino's subtly illuminated office/apartment in the skies above Atlantic City. She herself had waxed hyperbolic about those halogen globes concealed by white ceramic hands.

"Miracle lighting!" she had raved to Megaman.

He nodded appreciatively. However, Alisette knew he really thought she must be exaggerating. He was strictly a bottom-liner. So Aunt Dorothy's, where a six week gig got you just about as much as Alisette could earn for one weekend in Vegas, was out of the question.

Since Megaman wouldn't call Orpheo, Alisette did. From Detroit. At Christmastime. Told him she'd be real interested in a long summer run at what she heard was the best club in the Rockies.

Orpheo immediately told Megaman about Alisette's call; an act of solidarity, one businessman to another. Megaman sighed. She was getting to be quite a pain in the butt. Knowing that Megaman had been placed in a difficult position, Orpheo offered to forget the whole thing. But since they were already speaking, Orpheo really did want Megaman to know that he'd be happy to have Alisette headline at Aunt Dorothy's all through August, when the eccentric woodlands nightclub attracted a weekend crowd that came for the hiking, the rafting or the Shakespeare Festival nearby and then went home, a constantly changing crowd suitable for a long run by one artist. He promised to provide Alisette with a luxuriously appointed lodge on the edge of the great pine forest. It came with a pool and a hot tub and a sauna, as well as a woman to cook and clean and her husband to fix and drive and guard the premises. Alisette's sons could come and try the whitewater rafting, the spelunking, the exhilarating high of camping under the stars. She could write her songs and give her well-known parties, and Megaman himself could enjoy a luxurious vacation.

Megaman thanked Orpheo, who was not the sort of guy you wanted to treat ungraciously. However, he said, he had plans for Alisette to be in L.A. during the summer. So Orpheo offered Megaman Thanksgiving weekend for Alisette at the Imperial Hotel and Casino, which had been completely refurbished in the two seasons since the great tidal wave.

"You gonna have that little Jew comic there again?" asked Megaman.

"You mean Heimlich? I hear he's finished, hasn't worked since that night. Think about my offer. Call me next week."

In his tan marble office in Century City with the maroon tweed velvet crush carpet and the Swedish crystal bar set, Megaman lit a cigar to regain the sense of self-importance he still immediately lost at the mere mention of Heimlich's name. He was ashamed at himself for never having given Alisette the letters from Heimlich which arrived periodically, letters which would have informed Alisette that Heimlich was close by, only a couple of hours from the city, so close as to be almost touching all their lives.

He calmed himself with a glass of Chivas.

Maybe Alisette had managed to get back in touch with Heimlich herself.

Maybe the reason she wanted to spend six weeks earning squat in Nowheresville was that she expected Heimlich to join her there.

Bitch, thought Megaman, drinking.

★ ★ ★

When Alisette heard that Megaman had torpedoed her gig at Aunt Dorothy's, she had a major shit fit. The big German shepherd Hansie, whom Megaman employed to terrify and, if need be, disembowel prowlers, got so scared by her screaming and carrying on that he ran into the neighbor's pool house and wouldn't come out until Lettie fixed him a chopped sirloin with onions.

It was the morning on which Alisette was supposed to start recording the soundtrack for a major Hollywood movie. This movie had already fallen a couple of weeks behind schedule. With huge, state-of-the-art studios rented and 43 contract musicians waiting, with Bo Tye on the telephone yelling "Give the woman what she wants and get her ass over here!", with the agent who represented the producers on the other phone icily reminding Megaman that his client had a contract which he, Megaman, had personally negotiated (months of negotiations!), Alisette hurled her breakfast tray at the door to her bedroom, sending Kisha and the current housekeeper running for their lives.

The housekeeper promptly quit.

Alisette slammed the door shut and shoved the bedroom dressers in front of it, so nobody could even get in by picking the lock, and she hunkered herself down under the scarlet satin sheets, with her fat mouth narrowed to a minus sign, and refused to come out of the bed.

Megaman called Orpheo and said okay to Aunt Dorothy's. So then she got dressed and went to work.

He never spoke to Alisette about her mutiny, not for all the ensuing months of that profitable year. Right up to the night before she left for Orgeon, he kept his silence.

Alisette waited until after he was finished, when he was wet and weak, struggling to catch his breath, and then she figured it was the right time to say: "You're not still mad about this summer, are you?"

He laughed and heaved his arm over her body.

"Hell no, sweet thing, I love having my decisions overruled by you. I love being humiliated in front of earless ginny gunrunners. So does my dog. It's very often more fun than we can fucking stand."

★ ★ ★

Aunt Dorothy's existed because Orpheo Pastafino had visited the beautiful mountains thereabout when his wife died, to go hiking and breathe the unadulterated air. Those who knew him could not believe he had decided to take such a trip. His last nights in a tent had been spent on an island in the Pacific Ocean in the early 1940s, and he had often sworn that he would never wish to replicate one moment of that experience.

However, Dorothy's death altered his resolve.

In the final weeks of her life, his sweet Dorothy had grown cruel. She had hurled down anathema upon her surroundings, the house she lived in, the hotels she had vacationed in from Cape Cod to Florida to Cuba and Cannes, the women she had been forced to spend her life with and their husbands, Orpheo's friends and associates. With her mouth all twisted, she maligned the Italians. She had always hated their food, she snapped, their disgusting, oily peppers and their skinny, ugly bread, good only for mopping up the gallons of tomato sauce they so dearly loved to gobble because it reminded them of the gallons of blood they so dearly loved to shed. Most of all she hated Orpheo, hated his fluffy, fly-away hair, his mutilated hands, the way he hummed Sinatra while reading the morning papers.

She hated his children. If she only had the strength, she said, she would gladly murder her own sons just for looking so much like him and sharing his despicable values: these were the kinds of things Dorothy said at the end.

The doctor assured Orpheo that her horrible tirades were brought on by the disease which had eaten into her brain, and the drugs she was being given to ease her pain. Orpheo believed the doctor. He understood, he really did. However, the places where he might have sought comfort in his bereavement were now cursed for him by Dorothy. An *aficionado* of beaches, he felt robbed of Cape Cod and

Cannes. When he just stayed home and read the papers, he caught himself humming "I Get a Kick Out of You" and that made him feel bad. So he stopped humming. But then he couldn't read the papers.

She had attacked the unconscious details of his everyday life. He couldn't comb his hair now without thinking of how thoroughly she loathed the way he combed his hair. He was at a loss.

After the funeral, when Orpheo was with his family and friends, deaf to the small talk, deaf from his unhappiness — thirty-five years after all; one woman; thirty-five years — Candy Deal Shapiro sat down next to him and took his hand.

"It's me, Uncle Fayo," she murmured. "Candy. What can I do for you?"

She smelled wonderful. Her gentle eyes concentrated on his well-being.

"Tell me how I can forget the angry things your Aunt Dorothy said to me in her last days," he answered with a sad smile, as hopelessly as Maida requesting the resurrection her darling Sam, never expecting that there would be a response.

Candy thought for a minute.

"Go where Aunt Dorothy never was," she said. "And do things there that you never did with her. So that you can relax and think about her without also thinking of anything she was angry at. And you can remember her as she was before she got so sick and crazy."

Thus it came about that Orpheo Pastafino, at the age of 62, bought himself some gear and flew west to the Orgeon Coastal Range and rented a car and went camping. He pitched a tent and shivered in the night cold. He made fires and cooked for himself. His gray beard grew. His cream-softened palms reverted to the hardness of their early years. He almost killed himself a couple of times because he drove so fast on the hair-pin turns above the plunging hollows while being blinded by memories. His Peggy Lee tapes attracted owls. They stuck around all night, screeching. At dawn, he watched fascinated as a family of wild goats scaled the sheer wall of a mountain, foraging fearlessly above the canyons. With reverence and respect, he tiptoed past a bear so as not to disturb him while he ate his lunch of freshwater fish.

At the end of two weeks, he headed down from his heights, following the melodious hum of great machines, and eventually he came to a lumberyard. The owner complained that he would soon have to sell the place, for the environmentalists were making his life impossible with their suits against the logging industry.

Orpheo looked at a map. He made some calculations. He offered to buy the lumberyard and its excellent access roads. The owner named an outrageous price. Orpheo offered him five-eighths of it, now, in cash. The owner accepted. Orpheo dug his checkbook out of his knapsack and paid the entire amount on the spot. The owner of the lumberyard figured he was a schizophrenic on a buying spree. But an Italian name on a New Jersey check did kind of make you wonder whether you hadn't just by some stroke of excellent fortune fallen in with gangland megabucks, especially since the crazy guy with the two weeks' growth and the burrs in his shirt said he was planning to build a nightclub.

Orpheo named the new nightclub for his wife, his wonderful wife who had never been unhappy in these lovely mountains. And deep in his most secret heart of hearts, he dedicated it to Candy.

★ ★ ★

They arrived at Aunt Dorothy's the hard way, driving all the way up through California on the nice wide Interstate, because Alisette wouldn't fly. The chauffeur who came with the lodge had been instructed that Alisette was a world class acrophobic, so he stayed off the steeper mountain roads when she was in the car and never let her drive anywhere by herself.

On the first night of her gig, Alisette stood in the wings, looking out at the capacity crowd, and grasped Bo Tye's arm and murmured: "Lookit, there's whole tables full of women together, must be housewives on a night out. And look how many people of color there are! And mixed couples, Bo, black and white, just like Whoopi's audience in San Francisco! Oh, I am hot for this crowd, I am gonna be great with this crowd tonight!"

And she was. People who chanced to catch her show that summer still talk about how great she was. She sang for an hour. Then she sang three encores. Two times each night. Three nights a week for six weeks. Her face and her arms ran with sweat by the end of a set, but she was not tired.

In the morning she sat out on the wraparound deck of the lodge. The maid brought her coffee. The chauffeur brought her papers. And she wrote songs.

Jimbo and Ali came to visit for two weeks. How she loved to have them with her, dancing barefoot on the white shag carpet and ragging on their stepmothers to their main Mama who loved them the most! They learned to shoot the light rapids and then took her along for the ride. She was thrown out of the boat but the guide had instructed her to float on her back and relax in the rushing water, so she did what he said and she was not even hurt.

Ali had a romance with a pretty little girl from Portland.

Untroubled by fear of crime, Alisette eschewed the locks and alarms with which she had riddled her other homes and left her door open and the stewpot brimful and simmering. She was visited by the finest people in the mountains — poets who lived in neighboring lodges, Hollywood moguls up from the offshore islands to the west, horticulturists who worked the fields of roses on the sunny eastern slopes, actors and techies from the Shakespeare Festival. The band came and cooked and ate. Bo

Tye arranged the new songs, pencils protruding from his hair, his thin face twitching with concentration.

At Aunt Dorothy's, Lionel came up to visit and so did Joan, on the same night. Alisette called them onto the stage, and they all jammed until three. Couple of recently sprung Russian rockers dropped in. Their tunes were catchy but their songs still had Russian words. Alisette heard the words, transliterated them in her mind, and sang the songs with near-perfect pronunciation, amazing everyone.

Alisette's tapes and CDs sold off the shelves, up and down the coast.

A big, sweet-faced woman stood on line after the show one night and presented Alisette with every record she ever cut going back twenty years, even the sides where she had just been singing back-up, and asked Alisette to autograph the lot. This woman carried along a skinny husband who wore rimless glasses and a long gray pony tail and seemed embarrassed by her boldness. But Alisette told him never mind, a fan for twenty years was like a blood relative, she would be thrilled to autograph every single record, and what's more, she would give them a picture, and her new album too.

A famous novelist whom Alisette considered the greatest black literary voice of her generation embraced her after the show when she sang "Who is We?" for the first time.

"Never be lonely," whispered the writer. "For *we* are we."

It was the most wonderful summer of Alisette's life. Like Megaman had said, she had risen and converged. She called him all the time, pleaded with him to come see how good she was up here. Somehow he just couldn't ever get away.

On a certain Tuesday at sunset around seven o'clock, Alisette carried out a huge tray of fried chicken to the musicians on the deck. They were working on her latest song. Their music fanned out into the darkening forest. She looked up at the tall trees and saw, to her delight, a gathering of owls. She imagined the deer in the hollows, the campers by the lakes, the frogs on the river banks all listening to what she and her friends had created. And it came to her, the mumbo-jumbo that Abe Heimlich had uttered, it came to her as she had always it known would.

*Et imcha v' et achotcha shachachta*
*L' amal kapeihen laagta.*
*Chola ishtecha b' shel bgida*
*V' libi nikra l' kol bichiya.*
*Asse immah chessed*
*U' m' eyva shachrerenah.*
*Kra la ach b' terem tikra la kala*
*Pen tihiye l' matmon avud*
*K' dvash namess al chotot hamidbar.*
*V' akshe et libbah*
*V' et yeladeycha t'lammed et shimcha lishkoach.*

That was it. The whole thing. She had remembered every word. She laughed triumphantly. She saw Heimlich's delighted smile on an owl in the forest, and the love shining from his wise eyes. She knew, despite the fact that he had never called or written to her, that he still watched over her, that he truly loved her for every single thing she was. And she had the feeling that it really didn't matter what the mumbo-jumbo meant, as long as she possessed this new proof that she was a true genius, that her magic ear could remember all the songs of all the people in all the languages, no matter how ancient and strange. While the entertainers on her deck laid into the fried chicken, Alisette exulted in her special blessings, feeling that the whole earth was filled with the work of her hands.

★ ★ ★

One night, Nacoochee the drummer appeared in the audience. He had come all the way from San Francisco to see her. They drove slowly back from Aunt Dorothy's to her house, drinking kisses, staggered by the crowds of stars.

On the porch, they found a courier waiting with a letter only Alisette could sign for.

"This letter," it said, "will serve to give notice that according to the terms of the agreement between the parties and because of irreconcilable differences on essential questions, 30 days from the affixed date, Brancusi Management will terminate its association with Alisette Legrand."

Alisette called her people together and told them the news. It turned out that those who had been traveling down to L.A. during the course of the gig at Aunt Dorothy's had suspected something like this might happen. They had not told Alisette because they didn't want to worry her, especially since she was such a hit here, but meanwhile, Pablo the keyboard player and Bo Tye had already scouted out other jobs for themselves. Mouths to feed and all that. Maxine the drummer decided it would be an opportune time to have arthroscopic surgery on her wrist. She made arrangements with a clinic in Portland. The guitarists and the back-up singers and the road manager started making a lot of phone calls.

Upon checking further, Alisette discovered that Megaman had long before canceled all the other gigs he had lined up for her. There would be no Thanksgiving in Atlantic City. No Christmas appearance in Detroit. He had allowed her recording contract to lapse. Of course, she had completely forgotten it was up for renewal. So now she would have to get the lawyer and negotiate a whole new deal in order to record her just-written songs. Realizing that yes, she had probably made a terrible mistake by coming here to this remote place for the entire summer, with no possibility of arranging work for herself or replacing her defecting manager until she returned to Los Angeles, she still knew she would do the same thing all over again. It seemed surreal, to be here in the lofty mountains, laying the people in the aisles, accepting their cheers, their pleadings for more, while down there in the planetary world, her great career was history.

She called people she knew in Los Angeles and New York. Her calls were not returned, she assumed, out of respect for Megaman. The men who had produced her soundtrack recordings for the Hollywood movie told her frankly that since her shit fit, she was known in the industry as a hysterical prima dona whose talents could not justify all the trouble she made. Neither they nor anyone else in the entertainment industry blamed Megaman for dropping her. He had a business to run, after all, and an extremely good reputation to protect.

Alisette did not call Megaman. She took her bitter pill quietly, almost feeling that she was justified in having to take it. Almost. On the other hand, he had never understood how much the people loved her in those mountains. He had never even come here to see them dancing like converts in church to her melodies, throwing their arms around each other and swaying and singing along, bringing their old records like babies to a baptism, for the blessing and honor of her name.

Let him play his power games with less uncommon women.

She would arrive back in Los Angeles in her own good time and find herself another man, maybe the drummer Nacoochee, who wouldn't get all vengeful and nasty just because she knew what was best for her career.

★ ★ ★

Alisette played her last weekend to the usual sold out house. Orpheo sent her 36 long-stemmed scarlet roses, one for each set she had sung at Aunt Dorothy's. She assumed somebody would organize a farewell party or something. But everybody expected somebody to do that, so nobody did it.

Bo Tye had booked himself real tight. He flew out in a private plane an hour after their final curtain and was hard at work on an ad campaign in L.A. the next afternoon. He assumed Alisette would drive down with Maxine and Kisha and them.

Maxine went to Portland for her surgery, assuming that Alisette and Kisha would drive down together. Kisha asked if Alisette would mind if she and Pablo took a week off to test their new grown love. Alisette said she didn't mind. Kisha assumed Alisette would drive down with the band.

The rest of the band and the back-up singers and the road manager loaded their stuff into a trio of vans and drove south on the Interstate. The chauffeur and his wife, the maid, went on their day off, with Alisette's substantial tip money in their pockets, assuming she would leave as she had come, the long way, with plenty of company.

Assuming. All of them assuming.

Alisette waited a full extra day, letting them all go on ahead, hinting that she had some unfinished business yet to handle, so that they wouldn't feel guilty about leaving her (although to be honest, she detected not a glimmer of guilt in anyone). Even with her reality fix, her securities and real estate, she had a terrible pain in her heart.

The new caretaker, who had arrived for the winter, loaded her bags into the Volvo she had rented. Uninformed about her habits and phobias, he gave her maps and driving instructions for the westward route to the coast. Alisette didn't pay too much attention. She was thinking about how the damn analyst had been right after all, that her ego always ruined her relationships, and how much good Megaman had done for her and how she already missed his swagger and his suede, his excellent scotch and his mellow, patriarchal style.

With a stack of work tapes to listen to in the car, she set out in a westerly direction at ten in the morning on a sunny day. An especially comfortable Victorian inn near Eureka expected her by three that afternoon. She was wearing designer jeans, gym shoes, thick black and gray tweed socks, and a short-sleeved, navy shirt with pearl buttons. Her earrings and bracelets were handmade from New Mexican silver. Her sporty gold watch was engraved thus: "To Mama, With love, Jimbo and Ali." She was driving a rented blue Volvo which had a driver's side airbag but no phone. Her keyboard and a fat folder of arrangements (as well as a scarlet sweatshirt that said "Du Bois Academy") rode in the passenger seat. In the trunk of the car, she had three matching ivory colored parachute silk garment bags containing a couple of hundred thousand dollars worth of clothes. In her black faux alligator pocketbook, she had $1,200 in cash as well as $35,000 worth of diamond and gold jewelry, wrapped in an envelope of emerald green silk that rested inside a leather case, some photographs of her children and some letters from her fans, strapped together by a strong rubber band. She was alone. The local papers had dubbed her "The Queen of the Redwoods." Very often during the last six weeks, they had carried her picture.

CHAPTER FOURTEEN

# DOWN FROM THE MOUNTAINTOP

THE FOG ROSE UP AMONG THE PINE TOPS like an evil spirit. It leaked onto the road, making twilight of early afternoon.

Alisette had expected to be off the mountains by now. However, the going was slow, the route extraordinarily circuitous and narrow, only two lanes, and the outside lane abutted on oblivion. Periodically along the road, the winds had carved a scenic overlook where you could pull over and enjoy the view and maybe you could turn your car around and head up the mountain again. But you would have to be awful desperate to do that, and very, very lucky not to back right through the little fence that marked the edge of the abyss. Had she been a passenger, with those fog-filled chasms at her right hand, she would have pleaded with the driver to turn back. But now that she was all alone, and completely responsible for her fate, she saw that a driver often had no way to turn back, and had to keep going forward; had to.

When she was driving the straight way, Alisette looked into her rear view mirror. She saw nothing but seething gray sky behind her. What had happened to the sun? It was off to the left, behind the mountain. When she made the turn, she caught a glimpse of it, being clouded over. Oh shit, she thought. Bad weather coming. She looked again into her rear view mirror. She saw nothing but the pinnacles of thousands of thousand-year-old trees, getting a last gasp of the fresh mountain air before it was all gone.

Alisette tried to avoid obsessing about the dangers of the precipitous drive by playing her tapes. They proved too distracting. She needed every bit of concentration to negotiate the irregular ellipses by which the road made its way down the mountain. By the time the sun had disappeared and the fog had drifted across the road and she had to turn on her lights to see, Alisette was so scared that she was barely able to take her hand off the wheel to remove her sun glasses, which had almost fallen down to her upper lip on a waterslide of sweat.

She slowed down and put the Volvo into low gear. She could see maybe one hundred feet ahead. Her heart, unhinged, rose to great heights, then fell into her belly. Feeling that she might faint, she slowed down even more. A sudden sense memory of her body slipping out of control in labor reminded her of Lamaze, and she began to do her breathing, and God bless French medicine, it worked. Her eyes cleared. Her stomach unclenched. Counting down, she gulped the fog. It filled her up. It pressed her floating organs back into place, pressed especially hard on her bladder. Alisette peed just a little in her pants.

Had they told her this would happen? Had someone actually told her the road down from the mountaintop would be this dangerous? Had she been so deafened by the roar of abandonment that she had failed to listen to the warnings and read the damn maps?!

She sang to calm herself. She sang and prayed.

*Please Lord,*
*Let this mountain end.*
*Please Lord, stop this steep descent.*

*Let this be the final bend*
*In the highway*
*Let me go my way,*
*For my soul, my troubled soul,*
*And all my strength is spent.*

Not everywhere in the mountains, but on the stretch of road where Alisette was driving, it began to rain. She drove with her hazard lights blinking. The rain further blurred her vision. Once, on a turn, the Volvo hydroplaned just a tiny little bit horizontally into the ascending lane. Her heart stopped. She knew that because her fingers and toes, her ears and nose went all numb from her heart not pumping and the blood not reaching those far places. That's it, she said to herself. I've had it. I'm finding a place to call from, going to call Aunt Dorothy's, the police, somebody to come get me somehow.

But there was no phone. Not on the next turn or the next.

Out across the miles of mountains, she could see where the rain she was under left off, a square edge, and she deduced that she would be riding with the rain all the way into the valleys, that there would be no more sun, no dry level roadways, only rain and fog at twenty miles an hour all the way, and at that rate she'd still be here when night fell, a horrifying thought. If she pulled over and just waited for the rain to pass, she would *surely* be here when night fell.

Trapped by time and the weather, Alisette suddenly lost her choices, and with them, all the meaning of her wealth and success. More than anything in this world, she wanted to cry. She could not manage to say to herself: this mountain will not go on forever, that gray space yonder must be the flatlands of the coast, the Pacific coast must be lying out there with the whole American Navy going to bars and strip joints, the loggers must have wives and children down there, the gentry must have summer places close by for these are not the mighty Rocky Mountains that lie far inland, these are lousy little foothills.

None of these logical ideas occurred to Alisette. She was too close to hysteria. Nothing had prepared her for this ordeal. Her entire adult life had been ordered and arranged by people who waited on her every wish. When she was lonesome, they came and stayed in her house to keep her company. When she was frightened, they moved heaven and earth to reassure her that she was a major entertainer, one of a kind, Tina-scale, Aretha-like, so that she would go on singing and bringing joy into their lives. She wasn't prepared, she just wasn't prepared, and worst of all, she hadn't known that! She had thought she was, by virtue of her earnings and her houses and her charities and her children and her queenly titles, a strong woman. But look at this! Look how shameful! All she wanted to do was cry!

Once again, as with the Lamaze, Alisette accessed her hair-trigger gift for recovery. She reminded herself of a girl in the choir in Detroit who had a big solo and got stage fright and cried helplessly when it came time for her to perform. How could she be like that little fool blowing her big chance? Hadn't thousands of people driven these roads, at night in the dark in the rain in the snow, and come out safe? Hadn't hundreds of them driven up the ascending lane just to hear her sing at Aunt Dorothy's? Thus whipping herself back into shape, Alisette managed not to cry, which would only have further blurred her vision.

Suddenly, she glimpsed a turn off to the left. Whistling with excitement, she cut across the inside lane, entering a level stretch of dirt road that descended, not on the edge of the mountain but rather into it.

She glanced in her rear view mirror, and was shocked to see that a battered Isuzu truck was blithely continuing down the road she had just been traveling. The truck must have been behind her all the time, hidden behind the turns she had just made! How could the driver of that truck be so fearless?! How come he wasn't a coward like she was?!

The rain, which had seemed a treacherous, driving downpour on the road, turned into a gentle summer shower when sifted by the pine branches. Alisette stopped the car and for a whole half an hour, she did nothing but breathe deeply.

She was safe.

She wiped her face and whipped off her sweat-soaked shirt, wiped her armpits with it and pulled on the scarlet sweatshirt that said "Du Bois Academy." She combed her hair, replaced the lipstick she had bitten off, gave herself a big smile in the rear view mirror. Then she drove on slowly, and for the first time in this trip, enjoyed the beauty of her surroundings.

The unpaved road had been cut through a dense, dark forest of tall pine interlaced with dogwoods and huge thatches of mountain laurel. Alisette had never paid much attention to nature. As a child, she had seen, at the most, twenty-five maybe thirty trees in one place at a time. This was all new to her, these stately groves, this landscape beyond human tilling, this deep silence redolent with the overwhelming scent of pine. It was fabulous! No wonder they cleaned bathrooms with it! The needles crunched beneath her wheels. A leggy dark spider, pushed off a leaf by the rain, scampered around Alisette's windshield, looking for a way out. She tumbled him into a new life with her wipers. Figuring she'd find a bathroom someplace up ahead, where she could change her pants, and a phone from which to call and demand to be rescued, she popped in her work tapes and began to sing.

Soon she came to a log house in a clearing.

A cluster of similar houses stretched back into the forest, and in the distance, Alisette could see a lovely, rustic church. A blonde young woman was unpinning laundry from a line in the yard. The woman was pregnant. A dirty baby girl messed about in a sandbox nearby. She looked like the woman's daughter. Bad planning, Alisette thought sympathetically, for the girl would not be more than 18 months old before the new baby arrived.

Around the side of the house, three teenage boys played football. They were too old to be the pregnant woman's children; besides they did not look like her; but Alisette knew it was their clothes she was hanging on the line. The mother of sons recognizes those telltale briefs with the name written in magic marker on the waistband.

Alisette stopped her car and approached the woman with a smile.

"Excuse me," she said. "Can you help me? I'm lost."

"Well, I guess you sure must be," said the woman.

"I need to find a phone and a bathroom. Is there any kind of eating place around here?"

"Not real close."

"I don't mind driving on as long as it's in the direction I'm heading, toward the Coast."

"Where'd you come from?"

"Aunt Dorothy's, it's a nightclub up near. . . "

"I know where it is."

"I was singing there."

"I saw a picture of a woman like you who was singing there but she was all dressed in white with diamonds and sequins."

Alisette grinned, pleased to be recognized.

"That was me indeed," she said. "These are my driving clothes. Too bad about your wash. I guess the rain got it."

"I'll just do it over," the woman murmured.

Her blue eyes looked beyond Alisette's shoulder to the boys, so that Alisette felt compelled to turn and see them as well. Only two of the boys were still in the yard. They had stopped playing football and were standing still, staring at her. The third was running up the road toward the other houses. Running fast. A little pin prick of foreboding shocked Alisette in her neck, at her pulse.

"Why don't you come inside until the rain passes?" offered the woman.

"I would need to make a phone call."

"Sure thing," she said.

Alisette thanked her and followed her inside, smiling at the two boys who remained. They just gaped at her. Alisette had grown accustomed to a progressive, interracial crowd at Aunt Dorothy's. Was it possible that only a couple of hours away, there were teen-agers who had never met a black woman?

The living room of the log house had a sofa and two chairs and a table and a book case and a large, stone fireplace over which no less than three rifles were mounted. On the mantle, there were stacks of ammunition in boxes.

"I guess your husband is a hunter," Alisette said.

"Yes," answered the woman. "Sit down."

Alisette sat facing the fireplace. She now noticed that on one corner of the mantle, there hung by its strap a Vietnam-type military weapon. Surely this was not what a family man took out hunting.

"May I use the bathroom?" Alisette asked.

The woman looked frightened, as though she had never anticipated that question.

"It's broken. You just sit there."

"How about the phone?"

The woman smiled.

"I guess we don't really have a phone," she said softly.

Alisette sighed audibly. She surely had not needed this sort of aggravation at this particular time. On the table before her, there was a Bible. On the leatherette cover, a complex insignia was embossed — it took a few seconds for Alisette to realize that it was a cross interlaced with a swastika.

"So long," Alisette said.

"You've got to wait for my husband."

"Like hell I do."

Alisette headed out the front door. But the woman had locked her in.

"You sure did get yourself lost," she said.

Alisette looked out the window. In the two or three minutes she had been in this creepy house, the running boy had alerted the neighbors, and now they were all over the car, young white men, they had her music out and the Casio. One of the boys beat on the door. His stepmother let him in.

"Give us your car keys," he said to Alisette.

The woman who had half an hour earlier struggled not to cry hysterically over a steep road now reasoned that if she forced Mr. Hitler Youth here to take the keys from her, then he would get her whole purse. If she gave him the keys without trouble, she might be able to keep her purse for a few more minutes. So she gave him the keys. He ran out to his comrades. The pregnant woman re-locked the door.

"Let me go," said Alisette.

"They're not going to want me to do that."

"I'll give you my diamonds."

"Oh yeah?"

"You saw them in the newspaper, with your own eyes. They're real diamonds."

"Oh yeah, sure, I guess they are real, sure thing."

"You could sell them in Eureka. You'd never have to pin up the laundry again."

"I wouldn't be foolish enough to take your fake diamonds. You can't buy me. Don't try."

Alisette looked outside. The Volvo had become a hive swarming. They had her clothes out, the beautiful dresses, the shoes; they were laughing over her custom-made brassieres. They sprayed each other with her perfume. One of them, a handsome man, got into the car and drove it slowly down the road with all the others clinging to the bumpers and windows, whooping and screaming with sheer delight.

Alisette took the $1,200 in fifties and twenties out of her wallet and displayed it before the woman.

"This is real," she said. The woman hovered like a bird on the edge of its nest. "All they will do is hurt me, maybe kill me, and use my money to buy more guns. Now what good is that to you? Is that going to get you and your babies off this mountain?"

The bird flew.

The woman took Alisette through the kitchen and let her out the back door. Alisette thought of taking the frying pan, but it was full of grease. She grabbed a carving knife and a box of matches as she went. The woman took her to the edge of the forest. The rain had stopped falling on the warm forest floor, and now the deep woods oozed with fog. It was impossible to see anything.

"Follow the huckleberry bushes and the wild rose thickets," the woman said. "They'll take you straight down."

Alisette gave her the money. She slung the alligator purse diagonally across her body so it wouldn't flap and ran directly into the fog and disappeared.

* * *

With one scoop of her garden spade, the pregnant woman buried the money at the base of an old gnarled apple tree. She re-entered the house. She heated the grease in the frying pan until it sputtered. Then with all her strength, she crashed the pan down on the top of her head, burning off patches of hair, blistering her scalp, scarring her forehead and neck and shoulders. She screamed with pain. When she could move again, she staggered into her front yard. The Volvo and all who preyed upon it were gone up the road. Only her baby girl still played in the cruddy old sandbox. She struck the child hard on the bottom. Then she called her husband's name. He came running. He found the little girl screaming bloody murder, and his wife weeping, scarred for life. She told him that Alisette had done this to her and then run away.

★ ★ ★

As Alisette said goodbye to her summer friends and prepared to journey down from the mountains, and Alex Deal followed close behind on his way to meet Candy in Portland, so did Heimlich set forth from Playa del Ruach. They were all bound for the same place, for the cities of the northern coast, and could easily have met there.

Heimlich kissed Dr. Herskovits and all the orderlies goodbye. He kissed the patients who were less lucky than he, who were perhaps sicker, or who did not have such devoted children as Rivka and Rachel had proved to be. He rode toward Rachel's house in Mendocino, with Rivka and her boyfriend Chuck, in the blue Olds which Chuck's parents had given him when he received his appointment in physics at Yale.

Rivka observed how her father sat in the back seat with Chuck's cute dog Sakharov, how the two of them pushed their faces into the ocean air that buffeted by the window, enjoying the mussel shoal scents, the incomparably refreshing breeze. She squeezed Chuck's thigh and grinned. It seemed that whatever force had overtaken Heimlich had somehow been defeated and cast out, a dybbuk exorcised, and now he would be returned to them, father, grandfather, funny and philosophical and full of card tricks to teach the children. Everything was going to be okay, she thought. Maybe now she would get married.

Suddenly Heimlich demanded that Chuck stop the car.

He had turned pale. He was sweating.

The worldly mongrel Sakharov immediately understood that something was terribly wrong. He leaped into the front seat and huddled, trembling, on Rivka's lap.

"Listen to me, kids," Heimlich said, "I'm not having a fit, I'm not going crazy. But I know there is some terrific trouble very close by."

Chuck pulled off the highway onto a sandy shoulder.

It was early afternoon, and the fog lay to the east in the mountains. On the ocean, all was clear. Heimlich got out of the car and ran eastward. He ran so fast for a man of fifty who was really out of shape that Chuck and Rivka had a hard time keeping up with him. Sakharov didn't even try.

"Daddy, where are you going?! Get hold of yourself! What kind of trouble could be here?"

Heimlich raised his hand for silence. He squinted and leaned into the trees, listening hard.

"Do me a favor, Rivka, be quiet. I'm trying to catch a signal here."

"Daddy!"

"I hear a voice. . . "

"Stop this shit, Daddy! What you hear is the voice of the redwoods crying out to be spared! Hell, we all hear that voice!"

"What redwoods?!" yelled Heimlich. "Those murdering bastards are after my women again!"

Chuck said quietly to Rivka: "Bite the bullet, baby. Your father is certifiable."

Sakharov slumped against the fender of the Lincoln and nodded sadly: true true.

Heimlich got back in the car.

"Take me to a telephone," he said.

And they did, and he called the police.

This is what he said.

(They've got it on tape. It's a matter of record.)

"Hello? 911? My name is Heimlich. Abraham Heimlich. I am at the Point Reyes National Seashore driving north to Mendocino. A woman named Alisette Legrand, yeah the singer the singer right, she is in terrific trouble somewhere in the mountains to the northeast. Like in a forest. Somebody's chasing her.

"I don't know the names of the towns. . . Rivka. . . look at the map. . . what are the towns northeast of here?. . . Healdsburg, no, Boonville, no, I don't know the towns, I'm not from this area, I'm from Los Angeles, but I'm telling you, they're chasing her. . . What do you mean how do I know? I know because I know!"

The tape records sounds of a struggle, cries of "Come on, Abe, take it easy. . . " and "Give me the phone, Daddy. . . "

But the caller, this Heimlich (spelled HIGHLICK on the police report) persisted.

"She's on foot, she has no car. No, she's not hiking, she's running. The racist bastards, the lousy anti-Semites, the earth should swallow them, they're after her! I'm telling you!"

"Abe, listen to me. . . "

"My daughter has a boyfriend here who is eight feet tall and weighs four hundred pounds and he is wresting the phone from my grip but I am asking you, I am begging you, go and find Alisette! Send a truck, for God's sakes! Send a helicopter! And call me at my daughter Rachel's house. Her number is . . . what is Rachel's number?! Rachel and Bernard Levine in Mendocino, that's where I'll be!"

Another voice now takes over the talking.

"Operator, hello, this is Professor Charles Minskoff of Yale, I'm sorry about this. You should be aware: my fiancee's father has visions. He is thought by many to be insane. But to be completely honest, not by everybody. I am very sorry to have caused you all this trouble and taken so much of your time when there are probably so many real emergencies."

"This is real!" yelled Heimlich helplessly at the end of Chuck's strong long arm.

"Please just forget it, Operator," Chuck said.

★ ★ ★

Alisette was thinking now. Her brain had been working correctly ever since she had seen the desecrated Bible. No longer dependent on psychic mechanisms to control her panic, she could at last use her powers of logic. Running alongside an apparently endless hedge of hucklekberries, grabbing at the vine maples for guidance, she wondered why the Bible had frightened her so much more than the weapon. Probably because she had seen the weapon, an Uzi maybe, or an M16, on the news, and it was as familiar to her as an old friend. Oh, if only she had one now! Even just a little one with a fake mother-of-pearl handle like Megaman's secretary Lettie said she got used to carrying in the streets of Paterson.

Alisette's watch, another logical tool which she had completely forgotten, told her it was three o'clock in the afternoon. At this moment, the innkeepers near Eureka were expecting her. And her new housekeeper would be calling from Malibu to give her the messages. The current date and time no longer had any relevance, she knew. In less than an hour, the "Queen of the Redwoods" had become a hunted runaway like her great great grandfather, and that was all there was to it.

She had to believe the worst; that the woman had given her the wrong directions; that the Nazis would not be content with her car and her clothes but would follow her and shoot at her with their guns. No fear could compare with this fear. This was the first fear, the fear of white people. To escape them, she would climb the tallest tree on the mountain. She would hang by twigs above canyons. Fuck acrophobia. She had to deal with it being 1858 out there, and she had to find a weapon.

The berries, she reasoned, would not have grown so profusely in the shade. Therefore, the woman must have directed her onto a sun trail, distinct and familiar to those who knew the forest. What if the fog lifted and the sun came out as suddenly as it had disappeared? And what if the skies cleared at sunset? She might be caught in silhouette.

The wet pine needles under her feet tripped her up; she slipped and fell into a shallow ravine, banging her hips on stones. Her arm caught in a huge thicket of thorned bushes. It was like being torn by the claws of a wildcat. Little spigots of blood opened up on her flesh. She muffled her own cry of pain with the heel of her hand and blew against it. One by one, she pulled out the thorns.

She had found huge clumps of wild roses. The rain had stopped and the sun struggled to come back through the clouds. She knew she had to get away from the berry trail and the sun-seeking roses, but not before they justified the pain they had caused her. With the kitchen knife, she cut half a dozen long strong wands. She scraped the thorns off halfway up, giving herself a handle and leaving a foot or so of thorns at the end. Using the rubber band that was holding her packet of letters together, she now bound the thorny wands into a pack. This weapon could inflict terrible damage. But you'd have to aim for the face. Even light clothing might blunt the impact. Immediately the rose wand whip became a kind of extension of her right arm. It was all the comfort she had at that moment. She would have had to be dying to give it up.

Alisette took off her sweatshirt — too red, easy to spot — and stuffed it into her pants, padding her hips and belly in case she fell again. Thankfully, she was wearing a black lace camisole. She wasn't cold because she was so frightened.

Blessed with an especially sensitive ear, Alisette detected the sound of running water a quarter of a mile away, and immediately recognized her alternative to the sun trail. Water would flow downhill. Water would cover her tracks. Water would travel through the dark forest, out of the light. The mountain stream would guide her out of the trap.

She raced toward the stream, slipped and blundered down the steep bank, through barricades of branches, and felt the sting of the freezing water inside her socks. Behind her, she heard their voices. Hugging the bank, Alisette kept on running. Then suddenly she found an overhang under which a tree's roots had formed a little cave. A hiding place. A place to rest.

A snake was sleeping in the cave.

"Oh, get the fuck outa here," Alisette snapped, whipping at the slippery creature with her killer rose wand.

Terrified, he sped away.

She stayed there until past sunset, drinking mountain spring water and praying for clear skies so she would have a glow to follow in the night. Her pursuers never saw her. Their voices came closer — and then, finally, passed by.

So rested and sated and perfectly calm, Alisette followed the gleam of starlight on the stream water. She could not see the cities of the coast lying before her like paradise. No light of human habitation twinkled through the dark to tell her she was very very close to safety. All she could sense was water, and down.

As soon as she dared, she pulled on the sweatshirt. Since the stream had grown deeper and wider, she untangled a wide log from the shore grass and used it as a raft to float herself downward, trying to keep as much of her body as possible out of the water. She would not be able to remember just when the stream which had treated her so kindly and hidden her so well grew turbulent. All that would remain was a blur of embankment swishing by, offering outgrowing bushes that she grabbed at and missed. She tried to hook a cascade of briars with her rose wand, but the water was too strong, it carried her willy nilly over the rocks.

This was rapids, she realized. Whitewater. She tried to turn on her back, as she had learned to do while rafting with Jimbo and Ali, and she put her hand on her head to protect her brains, but realized immediately that the technique only worked if you were wearing a life preserver. *Grandma Blanche, I'm done for,* she thought. *Jimbo. Ali. God bless my babies. Abe,* she thought. *Abraham. Where are you? Will I find you in Heaven?*

Not seeing where she was headed, helpless to resist the powerfully running rapids, she relaxed her body and stopped trying to save herself from death. *Oh Lord, forgive me please for all the evil I have done.* The life-saving log and the rose wand flew off, and her body followed at wild water speed. *Do me how You will, Lord, I have loved You in my way.* And she fell sixteen feet over a waterfall considered one of the loveliest sights on the coastal range.

CHAPTER FIFTEEN

# LOST VOICES

IN LOS ANGELES, where Alisette occupied a permanent place in the back of his mind, Megaman told Lettie to try and reach her. He figured she must be back from Oregon by now, because members of her company were turning up at recording sessions all over town. It irritated him that she had never called in response to his letter, never cursed him out or wished him dead. He wondered what else could be occupying her mind.

The winter caretaker at the lodge could not be reached immediately for he was out splitting wood for the fire, shopping for groceries, having a few drinks with his friends. So Lettie began calling everybody else she could think of who might know when Alisette had left the mountains and where she was headed. By ten o'clock at night, she had reached everybody, even Maxine the drummer in her post-operative haze, even Kisha and Pablo at their love-nest by a roaring river. They had all left a day or two before Alisette. Nobody knew exactly where she was.

Finally, at 11:30 at night, the winter caretaker returned Lettie's call and described the time and circumstances of Alisette's departure. She should long ago have reached her destination, he reported. The innkeepers in Eureka declared peevishly that they had been waiting for her since three o'clock in the afternoon, and she had not even called, and now they were going to sleep. The new housekeeper in Malibu said she had not heard from Miss Legrand and had no idea when to expect her, but if Mr. Brancusi reached her, he should tell her to call home, for there were many messages.

Megaman took the Rolls and drove himself down to a recording studio where Bo Tye was pulling an all-nighter. The brilliant arranger did not look happy. He chain-smoked, professing to detest the music he had been given to process. He was especially pissed at the clarinets.

"You let her drive down from the mountains herself," Megaman said.

"Hey, she's past 40, man!" Bo Tye retorted. "She has a top of the line state of the art car. She's got money. If she wants to go out alone, nobody has to give her permission."

"She was expected in Eureka before three this afternoon!"

"I got to say, it is real touching how all of a sudden you are so worried about Al. Anyway. Kisha's with her."

"Kisha's with Pablo."

"Well then I don't know, maybe she drove down with the drummer and they stopped to enjoy the view."

"What drummer?"

"Leave me alone, Brancusi. I'm not the woman's keeper. I got an orchestra waiting for me in there."

"What drummer is this, you son-of-a-bitch?!"

Bo Tye smashed his butt into his other butts.

"Don't be calling me names," he growled. "You were the one who dropped her. You can lay it off on me all you like but if anybody left Al to fend for herself in the mountains, it was you!"

Megaman took a swing at him. Bo Tye hugged him, stopping the punch. They were both so scared, they couldn't even curse at each other.

Now nearly hysterical with worry, Lettie checked with the Coast Patrol. They said the weather on the mountains had been mixed that afternoon, some sun, some rain, and there were fog emergencies in the foothills, so people had been warned not to drive if at all possible until the fog cleared. Maybe Miss Legrand had got herself caught in the fog, the cops conjectured, and had pulled over in response to the message on the radio.

But Miss Legrand never listened to the radio! Lettie shrieked. She had tapes to study!

The Coast Patrol assured Lettie that a logical explanation would soon emerge. However, because it was a big talent involved here, and because Orpheo Pastafino himself called personally from New Jersey at what was four in the morning there and said they should go and find Alisette Legrand, the police dutifully set out in the starry dark, looking for her Volvo, skimming the road down from Aunt Dorothy's with the beams of their helicopters. By dawn, they too had begun to think that Alisette might have driven into a canyon in the fog, or maybe got herself mixed up with the goddamned white supremacists in the interior.

★ ★ ★

You run down a mountain, you're thrown by a waterfall, you think you're dead and who's there waiting? The Girl Scouts.

They were hanging out around a campfire, propped up in their sleeping bags, wearing their hair in curlers to look good for God only knows who in these rough woods in the morning. They were learning from their counselors (two college juniors, Ann and Harriet) how to assemble s'mores.

"First you take a sheet of tin foil," Ann said. "In the center of the foil, you place a Graham cracker. On top of it, you place a chocolate bar; on top of that three marshmallows, one for each section of the chocolate bar; finally another

Graham cracker. Then you fold up the sides of the tin foil to hold it together and lay it gently on the coals of the fire to roast. Gently! You don't want it to fall on its side, or else the marshmallows won't melt evenly."

That much Alisette heard. She must have heard it because the next day, she knew how to make s'mores, and she had never even heard their name before in her entire life.

The Girl Scouts sang campfire songs in three part harmony, one part for each section of the chocolate bar:

*Bree-zes*
*Blow-ing*
*Rivers*
*Flow-wing*
*Blackberry bushes*
*Grow-oh-woh-oh-woh-ing*
*Up in th' mountains*
*With you.*
*Ow-wels*
*Hoo-ting*
*Hunters*
*Shoo-ting*
*Ordinary folk*
*Pul-loo-oo-woo-oo-woo-ting*
*Up in the mountains*
*With you-oo-oo.*

Well, of course Alisette — who had been thinking she must be alive because somebody was talking about Graham crackers — knew she certainly must be dead and in hell getting punished when she heard that singing.

Every single one of the Girl Scouts said she was the one who saw Alisette first. They saw the moonlight gleaming on her wet face and thought for a moment that she was a plastic trash bag which some evil person who didn't love nature had carelessly tossed into this magnificent wilderness so that now, it had washed up on the stream bank. Their cries for Ann and Harriet jolted Alisette to consciousness. *Shhh,* she wanted to say, *quiet, quiet, they'll hear you.*

The counselors came running. They wore jeans torn at the knees and their brothers' plaid flannel shirts, and mighty-soled work boots like girls never used to wear when Alisette was a child. They pulled her up out of the water. Slapped her face gently. Breathed air into her lungs, making her cough and throw up the mountain stream. Dragged her onto a blanket and wrapped her up in it like she was a s'more. All around her, little girls ran here and there seeking blankets and towels, then hovered not too near, holding each other close to keep from weeping forth their own terror at finding a person so hurt and maybe even close to death in this idyllic place. In the moonlight, the Girl Scouts seemed translucent as aliens, their eyes huge with tenderness. They were all colors, like a bunch of flowers. These must be angels, Alisette thought. These are all the children who fell out of the sky because of the sins of someone who was flying on the same airplane, who turned immediately into angels while wearing sweatshirts that said "Lewis and Clark Naked Lacrosse" and "Rogue River Rapids" and "I Love My Country But I Fear My Government."

Ann and Harriet called for the Girl Scouts to carry Alisette into the warmth of their tent. Working all together, a determined solidarity of thin young arms, they raised her up, bearing her as Gulliver and Snow White before her had been borne to safety, an oversized traveler in the nation of the small. Many of the girls stayed in the tent, hugging its delicate sides, trying to give Ann and Harriet plenty of room. The counselors cut off Alisette's clothes and carefully saved them in a paper bag. They felt her body gently. When they saw that the lacerations were superficial, the big bones still unbroken, they rubbed her hard with towels to make her blood flow and then dressed her in dry clothing and wrapped her in blankets which had been brought by the little angels. They laid themselves down beside her and held her close to give her their warmth. Meanwhile one of the Girl Scouts dried Alisette's hair with a blow dryer which ran on batteries like a flashlight. Another brought in a cup of tea from outside.

Ann kneeled and propped Alisette's head against her thighs while Harriet spooned the tea into her mouth. It was heavy with sugar. Alisette could only manage two teaspoons. However, she would never forget the heavenly feeling of well-being which spread through her body with the sugar and the warmth.

For the first time, she opened her eyes to a full consciousness of her surroundings and her physical condition. Her legs were twitching as the muscles lost the fear signal and came to rest. She felt stinging pains in her arms and on her chest a great weight. The throbbing in her head grew unbearable. Harriet rubbed her forehead right above her brows, and then rubbed her sinuses.

A happy Girl Scout ran into the tent. "I found them!" she cried, producing a large pair of furry ear muffs which her mother had insisted she pack even though only a dweeb would bring ear muffs on an overnight but her mother had said "You never know how cold it's going to get in those mountains!" and despite the fact that the Girl Scout had unpacked the ear muffs twice, her mother had packed them three times.

Her wonderful smart mother.

Harriet tilted Alisette's head first one way, then the other, to see if maybe some more of the stream would dribble out, and it did. Finally, she put the ear muffs on Alisette and wrapped them in place with a towel. The tea angel brought a steaming bowl of water. Astounding the girls with the toughness of her hands, Ann dipped a cloth in the water and wrung it out until it was almost dry. She pressed it on Alisette's forehead. Again and again she heated the cloth. Again and again the campfire angels outside in the cold and dark built up the fire to heat water for these saving compresses.

They gave her a little more hot tea with sugar. They asked her no questions, opened her pocketbook seeking identification and finding none, closed it, leaving the jewels she had been ready to abandon safe and untouched in their sodden bag. Under and around her body, they tucked all the pillows they had brought with them, to keep her warm and comfortable. Alisette recognized the old pillowcases; familiar American no-iron patterns; Grandma Blanche had owned a couple of those; Alisette herself had bought the blue one with the big pink roses.

Her mind slid and flew like a leaf in a wind. Wouldn't it be funny if the damn sheets became classics in time? she asked herself. If Wamsutta stripes became as precious a symbol of African American culture as Grandma Blanche's antique cotton sun bonnet that her grandmama before her had sewed for sowing cotton?

Sowing and sewing. Woman's work.

*You don't do woman's work, you get punished, honey:* now who had told her that? Someone in her life before Grandma Blanche, someone she had to stay with because she had no Mama and no Daddy, a transient caretaker in some foster home expounding bygone philosophies. What if they were true? Maybe they were true, and she had been punished for being so high and mighty and refusing to do woman's work and climbing right up there onto the clouds with the gods.

Alisette began to throw up and run a fever. Ann held her head and Harriet bore off her vomit and the Girl Scouts watched, thinking: this is what you do for people, this is how you take care.

★ ★ ★

When the Girl Scouts first brought her into the hospital, Megaman rushed up the coast to Eureka to see her, overcome with guilt, falling on his knees to beg forgiveness for having left her in the lurch so that everybody else in the company took the cue and did the same. She couldn't talk yet. But she patted his head which lay on the mattress next to her arm and the patting said: "Don't you upset yourself about it, baby," like she hadn't been paying much attention to what he said anyway, like he was Jimbo or Ali admitting some trivial transgression. *I burned the pot you cook our dinner in, Mama. I'm sorry. . . Don't you upset yourself about it, baby. . .* Well, she had been through a terrible ordeal; she was sedated. How could he be mad at a sedated woman for patting him absently and making him feel like he was a kid again, with only one pot to cook in?

Alisette wanted to be reassured that Grandma Blanche had not died in the night, wanted to go to her immediately, to drive down Five Mile Road and see only black faces and surround herself with family, Zeke's kids, Hank's grandbabies, and visit her old church to give thanks. Of course, the doctors insisted that she must stay put in the hospital. She was suffering from exposure, several minor fractures, cracked ribs, smashed up teeth, lacerations and bruises of varying severity. It would take several weeks to fully rule out other more complicated internal injuries. No, the doctors said, they weren't even sure when she'd be able to take a slow drive home to Malibu. And Detroit, with its hard winter, was completely out of the question.

To calm down Alisette, Megaman had little old Grandma Blanche brought to the phone in her nursing home. She spoke in that high-pitched, upward sliding voice which certain black comedians parodied so well. "Alisette? Tha's you, baby? When you gonna com'n see me? You still singin'? You still fat? When you gonna lose some of your weight, girl? Don't you know the weight is what gets you round your heart? The weight is what's killing me, sure is. . . "

Saying only that Alisette was sick and needed them, Megaman flew in Ali and Jimbo from the homes of their stepmothers. He picked them up at the airport in his own car.

On the San Diego Freeway, he told them what had happened and made them promise to keep it a secret. Let the fuckers stew in their own suspicions for a while, he counseled. Let them wonder how she had escaped, who told her the way down the mountain, who among them was the traitor. Troop 34, assembled at their club house with their parents and Ann and Harriet, received the same message, differently couched, from the Coast Patrol. Don't tell, they were told. Now that you have told us, don't tell anyone else. Because you never know who's in on it, kids. You never know who might take vengeance *against you* for saving Alisette Legrand.

Thus terrified by the authorities, the girls and their families kept their silence. Word definitely did not get around.

★ ★ ★

Some microorganism from the stream water had lodged in Alisette's gut and now devastated her with diarrhea, weakening her so that she could not easily throw off the pneumonia she had contracted just from being wet and cold. She needed round-the-clock nurses, and couldn't be nourished except intravenously. When she finally came out of the hospital, she was too weak even to enjoy the view of the ocean on the way home. She took to her bed in Malibu. The first time she sat out on her terrace, she sat in a wheelchair.

Megaman and Bo Tye came around regularly. However, they put off other members of Alisette's troupe with false stories about how she was traveling here and there, visiting family, teaching seminars in Eastern Europe. Can't let people know you've had a run-in with the racists, they told Alisette, because people might be moved to act vengefully, and we've got to let the police continue their search without undue publicity or interference. So just at the time when she was needing them the most, Alisette was not overwhelmed with get-well cards and visitors.

She had begun to think of Megaman as her third ex-husband. He tried to explain that he had dropped her because she had ignored his advice, overruled his decisions, undermined his credibility with her fits and delays and unprofessional behavior and generally treated him like shit. Did she understand that she had treated him like shit?! By this time, Alisette was back with her old analyst (the one who had been right about everything), so she was now in an excellent position to understand exactly how she had treated Megaman, and why he was more than justified in having taken revenge on her. She declared that she certainly did not blame him for her encounter with the Aryan Christian Congregation, which could have happened even if she had been driving with Nacoochee, her new lover.

Megaman chortled. Even at thirty pounds below her normal weight, even from a wheelchair, Al could zap you like no other woman ever.

Alisette forgave Megaman so thoroughly that a press release went out announcing that they had patched up their differences and that Brancusi Management would continue to serve as her representatives. "Sure we made up," Megaman said to those who asked him for a more personal explanation. "Could I stay mad at my lovin' Al?"

Alisette started cooking chicken again. She bought a new keyboard and wrote down the music she had heard in her mind in the mountains. She allowed Brancusi Management to entertain offers to have all her works published in a series of songbooks. Her voice continued to be weak; she continued to rest it, unconcerned, sure it would come back to her.

Two nice fellows from the Coast Patrol brought hundreds of photographs into her living room to see if she might be able to identify someone. No luck. Although she was sure she remembered the faces of the blonde woman, her stepsons, her baby girl and many of the young men who had overrun the

Volvo, those faces did not appear in the police files. Somehow the car could not be found either. Or her clothes.

"How can you not find a dozen white sequinned ball gowns in the redwood forest?" Megaman asked Bo Tye Jamal.

* * *

The only other person in this world, besides the Girl Scouts and their counselors and parents and Jimbo and Ali and Megaman and Bo Tye and Lettie and some Coast Patrol cops and Orpheo Pastafino and the Aryan Christians, who knew about Alisette's escape down from the mountaintop was Abraham Heimlich. He knew without a doubt.

However, at his daughter Rachel's house in Mendocino, surrounded by traditional believers, he could not *swear* that he knew. These people trusted God; they thought history was reason; they thought that if they studied hard, all their lives, they could know some wisdom. As for the understanding that was beyond wisdom, they did not think that their father, an incidental rabbi, at heart a comedian from L.A.'s hot streets, schmoozer, womanizer, occasional *traife*-eater, would be privy to that. Like Rivka's darling Chuck, the man of science, these Torah observers thought Heimlich was crazy.

Heimlich sat at the table of his son-in-law Bernie the Furniture Maker and made a little suggestion.

"What if there's an accident?" he suggested. "Even just a little glitch? What if a crash occurs, a plane is late, somebody screws up, somebody forgets, a message isn't delivered, a great moment drowns? You think it doesn't happen? You think the words of the prophets are all revealed, that nothing remains to be intuited, invented? That nothing was lost forever that has to be found again and again?

"Look, I have some slight evidence that there was this woman in the time of Solomon. Maybe she made good honey cakes but otherwise, she was a terrific pain in the neck, complaining and raging all the time, impossible to live with. So her father or maybe her husband sold her into slavery. She was part of the cargo on a Phoenician ship that set out from the port of Eilath. How do I know? I saw the manifest. It's a shard in Jerusalem. It's also written that on the ship, she raised such hell that the ocean got all excited and the ship went down.

"Now, what could she have said, this woman, that her fury should have the power to create a tempest that would drown the sons of men? Maybe she wasn't just a complaining JAP. Maybe she had truth on her side. Maybe she had God on her side. Maybe she was a prophet.

"To feel so compelled to say what nobody wanted to hear, to be such a nudnick that she should endanger her security and her place in the household, something must have been driving her, some great pain. Maybe she was trying to warn us, that something we were doing was wrong and would destroy us. But her prophecy sank. Her fears became a gleam in the water. Fish ate it in the Gulf of Aqaba. Strong food; it gave them bright colors. Tides swept it so deep that today the only creatures who say what she said seem like monsters from the darkest parts of the ocean. And nobody listens to them. Because she drowned, the people of the world still go to war against women, still to this day. With no light to guide them in wiser ways, the cultures of the world tear at their girls with violence and ridicule, as though that could possibly not be a sin and an offense to God, as though it's a game, my children, when in fact the salvation of the very earth depends on the righting of this everyday wrong, which is so ordinary, so commonplace that we do not even recognize it as an abomination."

This story struck Rachel's friends as blasphemous, fatuous, laughable. Go imagine that a piece of ancient prophecy should be lost at sea until suddenly a few years ago in New Jersey, when it was washed up by a giant wave and tossed behind the eye of Heimlich. Please, Abe. . . they said. Please. You want to change the world? Make a movie. Write a book. Go teach in a day school.

So Heimlich was assailed by doubts. All the more so since he had never been able to remember the prophecy and had for proof of its existence only the eerie recollections of others who could not remember it. Surely the whole thing must be some mistake, he thought, hoping it was.

He could not have intuited Alisette's run-in with the racists any more than he could have spouted prophecy. It was impossible. Alisette had reunited with her manager; it was in print before his eyes; she was playing Budapest or someplace like that. She was fine! His fears and imaginings were so much depressive bullcrap. Forget it, he told himself.

And still he couldn't forget it.

Nagged by the feeling that he was right and everybody else was wrong, he called the Coast Patrol. They said they knew nothing about any trouble with Alisette Legrand. He called Brancusi Management. The receptionist told him: "It is the policy of Brancusi Management never to take phone messages for our clients. Please get in touch with us by mail. Our address is. . . . . " So once again, he wrote her a letter.

"This is my seventh letter to you," he wrote. "One for each day of creation. I took a rest in the middle between the third and fourth letters because not being God I was exhausted from creating without feedback.

"Why do you not answer me, Alisette? I am tormented by fears for your safety and your health. Maybe I got the wrong address. Maybe this person who controls Brancusi Management where I write you thinks I am a berserk fan and automatically shields you from mail such as mine.

"Maybe you have married or died, although I think I would have read it in the trades.

"Or maybe you would prefer not to hear from me again. Or you don't remember who I am.

"That's a possibility. Forgetting. Don't people keep coming in a steady stream to my old friend Eliezer AvShalom, asking what it was I said that night in Atlantic City? He told me you came too, dressed all in white, like a high priest.

"We all forgot what I said that night.

"But I cannot forget you, Alisette.

"You wore black silk pants and low gold shoes, sort of sandals with an open web of straps that showed the pink of your soles. You painted your toenails gold, you devil. And all these years, I have wondered what made the jingling sound that accompanied every step you took. Now I have decided that you wore bracelets with bells around your ankles like a Balinese dancer.

"I taste your feet in my dreams.

"You wore a black shirt with a gold design and around your arm a gold snake bracelet. You wore long gold earrings. I imagine them on my pillow. In my dream you watch over me while I sleep with your gold eyes.

"I think of you not as my sister, because only women think of sisters as equals, men find it hard to do so, that's just the way the language is; words have to be chosen carefully.

"I think of you as my brother.

"I dream of you as my bride.

"Eliezer and I have started a school for men in Israel. I am going there to teach. To be a student, you have to be past forty and at least previously married. Of course the rabbinical authorities refuse to accredit this school. They say it offers no degree and requires much too much music. But the students are coming to us in droves anyway, representing all the tribes.

"Spring will soon return.

"The voice of the turtle and all that.

"A *zissen Pesach,* that means have a joyful Passover. *Achi.* My brother. *Kalah.* My bride."

Heimlich noted the numbers and addresses where he could be reached in Mendocino and in New Haven and at the school for perplexed and suffering men which he and Eliezer had founded in the trackless Negev, near the American kibbutz at Keturah, on the road to Eilath and the crystal waters of Aqaba.

★ ★ ★

When he was first awakened by Megaman's secretary and told that Alisette was suspiciously delayed on her return trip from Aunt Dorothy's, Orpheo felt a tightening in his aorta. Once again, he was forced to consider the lessons of the Mednorth bust.

He had been deeply distressed by the television coverage of the bust. The sight of the Queens police and Carol O'Banyon posing in front of all those guns still lingered in his mind, making him philosophical, making him feel old. Obviously America had become an unsupervised arsenal, in which any paramilitary punk could acquire weapons only professionals should ever be allowed to touch. The police looked like fools, crediting a blonde politician with important intelligence. Why could she find out what they did not know? They should have been embarrassed to go public with this story, Orpheo felt.

And the stashers of the guns! What could they have been thinking?! Were they *taking* the drugs they had vowed to protect?! In his day, if you needed a garage to store weapons in, you asked the guy who owned the garage; you invited him to dinner maybe, worked out a legitimate rental arrangement. Here, these poor fools being loaded into cop vans on national television had so little rapport with the people in whose neighborhood they were operating that no one had warned them. During two full weeks of police surveillance, not one person had warned them! In his day, that would have been enough time for an intelligent person to find out the names and needs of every cop on the case, so everybody could be quietly paid off and the guns could slip out of town likes snakes in the night, not a sound.

This television fanfare, this bazaar of microphones and commentary and political hay-making, is what happens when democratic ideals fall into disrepair, he told his Japanese cook. Fools without training or discipline think they are safe just because they possess some high tech fire power. They forget the all-important principle that no one is safe without the consent of the people.

Orpheo hoped that the police in Oregon would be wiser and more efficient than the police of Queens. But no. The minute he heard their voices on the phone, he could tell: they were small timers; amateurs. Despite their helicopters and horses and high beam hunting trucks, they would never be able to find one famous woman on a foggy mountain.

Now his assessment had proven correct. To the shame of all concerned, Alisette had been found and saved by Girl Scouts.

Orpheo sighed and watered his gloxinias. The police said they would make arrests. As soon as Alisette could identify those who had abused her, they would make arrests. Meanwhile nothing. And more nothing. And the winter came, and still nothing. It was enough to make an old man descend from the safety of the clouds and take matters into his own hands.

⋆ ⋆ ⋆

Orpheo hitched a ride west on the private plane of a good friend, for he had no such vehicle of his own and preferred not to have his flight schedule observed. The chauffeur who had worked for Alisette at the lodge picked him up at the airport. It was a freezing cold day in March. The only road in the mountains not completely coated with ice was the especially well-maintained road to Aunt Dorothy's. The chauffeur had never been told of the trouble Alisette had encountered while leaving these parts so many months before. When he heard the story, tears of rage rolled from under his sunglasses down his ruddy face into his wispy beard.

Aunt Dorothy's was being cleaned and refurbished for the forthcoming spring-summer season. The chairs and tables had been stacked and covered with plastic to protect them from the spatter of new paint and the dust of plastering repairs. Crews of silent workmen were laying thin, tough, blue carpet. Five enterprising Tlingit sisters scrubbed every last trace of pasta sauce and mildew from the kitchen tiles. The black stoves gave off cleansing chemical steam. The silver pots hanging overhead shined like temple gongs.

In six weeks, the club would reopen. Bobby was coming to beat on his chest and make an echo chamber of his mouth and escort the patrons down to what Paul had named "the roots of rhythm." Bobby was coming with a band of astonishing musicians, most of them black. One or two of them might be gay. One or two of them might be Jews. And some might be women like Alisette, mothers like Alisette, intimate with important men as Alisette was with Megaman Brancusi. And still the police who were responsible for public safety in these remote mountains had made no arrests. They had taken no steps to adequately protect Bobby and his band and the other talented entertainers who trekked up to Aunt Dorothy's to bring happiness to the world.

Orpheo dismissed the Tlingit sisters with a friendly smile. "Take a break, kids," he said. "You're the best cleaning crew in the Pacific Northwest, you're going to be rich. Relax a couple of minutes now. Go for a walk in the woods. Don't come back until I send somebody to get you." And so they did, asking each other why everybody was afraid of the little man from New Jersey when he was actually so very pleasant and sweet?

He sat with a few friends in the gleaming kitchen to discuss the situation.

"To book a man's act is like agreeing to take care of a man's family," he told his friends. "I signed a deal with Megaman Brancusi and implicit in that deal was my obligation to protect those he entrusted to me. Who will come and entertain in my nightclubs if I sit by and put up with the bigotry or maybe the laziness or maybe just the incompetence of the police?"

★ ★ ★

In the early spring, a policeman who worked for Orpheo began nosing around the Coast Patrol files. It turned out to be very easy to find out who had connections with the Aryan Christian Congregation, who wanted certain mug shots pulled, the search for a certain Volvo abandoned. The particular officers who had effectuated the cover-up were easy to identify. Their records were secretly photocopied. Pictures of their houses, cars, families were placed in folders like academic research. But what was really interesting, this thorough workman reported, was that the emergency telephone operator had recorded a series of phone calls during the time that Alisette had spent running in the mountains. They were from a crazy guy who started out at Point Reyes and wound up in Mendocino. This man reported that Alisette was in trouble, and he gave his name and where he could be located as though he had nothing to hide. The guy with him said he was having a vision. He had called several more times during the following weeks, asking if they had heard from her, if she was okay. Of course, no one had told him anything because they had gag orders to abide by. But it sure was funny, noted Orpheo's spy, that this crazy guy would call. . . from so far down the coast. . . right at the exact moment when Alisette really was bribing the pregnant woman and running for her life into the fog-filled forest.

Orpheo showed this report to Megaman at a diner on a murky New Jersey highway, showed him pictures of the Volvo which had been gutted, then disfigured with paint, then hurled into a ravine and camouflaged by pines and roses. Deal by deal, he documented which parts of the car had reached the coast emporia serving thieves. Alisette's Casio had been fenced to a music student. The remains of her beautiful dresses were spotted by a Forest Ranger in the charcoal of a campfire pit because of the way the stray aurora beads glittered in the sun.

They had not been able to find the pregnant woman. Perhaps she had disguised or even disfigured herself in some way, to make good her escape. Whatever the case, Orpheo figured, she would not break the silence.

It was fortunate that Orpheo and his friends had always operated according to democratic principles, that they had paid rent and extended a lot of hospitality and had so much good will in the area. Because now Orpheo could count on the support of Aunt Dorothy's neighbors, and could be quite sure that under no circumstances would anybody tell some local political upstart where he kept his guns.

★ ★ ★

It was written in the papers that the backwoods settlement of the Aryan Christian Congregation had been invaded by a small army at midnight. They killed several men who tried to mount a defense and chased all the other inhabitants into the woods. After removing the settlement's large weapons stores, they burned the pretty church and all the cabins to the ground.

In the West 40s, in the rumor mills of the entertainment industry, Slim Price and Jock Silver heard that the event had occurred in response to an insult to the considerable person of Alisette Legrand. As a result of these rumors, Megaman Brancusi's business was flourishing, because after all, everybody wants a bloodthirsty manager. And old Pastafino, the gangland impresario who was said to have collaborated with

Megaman on this operation, had renewed his reputation for savagery. So now absolutely the biggest stars were fighting to play the Imperial Hotel and Casino.

Frantic, Alisette threw on her gray suit and the earrings nearest at hand, she barely even combed her hair and completely forgot her make-up and raced over to Megaman's office.

"Just tell me you didn't have anything to do with this!" she screamed.

"I know you've been feeling bad, sweet thing, but that's no reason for you to go around looking like hell. You're still an entertainer."

"Don't tell me how to look! Just tell me these murderers were not commissioned by mysterious power brokers in the music business!"

"Now how could I know anything about that?" Megaman answered, smiling. "I was fishing off the coast of Baja at the time."

Alisette glared at him.

"I hate revenge!" she yelled. "I hate it! I hate it! It's shameful and stupid and endless! My peace of mind is at stake here, and I am not going to stand for. . . "

She kept yelling but no sound came out. Rough little whispers. Wheezing. Nothing. Damn, damn, where was her voice?! She couldn't even have a shit fit anymore! WHAT THE HELL WAS HAPPENING TO HER VOICE?!

CHAPTER SIXTEEN

# SOLDIERS

CANDY'S DECISION TO GO INTO BUSINESS WITH SHAUL was based on her need to occupy herself during the tortuous process of getting a divorce. She decorated the office above the garage in Astoria and filled her days and nights with accounts and ledgers, instructing Shaul whom to hire and fire, dominating the staff with benevolent grandeur. Shaul figured it was okay for her to own Achim Movers and call the shots as long as nobody else really knew that she owned the company and called the shots. Because his brother Shimshon knew, he sent Shimshon home to Israel, sent him weighed down with appliances and athletic shoes.

In April, right after Passover, Candy took Ellen Vanczek to lunch and apologized for Shaul's foolish arrogance, blaming it on his ignorance of the country's ways, assuring Ellen that future relations between their two companies would be governed by American good manners and the understanding of professional women.

"She's a real classy broad," Ellen told Dominick. "She wore the most beautiful shoes I have ever seen on a real person in my whole life. I felt like we could be friends. Some day I'd love to buy her out."

Candy tried the same largesse with Lazard Goldberg, but he refused to meet with her.

"As far as I'm concerned, you're a pig, Mrs. Shapiro," he said on the telephone. "You shtup this guy in your husband's house and then you set him up like a whore on my territory. I don't want to know you."

Candy sighed. What could you do? Her mother had warned her that even the nicest people in the world inevitably acquired a couple of serious enemies.

Rather than compete directly with Fabrizi and Lazard Cares, Candy decided that Achim should invest heavily in insurance and cultivate the "priceless object" trade, moving spinets and lamps and statuary and candelabra for the hundreds of collectors she seemed to know. Her business solicitations were more like social calls than anything else, and they usually worked.

Shaul proudly wrote to his family that under Candy's magic spell, giant New York became a mere village, as small and friendly as Afula. She could not go anywhere without meeting someone she knew. Her classmates from high school had become the captains of industry, her bunkmates from camp controlled the city's politics, her occasional dates from college owned suburban shopping malls, her companions from Weight Watchers were stock manipulators. Her years of attending all functions, paying all minimums, springing for all tickets, serving on all boards — coupled with Shaul's charm and willingness to work until he dropped, and drive the other men at the same pace — now helped Achim Movers to carve out a profitable niche for itself on western Long Island.

Shaul hired Israelis who had just finished the Army and had come to America to take a look around the larger world. They loved working for him because he had learned from Lazard how to be a fair, straightforward boss in the American style. They carried goods and knowledge and very often wives as well back to Israel, a river of commerce that recalled the booming caravan days of Solomon.

It thrilled Candy that she was becoming a businesswoman, more and more frequently displaying the gifts of her father. She held out her hand, and there was Jack Deal, standing in her palm like Tinkerbell, a little man who had bled wonderful skills into her veins that now won her the respect — at long last! — of her community.

*I thought she was an idiot, and he thought she was a genius, Rabbi. How can one woman be such different people to two guys simultaneously? Was I born with this blindness or did some fool teach it to me?*

For the first time, Candy took Shaul out in public with her. At a special performance of the new Price, Silver & Deal show, "The Go Go Girls Turn Fifty," mounted to benefit the campaign treasury of Carol O'Banyon, Shaul sported a thick, well-shaped beard, dove gray slacks and a silk tweed jacket, and his chest hair bubbled out at the open neck of his silk shirt. He wore three gold rings in his ear, reminding those in their 60s of Alfred Drake in "Kismet." He held Candy's hand in his pocket.

Carol O'Banyon and the other women who had enjoyed the gossip at Crunchie's had to admit he had a sensational tush.

Maida came from Florida to protest the whole divorce thing. She said it was crazy and that Candy would regret it. She should stop with the Israeli boyfriend and get on a plane and go to Paris and beg Marty to return home.

However, Shaul softened Maida's heart by calling her *Ima.* And the children, my God, the children seemed so happy with him! Little Sam just adored him, and it was a melting sight for the grandmother to watch them playing ball and discussing public policy as the first Sam — *her* Sam — and Jack had often done in her salad days back in Gimbel's Inlet.

*I sat in Paris, Rabbi, eating myself up with guilt, and this stranger moved through my wife's belly into my son's heart.*

For Candy at 40, all the years of pain and silence seemed suddenly to fade away. Soon her monstrous marriage would be over. She was the envy of women who were a thousand times thinner and more successful than she. She had a great lover who made her feel both smart and desireable, and when she saw her children curled up on the sofa, sleeping under the arch of his strong arms, she felt at last the blessing of security.

From his Paris exile, Marty contested nothing. Yes yes, she could have the house, the cars, custody of the kids, a piece of the practice until the end of her days. Her lawyer, some guy named McCabe, seemed to be the most brilliant negotiator ever to pass through the family courts. Conversely, Phil Brinks turned out to be a lazy jerk, his incompetence *(I found out everything too late, Rabbi, everything. . . )* fueled by disgust with Marty's conduct and a great fondness for Candy's baking.

Beyond self-hatred, far beyond the reach of any comedian's parody now, she sat with her mother on a Sunday morning by the water, having worked an eighty hour week. She was tired but good tired. She confided to Maida that eventually she planned to give the business to Shaul and enroll at Stony Brook or Columbia and get a Masters in American History. Ethel played the guitar, which she had somehow picked up, and sang country and western songs, and Shaul and Little Sam plunged and whooped in the pool like dark brown seals. When they came out, Candy cloaked them with towels and sat them down to brunch with napkins she had embroidered, with jam she had made from berries she had grown. The sun illuminated all the golden threads that wound into her braid.

Everybody in the family, even her brother Alex, had to admit that Candy had finally grown up to be gorgeous, as Jack Deal had always wanted her to be.

★ ★ ★

Marty returned from Paris all gray. It devastated Candy to see him so unhappy. She longed to reach out for him, to hold him, to make him comfortable, to watch him sleep, to hear him yelling again on the phone at his nurses, to feel his iron hands on her hips on her shoulders in her hair, to sit in the room embroidering while he listened to Schumann. For a few minutes there, she wanted to plead with him to permit her to adore him once again. Then she reminded herself that it was another woman's pain which had turned him gray.

So be it, Candy thought, regret losing its grip, compassion retreating. So be it.

Marty's papers, his clothing and all his possessions down to the last book and tape had been neatly packed in cartons that said "Achim," ready for shipping anywhere he should decide to alight. At Candy's request, he took a last look around the house to see if there was anything else he wanted.

*What could I say, Rabbi? That I wanted everything? Her perfume on the dresser, her spices in the kitchen, her flowers in the garden, her mother on the phone. . .*

Long ago resigned to seeing him depart, Ethel behaved in a friendly manner. She seemed to have no idea how it crushed Marty to learn that she had changed her name to Dobkin, to commemorate a paternal great grandfather who reportedly had possessed a beautiful Irish-type tenor. Pinye Dobkin was the only other singer in the history of their family, Ethel explained. Since she had inherited his genes, why not his name as well? This was the name with which she had decided to launch her career in show business. Ethel Dobkin.

"Gee baby," Marty said, "with a name like that, you'd better be very good."

"I am," said Ethel.

Sam was not so friendly. Now eleven years old, he tended toward chubbiness. It looked like he would not grow very tall. He had Candy's voluminous chestnut hair and Marty's bright, stressed eyes. His glasses were already thick.

Lovely old Aunt Theresa, always trying to say something positive and nice, said: "Maybe you'll grow up to be a doctor, Sammy. Like your uncle. And your father."

"I'd rather do time in a Syrian jail," responded Little Sam.

Candy walked Marty down to the end of the driveway to his car, for old time's sake. All he could think of was the weekend at her parents' house in the Hamptons when he had proposed marriage to her, when her eyes were empty vessels that harbored no secrets from him. She had pressed his hands against her breast and promised that she would always love him, and he had believed that, he had counted on it. He knew, for he had seen them bear their suffering, that women were stronger than men; no one knew that better than Marty did. And he had thought his Candy must be the strongest of them all: comforter, guardian, caretaker, supporting the whole Jewish nation on her soft shoulders, cushioning the descent of his soul with her plump arms and plucking him out of his nightmares, protecting his sacred work, always waiting up, always worrying.

*I thought that nothing would shake her commitment to me, Rabbi. Nothing. Why did I think that? Who the fuck taught me to think that?!*

It seemed to him that his marriage, like his French baby, had been born under a sentence of death, that he had entered into his compact with Candy with so much pre-existing hatred for her breed and class of woman that there was never really any chance for survival. On the day their divorce papers were filed, Marty went home to California and called Rabbi Eliezer AvShalom and asked for help.

★ ★ ★

For all her elegance, for all her fabulous rhetoric, her celebrated warmth and wit, Carol O'Banyon lost the election. Men over thirty didn't vote for her; the poor didn't vote for her; and women, recalling the fuzzy record of Frank O'Banyon on the question of Choice, didn't vote for her either. The Mednorth Bust, which had won the nomination for her, had occurred more than a year ago, a long long time in the memory of a city routinely rocked by fresh disasters.

Some smart aleck journalist ran a story that Carol spent movie star amounts of money on clothes. The O'Banyon campaign countered with a proposal that the IRS should investigate how much money the journalist spent on bribes to elicit information from salesladies and busboys. However, charge always beats counter-charge, and the damage was done. The celebrity journalist who knew Roxie Kirsch admitted with a guilty giggle at a cocktail party that she had not voted for Carol even though she had donated money to her campaign. This was apparently the case across the board. Editorial writers noted that Carol O'Banyon had never held elective office and probably wouldn't know what to do with one. Better she should be appointed head of the city's Welcoming Committee, they said, something that required a woman with her looks and her wardrobe. But the United States Congress. . . come on. . . let's get real.

A year after her lunch at Crunchies, Carol wandered around an empty campaign headquarters on East 74th Street. It was a Saturday. She was all alone. Fenced in by her own picture blown up and plastered on every wall, she mentally tallied the dollars it had cost her to have that picture retouched, this large office rented, these thousands of flyers printed, these dozen phones installed. Soon the phone company would shut down the lines. The computers had been gone since early morning. She figured she was going to have to remortgage the house in Connecticut to pay off her campaign debt. Dizzy from loneliness, she longed for her youth and wished she were sucking up to Hitchcock again, flirting with Omar Sharif, she wished she were on the Riviera talking French and drinking wine with someone funny and diverting like Danton Moore.

She had offers to go to work as the Vice President of a big hotel chain and to become one of the heads of protocol at the U.N. Either way she would spend the rest of her career entertaining. That seemed to be her fate, the only thing she had ever really been good at. The Mednorth bust had given her one opportunity to break into Frank O'Banyon's world of make-a-difference power, and she had blown it. Admitted a political advisor with whom she had once been intimate: "Truth is, sweetheart, you never had a chance."

The sight of her wrinkled fingers made Carol sick. She had no experience with failure! She needed help handling this! Who would help her eradicate the misery of this terrible day?!

Candy Shapiro called from Astoria and said: "Not to worry, darling. Shaul is coming over to your place with a big red truck and a couple of guys who are going to move everything out, and after that, he is going to bring you over to Jimmy's where the three of us will have a wonderful lunch and plan the future."

"Oh Candy. . . "

"And Carol. . . please. . . don't try to give the guys any money, okay? This one's on me."

It was like a miracle. In all the years of her charmed and happy life, Carol O'Banyon had never actually possessed a woman friend, a good friend, who would come through and be there, sustaining and supportive, despite Carol's great beauty and her wit and her success. Candy Shapiro, who had gotten her the nomination with the Mednorth tip, who had planned her fundraisers and arranged her daises, Candy had actually remembered her in defeat! It was amazing but every word of flattery which she had cynically heaped upon Candy Shapiro had turned out to be true!

"I don't know how to thank you, Candy," she said, her voice cracking with emotion. "I will never forget this. Never."

"Gee, don't cry, Carol," Candy laughed. "You're supposed to be the toughest cookie in New York! I depend on you for inspiration! Now. Look for a bunch of dark, handsome guys with big muscles. They should be there any minute."

★ ★ ★

Candy laughed out loud when she hung up the phone. She had been recognized! Appreciated! Thanked, really thanked! It was a great moment in her life, a watershed. Her applications to grad schools, thick and complex and full of transcripts, were all packed up and stamped and ready to go. She thought of the shafts of light that fall from the high windows in libraries. How they vibrate with lively dust. How the heart can rest when the mind is distracted by tales of important events. She remembered studying with great fondness, the way she remembered her brother Sam. As with Sam, she had not paid enough attention when she had the chance. Well, she would pay attention now. She would get one of those nice, decorative chains to hold her reading glasses and a tiny little laptop and a big clunky briefcase to show she meant business. She would go back to Gettysburg to study all the things that were known now about that great battle that had not been known 20 years earlier. She would read the memoirs of President Grant and write papers about General Mead and then when she was finished with her Masters, she would get a job teaching high school history. Oh, she would make it so interesting! The kids would love her class! She could see them rushing through the halls, calling *I'll see you after Mrs. Shapiro's class!*

*Mrs. Shapiro's class.* It sang in her mind's ear. It was so much fun to imagine, to toy with fantastic ambitions. To have *any* ambition that was not a piece of furniture or a weight loss.

Gratitude to Carol, to Roxie Kirsch and Charlotte Glick and the girls at Hadassah, to Marie and the snow-flecked Dean in Boston and sunny Dalia on the bus to S'dom, and to Alisette with her incendiary songs, all the women who had picked at her with their fires until finally, finally! she too burned, gratitude to them filled her heart. For the first time in her life she felt that she owned a glorious future.

Whistling one of Ethel's happy tunes, Candy gathered up her applications and prepared to leave the office.

But then she had a visitor. It was Rita, Shaul's old across-the-street neighbor. From Mednorth.

"Where's Shaul?" she asked.

"He's not here. He's making a pick-up."

"You have got to warn him, lady. Right away. They're after him. They say he told that blonde politician about their guns and got their friends put in jail. They have been asking everybody on the street where he is. And somebody is going to tell them. And then all of us who didn't tell are gonna be in big trouble. If they find Shaul, they could hurt him, and all the nice boys who lived with him in that house. . . "

Candy sat down slowly.

"I got to go," Rita said.

"Yes. Yes, go go, right now. Use the back door."

"Are you gonna tell him? You got to tell him, right away."

"Yes. Don't go home, Rita. Hide yourself."

"You too, lady."

Rita hurried out of the office.

Candy gripped the edge of her desk, trying to force her hands to stop shaking. She was being seized by a terror such as she had never known. How could she have imagined that she would get away with it? Rescue the people, help the cops make the bust, and sneak away under cover, an anonymous tipster, forever unharmed — it had almost worked. But how could she, a businesswoman, ever have imagined that businessmen would forgive and forget the loss of so much money? Once again, innocent over-protected Candy had blundered into the whirlwind like Dorothy in Oz, and this time she had placed innocent people, people she loved, in mortal danger!

She had to warn Shaul! And Carol. . . she had to get through to Carol!

Her healed wrist seemed to break again; her right hand withered and lost its strength. She had to hold it with her left hand to make the fingers work to dial the numbers. She called O'Banyon headquarters. As the dead signal came on, she realized to her horror that by now all the phones there had probably been cut off. She tried to get through to Carol's friend at the Detective Bureau but he wasn't in, so she told whoever would listen that she had received a tip that Mrs. O'Banyon might be in danger because of the Mednorth bust and please please they had to go up to her headquarters and protect her right now and if they saw Mr. Beit-Halachmi and the Achim Truck there, they should protect them too! She called the only Achim truck that was out today, the one that was headed to Carol's office. "I have to talk to Shaul!" she screamed. The driver said that Shaul was not with them, that he had stopped off at that big toy store in the 50s to buy something for Sam's birthday and was planning to meet them at O'Banyon headquarters. "They'll be looking for our trucks!" Candy cried. "Park the truck in a place where there are no people and get out and leave it! Go!"

Imagining Shaul walking up to Carol's door in perfect ignorance only to have assassins mow him down, imagining his blood in the street, on her head, on her hands, Candy raced down the stairs, tripped and fell, ripped her stockings, scraped her shins, ran on, sweating. She was shaking so that she could hardly get the key into the door of the BMW. And then she thought No no no! not the BMW, they might know that car, it might be spotted! She tried to pull the key out of the door but it wouldn't come so she left it there and ran into the street and hailed a cab and told the driver to rush her into Manhattan. "Rush!" she screamed, throwing a couple of twenties at him. "Fast fast!" He hit the gas and ran the lights, heading for the Triboro. Candy could hardly breathe. As the cab flew out of the Midtown Tunnel and raced uptown, she began to weep and pray: "Oh God, please let me not have involved this woman I admire so much in an idiotic adventure that will get her killed, oh please God, let me not have endangered my wonderful lover who has brought me so much happiness, please please. . . " Scaring pedestrians, causing bike messengers to fly and tumble out of the way, the cab rocketed across Third Avenue then Second. . . and then she saw him. He was walking in crowds of midday shoppers, carrying packages from F.A.O. Schwarz, walking fast because he was a little late and craning his neck, looking for the Achim truck. Candy called to him but she was not close enough, he did not hear her. "Get closer to that man!" she hissed at her driver. "Cut off this asshole behind us! Get closer!" Shaul had slowed down. He was squinting at the police cars which had ganged up at the entrance to Carol's building. She threw open the door of the still-moving cab and reached out for him. *"Tikaness!"* she screamed in Hebrew. *"Achshav!* Now now now!" Shaul dropped everything, grabbed her hand and leaped into the cab. Candy slammed the door shut and pushed him onto the floor and shouted at the driver to "Go go go!" He had no choice anyway, because behind them an ambulance came howling and a cop in front of Carol's building waved them on. As they passed the headquarters, Candy turned and looked back. She saw the ambulance stop, saw the medics running into the building with their stretcher. The soccer ball which Shaul had bought for her little boy's birthday rolled unnoticed into the teeming street.

"Look for a bunch of dark handsome guys with big muscles," she herself had said. "They should be there any minute." And so her friend, from whom she had learned all she had ever known of self-respect, had flung open the door and welcomed them in.

"They got her," she whispered. "They got Carol."

★ ★ ★

Shaul pulled himself up from the floor onto the seat. He looked crushed and dusty like a smashed moth. *It was all a mistake; go back in the cocoon, close the hatch, bite the darkness.* He leaned against her, but she knew he did not feel her for he was numb, his moment of peace and productivity already slipping away. They would get him, Candy thought. They would hunt him down. It finally hit her, that they would find the cops who had staked out the neighborhood and the neighbors who had not warned them of the presence of the cops and Udi and his wife and Rita and Barbara and Lazard and Gad and Efi and Reuven, and oh my God, there would be no end to it, the long ripples of vengeance which could be taken against innocent people whom she had implicated. They would burn down the office and Barbara's house, maybe even the whole block, just as someone had burned down the settlement of those fascists in the northwest, an event which she had read about in the papers, seen featured on the evening news.

Heard rumors about.

A great quiet suddenly came over Candy. She felt as though she was dying. All her memories pressed in. The localities of her life, the vivid features of her friends and family, stood up like stalagtites around her, etched in black, and among these she saw the glasses on a chain. . . the sunbeams in the library. . . Mrs. Shapiro's class in American History. Her future, only just imagined, had already become a memory.

She heard the voices of her partners. *Old Pastafino, the gangland impresario, has renewed his reputation for savagery. . .* She heard the voice of her brother. *A crook. A goon. A two-bit hood. . .* The voice of her husband at breakfast; lace in the coffee. *A racketeer and a gambling czar, who is also thought to be a big dealer in stolen weapons.* The voices were not laughing, or screaming, or heavy with sarcasm. They were kind, and understanding, soldierly and thoroughly resigned.

They were all Sam's voice.

On the East Side Highway, she pressed two hundred dollar bills into the cabbie's hand. For the first time she noticed his African name and realized how lucky she had been, to pick up a driver who knew exactly how to flee. She instructed him to take Shaul to the airport.

"You gave me back my life," he said to her.

"You gave me back my life," she said to him.

One last time, they rocked in each other's arms. Then at 96th Street, Candy got out of the cab and let the men go on without her.

She called Marie. "*Écoute.* The key to the safe in my bedroom is in the silver Bible in the mirrored cabinets. Unlock the safe and take all the money and the jewelry too, all of it. Take the Volvo and pick up the kids at school and drive to the Imperial Hotel in Atlantic City." Marie started to protest. The butcher was delivering, the gardener needed instructions. "Just do it," Candy said.

★ ★ ★

In the peace of the lofty office, she tried to catch her breath. The best brandy in the world soothed her nerves. Her children were sleeping at last, guarded by armed men. Her house in Broadbeach was lit up like Vegas in the dead of night as a dozen careful men loaded her possessions into Dominick Fabrizi's trucks. Everything she owned had been saved, except herself, whom she no longer owned.

"Your brother Alex has the story wrong," Orpheo explained in his light, humorous way, his dimples winking. "When your father and your Uncle Milton broke into the butcher shop, it wasn't just pigs they found. It was me. Hanging from a meat hook. In the freezer. My enemies were angry because they felt I was moving in on their territory. So they executed me for trying to protect your Grandpa's store, in that extra special way Hitler liked to execute people who tried to assassinate him. So since it was a pretty slow way to die, I wasn't quite dead yet when your father busted in and cut me down.

"I know that my heart must have slowed down while I was hanging because the blood stopped pumping to the edges of my body. The ends of my fingers had to be trimmed a little and my toes and my earlobes and my nose."

"Believe it or not, this here is not my nose. Me and Michael Jackson, we got the same nose."

She leaned back in the chair, stretching and breathing deeply to unclench the muscles of her belly, and let her shoes slide off. He noticed that her leg was still jumping from the terror of her flight. So he put his hand on her knee.

"When your father cut me down, I must have been hallucinating because of my heart stopping, because I thought I was Jesus being hauled down from the cross. They put me in a sack. I thought it was a shroud. Then I thought I was in the grave, and these pigs had come to dig me up and eat my remains.

"That was why they stopped near the church. Not to drop off the pigs, who could have been released onto any highway, but to drop off your Uncle Fayo.

"And the next thing I knew, I was lying on a bed. Under a window of stained glass that poured down light upon me. Some kid upstairs was practicing the 'Ave Maria,' real high. And nuns who looked like Mary and Margaret in the old habits, they were bandaging my hands and feet.

"How do you like that? I said to myself. I turned out to be Jesus! Who would have believed it?"

She smiled, shaking her head, rubbing her eyes.

"When I woke up in the hospital, I saw the priest of the church. He was the one who filled me in who I really was. 'Your worthless life was saved by two Jewish brothers,' he says.

'They're going to jail for arson. The only good thing about all this is that you have lost enough of your fingers so you won't be able to shoot a gun again and bring any more bloodshed to our community.' "

Orpheo sighed. He poured them both another brandy.

"Those who tried to execute me became powerful in the meat business; they still terrorize decent butchers, to this day. Because they are insensitive people. To them, slaughter is slaughter, meat is meat.

"They don't understand kosher, what it means, the tenderness and the concern for mercy that kosher means. They don't understand that some ideas are so precious that they must be protected. Like kosher. And democracy. And some people have to be protected too. The righteous like your grandfather. The great talents like Alisette.

"Real soldiers, like me and your father, like you, Candice, we understand that the point of having guns and power is to defend the world's treasure, not to plunder it."

Orpheo limped over to an embankment of stars that hovered outside his window. He looked like Einstein, like Yoda; the least dangerous of men.

"I could never be in the meat business again so I went to work in a nightclub. In Detroit. In a place where black and white could have a few laughs and drink and dance together, because I always believed in the integration of the races.

"One night your father and your uncle brought in a big crowd. They were in town on business when the Israelis won a war, and so they were having a party to celebrate. I told my guy to give your father the check. And on the check there was a note from me. It said: 'This party is on Orpheo Pastafino, Jack.' And he embraced me. His eyes filled up with tears, Candice. Tears fell from his eyes.

"He said I thought you were dead and you're not. I thought our people would be defeated in this war and we were not. There is some justice in the world, your father said. Justice will be done.

"So you see, I know your father not just from the Pacific, but from the West 40s in the meat freezer. Your father saved my life. And it is my obligation to take care of you as your father would, even though your friends have been very foolish to mix into the business of these extremely dangerous gun-runners."

Candy leaned toward him. There seemed to be no alternative to absolute truthfulness at this point, so she did not mince words.

"It wasn't my friends, Fayo. It was me. I am a member of the conspiracy. I invented it. I notified Carol. I notified the press."

He chuckled.

"Oh I don't think that is possible, Candice. I think I would have known. . . "

"Maybe someone didn't think you had to know, thought you might feel hurt or sad to hear it and wanted to spare you. That sometimes happens. People are kind." She touched his jacket with one finger. "But the truth gets out. And when it does, my name will appear on the list of those to be punished."

"That is not possible!"

"Why not?! Did you think I would be a good little girl forever? Did you think a lifetime of humiliation would teach me nothing? That I would always look evil in the face and not deal?!"

He pushed her away from him. She lurched against the window. The black sky loomed.

"A treasure of weapons!" he shouted.

"A contradiction in terms," Candy answered.

For many minutes, Orpheo walked around his office, mopping his mouth with a handkerchief. Candy watched him. She was not afraid. Finally he came to a stop. He stood far away from her, under the white hands that held one of his lights. He looked at her for a long time, and then sighed, and smiled.

"What an interesting person you have turned out to be, Candice," he said. "Maybe you would consider staying here for a while. It would be such a change for me, to spend some time with a smart woman."

Candy walked over to him and took his hands, knowing how much power that gave her over him, knowing as Queen Esther must have known that, at least at this one moment, she had this much power.

"I will stay on certain conditions. Everyone is saved. Everyone. Give me your word that no one else will be destroyed like Carol O'Banyon, my friend that I loved, Orpheo, I loved her.

"I want Barbara's house to be bought by honest, harmless people and the neighbors to feel safe on their street again and no more trouble there in that place, no more trouble. I want Shaul and his friends to be protected from vengeance. I want him to be able to go home to Israel and to be like a river to his family." Her eyes were dark with tears. "Give me your word, Fayo. I won't be able to stand it, to see people I care about destroyed. How could I endure that? Give me your word that everyone will be saved, and I will stay here with you."

Orpheo shook his head. He could hardly believe this was happening. Was it possible that a man who had sinned so much, who had so little to hope for, should suddenly receive his life's greatest desire for such a paltry cost?! "Sure, you have my word, Candice," he answered. "You have my promise of protection."

With that, Candy kissed his hands, and held them to her breast as a promise. He was greatly moved. He touched her hair. Even with his mutilated fingers, it took him only a few seconds to loosen the complex braid, to unweave the hopes of Jack and the widsom of Maida and the righteousness of Reb

Ezra and the priceless, life-saving skills of Marty Shapiro and the courage of Shaul Beit-Halachmi and the loyalty of Marie and Roxie, the sacrifices of her brothers, the infinite love of her children and the patriotic yearnings of her own heart, the beauty of her gardens and the precious lessons she had learned from visiting battlefields, all the gold and granite strands unraveled there and then forever more.

"I have a lot of respect for you, Candice," whispered the old man.

CHAPTER SEVENTEEN

# ALISETTE'S SONGBOOK

ONCE HE HAD BEEN ASSURED BY THE WEATHERMAN that there would be nothing but sunshine and calm seas for days on end in Atlantic City, Heimlich sauntered into the Imperial Hotel and Casino without fear. He came straight from El Al, sporting a desert tan and heavy sandals but otherwise dressed as always like a Californian — golf shirt, sports jacket, pressed jeans, mauve eye patch. He had thickened with the years and now wore a white curly beard.

The weight of the yeshiva lifted off his head the minute he smelled the Casino.

Goodbye (for now) to deep silence, high winds, midnight cold, considerations of guilt and justice and relative guilt and relative justice. So long to anxious explorations of the war between sons and fathers, between brothers and other brothers, and the burden of remorse for bad behavior towards women that tormented men of conscience as they grew older. Here for the next hour or so, he might enjoy a respite from angst and become Heimlich the Comedian again, schmoozing, getting laughs, as though his jokebook had never drowned. Here, he was back with the easy stuff. Movie stars.

Pop songs. Fast foods. Small fortunes. Amicable divorce. Recreational sex. High rollers. Low fat. Lightness — America's gift to the Jews.

Jeez Louise, it's good to be home, said Eliezer as they encountered the bickering traffic and took on some cheap gas. But when they arrived in Atlantic City, he stayed out on the Boardwalk, grooving on the ocean air, buying taffy and fudge for his grandchildren, afraid to cross the threshold of the Casino. How come? Because the cathartic sojourn in the wilderness had changed Eliezer AvShalom, making him not a fundamentalist but a goody goody.

Himself, Heimlich looked forward to a triumphal return. All the way home on the long flight, he had imagined what a pleasure it would be, surprising Marge at her blackjack table, sneaking up in the dark behind Fred the Soundman and Fred the Lightman and hugging Fred the Waiter, his favorite Fred, the best straight man he had ever worked with until Eliezer came to Playa del Ruach and took over that role.

He raced into the Casino as into a fabulous old dream. . . and found to his surprise that the ceiling had changed from red to blue. BLUE! And the lascivious goddesses had given way to slender young pale-haired ladies, got up in pretty silks and laces like the rural sprites of Boucher and Watteau and the porcelain bases of certain insufferable lamps! And instead of lolling around naked, these Parisian pseudo-nymphs went swinging up to the cotton ball clouds on sylvan swings in the company of shrimp-pink cherubs while strumming mother-of-pearl lutes and fondling lambs! The ladies on the ceiling smiled sweetly without a trace of the old come-on. They had so many buttons and flounces and bows on their voluminous skirts, they were so thoroughly *dressed,* that you couldn't even imagine where the peepholes were.

Heimlich staggered! He reeled! It was horrible! A nightmare! He was so disappointed!

"What happened to the fat red goddesses?!" he whined to a croupier who was fanning his cards to pass the time at a slow table.

"Mr. Pastafino decided to get rid of them because Candy said they were vulgar."

Until that moment, it had never entered Heimlich's mind to be fearful of Candy. He had come to speak with her, that was all, a rabbi sent to bear a message from one of his students. But now that he knew they called her by her first name here, as though she were Evita, and now that he saw that she had enough influence to change the color of the sky, he thought maybe he should approach this woman with more caution than he had previously planned on.

"I'd like to see Mrs. Sha. . . Candy," he said to the man at the elevator.

"Oh yeah?"

"My name is Abe Heimlich, I used to work here in the Vancouver Lounge. A lot of people know me. Marge, Dr. Yablonsky."

"They quit. Marge became a kindergarten teacher. Yablonsky retired and raises orchids."

"Fred."

"All the old Freds quit."

"Oh. . . "

"We got new Freds."

"Well, maybe uh. . . maybe you could tell Candy that I am formerly Heimlich the Comedian, now once again Heimlich the Rabbi, and I have come from the Holy Land to bring her a message from the man who was formerly Shapiro Her Husband."

The elevator closed in his face. Either he could take that as a final rejection or hang out and wait. Heimlich decided to think positively. He waited, staring at the elevator. Finally, it opened. There stood Pozzo the Wimp of Bensonhurst. But thin. With wire-rimmed glasses.

"How you doing, Heimlich?" Pozzo said. "We thought you were dead."

"Almost. But not entirely. I just came from Israel, and I was hoping to speak with Candy."

"Why? You raising money for something?"

"No."

"Because if you are, you can just write it down on a piece of paper and she'll send you a check."

"No! No money. I uh I uh. . . I had her ex-husband in a Talmud class. . . he asked me to carry a message. . . "

"Forget it."

"Please Pozzo, how much time will I take? A couple of minutes maybe."

Pozzo's walkie talkie beeped him and he placed it next to his ear, all the while gazing at Heimlich with poisonous mistrust.

"Get in," Pozzo said.

Heimlich smiled and came on board. As soon as the elevator doors closed, he felt something, a hard sharp thing, jabbing firmly into his kidneys. He didn't dare turn to see what the jabbing thing was, but he assumed it was not Pozzo's dick.

They flew upward at terrifying speed. Heimlich's ears clogged. He began to perspire. Sweat collected in the empty socket where his eye had been. When it rolled out, it would look like tears. People would be baffled; can a missing eye weep?

Suddenly the doors flew open.

Two men surged into the elevator and began feeling his body up and down. When they ascertained that he was not armed, they swept him into Orpheo's office and seated him by force on some lawn furniture.

And then Candy appeared.

She looked terrific. Perhaps a little more *zaftig* than he remembered her; perhaps more conservatively dressed; one or two more diamonds. Her hair was knotted simply at her nape. She wore very little make-up. He had no reason to fear her, yet he trembled.

"Don't be scared by Pozzo," she said. "He got thin and he doesn't like you so he's acting tough but underneath, he's still the wimp and you're still the one with the talent. You want some coffee? I have good decaf, it tastes like real. You want rugulach?" The Japanese cook placed a platter before him. He ate one. It was delicious, thick with honey that sealed his teeth for a few seconds. "Do you need a job?" Candy asked.

"Mmmmnnn. . . "

"You don't want a contribution and you don't want a job."

"Nnnnmmmm. . . "

"You're really bringing me a message from Martin? That wasn't just a cover, a way to get in here?"

Heimlich finally swallowed the yummy cake.

"No! Honest! It never occurred to me that I would have trouble getting in here."

Candy laughed heartily. "Gee, you are ill-informed, Rabbi."

"Mrs. Shapiro. . . please. . . hear me out. . . "

"How is it possible that Martin is studying Talmud? Are men like him allowed to do that? I mean, don't you have to be a good person, sort of qualified morally, to study the holy books?"

"Uh. . . no," Heimlich managed.

"No, huh? So I guess any son-of-a-bitch can become a *tzaddik* these days, right?"

Heimlich stood up.

It seemed necessary to do that.

He wished he had worn a tie.

"Martin would like to arrange to see his children," Heimlich said.

"He arranged that infrequently enough when they were under his roof."

"Please, Candy. Please. A week, even just a few days, even just once in a while. Children need a father's love."

"You'll have to think of something a lot more tempting than that to get me to release a child of mine into Martin's custody, no matter how briefly."

"He has changed, Candy."

"Oh bullshit, Rabbi, if I may be so bold."

"Why not? It's possible. Look at you. You've changed."

"No, I haven't," Candy said. "I was always like this. I sometimes think I was actually raised with this eventuality in mind."

She smiled just a little, ironic and resigned, the way the old Jews used to smile. Heimlich could barely repress a cry of despair. He saw the desert, the bowl of honey tipped over, the honey pouring out, melting on the burning sands. He saw poor gorgeous Esther in Shushan — but late in her life, when the crisis was over and her courage had long ago entered history and she was just the Queen, making the best of it in the castle of the King, doing life for her people. It seemed to Heimlich in that moment that all the jokes he had ever told about Stacey and Barbara were really about Esther the Queen, and his heart broke.

Candy turned her face — not even her whole body, just her face! — and that was enough to signal dismissal. Her guards packed Heimlich into the elevator like old material into a time capsule. Earthward he rushed.

"What was she like?" asked Eliezer on the Boardwalk.

"An irreplaceable loss!" Heimlich wept. "A wasted fortune!" Tears rolled through his white beard onto his shirt collar, tears from the good eye, and tears from the socket. He beat himself on the chest, like a sinner atoning on Yom Kippur, for sins committed in ignorance, by mistake, because the light failed.

"The minute I saw her," he cried to his friend, "I remembered the words of the prophecy. I remembered the drowned prophet's voice that came up from the deep and what it caused me to say."

★ ★ ★

A physical therapist told Alisette to try heat packs on the throat and chest twice a day. Lot of good that did. At the suggestion of a Chinese flutist who purported to have worked with the Peking Opera, she went on a diet of brown rice and steamed vegetables and great draughts of hot water containing the juice and pulp of lemons. She lost weight but she still couldn't sing for more than an hour or so without starting to rasp.

A neighbor from down the beach recommended long sessions of yoga with attendant breathing exercises and monotone humming to produce a state of bliss, for it was bliss, this neighbor said, which had cured her cancer. The yoga didn't work for Alisette. So she solicited bliss in Baskin Robbins, and gained back all the weight she had lost.

At a party, she met an Italian tenor (formerly a baritone) who had lost his voice and returned to music by cultivating a whole new register.

"You are like a blind person who must develop a strong sense of smell to compensate for the loss of your sight," he said. "You are like a cripple without legs, and your soft weak arms must grow new muscles to pull you along."

Alisette took his advice. Networking through the musical community, she found teachers with whom she could study *lieder* and *bel canto.* To bypass the badly scarred parts, she raised herself up on high notes which she personally had never encountered before. The throat doctors told her these regimens and exercises couldn't hurt. However, they held out little hope. The Italian tenor said not to listen to them, that they were all assholes. He pronounced it "ess-ho-less." Alisette loved to hear him say that so much that she encouraged him in his diatribes against the doctors, even though she knew damn well they were right.

When she visualized her voice, she saw a chubby little black girl chewing on her hair, scared to raise her face up from the floor, orphaned daughter from random loins, brought to live with the family and given a bed in Grandma Blanche's house, given food and love and joyful instruction, so she could grow up and inhabit Alisette's body. Her voice was herself as a child, her sweet sense of resurrection from being cast out and alone, her rapture of self-discovery. How could she live without her voice?! Who would love her if she couldn't sing?! Day after day she paced along on the gray beach at Malibu, and mourned for her little girl: *Ah sweet baby Al, why have you gone and died?!*

She was so obsessed with the loss of her voice that she forgot the rest of her body. So it came as a complete surprise that, when she turned and walked back toward her house, she seemed to be walking on a trail of black spots. Black and scarlet spots in the sand. She broke into a run. As she staggered up the back steps, she began pulling off her pants. As she yelled for help into the phone, she saw that the blood was pouring down her legs in rivers and chunks. Marty Shapiro, covering for Alisette's doctor who was off fishing in Baja, cut out her ovaries and her uterus and tied off all the rupturing blood vessels thereabout and, with the help of many many pints of certified pure blood, saved her life.

★ ★ ★

Alisette disliked the substitute doctor. He didn't smile, he wasn't cute; the only man in California without a tan. His faded hair stuck up in spikes like he hadn't combed it that morning. His shirts were wrinkled. His awful, old fashioned paisley ties never quite closed at the collar, and very often he needed a shave. He smelled bad. It wasn't that he was dirty;

no, Dr. Shapiro was clean as a scrubbed kitchen sink and just about as cuddly. But he smelled of medicine. He smelled of neglect. The only thing remotely ingratiating about him were the dark pouches of suffering under his eyes under his glasses.

On the crown of his head, he wore a black skullcap. Alisette assumed he must be an Orthodox Jew. She was told by her own doctor that actually he was a born-again Jew who had screwed up his marriage and lost his family back in New York and had recently returned from a retreat in Israel where he had sought solace in the old religion. Apparently, he had not found what he was looking for. Shapiro's body, his whole personality, seemed caved in; bitter and boring like juice without pulp, soup without veggies. Alisette called him "Dr. Thin."

When he came around to check on her in the dawn hours, she smiled insincerely and said "Well hey, Dr. Thin, how you feeling today?"

"Better thin than fat like you," he said.

"I like the way I look."

"Okay, g'head, delude yourself, it's not my business."

"Damn straight! So butt out!"

"You'll calm down when the estrogen kicks in."

"I'll calm down when you get yourself out of my face!" she yelled, knocking the water pitcher off her tray and onto her doctor.

She was very depressed. Sure, it was the pain; it was hormonal upheaval and its attendant mood displacement. But it was also the plain facts of her life. To cheer her up, Megaman bought her masses of roses like she was a dead Mafia wife and the thrilling news that her new songs were being recorded by Joan and Whitney. She would probably make as much money, maybe more, than she ever had recording her songs herself, and look, she didn't even have to go to the trouble of showing up at the studio, she could just lie there and smell the roses and rest and relax and get her strength back.

Alisette wanted to choke him.

Her sons, home from college, didn't show up to console her as often as they should have.

"I hate my kids," Alisette said to Marty.

"Be thankful they don't hate you."

"I hate my manager. He treats me like an invalid."

"You *are* an invalid."

"Thanks a lot, Doc. What happened to old fashioned encouragement, hanh? What happened to 'You're gonna be out of here in no time, Al?' "

"Actually, you're not going to feel like a human being again for six months," Marty said.

"You sure do know how to make a recovering woman wish she had died under the knife!"

He winced and looked like he was going to cry. "I'm really sorry," he said, and quickly left the room.

It took her six months to feel like a human being again. Everybody tried to help. Megaman and Bo Tye, the musicians and the back-up singers, Lettie and Nacoochee filled the Malibu house, making music day and night, bringing her worshipful students who wanted only to emulate her and pay homage to her brilliance, to assure her that even if sweet baby Al could only write it and not sing it, there would always be music in her life, always voices raised in song.

Their attentiveness didn't help. For Alisette's old vision of hell had mutated through fear and physical constriction and age and descent. In hell, there is music, she told her shrink, but no love.

One day she went for her regular appointment to Dr. Thin.

"You look worse than usual," she said, lifting her feet into the stirrups.

"I'm worried about my children."

"Why? They doing drugs?"

"Relax," he said, inserting the speculum.

"Oh, I hate this," Alisette murmured, covering her eyes.

"They don't do drugs," he said. "RELAX! The girl sings. The boy is just a nice regular boy. But their mother has taken them to live with a murderer."

"Some people have unusually terrible problems," she said, trying not to think about the little spatula scraping the goo off the inside of her vaginal orifice into a piece of glass for testing.

While he poked around in the neighborhood where her ovaries had once done their monthly stunts, Marty Shapiro said: "I write to them. I plead. My ex-wife made this incredible bat mitzvah, a kind of great maturation ceremony where a girl gets up in the synagogue and shows her mastery of Hebrew and the Bible, oh Ethel was sensational, and I went and I pleaded with my ex-wife, I even begged the man, this. . . this. . . this man she uh. . . " Marty's voice faltered; he still could not bear to think of Candy in Orpheo's life, in his bed, in his will. "I sent my teacher to plead for me. But she will not let the children come. I write to my son. He doesn't even answer. He has changed his name to Deal. Sam Deal Two, he calls himself. Like he's the son of his uncle."

"Do you soak that goddamn thing in ice water?!" Alisette yelled.

"But the girl, the girl might. . . " he murmured, peering into her body like a spelunker.

"Oh Jesus. . . "

"The girl, my daughter, she's a great fan of yours," he said, widening the speculum. "So is my wife and the man, this. . . this. . . this man. . . I heard that you are taking on some students. Would you allow me to say that if my daughter came to visit, she could meet you and sing for you, maybe study with you? It might be an enticement. . . to her. . . to her mother. . . "

"Anything! I'll allow you to say anything!" Alisette hollered. "Just get that damn machine outa my snatch!"

★ ★ ★

In this way Marty Shapiro came up with something that really did tempt Candy and induce her to allow her daughter Ethel Dobkin to visit him in California.

Ethel arrived with a bodyguard, a discreet young man who kept out of the way so cleverly that people in whose living rooms he had been sitting for hours didn't know he had been there.

She was friendly, Ethel. A little tough maybe. Martin introduced her with the same baffled joy he might have used to present the sole survivor of a great battle. At fourteen, she was taller than he and gangly, leggy as a spider. Her nose was long, her face was covered with freckles, a rare skin type in such a dark-haired child. She had a big toothy smile that revealed her gums. No, she wasn't a pretty girl, but then again, when you could sing like Ethel, you were a knockout.

She sang "Who Are We?" and *"Erev Shel Shoshanim"* a Hebrew love song. She was real good. Alisette agreed to be her teacher. She found that the girl could capture the participles of the Middle Eastern scale like a Yemenite, that she could make her voice weep like a gypsy violin. But she could not really sing the blues just yet because she was white and so very young and so very fortunate. "Don't you upset yourself about that, honey," Alisette said. "The blues will come to you, in time."

★ ★ ★

Megaman had instructed the mail room personnel at Brancusi Management to give all Alisette's fan letters to him so he could screen out the bad ones, and he had burned up the first six of Heimlich's letters, hoping that Alisette would just forget the bizarre comic and concentrate on being devoted to the one person who knew what was good for her.

But it never had worked anyway, had it?

Seeing the report of Orpheo's spy, reading the taped transcript of the vision at Point Reyes, Megaman realized that Abe Heimlich probably loved Alisette more than anybody, loved her far beyond the bounds of wisdom and reason, and despite the passage of considerable time. And since she would now have to deal with the loss of her powerful voice and the cessation of her career as an entertainer, and would need all the love and support she could get from any source, he did not burn the seventh letter but rather sent it on to Alisette herself. And then he wrote to Heimlich, to the Mendocino address, admitting all that he had done and apologizing for having been such a desperate and foolish and jealous man and offering by way of recompense Alisette's personal unlisted phone numbers and a key to the beach in Malibu.

Heimlich found Megaman's confessional when he returned to Mendocino, after Rivka's wedding in New Haven. He read it over and over, his heart singing. For it was some evidence after all that men could come to comprehend each other's suffering and passion, that there was indeed a multi-colored race called Lover, if only in one little corner of the entertainment business.

* * *

One day, while Alisette was walking on the beach under a clouded-over, autumn sky, a chicken fell into step beside her.

He was dressed as an observant Jew. He had a prayer shawl secured around his orange wings with a safety pin and a *kipah* the size of a bottle cap on his cockscomb.

"Well hi," Alisette said.

"Hi," said the chicken.

"You going to the Grammies?" she asked.

"A chick has to be able to sing to go to the Grammies. Besides I don't have a date."

"You could go with me."

"You would be seen with a chicken in front of all those people on national television?"

"Hell, I been seen with worse shit than that on national television, honey," Alisette laughed.

"Okay I'll go," said the chicken. "But we've got to do this right. First you call your agent. You say I've got a date for the Grammies with a talking chicken. Wait'll you hear this bird rap, you say."

"But does he have a tuxedo?" asked Alisette.

"Your agent gets him a tuxedo. Your agent calls the papers. The papers run titillating promises of chickens to come at the Grammies. The talk shows try to get a talking chicken preview. But we are aloof. Stand-offish. We feather our nest with rumors. Jimmy the Greek is taking bets. Will the strange bird speak? Will he lay an egg? Then we go to the Grammies, me in my tiny chicken tux, you in your gold sandals with your gold toenails. They say: speak, strange bird! But I am silent.

"Speak! they insist. I maybe give a little peep. The whole world is pissed and miffed with disappointment. So what happens then?"

"We get even better odds at the Academy Awards," Alisette said, wiping her eyes, holding Heimlich close.

★ ★ ★

Alisette liked the idea of people sitting around in living rooms singing her songs, so she finally said yes to a deal Megaman had found for her and allowed the publication of *Alisette's Songbook.* Special for this occasion, she set some of Heimlich's words to music. Not the prophecy. She and Heimlich agreed it was too damn sad to be sung and should better be intoned in the old way as the ancient Hebrews had done it in the days when the seas and the fish were Phoenician.

However, Heimlich gladly gave up some of the words of his seventh letter, and Alisette laid them onto a Flamenco-type tune.

This was her first Jewish love song.

Since it was written in English, there was some confusion about who was speaking, the man or the woman. But as with King Solomon's Song of Songs, when it was translated into Hebrew, the gender of the voices became abundantly clear.

Luckily, the song especially suited the vocal abilities of Dr. Thin's gifted daughter, who now came bounding down the beach like a colt, with her bodyguard in the shadows and her music in her knapsack, wearing shiny Lakers shorts and thick purple socks and baby blue sneakers, ready to try anything.